"For the Benifit
of all the people"
Leave it as it is! + a
On Yellow Stone
National Park Bark Entrance

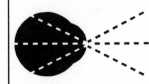

This Large Print Book carries the
Seal of Approval of N.A.V.H.

TREASURE

TREASURE

CLIVE CUSSLER

THORNDIKE PRESS

A part of Gale, Cengage Learning

Detroit • New York • San Francisco • New Haven, Conn • Waterville, Maine • London

GALE
CENGAGE Learning

LIBRARY OF CONGRESS CATALOGING-IN-PUBLICATION DATA

Cussler, Clive.
    Treasure / by Clive Cussler.
        p. cm. — (A Dirk Pitt Adventure series.) (Thorndike Press
    large print famous authors)
    ISBN-13: 978-1-4104-0404-6 (alk. paper)
    ISBN-10: 1-4104-0404-8 (alk. paper)
    1. Greenland — Fiction. 2. Treasure troves — Fiction.
    3. United States — History — Invasions — Fiction. 4. Large type
    books. I. Title.
    PS3553.U75T7 2008
    813'.54—dc22   2007038564

Published in 2008 by arrangement with Pocket Books,
a division of Simon & Schuster, Inc.

Printed in the United States of America
2 3 4 5 6 7 12 11 10 09 08

In memory of
Robert Esbenson

No man had a truer friend

A NOTE TO THE READER

Please forgive the inconvenience of converting measurements from what most Americans are used to. But in 1991 the United States finally became the last nation on earth to convert to the metric system.

It's easy.

- 1 kilometer roughly equals a little more than 1/2 mile.
- 1 meter is slightly more than 1 yard, about 39 inches.
- 2 centimeters to the inch.

And there you have it.

The Alexandria Library truly existed, and if it had remained unravaged by wars and religious zealots it would have given us not only the knowledge of the Egyptian, Greek and Roman empires, but those little-known civilizations that rose and fell far beyond the shores of the Mediterranean.

In A.D. 391 Christian Emperor Theodosius ordered all books and art depicting anything remotely pagan, which included the teachings of the immortal Greek philosophers, burned and destroyed.

Much of the collection was thought to have been secretly saved and spirited away. What became of it, or where it was hidden, remains a mystery sixteen centuries later.

THE PRECURSORS

July 15, A.D. 391
A land unknown

A small, flickering light danced eerily through the black of the tunneled passageway. A man dressed in a woolen tunic that dropped below his knees paused and raised an oil lamp above his head. The dim glow illuminated a human figure inside a gold-and-crystal casket while casting a grotesque, wavering shadow against the smoothly cut wall behind. The man in the tunic stared into the sightless eyes for a few moments, and then he lowered the lamp and turned away.

He studied the long line of stationary forms that stood in deathlike silence, so great in number they seemed to trail off into infinity before vanishing in the darkness of the long cavern.

Junius Venator moved on, his strap sandals scraping over the uneven floor with a bare whisper of sound. Gradually, the tunnel widened into a vast gallery. Soaring to a

13

height of nearly thirty feet, the domed ceiling was divided by a series of arches to give it structural strength. Gutters carved in the limestone spiraled down the walls so water seepage could run into deep drainage basins. The walls were laced with cavities filled with thousands of strange-looking circular containers made of bronze. Except for the large wooden crates stacked uniformly in the center of the carved chamber, the forbidding place might have been mistaken for the catacombs beneath Rome.

Venator peered at the copper tags attached to the crates, checking their numbers against those on a scroll he flattened on a small folding table. The air was dry and heavy, and sweat began to course through the layers of dust that blanketed his skin. Two hours later, satisfied everything was catalogued and in proper order, he rolled up the scroll and slid it into a sash at his waist.

He took one final, solemn look at the objects in the gallery and exhaled a sigh of regret. He knew he would never see or touch them again. Tiredly, he turned, held the little lamp in front of him and retraced his steps through the tunnel.

Venator was not a young man; he was approaching his fifty-seventh year — old for his time. The gray, lined face, the sunken cheeks, the tired dragging steps reflected the weariness of a man who had no more heart for life. And yet, down deep, he felt a glow of warmth from an inner satisfaction. The immense project was successfully completed; the great burden lifted from his bent shoulders. All that remained for him was to survive the long voyage to Rome.

He passed four other tunnels leading off into the hill. One had been blocked off by a great pile of rubble. Twelve slaves excavating deep inside had perished when the roof collapsed. They were still in there, crushed and buried where they fell. Venator felt little remorse. Better for them to have died quickly than suffer years of misery in the mines of the Empire on a bare subsistence diet before dropping from disease or being abandoned when they were too old to work.

He took the far passage on the left and walked toward a pale glimmer of daylight. The entrance shaft had been hand-cut inside a small grotto and measured two-and-a-half meters in diameter — just wide enough to permit entry of the largest crates.

Suddenly the sound of a faraway scream echoed down the shaft from the outside. A frown of concern furrowed Venator's forehead, and he increased his pace. Out of habit he squinted his eyes against the brilliance of the sun as he stepped into its light. He hesitated and studied the camp that lay a short distance away on a sloping plain. A group of Roman legionaries stood around several barbarian women. One young girl screamed again and tried to scramble away. She almost broke through the cordon of soldiers, but one of them grabbed her by her long flowing black hair. He pulled her back, and she stumbled to her knees in the coarse dirt.

A huge, hard-bitten character spied Venator and approached. The man was a giant, standing a good full head above everyone else in camp, with great shoulders and hips joined nearly as one, and a pair of oak-beam arms ending in hands that dropped almost to his knees.

Latinius Macer, a Gaul, was the chief overseer of the slaves. He waved a greeting and spoke in a voice that was surprisingly high-pitched.

"Is all in readiness?" he asked.

Venator nodded. "The tally is finished. You can seal off the entrance."

"Consider it done."

"What is the disturbance in camp?"

Macer glanced at the soldiers, peering through black, cold eyes, and spat on the ground. "Stupid legionaries became restless and raided a village five leagues north of here. The massacre was senseless. At least forty barbarians were killed. Only ten were men, the rest women and children. And for no good reason. No gold, no booty worth mule dung. Returned with a few ugly women to

16

gamble over. Little else."

Venator's face tensed. "Were there any other survivors?"

"I was told two of the men escaped into the brush."

"They will sound the alarm in other villages. I fear Severus has kicked a hornet's nest."

"Severus!" Macer spat the word in unison with another salvo of saliva. "That damned centurion and his lot do nothing but sleep and drink our wine supply. A pain in the buttocks to bring the lazy baggage along, in my judgment."

"They were hired to protect us," Venator reminded him.

"From what?" Macer demanded. "Primitive heathen who eat insects and reptiles?"

"Gather the slaves and seal off the tunnel quickly. And make a good job of it. The barbarians must not be able to dig through after we leave."

"Little fear of that. From what I've seen, no one around this cursed land has mastered the art of metalworking." Macer paused and pointed to the massive heap of excavated tailings poised above the entrance to the shaft, precariously held in place by a giant crib of logs. "Once that falls, you can stop worrying about your precious antiquities. No barbarian will ever get to them. Not by scratching with his bare hands."

Reassured, Venator dismissed the overseer and strode angrily toward the tent of Domitius Severus. He passed the personal emblem of the military detachment, a silver symbol of Taurus the bull atop a lance, and brushed aside the sentry who attempted to block his passage.

He found the centurion seated in a camp chair, contemplating a naked, unwashed barbarian woman, who sat on her haunches, uttering a chorus of strange vowel sounds. She was young, no more than fourteen. Severus was wearing a brief red tunic clasp over his left shoulder. His bare arms were ornamented with two bronze bands fastened around his biceps. They were the muscled arms of a soldier, trained for the sword and shield. Severus did not bother to look up at Venator's sudden appearance.

"This is how you pass your time, Domitius?" snapped Venator, his voice coldly sarcastic. "Scorning God's will by raping a heathen child?"

Severus slowly turned his hard gray eyes to Venator. "The day is too warm to listen to your Christian tripe. My god is more tolerant than your god."

"True, but you worship a pagan."

"Purely a matter of preference. Neither of us has met our gods face to face. Who is to say who is right?"

"Christ was the son of the true God."

Severus gave Venator a look of exasperation. "You have invaded my privacy. State your case and leave."

"So you can ravage this poor heathen?"

Severus did not answer. He rose, grabbed the chanting girl by the arm and threw her roughly on his camp cot.

"Would you care to join me, Junius? You may go first."

Venator stared at the centurion. A chill of fear ran through him. The Roman centurion who led an infantry unit was expected to be a hard master. This man was merciless, a savage.

"Our mission here is finished," said Venator. "Macer and the slaves are preparing to seal off the storage cave. We can strike camp and return to the ships."

"Eleven months tomorrow since we left Egypt. One more day to enjoy the local pleasures will not matter."

"Our mission was not to pillage. The barbarians will seek revenge. We are few, they are many."

"I'll match my legionaries against any horde the barbarians can throw against us."

"Your men have grown soft as mercenaries."

"They haven't forgotten how to fight," Severus said with a confident smile.

"But will they die for the honor of Rome?"

"Why should they? Why should any of us?

The great years of the Empire have come and gone. Our once glorious city on the Tiber has turned into a slum. Little Roman blood runs in our veins. Most of my men are natives of the provinces. I am a Spaniard and you are Greek, Junius. In these chaotic days who can feel an ounce of loyalty toward an emperor who rules far to the east in a city none of us have ever seen? No, Junius, my soldiers will fight because they are professionals and because they are paid to fight."

"It may be the barbarians will give them no choice."

"We'll deal with that scum when the time comes."

"Better to avoid conflict. I say we leave before dark —"

Venator was interrupted by a loud rumble that shook the ground. He rushed from the tent and stared at the cliff wall. The slaves had pulled the supports from under the crib, releasing a thundering avalanche that plunged over the cave opening, burying it beneath tons of massive boulders. A great dust cloud erupted and spilled into the ravine. The echoing rumble was followed by cheers from the slaves and legionaries.

"It's done," said Venator, his voice solemn, his face weary. "The wisdom of the ages is safe."

Severus came and stood beside him. "A pity the same can't be said for us."

Venator turned. "If God grants us a smooth voyage home, what have we to fear?"

"Torture and execution," said Severus flatly. "We have defied the Emperor. Theodosius does not forgive easily. There will be no place for us to hide in the Empire. Better we find refuge in a foreign land."

"My wife and daughter . . . they were to meet me at our family villa at Antioch."

"The Emperor's agents have probably intercepted them by now. They are either dead or sold into slavery."

Venator shook his head disbelievingly. "I have friends in power who will protect them until my return."

"Friends can be threatened and bought."

Venator's eyes widened in sudden defiance. "No sacrifice is too heavy for what we have achieved. All would be for nothing if we did not return with a record and chart of the voyage."

Severus was about to reply when he observed his second in command, Artorius Noricus, running up the slight grade toward the tent. The young legionary's dark face glistened in the noonday heat, and he was gesturing up at the edge of the low cliffs.

Venator held up a hand to ward off the sun and stared upward. His mouth pressed into a tight line.

"The barbarians, Severus. They have come to pay back the sack of their village."

It was as if the hills swarmed with ants. Over a thousand barbarian men and women stared down at the cruel intruders of their land. They were armed with bows and arrows, shields of leather hide and spears with chipped obsidian points. Some gripped clubs of rock tied to short wooden handles. The men wore only waistcloths.

They stood in stony silence, expressionless, savage, and as ominous as an approaching storm.

"Another force of barbarians has massed between us and our ships!" Noricus shouted.

Venator turned, his face ashen. "This is the result of your stupidity, Severus." His voice was vicious with anger. "You have killed us all." Then he dropped to his knees and began to pray.

"Your divinity will not turn the barbarians into sheep, old man," Severus said sarcastically. "Only the sword can provide deliverance." He turned and took Noricus by the arm and began issuing commands. "Order the bucinator* to sound battle assembly. Tell Latinius Macer to arm the slaves. Form the men in a tight fighting square. We'll march in formation to the river."

Noricus threw a taut salute and ran for the center of the camp.

The infantry unit of sixty soldiers quickly

* Bugler.

formed in a hollow square. The Syrian archers took their place on the flanks between the armed slaves, facing outward, while the Romans formed on front and rear. Screened in the center were Venator and his small staff of Egyptian and Greek aides and a three-man medical unit.

The main infantry weapons of fourth-century Rome were the gladius, a double-edged pointed sword eighty-two centimeters long, and the pilum, a two-meter throwing and thrusting spear. For protection and armor, the soldiers wore an iron helmet with hinged cheek pieces that tied under the chin with a strap and looked like a jockey cap with the brim turned backward, a cuirass made up of overlapping metal plates encircling the body and covering the shoulders, and a guard worn over the shins called a greave. Their defensive tool was an oval shield made out of laminated wood.

Instead of rushing in to attack, the barbarians took their time and slowly encircled the column. At first they tried to draw the soldiers out of the solid lines by sending a few men up close who shouted strange words and made threatening gestures. But their heavily outnumbered foe did not panic and run as expected.

Centurion Severus was too much a veteran to feel fear. He stepped ahead of his front line and surveyed the terrain crawling with barbarians.

He waved derisively at them. This was not the first time he had faced overwhelming odds in a fight. Severus had volunteered for the legion when he was sixteen. He advanced from common soldier, winning several decorations for distinguished bravery in battles against the Goths along the Danube and the Franks at the Rhine. After his retirement, he had become a mercenary, hiring out to the highest bidder, in this case Junius Venator.

Severus had unswerving confidence in his legionaries. The sun gilded their helmets and unsheathed swords. They were strong fighters and battle-hardened men who knew victory without ever enduring defeat.

Most of the livestock, including his horse, had died on the grueling voyage from Egypt, so he walked at the head of the square, turning every few steps so as to keep a constant, wary eye on the enemy.

With a roar that rose and broke like crashing surf, the barbarians rushed down the sun-baked incline and fell on the Romans. The first wave was decimated, pierced by the long throwing spears of the soldiers and the arrows from the Syrian archers. The second wave burst forward, crashed into the thin ranks, and were cut down like wheat before a scythe. The gleaming swords dulled and turned red with barbarian blood. Driven by a stream of salty oaths, and threatened by the scourging lash of Latinius Macer, the slaves gave a good account of themselves and stood firm.

The formation moved forward at a crawl as the barbarians pressed from all sides, fed by continuous reserves. Great red stains formed on the dirt of the arid slope. More and more naked bodies dropped and crumpled lifeless. Those who surged from behind fought on their comrades' corpses, slicing bare feet on shattered weapons, throwing flesh against the terrible shafts of iron that thrust into breasts and stomachs, then falling on the death heap. At close quarters they were no match for Roman discipline.

The battle now took a different turn. Realizing they could make no headway against the swords and spears of the foreigners, the barbarians pulled back and regrouped. Then they began shooting flights of arrows and throwing their crude spears while their women hurled rocks.

The Romans closed shields over their heads like large tortoiseshells and stoutly maintained their march for the river and the safety of their ships. Only the Syrian archers were able to cause casualties among the barbarians. There were not enough shields to go around for the slaves, and they fought open and unprotected from the hail of missiles. They were weakened from the long, tiring voyage and the exhausting excavation of the cavern. Many fell and were left behind, their bodies immediately stripped and horribly mutilated.

Severus was an old hand at this style of fighting; he had experienced it against the Britons. Noting that his enemy was reckless and untrained, he called a halt and ordered all weapons be dropped on the ground. The barbarians, taking it as a gesture of surrender, were deceived into making a rash charge. Then, at Severus's order, the swords were snatched up and the Romans counterattacked.

Straddling two rocks, the centurion swung his sword in almost measured, metronomic strokes. Four barbarians dropped at his feet. He knocked another one sprawling with the flat of his sword and slashed the throat of one who lunged against his side. Then the frenzied tide receded and the naked horde retreated out of hand-to-hand range.

Severus took advantage of the breathing spell to count his casualties. Out of sixty of his soldiers, twelve lay dead or were dying. Fourteen more sustained various wounds. The slaves had suffered the worst. More than half were killed or missing.

He approached Venator, who was binding up a gash on one arm with a torn piece of his tunic. The Greek wise man still carried his precious tally sheet securely under his sash.

"Still with us, old man?"

Venator looked up, his eyes brimming with fear mixed with determination. "You'll die before me, Severus."

"Is that a threat or a prophecy?"

"Does it matter? None of us will see the Empire again."

Severus did not reply. The fight abruptly resumed as the barbarians unleashed another discharge of spears and rocks that darkened the air and thumped against the shields. He quickly returned to his place in front of the depleted square.

The Romans fought viciously, but their numbers were dwindling. Almost all of the Syrian archers were down. The square was closing in on itself as the withering assault continued unabated. The survivors, many of them wounded, were exhausted and suffered from the heat and thirst. Their swords began to sag and they switched them from one hand to the other.

The barbarians were equally exhausted and taking huge losses, yet they stubbornly contested every foot of the gradual slope to the river. Half a dozen of their corpses could be counted around every slain legionary. The mercenaries' bodies, pierced by scores of arrows, looked like pincushions.

The giant overseer Macer was struck in one knee and the thigh. He stayed on his feet but could not keep up with the moving formation. He dropped behind and soon attracted a group of twenty barbarians who swiftly surrounded him. He turned, at bay, waved his sword like a windmill and cut three of them completely in two before the rest drew back and hesitated in respect of his awesome strength. He shouted and motioned for them to come close and fight.

The barbarians had learned their lesson the hard way and refused to be drawn into arms-length combat. They stood back and launched a torrent of spears at Macer. In seconds, blood gushed from five wounds on his body. He grasped the shafts and pulled out the points. A barbarian ran close and hurled his spear, striking Macer in the throat. Slowly he toppled over from the loss of blood and dropped into the dust. The barbarian women rushed in like a pack of mad wolves and stoned him to pulp.

Only a high sandstone bluff separated the Romans from the river's edge. Beyond, it seemed that the sky had suddenly turned from blue to orange. Then a column of smoke rolled upward, black and heavy, and the wind brought the smell of burning wood.

Shock gripped Venator, quickly replaced with despair.

"The ships!" he shouted. "The barbarians are attacking the ships!"

The bloodied slaves panicked and made a suicidal dash for the river. The barbarians rushed in from the flanks and viciously assaulted them. Several of the slaves threw down their arms in surrender and were slaughtered. The rest tried to make a fight of it from behind a grove of small trees, but their pursuers cut them down to a man. The dust of the strange land became their shroud, the dry brush their sepulcher.

Severus and his surviving legionaries fought their way to the summit of the bluff and suddenly halted, oblivious to the murderous onslaught raging around them, and stared in stunned fascination at the disaster below.

Pillars of fire rose and merged into a coil of smoke that unwound and reached upward like a serpent. The fleet, their only hope of escape, was burning along the river's edge. The enormous grain ships they had commandeered in Egypt were being incinerated under great sheets of rolling flame.

Venator pushed his way through the front rank and stood beside Severus. The centurion was silent; blood and sweat stained his tunic and armor. He gazed in frustration at the sea of flame and smoke, seeing the blazing sails disintegrate in a maelstrom of sparks, the dreadful reality of defeat branded in his eyes.

The ships had been anchored on the shoreline and lay naked and exposed. A force of barbarians had engulfed the small body of seamen and torched everything that could burn. Only a small merchant ship had escaped the conflagration, its crew somehow beating off their attackers. Four seamen were struggling to raise the sails while several of their shipmates strained at the oars in their struggle to reach the safety of deep water.

Venator tasted the falling soot and the bitterness of calamity in his mouth. Even the sky itself seemed red to him. He stood there in helpless rage. The faith he had placed in his carefully executed plan to safeguard the priceless knowledge of the past died in his heart.

A hand was laid on his shoulder and he turned and stared into the strange expression of cold amusement on Severus's face.

"I had always hoped to die," said the centurion, "drunk on good wine while lying on a good woman."

"Only God can choose a man's death," Venator replied vaguely.

"I rather think luck plays a heavy role."

"A waste, a terrible waste."

"At least your goods are safely hidden," said Severus. "And those escaping sailors will tell the scholars of the Empire what we did here."

"No," said Venator shaking his head. "No one will believe the fanciful tales of ignorant seamen." He turned and gazed back at the low hills in the distance. "It will remain lost for all time."

"Can you swim?"

Venator's eyes returned to Severus. "Swim?"

"I'll give you five of my best men to cut a passage to the water if you think you can reach the ship."

"I . . . I'm not certain." He studied the waters of the river and the widening gap between the ship and shoreline.

"Use a piece of debris for a raft if you have to," Severus said harshly. "But hurry, we'll all be meeting our gods in a few more minutes."

"What about you?"

"This hill is as good a place as any to make a stand."

Venator embraced the centurion. "God be with you."

"Better he walk with you."

Severus turned and swiftly selected five soldiers who were unwounded and ordered them to protect Venator on their run for the river. Then he went about the business of re-forming his ravaged unit for a final defense.

The pitifully few legionaries clustered around Venator. Then they made their dash for the river, shouting, and hacking their way through a loose line of startled barbarians. They thrust and slashed like madmen on a bloody rampage.

Venator was exhausted beyond feeling, but his sword never hesitated, his step never faltered. He was a scholar who had become an exterminator. He was long past the point of no return. There was only grim stubbornness left now; any fear of dying had disappeared.

They fought through the mad whirl of fiery heat. Venator could smell the odor of burnt flesh. He tore off another shred of his tunic and covered his nose and mouth as they battled through the smoke.

The soldiers went down, protecting Venator to their last breath. Suddenly his feet were in the water, and he sprang forward, diving the instant it rose above his knees. He glimpsed a spar that had fallen free of a burning ship and feverishly paddled toward it, not daring to look back.

The soldiers still on the bluff countered everything that was thrown at them. The barbarians dodged and chanted defiance while probing for a weak spot in the Roman defenses. Four times they grouped in mass formations and charged, and four times they were hurled back, but not before whittling down a few more of the exhausted legionaries. The square became a small knot as the few survivors closed ranks and fought shoulder to shoulder. Bloody heaps of dead and dying carpeted the summit, their blood flowing in streams down the slopes. And still the Romans resisted.

The battle had been raging without let-up for nearly two hours, but the barbarians were still attacking with the same intensity as at the beginning. They began to smell victory and massed for one last charge.

Severus broke off the arrow shafts that protruded from his exposed flesh and fought on. Barbarian corpses carpeted the ground around him. Only a handful of his legionaries remained at his side. One by one they perished, sword in hand, buried beneath swarms of rocks, arrows and spears.

Severus was the last to fall. His legs folded under him and his arm could no longer lift his sword. He swayed on his knees, made a futile effort to rise, then looked up to the sky and muttered softly, "Mother, Father, carry me to your arms."

As if in answer to his plea, the barbarians rushed forward and savagely clubbed him until death released his agony.

In the water, Venator grimly clutched the spar and kicked his legs in a desperate attempt to reach the retreating ship. His effort was in vain. The river's current and a puff of wind pushed the merchant vessel further away.

He shouted to the crew and frantically waved his free arm. A group of seamen and a young girl holding a dog stood on the stern, staring at him without compassion, making no move to bring the ship around. They continued their escape downriver as if Venator did not exist.

They were abandoning him, he realized helplessly. There would be no rescue. He beat a fist on the spar in anguish and sobbed uncontrollably, convinced that his God had forsaken him. Finally he turned his eyes toward shore and gazed at the carnage and devastation.

The expedition was gone, vanished in a nightmare.

■ ■ ■ ■

PART I:
NEBULA FLIGHT 106

■ ■ ■ ■

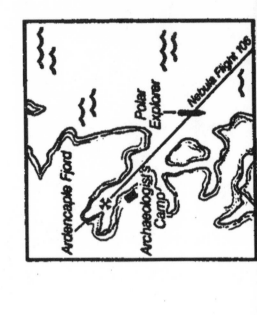

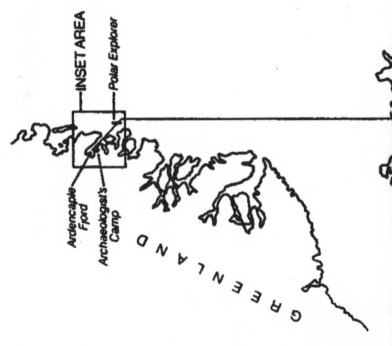

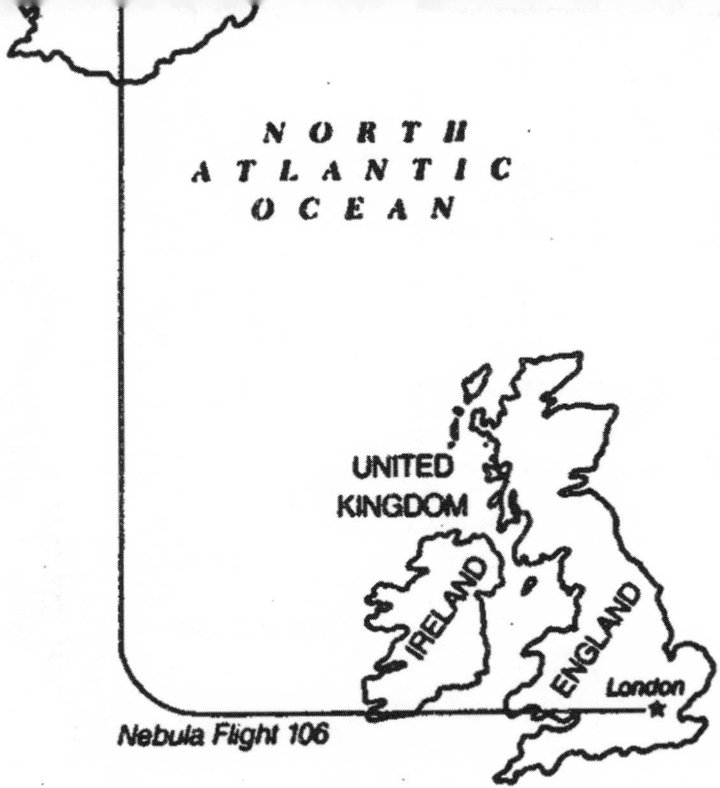
NORTH
ATLANTIC
OCEAN
UNITED
KINGDOM
IRELAND
ENGLAND
London
Nebula Flight 106

1

October 12, 1991
Heathrow Airport, London

No one paid the slightest attention to the pilot as he slipped around the crowd of media correspondents who overflowed from the interior of the VIP lounge. Nor did any of the passengers sitting in the waiting area of gate 14 notice that he carried a large duffel bag instead of a briefcase. He kept his head down, eyes straight ahead, carefully avoiding the battery of TV cameras aimed at a tall attractive woman with a smooth brown face and compelling coal-black eyes, who was the hub of the noisy activity.

The pilot quickly walked through the enclosed boarding ramp and halted in front of a pair of airport security agents. They wore plain clothes and blocked the aircraft door. He threw a casual wave and tried to shoulder his way past them, but a hand firmly grasped his arm.

"One moment, Captain."

The pilot stopped, a questioning but friendly expression on his dark-skinned face. He seemed mildly amused at the inconvenience.

His olive-brown eyes had a gypsylike piercing quality about them. The nose had been broken more than once, and a long scar ran down the base of his left jaw. The closely cropped gray hair beneath the cap and the lines etching his face suggested an age somewhere in the late fifties. He stood nearly six feet four inches, thickset, with a slightly rounded paunch. Seasoned, confident, and standing straight in a tailored uniform, he looked like any one of ten thousand airline pilots who captained international passenger jets.

He removed his identification from a breast pocket and handed it to the security agent.

"Carrying VIPs this trip?" he asked innocently.

The British guard, correct, immaculately dressed, nodded. "A body of United Nations people returning to New York — including the new Secretary-General."

"Hala Kamil?"

"Yes."

"Hardly the job for a woman."

"Sex didn't prove a hindrance for Prime Minister Thatcher."

"She wasn't in water over her head."

"Kamil is an astute lady. She'll do all right."

"Providing Moslem fanatics from her own country don't blow her away," replied the pilot in a decided American accent.

The Britisher gave him a strange look indeed but made no further comment as he compared the photo on the I.D. card with the face before him and read the name aloud. "Captain Dale Lemke."

"Any problem?"

"No, simply preventing any," the guard replied flatly.

Lemke extended his arms. "Do you want to frisk me too?"

"Not necessary. A pilot would hardly hijack his own airplane. But we must check your credentials, to be certain you're a genuine crew member."

"I'm not wearing this uniform for a costume party."

"May we see your carry bag?"

"Be my guest." He set the blue nylon bag on the floor and opened it. The second agent lifted out and riffled the pages of the standard pilot's aircraft and flight operations manuals and then held up a mechanical device with a small hydraulic cylinder.

"Mind telling us what this is?"

"An actuator arm for an oil-cooling door. It stuck in the open position, and our maintenance people at Kennedy asked me to hand-carry it home for inspection."

The agent poked at a bulky object tightly

packed on the bottom of the bag. "Hello, what do we have here?" Then he looked up, a curious expression in his eyes. "Since when do airline pilots carry parachutes?"

Lemke laughed. "My hobby is skydiving. Whenever I have an extended layover, I jump with friends at Croydon."

"I don't suppose you would consider jumping from a jetliner?"

"Not from one flying five hundred knots at thirty-five thousand feet over the Atlantic Ocean."

The agents exchanged satisfied glances. The duffel bag was closed and the I.D. card was passed back.

"Sorry to have delayed you, Captain Lemke."

"I enjoyed the chat."

"Have a good flight to New York."

"Thank you."

Lemke ducked into the plane and entered the cockpit. He locked the door and switched off the cabin lights so any casual observer could not view his movements through the windows from the concourse above. In well-rehearsed sequence, he knelt behind the seats, pulled a small flashlight from his coat pocket and raised a trapdoor leading to the electronics bay below the cockpit, a compartment that was named by some long-forgotten joker as the "hell hole." He dropped down the ladder into pure darkness, underscored by the murmur of the flight attendants' voices as they prepared the main cabin for boarding and the thump of the luggage being loaded in the rear by the baggage handlers.

Lemke reached up and tugged the duffel bag down after him and switched on the penlight. A glance at his watch told him he had about five minutes before his flight crew arrived. In an exercise he had practiced nearly fifty times, he retrieved the actuator arm from the bag and connected it to a miniature timing device he had concealed in his flight cap. He attached the assembled unit to the hinges of a small access door to the outside used by ground/maintenance mechanics. Then he laid out the parachute.

When his first and second officers arrived, Lemke was sitting in the pilot's seat, his face buried in an airport information manual. They exchanged casual greetings and began running through their preflight check routine. Neither the copilot nor the engineer perceived that Lemke seemed unusually quiet and withdrawn.

Their senses might have been sharper if they had known this was to be their last night on earth.

Inside the crowded lounge, Hala Kamil faced a forest of microphones and glaring camera lights. With seemingly inexhaustible patience, she fielded the barrage of questions thrown at her by the mob of inquisitive reporters.

Few asked about her sweep through Europe and the nonstop meetings with heads of state. Most probed for insights on the imminent overthrow of her Egyptian government by Moslem fundamentalists.

The extent of the turmoil was unclear to her. Fanatical mullahs, led by Akhmad Yazid, an Islamic law scholar, had ignited religious passions that ran through the millions of destitute villagers of the Nile and the impoverished masses in the slums of Cairo. High-ranking officers in the army and air force were openly conspiring with the Islamic radicals to remove the recently installed president, Nadav Hasan. The situation was extremely volatile, but Hala had received no up-to-the-minute intelligence from her government, and she was forced to keep her answers vague and ambiguous.

On the surface Hala appeared infinitely poised and sphinx-like as she replied calmly, without emotion. Inwardly she floated between confusion and spiritual shock. She felt distant and alone, as though uncontrollable events were swirling around someone else, someone beyond help for whom she could only feel sorrow.

She could have posed for the painted portrait bust of Queen Nefertiti in the Berlin museum. They both possessed the same long-stemmed neck, delicate features and haunting look. Forty-two years old, slim, black eyes, flawless tawny complexion and long jet-black silken hair brushed straight and falling down to her shoulders. She stood five feet eleven inches in heels, and her lithe, shapely body was enhanced by a designer suit with pleated skirt.

Hala had enjoyed the attentions of four lovers over the years but had never married. A husband and children seemed foreign to her. She refused to spare the time for long-term attachments, and making love held little more ecstasy for her than buying a ticket and attending the ballet.

As a child in Cairo, where her mother was a teacher and her father a filmmaker, she had spent every minute of her free time sketching and digging in the ancient ruins within bicycle distance of her home. A gourmet cook and an artist with a Ph.D. in Egyptian antiquities, she had landed one of the few jobs open to Moslem women, as researcher for the Ministry of Culture.

With great individual effort and prodigious energy, she then successfully fought Islamic discrimination and worked up to Director of Antiquities and later head of the Department of Information. She caught the eye of then President Mubarak, who asked her to serve on the Egyptian delegation to the United Nations General Assembly. Five years later, Hala was named Vice Chairman when Javier Pérez de Cuéllar stepped down in the middle of his second term during an upheaval when five Moslem-run nations withdrew from the charter during a controversy over demands for religious reform. Because the men in line ahead of her refused the job, she was appointed to serve as Secretary-General in a tenuous hope she might mend the widening cracks in the organization's foundation.

Now, with her own government teetering on the brink of disintegration, there was a good chance she might become the first chief representative of the United Nations without a country.

An aide came up and whispered in her ear. She nodded and held up one hand.

"I'm told the plane is ready to take off," she said. "I'll take one more question."

Hands flew up and a dozen queries filled the air at once. Hala pointed to a man standing at the doorway holding a tape recorder.

"Leigh Hunt of BBC, Madame Kamil. If Akhmad Yazid replaces President Hasan's democratic government with an Islamic republic, will you return to Egypt?"

"I am a Moslem and an Egyptian. If my country's leaders, regardless of the government in power, wish me to come home, I will comply."

"Even though Akhmad Yazid has called you a heretic and a traitor?"

"Yes," Hala replied evenly.

46

"If he's half as fanatical as the Ayatollah Khomeini, you might be walking into an execution. Would you care to comment?" Hala shook her head, smiled gracefully and said, "I must leave now. Thank you."

A circle of security guards escorted her from the throng of reporters and onto the boarding ramp. Her aides and a large delegation from UNESCO were already seated. Four members of the World Bank were sharing a bottle of champagne and conversing in low tones in the pantry. The main cabin smelled of jet fuel and Beef Wellington.

Wearily Hala fastened the catch of her seat belt and glanced out the window. There was a light mist and the blue lights along the taxi strips blurred into a dull glow before disappearing completely. She removed her shoes, closed her eyes and gratefully dozed off before the stewardess could offer her a cocktail.

After waiting its turn behind the warm exhaust of a TWA 747, United Nations charter Flight 106 finally moved onto the end of the runway. When takeoff clearance came down from the control tower, Lemke eased the thrust levers forward and the Boeing 720-B rolled over the damp concrete and rose into the soggy air.

As soon as he reached his cruising a of 10,500 meters and engaged the au

47

Lemke unbuckled his belt and rose from his seat.

"A call of nature," he said, heading for the cabin door. His second officer and engineer, a freckle-faced man with sandy hair, smiled without turning from the instrument panel. "I'll wait right here."

Lemke forced a short laugh and stepped into the passenger cabin. The flight attendants were preparing the meal service. The aroma of Beef Wellington came stronger than ever. He made a gesture and drew the chief steward aside.

"Can I get you anything, Captain?"

"Just a cup of coffee," replied Lemke. "But don't bother, I can manage."

"No bother." The steward stepped into the pantry and poured a cup.

"There is one other thing."

"Sir?"

"The company has asked us to take part in a government-sponsored meteorology study. When we're twenty-eight hundred kilometers out from London, I'm going to drop down to fifteen-hundred meters for about ten minutes while we record wind and temperature readings. Then return to our normal altitude."

"Hard to believe the company went along. I wish my bank account totaled what it will cost in lost fuel."

"You can bet those cheap bastards in top management will send a bill to Washington."

"I'll inform the passengers when the time comes so they won't be alarmed."

"You might also announce that if anyone spots any lights through the windows, they'll be coming from a fishing fleet."

"I'll see to it."

Lemke's eyes swept the main cabin, pausing for an instant on the sleeping form of Hala Kamil before moving on. "Did it strike you that security was unusually heavy?" Lemke asked conversationally.

"One of those reporters told me Scotland Yard caught wind of a plot to assassinate the Secretary-General."

"They act as though there's a terrorist plot under every rock. I had to show my identification while they searched my flight bag."

The steward shrugged. "What the hell, it's for our protection as well as the passengers'."

Lemke motioned down the aisle. "At least none of them looks like a hijacker."

"Not unless they've taken to wearing three-piece suits."

"Just to be on the safe side, I'll keep the cockpit door locked. Call me on the intercom only if it's important."

"Will do."

Lemke took a sip of his coffee, set it aside and returned to the cockpit. The first officer, his copilot, was gazing out the side window at the lights of Wales to the north, while behind him the engineer was occupied with

49

computing fuel consumption.

Lemke turned his back to the others and slipped a small case from the breast pocket of his coat. He opened it and readied a syringe containing a highly lethal nerve agent called sarin. Then he faced his crew again and made a fumbling step as if losing his balance and grabbed the arm of the second officer for support.

"Sorry, Frank, I tripped on the carpet."

Frank Hartley wore a bushy moustache, had thin gray hair and a long, handsome face. He never felt the needle enter his shoulder. He looked up from the gauges and lights of his engineer's panel and laughed easily. "You're going to have to lay off the sauce, Dale."

"I can fly straight," Lemke replied good-naturedly. "It's walking that gives me a hard time."

Hartley opened his mouth as if to say something, but suddenly a blank expression crossed his face. He shook his head as if to clear his vision. Then his eyes rolled upward, and he went limp.

Leaning his body against Hartley so the engineer would not fall to one side, Lemke withdrew the syringe and quickly replaced it with another. "I think something is wrong with Frank."

Jerry Oswald swung around in the copilot's seat. A big man with the pinched features of a desert prospector, he stared questioningly. "What ails him?"

"Better come take a look."

Oswald twisted his bulk past the seat and bent over Hartley. Lemke jabbed the needle and pushed the plunger, but Oswald felt the prick.

"What the hell was that?" he blurted, whirling around and gazing dumbly at the hypodermic needle in Lemke's hand. He was far heavier and more muscular than Hartley, and the toxin did not take effect immediately. His eyes widened in sudden comprehension, and then he lurched forward, gripping Lemke by the neck.

"You're not Dale Lemke," he snarled. "Why are you made up to look like him?"

The man who called himself Lemke could not have answered if he wanted. The great hands were choking the breath out of him. Crammed against a bulkhead by the immense weight of Oswald, he tried to gasp out the words of a lie, but no words could come. He rammed his knee into the engineer's groin. The only reaction was a short grunt. Blackness began to creep into the corners of his vision.

Then, slowly, the pressure was released and Oswald reeled backward. His eyes became terror-stricken as he realized he was dying. He looked at Lemke in confused hatred. With the few final beats left in his heart he swung his fist, landing a solid blow into Lemke's stomach.

Lemke drifted to his knees, dazed, the breath punched out of him. He watched as if looking through fog as Oswald fell against the pilot's seat and crashed to the cockpit floor. Lemke slid to a sitting position and rested for a minute, gasping for air, massaging the pain in his gut.

He rose awkwardly to his feet and listened for any curious voices coming from the other side of the door. The main cabin seemed quiet. None of the passengers or flight crew had heard anything unusual above the monotonous whine of the engines.

He was drenched in sweat by the time he manhandled Oswald into the copilot's seat and strapped him in. Hartley's safety belt was already fastened so Lemke ignored him. At last he settled behind the control column on the pilot's side of the cockpit and plotted the aircraft's position.

Forty-five minutes later, Lemke banked the plane from its scheduled flight path to New York onto a new heading, toward the frozen Arctic.

2

It is one of the most barren spots on the earth and one never seen or experienced by tourists. In the last hundred years, only a handful of explorers and scientists have trod its forbidding landscape. The sea along the rugged shore is frozen for all but a few weeks each year, and in the early fall temperatures hover around — 73 F. Darkness grips the cold skies for the long winter months, and even in summer, dazzling sunshine can be replaced by an impenetrable blizzard in less than an hour.

Yet, shadowed by glacial scarred mountains and swept by a constant wind, this magnificent desolation in the upper reaches of Ardencaple Fjord on the northeast coast of Greenland was inhabited nearly two thousand years ago by a band of hunters. Radiocarbon dating on excavated relics indicated the site was occupied from A.D. 200 to A.D. 400, a short time span for the archaeological clock. But they left behind twenty dwellings which had been beautifully preserved by the frigid climate.

A prefabricated aluminum structure had been airlifted by helicopter and assembled over the ancient village by scientists from the University of Colorado. A balky heating arrangement and foam-glass insulation fought a lopsided battle against the cold, but at least denied entry to the never-ending wind moaning eerily around the outside walls. The shelter also enabled an archaeological team to work the site into the beginning stages of winter.

Lily Sharp, a professor of anthropology at Colorado, was oblivious to the cold that seeped into the covered village. She rested on her knees on the floor of a single-family dwelling, carefully scraping away the frozen earth with a small hand trowel. She was alone and lost in deep concentration as she probed the distant past belonging to the prehistoric people.

They were sea-mammal hunters who spent the harsh Arctic winters in dwellings dug partially into the ground, with low walls of rock and turf roofs often supported by whale bones. They warmed themselves with oil lamps, passing the long dark months carving miniature sculptures out of driftwood, ivory and antlers.

They had settled this part of Greenland during the first centuries after Christ. Then,

54

inexplicably, at the height of their culture, they pulled up stakes and vanished, leaving behind a revealing cache of relics.

Lily's perseverance paid off. While the three men on the archaeology team relaxed after dinner in the hut that was their living quarters, she had returned to the protected settlement and continued to excavate, unearthing a length of caribou antler with twenty bearlike figures sculpted on its surface, a delicately carved woman's comb and a stone cooking pot.

Suddenly Lily's trowel clinked on something. She repeated the movement and listened carefully. Fascinated, she tapped again. It was not the familiar sound from the edge of the trowel striking a rock. Though a bit flat, it had a definite metallic ring to it.

She straightened and stretched her back. Strands of her dark red hair, long and thick, shining under the glare from the Coleman lantern, fell from under her heavy woolen cap. Her blue-green eyes mirrored skeptical curiosity as she gazed at the tiny speck protruding from the charcoal-black earth.

A prehistoric people lived here, she pondered. They never knew iron or bronze.

Lily tried to stay calm, but a feeling of astonishment crept over her. Then excitement, followed by urgency. She dismissed the archaeologist's fussbudget passion for prudence. She scraped and dug furiously at the hard-crusted soil. Every few minutes she stopped and painstakingly brushed away the loose dirt with a small painter's brush.

At last the artifact lay fully exposed. She leaned over for a closer look, staring in awe as it glimmered yellow under the bright white from the Coleman lantern.

Lily had excavated a gold coin.

A very old one, by the look of the worn edges. There was a tiny hole and a piece of rotted leather thong on one side, suggesting that it had once been worn as a pendant or personal amulet.

She sat back and took a deep breath, almost afraid to reach down and touch it.

Five minutes later, Lily was still crouched there on her knees, her mind trying to create a solution, when abruptly the shelter's door opened and a large-bellied man with a black-whiskered, kindly-looking face stepped in from the cold, accompanied by a swirl of snow. He exhaled clouds of steam as he breathed. His eyebrows and beard were matted with ice, which made him look like some frozen monster from a science-fiction movie until he broke into a great toothy smile.

It was Dr. Hiram Gronquist, the chief archaeologist of the four-person dig.

"Sorry to interrupt, Lily," he said in his soft, deep voice, "but you've been pushing too hard. Take a break. Come back to the hut, warm up and let me pour you a good stiff brandy."

"Hiram," said Lily, doing her best to stifle the excitement in her voice, "I want you to see something."

Gronquist moved closer and knelt down beside her. "What have you found?"

"See for yourself."

Gronquist fumbled for his reading glasses inside his parka and slid them over his red nose. He bent over the coin until his face was only inches away and studied it from every angle. After several moments, he looked up at Lily, an amused twinkle in his eyes.

"You putting me on, lady?"

Lily looked at him sternly, then relaxed and laughed. "Oh, my God, you think I salted it?"

"You've got to admit, it's like finding a virgin in a bordello."

"Cute."

He gave her a friendly pat on one knee. "Congratulations, this is a rare discovery."

"How do you suppose it got here?"

"There isn't a workable gold deposit within a thousand miles, and it certainly wasn't minted by the early inhabitants. Their level of development was only a notch above Stone Age. The coin obviously came from another source at a later date."

"How do you explain the fact it was buried with artifacts we've dated within a century either side of A.D. 300?"

Gronquist shrugged. "I can't."

"What's your best guess?" asked Lily.

"Off the top of my head, I'd say the coin was probably traded or lost by a Viking."

"There is no record of Vikings sailing this far north along the East Coast," said Lily.

"Okay, maybe Eskimos from a more recent time frame traded goods with the Norse settlements to the south and used this site to camp during hunting expeditions."

"You know better, Hiram. We've found no evidence of habitation after A.D. four hundred."

Gronquist gave Lily a scolding look. "You never give in, do you? We don't even have a date on the coin."

"Mike Graham is an expert on ancient coins. One of his specialties is dating sites around the Mediterranean. He might identify it."

"Won't cost us a nickel for an appraisal," said Gronquist agreeably. "Come along. Mike can examine it while we have that brandy."

Lily donned her heavy fur-lined gloves, adjusted the hood of her parka and turned down the Coleman. Gronquist switched on a flashlight and held the door open for her. She stepped into the agony of the numbing cold and wind that groaned like a ghost in a churchyard. The freezing air stuck her exposed cheeks and made her shudder, a reaction that always seemed to sneak up on her

58

even though she should have been quite used to it by now.

She grasped the rope that led to the living quarters and groped along behind the protecting bulk of Gronquist. She stole a glance upward. The sky was unclouded and the stars seemed to melt into one vast carpet of shimmering diamonds illuminating the barren mountains to the west and the sheet of ice that ran down the fjord to sea in the east. The strange beauty of the Arctic was a compelling mistress, Lily decided. She could understand why men lost their souls to its spell.

After a thirty-yard hike through the dark, they entered the storm corridor of their hut, walked another ten feet and opened a second door to the living quarters inside. To Lily, after the abominable cold outside, it was like stepping inside a furnace. The aroma of coffee caressed her nostrils like perfume and she immediately pulled off her parka and gloves and poured herself a cup.

Sam Hoskins, neck-length blond hair matching an enormous blond handlebar moustache, was hunched over a drafting board. A New York architect with a love for archaeology, Hoskins allowed two months a year out of his busy schedule to rough it on digs around the world. He provided invaluable assistance by rendering detailed drawings of how the prehistoric village might have looked seventeen hundred years ago.

The other team member, a light-skinned man with thinning sandy hair, reclined on a cot, reading a dog-eared paperback novel. Lily couldn't remember seeing Mike Graham without an adventure book in one hand or stuffed in a coat pocket. One of the leading field archaeologists in the country, Graham was as laid back as a mortician.

"Hey, Mike!" Gronquist boomed. "Take a look at what Lily dug up."

He flipped the coin across the room. Lily gasped in shock, but Graham expertly snatched it out of the air and peered at the face.

After a moment he looked up, his eyes narrowed doubtfully. "You're putting me on."

Gronquist laughed heartily. "My exact words when I laid eyes on it. No gag. She excavated it at site eight."

Graham pulled a briefcase from under his cot and retrieved a magnifying glass. He held the coin under the lens, examining it from every angle.

"Well, what's the verdict?" Lily asked impatiently.

"Incredible," murmured Graham, captivated. "A Gold Miliarensia. About thirteen and a half grams. I've never seen one before. They're quite rare. A collector would probably pay between six and eight thousand dollars for it."

"Who is the likeness on the face?"

"A standing figure of Theodosius the Great, Emperor of the Roman and Byzantine Empires. His position is a common motif found on the face of coins from that era. If you look closely, you can make out captives at his feet while his hands hold a globe and a labarum."

"A labarum?"

"Yes, a banner bearing the Greek letters XP and forming a kind of monogram meaning 'in the name of Christ.' The Emperor Constantine adopted it after his conversion to Christianity and it was handed down through his successors."

"What do you make of the lettering on the reverse?" asked Gronquist.

Graham's eyeball enlarged out of proportion through the glass as he studied the coin. "Three words. First one looks like TRIVMFATOR. Can't make out the other two. They're nearly worn smooth. A collector's catalogue should give a description and Latin translation. I'll have to wait until we return to civilization before I can look them up."

"Can you date it?"

Graham stared at the ceiling thoughtfully. "Coined during the reign of Theodosius, which, if I remember correctly, was from A.D. 379 to 395."

Lily stared at Gronquist. "Right in the ballpark."

He shook his head. "Sheer fantasy, to suggest fourth-century Eskimos had contact with the Roman Empire."

"We can't rule out the infinity of chance," Lily persisted.

"Once this gets out, there will be a flood of speculation and hype by the news media," said Hoskins, inspecting the coin for the first time.

Gronquist took a swallow of his brandy. "Ancient coinage has turned up in odd places before. But the date and source of its deposit could rarely be proven to the full satisfaction of the archaeologists' community."

"Perhaps," said Graham slowly. "But I'd give my Mercedes convertible to know how it turned up here."

They all gazed at the coin for a few moments without speaking, each lost in their own thoughts.

Finally Gronquist broke the silence. "It seems the only thing we know for certain is that we have a real mystery on our hands."

3

Shortly before midnight, the imposter began his practiced drill to abandon the jetliner. The air was sparkling clear and the dim smudge that was Iceland rose above the flat, black horizon line of the sea. The small island country was outlined by a faint but eerie display of greenish rays from the Aurora Borealis.

He was oblivious to the dead men around him. He had grown used to the smell of blood and it no longer sickened him. Death and gore simply went with the job. He was as indifferent to mutilated bodies as a pathologist or the neighborhood butcher.

The imposter was quite clinical about killing. Numbers of dead were merely mathematical sums. He was paid well; he was a mercenary, as well as a religious fanatic who murdered for a cause. Oddly, the only part of his work that offended him was being called an assassin or a terrorist. He detested the words. They had a political ring about them, and he nurtured a passionate dislike for politicians.

He was a man of a thousand identities, a perfectionist who rejected random gunfire in crowds or sloppy car bombs, considering them tools for juvenile idiots. His methods were far more subtle. He never left anything to chance. International investigators found it difficult to separate many of his hits from what appeared to be accidents.

The death of Hala Kamil was more than an assigned task. He considered it a duty. His elaborate plan had taken five months to perfect, followed by the patient wait for the opportune moment.

Almost a waste, he mused. Kamil was a beautiful woman. But she was a threat that had to be nullified.

He gently eased back on the throttles and nudged the control column forward, beginning a shallow rate of descent. To anyone but another pilot the slight drop in speed and altitude was imperceptible.

The main cabin crew had not troubled him. By now the passengers were dozing, attempting but failing to fall into the deep sleep so elusive on long aircraft flights.

For the twentieth time he rechecked his heading and studied the dwindling numbers on the panel computer, which he had reprogrammed to indicate the time and distance to his drop zone.

Fifteen minutes later the jetliner crossed over an uninhabited section of Iceland's southern coastline and headed inland. The landscape below became a montage of gray rock and white snow. He lowered the flaps and reduced speed until the Boeing 720-B was flying at 352 kilometers an hour.

He reengaged the auto pilot on a new radio frequency transmitted from a beacon placed on the Hofsjokull, a glacier rising 1,737 meters from the center of the island. Then he set the altitude so the aircraft would impact 150 meters below the peak.

Methodically he smashed and disabled the communication and direction indicators. He also began dumping fuel as a backup in case a flaw somehow marred his carefully conceived plan.

Eight minutes to go.

He dropped through the trapdoor into the hell hole. He already wore a pair of French paraboots with thick, elastic soles. He hurriedly removed a jumpsuit from the duffel bag and slipped into it. There had been no room for a helmet so he pulled on a ski mask and stocking cap. Next came a pair of gloves, goggles and an altimeter, which he strapped to one wrist.

He clipped the harness snaps and checked the straps for snugness. He wore a piggyback rig where the reserve sat on his shoulder blades and the main chute fit into the small of his back. He relied on a ram air canopy, a square air foil that is more flown than jumped.

He glanced at the dial of his watch. One minute, twenty seconds. He opened the escape door and a rush of air swept through the hell hole. He studied the sweep second hand on the watch and began counting down.

When he reached zero he launched his body through the narrow opening feet first, facing in the direction of flight. The velocity of the airstream struck him with the icy force of an avalanche, crushing the breath from his lungs. The plane soared past with a deafening roar. For a brief instant he felt the heat from the turbine's exhaust, and then he was away and falling.

Face down in a stable arched and spread position, knees slightly flexed, hands spread in front, Lemke looked down and saw only blackness. No lights burned on the ground.

He assumed the worst; his crew had failed to reach the correct rendezvous point. Without a defined target zone he could not gauge his wind drift or direction. He might land kilometers away, or worse, impact in the middle of jagged ice with serious injury and never be found in time.

In ten seconds he had already dropped nearly 360 meters. The needle on the luminous dial of his altimeter was crossing into the red. He could not wait any longer. He pulled the pilot chute from a pouch and threw it into the wind. It anchored to the sky and strung out the main canopy.

He heard the chute open with a satisfying thump, and he was jerked into an upright position. He took his penlight and aimed the narrow beam over his head. The canopy blossomed above him.

Suddenly a small circle of lights blinked on about one mile away to his right. Then a flare went up and hung for several seconds, just long enough for him to judge wind direction and speed. He pulled on the right steering toggle and began gliding toward the lights.

Another flare went up. The wind held steady with no fluctuation as he neared the ground. He could clearly see his crew now. They had laid out another line of lights leading to the previously lit circle. He jockeyed the steering toggles and made a 180-degree bank into the wind.

Lemke prepared to strike the ground. His crew had chosen the terrain well. The balls of his feet made contact with soft tundra, and he made a perfect stand-up landing in the center of the circle.

Without a word, he unsnapped the harness and walked outside the glare of the lights. He looked up at the sky.

The aircraft with its unsuspecting crew and passengers flew straight toward the glacier that gradually rose, closing the gap between ice and metal.

He stood there watching as the faint sound of the jet engines died and the blinking navigation lights melted into the black night.

4

Back in the galley, one of the flight attendants tilted her head, listening.

"What's that funny noise coming from the cockpit?" she asked.

Gary Rubin, the chief steward, stepped into the aisle and faced toward the bow of the plane. He could hear what sounded like a continuous, muffled roar, almost like rushing water in the distance.

Ten seconds after the imposter's exodus, the timer on the actuator set the hydraulic arm in motion, closing the hatch in the hell hole and cutting off the strange sound.

"It stopped," he said. "I don't hear it any more."

"What do you suppose it was?"

"Can't say. I've never heard anything quite like it. For a moment I thought we might have suffered a pressure leak."

A passenger call light came on and the flight attendant brushed back her blond hair and stepped into the main cabin. "Maybe you better check it out with the captain," she said over her shoulder.

Rubin hesitated, remembering Lemke's order not to bother the flight crew except for a matter of importance. Better safe than sorry. The welfare of the passengers came first. He lifted the intercom phone to his ear and pressed the cockpit call button.

"Captain, Chief Steward here. We've just experienced a weird noise forward of the main cabin. Is there a problem?"

He received no reply.

He tried three times, but the receiver remained dead. He stood there at a loss for several moments, wondering why the flight cabin did not respond. In twelve years of flying, this was a new experience for him.

He was still trying to fathom the mystery when the flight attendant rushed up and said something. At first he ignored her, but the urgency in her voice got through to him.

"What . . . what did you say?"

"We're over land!"

"Land?"

"Directly beneath us," she said, eyes blank with confusion. "A passenger pointed it out to me."

Rubin shook his head doubtfully. "Impossible. We have to be over the middle of the ocean. He probably saw lights from fishing boats. The captain said we might spot them

70

during our descent for the meteorology study."

"See for yourself," she pleaded. "The ground is coming up fast. I think we're landing."

He stepped over to the galley window and looked down. Instead of the dark waters of the Atlantic there was a glimmer of white. A vast sheet of ice was slipping under the aircraft no more than 240 meters below. It was near enough for the ice crystals to reflect the strobe flashes from the navigation lights. He froze, uncomprehending, trying to make some sense out of what his eyes told him was true.

If this was an emergency landing, why hadn't the captain alerted the main cabin crew? The "Fasten Seat Belts" and "No Smoking" signs had not been turned on.

Almost all of the U.N. passengers were awake, reading or engaged in conversation. Only Hala Kamil was sound asleep. Several representatives from Mexico, returning from an economic mission to the World Bank headquarters, were huddled around a table in the tail section. Director of Foreign Financing Miguel Salazar talked in grim undertones. The atmosphere around the table was dampened by defeat. Mexico had suffered a disastrous economic collapse and was going through technical bankruptcy with no monetary aid in sight.

Dread flared within Rubin, and the words rushed from his mouth: "What in hell is going on?"

The flight attendant mirrored his dread. Her face paled and her eyes widened. "Shouldn't we begin emergency procedures?"

"Don't alarm the passengers. Not yet anyway. Let me check with the captain first."

"Is there time?"

"I don't know."

Controlling his fear, Rubin walked quickly, almost at a jog, toward the cockpit, faking a bored yawn to divert any passenger's curiosity at his rapid step. He whipped the curtain closed that shielded the boarding entryway from the main cabin. Then he tried the door. It was locked.

He frantically rapped his knuckles against the door. No one answered from inside. He stared dumbly at the thin barrier that blocked the cockpit, his mind an incredulous blank; and then, in a flash of desperation, he lashed out his foot and kicked in the door.

The flimsy panel was built to open outward, but the blow smashed it against the inner bulkhead. Rubin stepped over the threshold and stared into the cramped space of the cockpit.

Disbelief, bewilderment, fear, horror: they swirled through his mind like a flood hurtling through a shattered dam.

One swift glance took in Hartley slumped

at his panel, Oswald stretched on the floor, face up, eyes staring sightlessly at the cabin roof. Lemke had seemingly vanished.

Rubin stumbled over Oswald's body, leaned across the empty pilot's seat, and stared terror-struck through the windshield.

The massive summit of the Hofsjokull glacier loomed beyond the bow of the aircraft less than ten miles away. The flickering northern lights silhouetted the rising ice, staining the uneven surface with ghostly shades of gray and green.

Driven by desperation and panic, the steward threw himself into the pilot's seat and grimly clutched the control column. He pulled the wheel toward his chest.

Nothing happened.

The column refused to give, yet, strangely, the altimeter showed a slow but steady increase in altitude. He yanked at the wheel again, but harder this time. It gave slightly. He was stunned by the unyielding pressure.

There was no time to think straight. He was too inexperienced to realize he was trying to override the automatic pilot with brute strength when only twenty-five pounds of pressure was required to overpower it.

The sharp, cold air made the glacier appear near enough to reach out and touch. He pushed the throttles forward and hauled back on the control column again. It gave sluggishly, like the wheel of a speeding car that lost its power steering, and inched back.

With agonizing slowness the Boeing lifted its nose and swept past the icy peak with less than a hundred feet to spare.

Down on the glacier, the man who had murdered the bona fide Flight 106 pilot, Dale Lemke, in London and taken his place, peered into the distance through a pair of night glasses. The northern lights had faded to a dim glow, but the uneven rim of the Hofsjokull still showed against the sky.

The air was hushed with expectancy. The only sounds came from the two-man crew who were loading the lights and transmitter beacon into the hull of a helicopter.

Suleiman Aziz Ammar's eyes became accustomed to the darkness, and he could make out the broken ridges scarring the wall of the ice floe.

Ammar stood like a statue, counting the seconds, waiting for the small speck of flame that would mark the crash of Flight 106.

But the distant fireball did not materialize.

Finally Ammar lowered the glasses and sighed. The stillness of the glacier spread around him, cold and remote. He pulled off the gray-haired wig and threw it into the darkness. Next he removed a pair of specially handcrafted boots and took out the four-inch risers in the heels. He became aware of his servant and friend, Ibn Telmuk, standing beside him.

"Good makeup job, Suleiman, I wouldn't recognize you," said Ibn, a swarthy type with a curly mass of ebony hair.

"The equipment loaded?" Ammar asked.

"All secured. Was the mission a success?"

"A minor miscalculation. The plane somehow cleared the crest. Allah has given Miss Kamil a few more minutes of life."

"Akhmad Yazid will not be pleased."

"Kamil will die as planned," Ammar said confidently. "Nothing was left to chance."

"The plane still flies."

"Even Allah can't keep it in the air indefinitely."

"You have failed," said a new voice.

Ammar swung and stared into the frozen scowl of Muhammad Ismail. The Egyptian's round face was a curious blend of malevolence and childish innocence. The beady black eyes gazed with evil intensity over a heavy moustache, but they lacked the power of penetration. Bravado without substance, a facade of toughness, pulling a trigger was his only skill.

Ammar had had little choice in working with Ismail. The obscure village mullah had been forced on him by Akhmad Yazid. The Islamic idol hoarded his trust like a miser, rationing it out only to those he believed possessed a fighting spirit and a traditionalist's devotion to the original laws of Islam. Firm

75

religious traits meant more to Yazid than competency and professionalism.

Ammar professed to being a true believer of the faith, but Yazid was wary of him. The assassin's habit of talking to Moslem leaders as though they were mortal equals did not sit well with Yazid. He insisted that Ammar carry out his death missions under the guarded eye of Ismail.

Ammar had accepted his watchdog without protest. He was a master at the game of deceit. He quickly reversed Ismail's role into that of a dupe for his own intelligence purposes.

But the stupidity of Arabs was a constant irritation to Ammar. Cold, analytical reasoning was beyond them. He shook his head wearily and then patiently explained the situation to Ismail.

"Events can happen beyond our control. An updraft, a malfunction in the automatic pilot or altimeters, a sudden change in the wind. A hundred different variables could have caused the plane to miss the peak. But all probabilities were considered. The automatic pilot is locked on a course toward the pole. No more than ninety minutes of air time is left."

"And if someone discovers the bodies in the cockpit and one of the passengers knows how to fly?" Ismail persisted.

"The dossiers of all on the plane were carefully examined. None indicated any pilot experience. Besides, I smashed the radio and navigation instruments. Anyone attempting to take control will be lost. No compass, no landmarks to give them a direction. Hala Kamil and her U.N. bedfellows will vanish in the cold waters of the Arctic sea."

"There is no hope for survival?" asked Ismail.

"None," said Ammar firmly. "Absolutely none."

5

Dirk Pitt relaxed and slouched in a swivel chair, stretching out his legs until his six-foot-three-inch body was on a near-horizontal plane. Then he yawned and ran his hands through a thick mat of wavy black hair.

Pitt was a lean, firm-muscled man in prime physical shape for someone who didn't run ten miles every day or look upon the exertion and sweat of bodybuilding as a celestial tonic against old age. His face wore the tanned, weathered skin of an outdoorsman who preferred the sun to the fluorescent lighting of an office. His deep green, opaline eyes radiated a strange combination of warmth and cruelty while his lips seemed eternally locked in a friendly grin.

He was a smooth article who moved easily among the rich and powerful, but preferred the company of men and women who drank their liquor straight up and liked to get their hands dirty.

A product of the Air Force Academy, he

was listed on active status with the rank of Major, although he had been on loan to the National Underwater & Marine Agency (NUMA) for nearly six years as their Special Projects Director.

Along with Al Giordino, his closest friend since childhood, he had lived and adventured in every sea, on the surface and in the depths, encountering in half a decade more wild experiences than most men would see in ten lifetimes. He had found the vanished Manhattan Limited express train after swimming through an underground cavern in New York, salvaged the passenger liner *Empress of Ireland* sent to the bottom of the Saint Lawrence River with a thousand souls. He had hunted down the lost nuclear submarine *Starbuck* in the middle of the Pacific and tracked the ghost ship *Cyclops* to her grave under the Caribbean. And he raised the *Titanic.*

He was, Giordino often mused, a man driven to rediscover the past, born eighty years too late.

"You might want to see this," Giordino said suddenly from the other side of the room.

Pitt turned from a color video monitor that displayed a view of the seascape one hundred meters beneath the hull of the icebreaker survey ship *Polar Explorer.* She was a sturdy new vessel especially built for sailing through ice-covered waters. The massive boxlike superstructure towering above the hull resembled a five-story office building, and her great bow, pushed by 80,000-horsepower engines, could pound a path through ice up to one-and-a-half meters thick.

Pitt placed one foot against a counter, flexed his knee and pushed. The motion was honed through weeks of practice and timed with the gentle roll of the ship for momentum. He twisted 180 degrees in his swivel chair as its castors carried him three meters across the slanting deck of the electronics compartment.

"Looks like a crater coming up."

Al Giordino sat at a console studying an image on the Klein sidescan sonar recorder. Short, standing a little over 162 centimeters in stockinged size-eleven feet, broadened with beefy shoulders in the shape of a wedge, he looked as if he were assembled out of spare bulldozer parts. His hair was dark and curly, an inheritance from Italian ancestry, and if he had worn a bandanna and an earring he could have moonlighted as an organ-grinder. Dry-humored, steadfast and reliable as the tides, Giordino was Pitt's insurance policy against Murphy's Law.

His concentration never flickered while Pitt, feet extended as bumpers, came to an abrupt stop against the console beside him.

Pitt watched the computer-enhanced sonograph as the ridge of a crater slowly rose to a crest and then made a steep descent into the interior void.

"She's dropping fast," said Giordino.

Pitt glanced at the echo sounder. "Down from 140 to 180 meters."

"Hardly any slope to the outer rim."

"Two hundred and still falling."

"Weird formation for a volcano," said Giordino. "No sign of lava rock."

A tall, florid-faced man with thick graying brown hair that struggled to escape from a baseball cap tilted toward the back of his head, opened the door and leaned in the compartment.

"You night owls in the mood for food or drink?"

"Peanut-butter sandwich and a cup of black coffee sounds good," Pitt replied without turning. "Leveling out at 220 meters."

"A couple of doughnuts with milk," Giordino answered.

Navy Commander Byron Knight, skipper of the survey vessel, nodded. Besides Pitt and Giordino, he was the only man with access to the electronics compartment. It was off limits to the rest of the officers and crew.

"I'll have your orders rustled up from the galley."

"You're a wonderful human being, Byron," Pitt said with a sarcastic smile. "I don't care what the rest of the navy says about you."

"You ever try peanut butter with arsenic?" Knight threw at him over his shoulder.

81

Giordino watched intently as the arc of the formation spread and widened. "Diameter almost two kilometers."

"Interior is smooth sediment," said Pitt. "No breakup of the floor."

"Must have been one gigantic volcano."

"Not a volcano."

Giordino faced Pitt, a curious look in his eyes. "You have another name for a submerged pockmark?"

"How about meteor impact?"

Giordino looked skeptical. "A meteor crater this deep on the sea bottom?"

"Probably struck thousands, maybe millions of years ago, at a time when the sea level was lower."

"What led you up that street?"

"Three clues," Pitt explained. "First, we have a well-defined rim without a prominent outer upslope. Second, the sub-bottom profiler indicates a bowl-shaped cross section. And third —" he paused, pointing at a stylus that was making furious sweeps across a roll of graph paper — "the magnetometer is having a spasm. There's enough iron down there to build a fleet of battleships."

Suddenly Giordino stiffened. "We have a target!"

"Where away?"

"Two hundred meters to starboard, lying perpendicular on the crater's slope. Pretty vague reading. The object is partly obscured by the geology."

Pitt snatched the phone and rang the bridge. "We've had a malfunction in the equipment. Continue our heading to the end of the run. If we can make the repair in time, come around and repeat the track."

"Will do, sir," replied the watch officer.

"You should have sold snake oil," said Giordino, smiling.

"No telling the size of Soviet ears."

"Anything from the video cameras?"

Pitt glanced at the monitors. "Just out of range. They should pick it up on the next pass."

The initial sonar image that appeared on the recording paper looked like a brown smudge against the lighter geology of the crater's wall. Then it slipped past the side-scan's viewing window and disappeared into a computer that enhanced the detail. The finished picture came out on a special large high-resolution color video monitor. The smudge had become a well-defined shape.

Using a joystick, Pitt moved a pair of crosshairs to the center of the image and clicked the button to expand the image.

The computer churned away for a few seconds, and then a new, larger, even more detailed image appeared on the screen. A rectangle automatically appeared around the target and showed the dimensions. At the same time another machine reproduced the color image on a sheet of glossy paper.

Commander Knight came rushing back into the compartment. After days of tedium, cruising back and forth as though mowing a vast lawn, staring for hours on end at the video display and sidescan readings, he was galvanized, anticipation written in every line of his face.

"I was given your message about a malfunction. You have a target?"

Neither Pitt nor Giordino answered. They smiled like prospectors who have hit the mother lode. Knight, staring at them, suddenly knew.

"Good God above!" he blurted. "We've found her, really found her?"

"Hiding in the seascape," said Pitt, pointing to the monitor while handing Knight the photo. "The perfect image of one Alfa-class Soviet submarine."

Knight stared, fascinated, at both sonar images. "The Russians probed all around this section of the sea. Incredible they didn't find her."

"She's easy to miss," said Pitt. "The ice pack was heavier when they conducted their search. They couldn't maintain a straight track. Probably skirted the opposite side of the upslope, and their sonar beams only showed a shadow where the sub was lying. Also, the unusually heavy concentration of iron under the crater would have thrown off their magnetic profile."

"Our intelligence people will dance on the ceiling when they see this."

"Not if the Reds get wise," said Giordino. "They'll hardly stand idle and watch us repeat our 'Seventy-five snatch of their 'Golf' class sub with the Glomar Explorer."

"You suggesting they haven't swallowed our story about conducting a geological survey of the seafloor?" Pitt asked with deep sarcasm.

Giordino gave Pitt a sour look indeed. "Intelligence is a weird business," he said. "The crew on the other side of these bulkheads has no idea of what we're up to, yet Soviet agents in Washington smelled out our mission weeks ago. The only reason they haven't interfered is because our undersea technology is better and they want us to lead the way to their sub."

"Won't be easy to deceive them," agreed Knight. "Two of their trawlers have been shadowing our every move since we left port."

"So have their surveillance satellites," added Giordino.

Pitt said, "All reasons why I asked the bridge to run out our last track before coming about for a closer look."

"Good try, but the Russians will pick up our track rerun."

"No doubt, except once we pass over the sub we go on and turn onto the next lane, continuing as before. Then I'll radio our

85

engineers in Washington to complain of equipment problems and ask for maintenance instructions. Every couple of miles we'll rerun a lane to reinforce the ruse."

Giordino looked at Knight. "They might buy it. It's believable enough."

Knight considered that. "Okay, we won't hang around. This will be our last look at the target. Then we continue on, acting as if we've found nothing."

"And after we've finished this grid," Pitt said, "we can start a new one thirty miles away and fake a discovery."

"A nice added touch," Giordino said approvingly. "Drop a red herring across our trail."

Knight smiled wryly. "Sounds like a good script. Let's go for it."

The ship rolled and the deck canted slightly to starboard as the helmsman brought her around on a reverse course. Far behind the stern, like an obstinate dog on a long leash, a robot submersible called *Sherlock* automatically refocused its two movie cameras and one still camera while continuing to send out probing sonar waves. Presumedly named by its designer after the fictional detective, *Sherlock* revealed detailed features of the seafloor previously unseen by man.

Minutes ticked by with the slowness of hours until at last the crest of the crater began slipping across the sidescan. The *Polar Explor-*

er's course towed *Sherlock* along the plunging slope of the crater's interior. Three pairs of eyes locked on the sidescan recorder.

"Here she comes," Giord..io said with the barest tremor of excitement.

The Soviet submarine nearly filled the port side of the sonograph. She was lying on a steep angle with her stern toward the center of the crater, her bow pointing at the rim. The hull was upright and she was in one piece, unlike the U.S. submarines *Thresher* and *Scorpion,* which had imploded into hundreds of pieces when they sank in the 1960s. The slight list to her starboard side was no more than two or three degrees. Ten months had passed since she went missing, but her outer works were free of growth and rust in the frigid Arctic waters.

"No doubt of her being an 'Alfa' class," said Knight. "Nuclear-powered, titanium hull, nonmagnetic and noncorrosive in salt water, latest silent-propellor technology, the deepest-diving and fastest submarines in both the Soviet and U.S. navies."

The lag between the sonar recording and the video view was around thirty seconds. As if watching a tennis match, their heads turned in unison from the sonar as they stared intently at the TV monitors.

The sub's smooth lines slid into view under the camera's lights and were revealed in a ghostly bluish-gray hue. The Americans found it hard to believe the Russian vessel was a graveyard with over a hundred and fifty men resting inside. It looked like a child's toy sitting on the bottom of a wading pool.

"Any indication of unusual radioactivity?" asked Knight.

"Very slight rise," answered Giordino. "Probably from the sub's reactor."

"She didn't suffer a meltdown," Pitt surmised.

"Not according to the readings."

Knight stared at the monitors and made a cursory damage report. "Some damage to the bow. Port diving plane torn away. A long gouge in her port bottom, running for about twenty meters."

"A deep one by the looks of it," observed Pitt. "Penetrated her ballast tanks into the inner pressure hull. She must have struck the opposite rim of the crater, tearing the guts out of her. Easy to imagine the crew struggling to raise her to the surface as she kept running across the center of the crater. But she took in more water than she could blow off and lost depth, finally impacting about halfway up the slope on this side."

The compartment fell into a momentary silence as the submarine dropped astern of the *Sherlock* and slowly faded from view of the cameras. They continued to gaze at the monitors as the broken contour of the sea bottom glided past, their minds visualizing the horrible death that stalked men who sailed the hostile depths beneath the sea.

For nearly half a minute no one spoke, they hardly breathed. Then slowly each shook off the nightmare and turned away from the monitors. The ice was broken. They began to relax and laugh with all the spontaneous enthusiasm of saloon patrons celebrating a winning touchdown by the home team.

Pitt and Giordino could sit back and take it easy for the rest of the voyage. Their part in the search project was over. They had found a needle in a haystack. Then slowly Pitt's expression turned serious and he stared off into space.

Giordino knew the symptoms from long experience. Once a project was successfully completed, Pitt suffered a letdown. The challenge was gone, and his restless mind quickly turned to the next one.

"Damn fine job, Dirk, and you too, Al," Knight said warmly. "You NUMA people know your search techniques. This has to be the most remarkable intelligence coup in twenty years."

"Don't get carried away," said Pitt. "The tough part is yet to come. Recovering the sub under Russian noses will be a delicate operation. No *Glomar Explorer* this time. No salvage from highly visible surface ships. The entire operation will have to be carried out underwater —"

"What the hell is that?" Giordino's eyes had returned to the monitor. "Looks like a fat jug."

"More like an urn," Knight confirmed.

Pitt stared into the monitor for a long moment, his face thoughtful, his eyes tired, red and suddenly intense. The object was standing straight up. Two handles protruded from opposite sides of a narrow neck, flaring sharply into a broad, oval body that in turn tapered toward the base buried in the silt.

"A terra-cotta amphora," Pitt announced finally.

"I believe you're right," said Knight. "The Greeks and Romans used them to transport wine and olive oil. They've been recovered all over the bottom of the Mediterranean." .

"What's one doing in the Greenland Sea?" Giordino asked no one in particular. "There, to the left of the picture, we've picked up a second."

Then a cluster of three drifted under the cameras, followed by five more running in a ragged line from southeast to northwest.

Knight turned to Pitt. "You're the ship-wreck expert. How do you read it?"

A good ten seconds passed before Pitt replied. When at last he did, his voice was distant, as though it came from someone in the next compartment.

"My guess is they lead toward an ancient shipwreck the history books say isn't supposed to be here."

6

Rubin would have traded his soul to abandon the impossible task, remove hands slick with sweat from the control column, close tired eyes and accept death, but his sense of responsibility to the flight crew and passengers drove him on.

Never in his wildest nightmares did he see himself in such a crazy predicament. One wrong physical movement, a slight error in judgment and fifty people would find a deep, unknown grave in the sea. Not fair, he cried in his mind over and over. Not fair.

None of the navigation instruments was functioning. All communications equipment was dead. Not one of the passengers had ever flown an aircraft, even a light plane. He was totally disoriented and hopelessly lost. Inexplicably the needles on the fuel gauges wavered on "Empty." His mind strained at the confusion of it all.

Where was the pilot? What caused the flight officers' deaths? Who was behind this insane madness?

The questions swarmed in his mind, but the answers remained wrapped in frustration.

Rubin's only consolation was that he was not alone. Another man shared the cockpit.

Eduardo Ybarra, a member of the Mexican delegation, had once served as a mechanic in his country's air force. Thirty years had passed since he wielded a wrench on propeller-driven aircraft, but bits and pieces of the old knowledge had returned to him as he sat in the copilot's seat reading the instruments for Rubin and taking command of the throttles.

Ybarra's face was round and brown, the hair thick and black with traces of gray, the brown eyes widely spaced and expressionless. In his three-piece suit, he seemed out of place in the cockpit. Oddly there was no beaded perspiration on his forehead, and he had not loosened his tie or removed his coat.

He motioned upward at the sky through the windshield. "Judging from the stars, I'd say we're on a heading toward the North Pole."

"Probably flying east over Russia for all I know," Rubin said grimly. "I haven't a vague idea of our direction."

"That was an island we left behind us."

"Think it was Greenland?"

Ybarra shook his head. "We've had water under us for the last few hours. We'd still be over the icecap if it was Greenland. My guess is we crossed Iceland."

"My God, how long have we been heading north?"

"No telling when the pilot turned off his London-to-New York course."

Another fear added to Rubin's aching confusion. Calamity was piling on calamity. The one-in-a-thousand chance of coming through alive had rapidly risen to one in a million. He had to make a desperate decision, the only decision.

"I'm going to bring her around ninety degrees to port."

"We have no other choice," Ybarra agreed solemnly.

"A few might survive if we crash on land. Near impossible to pull off a water landing on high waves in the dark, even by an experienced pilot. And if by some miracle we set her down intact, no human dressed in street clothes could last more than a few minutes in a freezing sea."

"We may already be too late." The U.N. delegate from Mexico nodded at the instrument panel. The red fuel warning lights were flashing across the board. "I fear our time in the air has run out."

Rubin stared in astonishment at the telltale instruments. He did not realize that the Boeing flying 200 knots at 1,500 meters ate up the same amount of fuel as it did when flying

500 knots at 10,500 meters. "Okay we head west until she drops from under us."

Rubin rubbed his palms on his pants legs and gripped the control column. He had not taken command of the aircraft again since climbing over the glacier's peak. He took a deep breath and pressed the "Autopilot Release" button on the control column. He was too unsure of himself to slip the Boeing into a bank with the ailerons so he used only the rudder controls to gently crab around in a flat turn. As soon as the nose came onto a straight course he felt something was wrong.

"Rpms dropping on number four engine," said Ybarra with a noticeable tremor in his voice. "It's starving for fuel."

"Shouldn't we shut it down or something?"

"I don't know the procedure," Ybarra replied dumbly.

Oh, dear Lord, Rubin thought to himself, the blind leading the blind. The altimeter began to register a steady drop. The airspeed indicated a decrease too. His mind strained beyond reason, Rubin tried to will the plane in the air rather than fly it.

He also tried to fight time as the distance between the plane and the sea slowly, relentlessly narrowed. Then, without warning, the control column began to grow sluggish and vibrate in his hands.

"She's stalling," shouted Ybarra, his stoic

face showing fear at last. "Push the nose down."

Rubin eased the control column forward, fully aware he was hastening the inevitable. "Lower the flaps to increase our lift!" he ordered Ybarra.

"Flaps coming down," Ybarra replied through pursed lips.

"This is it," Rubin muttered. "We're going in."

A stewardess stood in the open cockpit door listening to the exchange, eyes wide with fright, face pale as a sheet of paper.

"Are we going to crash?" she asked, barely above a whisper.

Rubin tensed in his seat, too busy to turn. "Yes, dammit!" he swore. "Strap yourself in."

She spun and nearly fell down as she raced back to the main cabin to alert the other flight attendants and passengers for the worst. Everyone realized there was no putting off the inevitable, and thankfully there was no panic or hysterical outcry. Even the prayers came softly.

Ybarra twisted in his seat and stared down the aisle. Kamil was comforting an older man who was shaking uncontrollably. Her face was completely calm and seemed to bear a strange expression of contentment. She was truly a lovely woman, Ybarra thought. A pity her beauty would soon be erased. He sighed and turned back to the instrument panel.

The altimeter was falling past two hundred meters. Ybarra took a great risk and increased the throttle settings on the three remaining engines. It was a useless gesture born of desperation. The engines would burn their last few gallons of fuel at a faster rate and die sooner. But Ybarra wasn't thinking logically. He could not sit and do nothing. He felt he had to perform one final, defiant act, anything, even if it meant hastening his own death.

Five tormenting minutes passed as one. The black sea reached up to clutch the aircraft.

"I see lights!" Rubin blurted suddenly. "Dead ahead!"

Ybarra's eyes instantly flicked up and focused through the windshield. "A ship!" he cried. "It's a ship!"

Almost as he shouted, the plane roared over the *Polar Explorer,* missing the radar mast by less than ten meters.

7

The crew of the icebreaker had been alerted by radar to the approaching aircraft. The men standing inside the bridge involuntarily ducked as the airliner, exhaust from its two straining engines screaming like an army of banshees, swept overhead toward the Greenland coast to the west.

The roar filled the electronics compartment, and it emptied like a lake through a split dam. Knight took off for the bridge at a dead run with Pitt and Giordino right behind him. None of the men manning the bridge as much as turned as the captain burst past the door. Everyone was peering in the direction of the receding aircraft.

"What in hell was that?" Knight demanded from the officer on watch.

"An unidentified aircraft nearly rammed the ship, Captain."

"Military?"

"No, sir. I caught a quick glimpse of the lower wings as she flashed overhead. She bore no markings."

"A spy plane maybe?"

"I doubt it. All her windows were lit up."

"A commercial airliner," Giordino suggested.

Knight's expression became vague and a trifle irritated. "Where does the pilot get off, endangering my ship? What's he doing around here anyway? We're hundreds of miles off commercial flight paths."

"She's losing altitude," said Pitt, staring at the blinking lights as they grew smaller in the east. "I'd say she's going in."

"God help them if they set down on this sea in the dark."

"Strange he hasn't turned on the landing lights."

The watch officer nodded his head in agreement. "Strange is the word. A pilot in trouble would surely send out a distress signal. The communications room hasn't heard a peep."

"You tried to raise him?" asked Knight.

"As soon as they came at us on radar. No reply."

Knight stepped to the window and gazed out. He drummed his fingertips thoughtfully for no more than four seconds. Then he turned and faced the watch officer.

"Maintain course, continue the grid pattern."

Pitt looked at him. "I understand your decision, but I can't say I applaud it."

"You're on a Navy ship, Mr. Pitt," said Knight sternly. "We're not the Coast Guard. Our mission takes first priority."

"There could be women and children on board that plane."

"The facts don't spell tragedy. She's still in the air. If the *Polar Explorer* is the only hope of rescue in this part of the sea, why no distress call, no attempt to signal us with his landing lights, no sign of preparations to ditch? You're a flyer, you tell me why the pilot hasn't circled the ship if he's in trouble."

"Could be he's trying for land."

"Begging the Captain's pardon," interrupted the watch officer, "I forgot to mention the landing flaps were down."

"Still no proof of an imminent crash," Knight said stubbornly.

"Damn the compassion, full steam ahead," Pitt said coldly. "This isn't war, Captain. We're talking about a mission of mercy. I wouldn't want it on my conscience if a hundred people died because I failed to act. The Navy can well afford the fuel it takes to investigate."

Knight tilted his head toward the empty chart room, closing the door after Pitt and Giordino entered. "We have our own mission to consider," he persisted calmly. "We turn off course now and the Russians will suspect we found their sub and home in on this area."

"Solid point," Pitt acknowledged. "But you

can still send Giordino and me into the game."

"I'm listening."

"We use our NUMA helicopter on the aft deck and you supply your medical people and a couple of strong bodies. We'll chase the aircraft while the *Polar Explorer* keeps running search lanes."

"And Russian surveillance? What will their intelligence analysts make of it?"

"At first they won't see it as a coincidence. They're already probably trying to paint a connection. But if, God forbid, the plane crashes, and proves out to be a commercial airliner, then at least you'll have a legitimate reason for turning off course to launch a rescue mission. Afterward we resume our search pattern, fake out the Russians and gamble on turning a disaster into a windfall."

"And your helicopter flight, they'll monitor your every move."

"Al and I will use open communications and keep a running dialogue of our search for the downed mystery plane. That should pacify their suspicions."

Knight's eyes turned downward, staring at something beyond the deck. Then he sighed and raised his head to look at Pitt.

"We're wasting time. Get your bird untied and warmed up. I'll see to the medical personnel and a team of volunteers."

■ ■ ■ ■

Rubin made no attempt to circle the *Polar Explorer* because of the almost nonexistent altitude and his sad lack of flying talent. There was every chance he would stall the plane and send it cartwheeling into the rolling swells.

The mere sight of the ship had ignited a small glimmer of hope in the cockpit. Now they had been sighted and rescuers would know where to look for survivors. A small comfort, but better than none at all.

The black sea abruptly turned to solid pack ice and, magnified by starlight, whirled crazily beneath the windshield. Rubin almost felt as if he were sledding through it. With the final impact only minutes away, it finally occurred to him to order Ybarra to turn on the landing lights.

The Mexican feverishly scanned the instrument panel, found the marked switches and flicked them to "ON." A startled polar bear was caught in the sudden glare before he vanished beneath and behind the aircraft. They were hurtling over a dead, frozen plain.

"Mother of Jesus," murmured Ybarra. "I see hills on our right. We've crossed over land."

Luck's pendulum had finally swung in Rubin's favor. Ybarra's hills were a desolate range

102

of mountains that swept above the jagged Greenland coast for a hundred miles in both directions. But Rubin had somehow missed them and miraculously manhandled the descending Boeing into the middle of Arden-caple Fjord. He was flying up the narrow inlet to the sea below and between the summits of steep sloping cliffs. Luck also conjured up a headwind, which gave the aircraft added lift.

The ice seemed close enough for him to reach out and drag his hand over it. The lights reflected a kaleidoscope of shivering colors. A dark mass loomed ahead. He gently pushed the right rudder pedal and the mass slid away to his port side.

"Lower the landing gear!" Rubin shouted.

Ybarra wordlessly complied. Under normal emergency landing procedures it was the worst possible action to take, but in their ignorance they unwittingly made the correct decision for the terrain. The landing gear dropped from their wheel wells and the plane quickly lost speed due to the added wind resistance.

Rubin gripped the control wheel until his knuckles turned ivory, and he glanced down directly at the ice flashing past. The blazing crystals seemed to be rising up to meet him, spreading as they came.

Rubin closed his eyes, praying they would come down in soft snow instead of striking unyielding ice. There was nothing more he and Ybarra could do. The end was approaching with horrifying speed.

Mercifully, he did not know, could not know, the ice was only one meter thick, far too thin to support the weight of a Boeing 720-B.

The maze of instrument lights had gone crazy, and the lights were flashing red. The ice rushed out of the darkness. Rubin had the sensation of bursting through a black curtain into a white void. He pulled back on the control column and the speed of the Boeing fell away as the nose rose up for the last time in a feeble attempt to cling to the sky.

Ybarra sat terrified. Oblivious to the 320-kilometer-an-hour airspeed, frozen in shock, he made no attempt to yank back the throttles. Nor did his dazed mind think to cut the fuel and electrical switches.

Then came the impact.

On reflex, Rubin and Ybarra flung up their hands and closed their eyes. The tires touched, slid, and gouged twin trails through the ice. The port inboard engine buckled and was torn from its mounts, madly gyrating into the darkness. Both starboard engines dug in at the same time, caught and twisted the wing away in a shrieking, mangled mass. Then all power was lost and the lights went dark.

The Boeing careened across the fjord's ice sheet, shedding pieces of protesting metal like particles behind a comet. It smashed into a pressure ridge that had been thrust up when the pack ice collided. The nose gear was crushed back against the forward belly, tearing into the hell hole. The bow dropped and plowed through the ice, crushing the thin aluminum plates inward against the cockpit. At last the momentum fell off, and the crumpled plane, distorted and dismembered, came to the end of its shattering journey. It came to a stop just thirty meters short of a jumbled group of large rocks near the ice-bound shore.

For a brief few seconds there was a deathly silence. Then the ice made a loud series of cracking sounds, metal groaned as it twisted against metal, and the battered aircraft slowly settled through the ice into the frigid water.

8

The archaeologists heard the Boeing fly up the fjord too.

They rushed out of their hut in time to catch a brief look at the plane's outline reflected in the ice glare by the landing lights. They could clearly make out the illuminated cabin windows and the extended landing gear. Almost immediately came the sound of shrieking metal, and a scant instant later the vibration of the impact carried through the frozen surface. The lights went dead, but the protest of tortured metal continued for several seconds. Then, suddenly, a dead silence swept out of the darkness, a silence that overpowered the dreary moan of the wind.

The archaeologists stood in disbelieving shock. Stunned, frozen immobile, immune to the cold, they stared into the black night like haunted statues.

"Good lord," Gronquist finally muttered in awe, "it crashed in the fjord."

Lily could not conceal the shock in her voice. "Horrible! No one could have survived uninjured."

"More than likely dead if they went in the water."

"Probably why there's no fire," added Graham.

"Did anyone see what kind of plane it was?" asked Hoskins.

Graham shook his head. "Happened too fast. Good size, though. Looked to be multi-engine. Might be an ice recon patrol."

"How far do you make it?" asked Gronquist.

"Roughly a kilometer, a kilometer and a quarter."

Lily's expression was pale and strained. "We've got to do something to help them."

Gronquist took a visual bearing and rubbed his unprotected cheeks. "Let's get back inside before we freeze, and form a plan before we charge off half-cocked."

Lily began to come back on track. "Gather up blankets, any extra warm clothing," she said brusquely. "I'll see to the medical supplies."

"Mike, get on the radio," Gronquist ordered. "Notify the weather station at Daneborg. They'll spread the word to Air Force rescue units at Thule."

Graham made an affirmative motion with his hand and was the first one inside the hut.

"We'd better bring along tools for prying any survivors from the wreckage," said Hoskins.

Gronquist nodded as he yanked on his parka and gloves. "Good thinking. Figure out whatever else we'll require. I'll hook up the sled to one of the snowmobiles. We can pile all the stuff in that."

Five minutes ago they had all been asleep. Now they were throwing on cold-weather gear and hurriedly rushing about their respective chores. Forgotten was the enigmatic Byzantine coin, forgotten was the warm comfort of sleep; all that mattered was the urgency of getting to the downed plane as quickly as possible.

Returning outside, head against a sudden shift of wind, Gronquist dashed around the hut to a small snow-covered shed that protected the project's two snowmobiles. He kicked away the ice that had formed around the bottom of the door and pulled it open. Inside, a small oil heater struggled with all the efficiency of a candle inside a freezer to keep the interior air twenty degrees above the temperature outside. He tried the starter buttons, but the batteries were badly drained after months of hard use, and both engines balked at turning over. Cursing in vapored breaths, he removed his heavy gloves with his teeth and began yanking on the manual pull ropes. The engine on the first snowmobile caught on the fifth attempt, but the second played stubborn. Finally, after thirty-two pulls (Gronquist counted them), the engine obstinately coughed to life.

He hitched the tongue of a large sled to the rear catch on the snowmobile whose engine had had extra time to warm up. He finished none too soon, as his fingers were beginning to turn numb.

The others had already stacked the supplies and equipment outside the entryway to the hut when he rode up. Except for Gronquist, they were all bundled up in down-filled jumpsuits. The sled was loaded to the top of its sideboards in less than two minutes. Graham passed everyone a heavy-duty flashlight, and they were ready to set off.

"If they crashed through the ice," shouted Hoskins above the wind, "we might as well forget it."

"He's right," Graham shouted back. "They'd be dead from hypothermia by now."

Lily's eyes turned hard behind her ski mask. "Pessimism never saved anybody. I suggest you big jocks get a move on."

Gronquist grabbed her by the waist and lifted her onto the snowmobile. "Do what the lady says, boys. There're people dying out there."

He swung a leg over the seat in front of Lily and cracked the throttle as Hoskins and Graham raced for the idling snowmobile in the shed. The engine's exhaust purred and the rear tread gripped the snow. He cut a sharp U-turn and took off toward the shore, the sled bouncing along behind.

They swept over the uneven ice-covered stones of the beach onto the frozen fjord. It was dangerous going. The beam from the single light mounted in front of the hand-grips wavered over the ice pack in a crazy jumble of white flashes against black shadows, making it nearly impossible for Gronquist to see any pressure ridges until they were plowing up and over them like a lifeguard boat through heavy surf. And no amount of driving skill could prevent the heavily laden sled from veering and seesawing in their wake.

Lily clasped her hands around Gronquist's great stomach in a death grip, her eyes closed, head buried against his shoulder. She yelled for him to slow down, but he ignored her. She turned and spied the bobbing light of the other snowmobile rapidly closing on their tail.

Without the drag of the sled, the overtaking vehicle, with Hoskins steering and Graham behind, quickly caught up and passed. Soon all Lily could see of the other two men was an indistinct blur of hunched figures through a trailing cloud of fine surface snow.

She felt Gronquist tense as a large metal object rose up out of the darkness at the far edge of the light's ray. Gronquist abruptly jammed the handgrips around to his left. The edges of the front skis dug into the ice and the snowmobile swerved away just one meter from striking a piece of the plane's shattered wing. He made a frantic attempt to straighten out, but the sudden twist of centrifugal force whipped the sled around like the tail of a maddened rattlesnake. The top-heavy sled went into a wild skid, jackknifed against the snowmobile and snapped the hitch. The tips of the runners dug in and it flipped upside down, scattering its load in the air like debris from an explosion.

Gronquist shouted something, but the words were cut off as the flat side of a runner unerringly caught him on the shoulder, knocking him off the snowmobile. He was thrown in a wide arc like a demolition ball about to smash a wall. The hood of his coat was jerked back and the ice rose up and struck his unprotected head.

Lily's arms were torn from around Gronquist's waist as he vanished into the darkness. She thought she might be thrown clear. The sled missed her, crashing to a stop a few meters away, but the snowmobile had other ideas. Without Gronquist's hands on the clutch lever and throttle, it came to a stop, teetering precariously at a forty-five-degree angle, engine popping at idle.

It hung there for a brief moment, and then slowly heeled over to one side, falling on

Lily's legs from her hips down and pinning her helplessly against the ice sheet.

Hoskins and Graham were not immediately aware of the accident behind them, but they were about to run into a disaster of their own. After covering another two hundred meters, Graham turned, more out of curiosity than intuition, to check how far they had outdistanced Lily and Gronquist. He was surprised to see their light beam far to the rear, stationary and pointing downward.

He pounded Hoskins's shoulder and shouted in his ear, "I think something's happened to the others."

It had been Hoskins's original intention to find the depression in the ice carved by the plane after it touched down and then follow it to the final crash site. His eyes were straining to penetrate the gloom beyond when Graham interrupted his concentration.

The words came indistinct over the growl of the snowmobile's exhaust. He twisted his head and shouted back at Graham.

"I can't hear you."

"Turn back. Something's wrong."

Hoskins nodded in understanding and refocused his attention on the terrain ahead. The distraction was to cost them. Too late, he glimpsed one of the troughs gouged by the landing gear almost as he was on it.

The snowmobile flew over the two-meter opening in the ice and became airborne. The weight of the two riders forced the nose to dip down and it collided against the opposite wall with a sharp crack like the blast of a pistol. Fortunately for Hoskins and Graham, they were pitched over the edge and onto the ice surface, their bodies tumbling crazily as if they were cotton-stuffed dolls thrown across a waxed floor.

Thirty seconds later a stunned Graham, moving like a ninety-year-old man, stiffly lifted himself to his hands and knees. He sat there dazed, not fully aware of how he got there. He heard a strange hissing sound and looked around.

Hoskins was sitting in an upright position, doubled up in agony with both hands tightly pressed against his groin. He was sucking and exhaling air through clenched teeth while rocking back and forth.

Graham removed his outer mitten and lightly touched his nose. It didn't feel broken, but blood was flowing from the nostrils, forcing him to breathe through his mouth. A series of stretches indicated all joints were still mobile, all limbs in place. Not too surprising, considering the heavy padding of his clothing. He crawled over to Hoskins, whose tortured hissing had become a string of mournful groans.

"What happened?" Graham asked, regretting such a stupid question the instant he uttered it.

"We hit a gash furrowed in the ice by the aircraft," Hoskins managed between groans. "Jesus, I think I've been castrated."

"Let me have a look." Graham pried away the hands and unzipped the front of Hoskins's jumpsuit. He took a flashlight from a pocket and pushed the switch. He could not suppress a smile. "Your wife will need another excuse to dump you. There's no sign of blood. Your sex life is secure."

"Where's Lily . . . and Gronquist?" Hoskins asked haltingly.

"About two hundred meters back. We've got to make our way around the ice opening and check out their situation."

Hoskins rose painfully to his feet and hobbled to the edge of the ice break. Amazingly, the snowmobile's headlamp was still burning, its dim glow playing on the bottom of the fjord while backlighting the bubbles that traveled up six meters to the surface. Graham walked over and peered down. Then they looked at each other.

"As lifesavers," said Hoskins dejectedly, "we'd better stick with archaeology —"

"Quiet!" Graham snapped suddenly. He cupped his mittens to his ears and turned from side to side like a radar dish. Then he stopped and pointed excitedly at flashing lights in the distance. "Hot damn!" he shouted. "There's a helicopter coming up the fjord."

■ ■ ■ ■

Lily floated in and out of reality.

She could not understand why it became increasingly difficult for her to think straight. She lifted her head and looked around for Gronquist. He lay unmoving several meters away. She shouted, desperately trying to get a response, but he lay as though dead. She gave up and gradually entered a half-dream world as her legs lost all sensation of feeling. Only when she began to shiver did Lily realize she was in a mild state of shock.

She was certain Graham and Hoskins would return any moment, but the moments soon grew into painful minutes, and they did not show. She felt very tired and was about to gratefully slip away into sleep when she heard a strange thumping sound approaching from overhead. Then a dazzling light cut the dark sky and blinded her eyes. Loose snow was kicked up by a sudden windstorm and swept around her. The thumping sound died in intensity and a vague figure, encircled by the light, came toward her.

The figure became a man in a heavy fur parka who immediately summed up the situation, took a strong grip on the snowmobile and heaved it off her legs to an upright position.

He walked around her until the light il-

115

luminated his face. Lily's eyes weren't focusing as they should but they stared into a pair of sparkling green eyes that took her breath away. They seemed to reflect hardness, gentleness and sincere concern in one glinting montage. They narrowed a fraction when he saw that she was a woman. She wondered dizzily where he came from.

Lily couldn't think of anything to say except, "Oh, am I ever glad to see you."

"Name's Dirk Pitt," answered a warm voice. "If you're not busy, why don't you have dinner with me tomorrow night?"

9

Lily looked up at Pitt, trying to read him, not sure she had heard him correctly. "I may not be up to it."

He pushed back the hood of his parka and ran his hands up and down her legs. He gently squeezed her ankles. "No apparent breaks or swelling," he said in a friendly voice. "Are you in pain?"

"I'm too cold to hurt."

Pitt retrieved a pair of blankets that had been pitched from the sled and covered her. "You're not from the aircraft. How did you get here?" he asked her.

"I'm one of a team of archaeologists doing an excavation on an ancient Eskimo village. We heard the plane come up the fjord and ran out of our hut in time to see it land on the ice. We were heading for the crash site with blankets and medical supplies when we . . ." Lily's words became vague and she weakly gestured toward the overturned sled.

"We?"

In the light from the helicopter Pitt quickly read the accident in the snow coating the ice: the straight trail of the snowmobile, the abrupt swerve around the severed aircraft wing, the sharp cuts made by the runners of the out-of-control sled — only then did he glimpse another human form lying nearly ten meters beyond the wing.

"Hold on."

Pitt walked over and knelt down beside Gronquist. The big archaeologist was breathing evenly. Pitt gave him a cursory examination.

Lily watched for a few moments, and then asked anxiously, "Is he dead?"

"Hardly. A nasty contusion on his forehead. Concussion, most likely. Possible fracture, but I doubt it. He has a head like a bank vault."

Graham came trudging up, Hoskins limping along behind, both looking like snowmen, their Arctic jumpsuits dusted white, their face masks plastered with ice from their breathing. Graham lifted his mask, exposing his bloodied face and studied Pitt blankly for a moment, then he smiled bleakly.

"Welcome, stranger. Your timing was perfect."

No one on the helicopter had seen the other two members of the archaeology expedition from the air, and Pitt began to wonder how many other ambulance cases were wandering around the fjord.

"We have an injured man and lady here," Pitt said without formalities. "Are they part of your group?"

The smile fell from Graham's face. "What happened?"

"They took a bad spill."

"We took one too."

"You see the aircraft?"

"Saw it go down, but we didn't reach it."

Hoskins moved around Graham and stared down at Lily and then glanced around until he spied Gronquist. "How badly are they hurt?"

"Know better after they've had X-rays."

"We've got to help them."

"I have a team of medics on board the helicopter —"

"Then what in hell are you waiting for?" Hoskins cut him off. "Call them out here." He made as if to brush past Pitt, but he was stopped dead by an iron grip on his arm. He stared uncomprehending into a pair of unblinking eyes.

"Your friends will have to wait," Pitt said firmly. "Any survivors on the downed aircraft must come first. How far to your camp?"

"A kilometer to the south," Hoskins answered compliantly.

"The snowmobile is still operable. You and your partner rehitch the sled and carry them back to your camp. Go easy in case they have any internal injuries. You have a radio?"

"Yes."

"Keep it set on frequency thirty-two and stand by," said Pitt. "If the plane was a commercial jetliner loaded with passengers, we'll have a real mess on our hands."

"We'll stand by," Graham assured him.

Pitt leaned over Lily and squeezed her hand. "Don't forget our date," he said.

Then he yanked the parka hood over his head, turned and jogged back to the helicopter.

Rubin felt a great weight smothering him from all sides as if some relentless force was driving him backward. The seat belt and harness pressed cruelly into his gut and shoulders. He opened his eyes and saw only vague and shadowy images. As he waited for his vision to clear he tried to move his hands and arms, but they seemed locked in place.

Then his eyes gradually focused and he saw why.

An avalanche of snow and ice had forged through the shattered windshield, entrapping his body up to the chest. He made a desperate attempt to free himself. After a few minutes of struggling, he gave up. The unyielding pressure held him like a straitjacket. There was no way he could escape the cockpit without help.

The shock slowly began to fade and he gritted his teeth from the pain that erupted from his broken legs. Rubin thought it strange that his feet felt as though they were immersed in water. He rationalized that it was his own blood.

Rubin was wrong. The plane had settled through the ice in water nearly three meters deep and it had flooded the cabin floor up to the seats.

Only then did he remember Ybarra. He turned his head to his right and squinted through the darkness. The starboard side of the aircraft's bow had been crushed inward almost to the engineer's panel. All he could see of the Mexican delegate was a rigid, upraised arm protruding from the snow and telescoped wreckage.

Rubin turned away, sick in the sudden realization that the little man who had sat at his side throughout the terrible ordeal was dead, every bone crushed. Rubin also realized he had only a short time to live before he froze to death.

He began to cry.

"She should be coming up!" Giordino shouted over the engine and rotor noise.

Pitt nodded and stared down at the gouge that cut across the merciless ice, its sides littered with bits and pieces of jagged debris. He saw it now. A tangible object with man-made straight lines imperceptibly appeared in the gloom ahead. Then they were on top of it.

There was a sad and ominous appearance about the crumpled aircraft. One wing had completely ripped off and the other was twisted back against the fuselage. The tail section was buckled at a pathetic angle. The remains had the look of a mashed bug on a white carpet.

"The fuselage sank through the ice and two-thirds of it is immersed in water," Pitt observed.

"She didn't burn," said Giordino. "That's a piece of luck." He held up his hand to shade his eyes from the dazzling reflection as the helicopter's lights swept the airliner's length. "Talk about highly polished skin. Her maintenance people took good care of her. I'd guess she was a Boeing 720-B. Any sign of life?"

"None," replied Pitt. "It doesn't look good."

"How about identification markings?"

"Three stripes running down the hull, light blue and purple separated by a band of gold."

"Not the colors of any airline I'm familiar with."

"Drop down and circle her," said Pitt. "While you spot a landing site, I'll try and read her lettering."

Giordino banked and spiraled toward the wreckage. The landing lights, mounted on bow and tail of the helicopter, exposed the half-sunken aircraft in a sea of brilliance. The name above the decorative stripes was in a slanted-style script instead of the usual easier to read block-type letters.

"NEBULA," Pitt read aloud. "NEBULA AIR."

"Never heard of it," said Giordino, his eyes fixed on the ice.

"A plush airline that caters to VIPs. Operates on charter only."

"What in hell is it doing so far from the beaten track?"

"We'll soon know if anybody's alive to tell us."

Pitt turned to the eight men sitting comfortably in the warm belly of the copter. They were all appropriately clothed in blue Navy Arctic weather gear. One was the ship's surgeon, three were medics, and four were damage-control experts. They chatted back and forth as casually as if they were on a bus trip to Denver. Between them, tied down by straps in the center of the floor, boxes of medical supplies, bundles of blankets and a rack of stretchers sat stacked beside asbestos suits and a crate of fire-fighting equipment.

An auxiliary-powered heating unit was secured opposite the main door, its hoisting cables attached to an overhead winch. Next to it stood a compact snowmobile with an enclosed cabin and side tracks.

The gray-haired man seated just aft of the cockpit, with gray moustache and beard to match, looked back at Pitt and grinned. "About time for us to earn our pay?" he asked cheerfully.

Nothing, it seemed, could dim Dr. Jack Gale's merry disposition.

"We're setting down now," answered Pitt. "Nothing stirring around the plane. No indication of fire. The cockpit is buried and the fuselage looks distorted but intact."

"Nothing ever comes easy." Gale shrugged. "Still, it beats hell out of treating burn cases."

"That's the fun news. The tough news is the main cabin is filled with nearly a meter of water, and we didn't bring our galoshes."

Gale's face turned serious. "God help any injured who didn't stay dry. They wouldn't have lasted eight minutes in freezing water."

"If none of the survivors can open an emergency exit, we may have to cut our way inside."

"Sparks from cutting equipment have a nasty habit of igniting sloshing jet fuel," said Lieutenant Cork Simon, the stocky leader of the *Polar Explorer's* damage-control team. He bore the confident look of a man who knew his job inside out and then some. "Better we go in through the main cabin door. Doc Gale, here, will need all the space he can get to remove any stretcher cases."

"I agree," said Pitt. "But a pressurized door that's been jammed against its stops by the distortion of the crash will take time to force open. People may be freezing to death in there. Our first job is to make an opening to insert the vent pipe from the heater —"

He broke off as Giordino cut a steep turn and dropped down toward a flat area only a stone's throw from the wreck. Everyone tensed in readiness. Outside, the beat of the rotor blades whipped up a small blizzard of snow and ice particles, turning the landing site into an alabaster-colored stew that wiped out all vision.

Giordino had barely touched the wheels to the ice and set the throttles on idle when Pitt shoved open the loading door, jumped into the cold and headed toward the wreckage. Behind him Doc Gale began directing the unloading of supplies while Cork Simon and his team winched the auxiliary heater and the snowmobile onto the ice.

Half-running, half-slipping, Pitt made a circle of the fuselage, carefully avoiding open breaks in the ice. The air reeked with the unwelcome smell of jet fuel. He climbed up the ice mound that was piled a meter thick over the cockpit windows. Climbing the slick surface was like crawling up a greased ramp. He tried to scoop an opening into the cockpit, but quickly gave it up: it would have taken an hour or more to dig through the packed ice and then tunnel inside.

He slid down and ran around to the remaining wing. The main section was twisted and

125

broken from its supporting mounts, the tip pointing toward the tail. It lay on the ice, crushed against the sunken fuselage only an arm's length below the row of windows. Using the wing as a platform over the open water, Pitt dropped to his hands and knees and tried to peer inside. The lights from the helicopter reflected off the Plexiglas, and he had to cup his hands around his eyes to close out the glare.

At first he could not detect any movement, only darkness and a deathly stillness.

Then, quite suddenly, a grotesque face materialized on the other side of the window, scant centimeters from Pitt's eyes.

He unconsciously stepped back. The sudden appearance of a woman with a cut over one eye and blood flowing over half the features, all distorted by the hairline cracks running through the window, startled Pitt momentarily.

He quickly shook off the shock and studied the unblemished side of the face. The high cheekbones, the long dark hair, and one olive-brown eye was enough to suggest a very beautiful woman, Pitt thought charitably.

He leaned close to the window and yelled, "Can you open an emergency exit hatch?"

The plucked eyebrow raised a fraction, but the eye looked blank.

"Do you hear me?"

At that instant, Simon's men fired up the

auxiliary power unit, and a stand of flood-lights flashed on, illuminating the aircraft in a glare as bright as daylight. They quickly connected the heater unit and Simon began dragging the flexible hose across the ice.

"Over here, on the wing," Pitt waved. "And bring something to cut through a window."

The damage-control team had been trained for emergency ship repair, and they went about their trade, competent and without wasted movement, as if rescuing trapped passengers from a downed airplane was an everyday exercise.

When Pitt turned back, the woman's face was gone.

Simon and one of his team scrambled up on the twisted wing, struggling to keep their footing while tugging the wide-mouthed heater hose behind. Pitt felt a blast of hot air and was amazed that the heating unit required so little time to warm up.

"We'll need a fire ax to break through," said Pitt.

Simon feigned a haughty look. "Give the U.S. Navy credit for a touch of finesse. We've advanced far beyond crude chopping methods." He removed a compact battery-powered tool from his coat pocket. He pushed the switch and a small abrasive wheel on one end began to spin. "Goes through aluminum and Plexiglas like butter."

"Do your stuff," Pitt said dryly, moving

back out of the way.

Simon was as good as his word; the little cutting device sliced through the thick exterior window in less than two minutes. The thinner sheet inside took only thirty seconds.

Pitt hunched down and extended his arm inside and beamed a flashlight. There was no sign of the woman. The cold water of the fjord glittered under the light's ray. The water lapped at the edge of empty, nearby seats.

Simon and Pitt inserted the end of the heater hose through the window and then hurried around to the forward section of the aircraft. The navy men had reached under the water and released the latch to the main exit door, but, as expected, it was jammed. They rapidly drilled holes and screwed in stainless-steel hooks which were attached to cables leading to the snowmobile.

The driver engaged the clutch and the snowmobile slowly inched ahead until the slack was taken up. Then he revved the engine, the metal spikes of the treads dug in, and the little snowmobile strained forward. For a few seconds nothing seemed to happen. There was only the growl of the exhaust and the crunching noise of the treads as they chiseled their way into the ice.

After an anxious wait, a new sound broke the cold — an unearthly screeching of protesting metal, and then the lower edge of the cabin door raised out of the water. The cables were unhooked and the entire rescue crew crouched down, set their shoulders against the door and heaved upward until it creaked almost to a full open position.

The inside of the plane was dark and ominous.

Pitt leaned across the narrow stretch of open water and stared into the unknown, his stomach churning with morbid curiosity. His figure threw a shadow over the water in the aisle of the main cabin, and at first he saw nothing but the gleam from the walls of the galley.

It was strangely quiet and there was no sign of human remains.

Pitt hesitated and looked back. Doc Gale and his medical team were standing behind him, staring in grim anticipation, while Simon's men were unreeling cable from the power unit to light the plane's interior.

"Going in," Pitt said.

He jumped across the opening into the plane. He landed on the deck in water that splashed over his knees. His legs felt like they had been suddenly stabbed by a thousand needles. He waded around the bulkhead and into the aisle separating the seats of the passenger cabin. The eerie silence was unnerving; the only sound came from the sloshing of his movement.

Then he froze in shock, his worst fears

unfolding like the petals of a poisonous flower.

Pitt found himself exchanging blank looks with a sea of ghostly white faces. None moved, none blinked, none spoke. They just sat strapped in their seats and stared at him with the sightless expression of the dead.

10

A chill colder than the freezing air spread over the back of Pitt's neck. The light from outside filtered through the windows, casting eerie shadows on the walls. He looked from seat to seat as if expecting one of the passengers to wave a greeting or say something, but they sat as still as mummies in a tomb.

He leaned over a man with slicked-back red-blond hair precisely parted down the middle of the skull, who sat in an aisle seat. There was no expression of agony on the face. The eyes were half open as if they were about to close in sleep, the lips met naturally, the jaw slightly loose.

Pitt lifted a limp hand and placed his fingertips just below the base of the thumb and pressed against the artery running beneath the skin on the inner side of the wrist. His touch felt no pulsations — the heart had stopped.

"Anything?" asked Doc Gale, wading past him and examining another passenger.

"He's gone," replied Pitt.

"So's this one."

"From what cause?"

"Can't tell yet. No apparent injuries. Dead only a short time. No indication of intense pain or struggle. Skin coloring doesn't suggest asphyxiation."

"The last fits," said Pitt. "The oxygen masks are still in the overhead panels."

Gale quickly moved from body to body. "I'll know better after a more thorough examination."

He paused as Simon finished mounting a light unit above the doorway and safely above the water. The naval officer motioned outside, and suddenly the interior of the passenger cabin was flooded with light.

Pitt surveyed the cabin. The only noticeable damage was a slight distortion in the ceiling. All seats were in an upright position and the seat belts buckled.

"Impossible to believe they just sat here half immersed in ice water and died from hypothermia without making any movement," he said while checking an elderly brown-haired woman for life signs. There was no hint of suffering in her face. She looked as if she had simply fallen asleep. A small rosary hung loosely from her fingers.

"Obviously all were dead before the plane struck the ice," offered Gale.

"A valid answer," Pitt murmured, rapidly

scanning the seat rows as if searching for someone.

"Death probably came from toxic fumes."

"Smell anything?"

"No."

"Neither do I."

"What does that leave us?"

"Digested poison."

Gale stared at Pitt a long, hard moment. "You're talking mass murder."

"We appear to be headed in that direction."

"Might help if we had a witness."

"We do."

Gale stiffened and hurriedly looked over the white faces. "You spot someone still breathing? Point him out."

"Before we broke inside," Pitt explained, "a woman stared at me through a window. She was alive. I don't see her now."

Before Gale could reply, Simon sloshed down the aisle and stopped, his eyes bulging with shock and incomprehension. "What in hell?" He stiffened and stared wildly around the cabin. "They look like figures in a wax museum."

"Try cadavers in a morgue," said Pitt dryly.

"They're dead? Everyone? You're absolutely sure?"

"Someone is alive," answered Pitt, "either in the cockpit or hiding out in the bathrooms to the rear."

"Then they're in need of my attention,"

said Gale.

Pitt nodded. "I think it best if you continue your examination in the slim chance there's a spark of life in any of these people. Simon can check the cockpit area. I'll head aft and search the bathrooms."

"What about all these stiffs?" asked Simon irreverently. "Shouldn't we alert Commander Knight and begin evacuating them?"

"Leave them be," Pitt said quietly, "and stay off the radio. We'll make our report to Commander Knight in person. Keep your men outside. Seal the door and place the interior of the aircraft off limits. Same goes for your medical team, Doc. Touch nothing unless it's absolutely necessary. Something's happened here beyond our depth. Word of the crash has already gone out. Within hours air-crash investigators and the news media will be swarming around like locusts. Best to keep what we've found under wraps until we hear from the proper authorities."

Simon weighed Pitt's words for a moment. "I get the picture."

"Then let's get a move on and find a survivor."

What was normally a twenty-second walk took Pitt nearly two minutes of struggle through the thigh-high water before he reached the bathrooms. His feet had already turned numb and he didn't require the services of Doc Gale to tell him he'd have to dry and warm them in the next half hour or risk frostbite.

The death toll would have been much higher if the plane had carried a full load of passengers. But even with many of the seats vacant, he still counted fifty-three bodies.

He paused to examine a female flight attendant seated against the rear bulkhead. Her head was tilted forward and blond hair spilled across her face. He felt no pulse.

He reached the compartment containing the bathrooms. Three had the VACANT sign showing and he peered inside. They were empty. The fourth read OCCUPIED and was locked. Someone had to be inside to have slipped the latch.

He knocked loudly on the door and said, "Can you understand me? Help is here. Please try to unlock the door."

Pitt put his ear to the panel and thought he heard a soft sobbing from the other side, followed by low murmurs as if two people were conversing in hushed tones.

He raised his voice. "Stand back. I'm going to force the door."

Pitt raised his dripping leg and gave a sharp but controlled kick, just enough to break the latch without smashing the door against whoever was inside. His heel impacted just above the knob and the catch ripped from the frame. The door gave about an inch. A gentle nudge with his shoulder and it swung inward.

Two women were huddled in the cramped rear of the bathroom, standing on top of the toilet platform out of the water, shivering and clutching each other for support. Actually, the one doing the clutching was a uniformed flight attendant, her eyes wide with alarm and the fear of a trapped doe. She was standing on her right leg, the left was stiffly extended to the side. A wrenched knee, Pitt guessed.

The other woman straightened and stared back at Pitt defiantly. Pitt immediately recognized her as the apparition at the window. Part of her face was still masked with coagulated blood, but both eyes were open now and had the cold look of hatred. Pitt was surprised at her hostility.

"Who are you and what do you want?" she demanded in a husky voice with a slight trace of an accent.

A dumb question was the first thought that crossed Pitt's mind, but he quickly wrote off the woman's testy challenge to shock. He smiled his best Boy Scout trustworthy smile.

"My name is Dirk Pitt. I'm part of a rescue team from the United States ship *Polar Explorer.*"

"Can you prove it?"

"Sorry, I left my driver's license at home." This was bordering on the ridiculous. He tried another tack and leaned against the

136

door frame and casually crossed his arms. "Please rest easy," he said soothingly. "I want to help, not harm you."

The flight attendant seemed to relax for an instant, her eyes softened and the edges of her lips lifted in a timid smile. Then abruptly the fear returned and she sobbed hysterically.

"They're all dead, murdered!"

"Yes, I know," said Pitt gently. He held out his hand. "Let me take you where it's warm and the ship's doctor can tend your injuries."

Pitt's face was shadowed by the floodlights in the forward part of the cabin, and the stronger woman of the two could not read his eyes. "You might be one of the terrorists who caused all this," she said in a controlled tone. "Why should we trust you?"

"Because you'll freeze to death if you don't."

Pitt tired of the word games. He stepped forward, carefully lifted the flight attendant in his arms and eased her out into the aisle. She offered him no resistance, but her body was stiff with apprehension.

"Just relax," he said. "Pretend you're Scarlett O'Hara and I'm Rhett Butler come to sweep you off your feet."

"I don't feel much like Scarlett. I must look a mess."

"Not to me," Pitt grinned. "How about dinner some night?"

"Can my husband come along?"

"Only if he picks up the check."

She gave in then and he felt her body sag in exhausted relief. Slowly her arms circled his neck and she buried her head in his shoulder. He paused and turned to the other woman. The warmth of his smile was revealed and his eyes glinted in the light. "Hang tight. I'll be right back for you."

For the first time Hala knew she was safe. Only then did the dam holding back the nightmare of fright, the stunning disbelief that any of this was happening to her, flood over the gates.

The suppressed emotions ran free, and she wept.

Rubin knew he was slipping away. The cold and the pain had ceased to exist. The strange voices, the sudden display of light, formed no meaning for him. He felt detached. To his confused mind they were like obscure recollections from a distant place, a former time.

Suddenly a white brilliance filled the shattered cockpit. He wondered if this was the light at the end of the tunnel people who had died and returned claimed to have experienced.

A disembodied voice nearby said, "Take it easy, take it easy."

Rubin tried to focus his eyes on a vague figure hovering over him. "Are you God?"

Simon's face went blank for a brief moment. Then he smiled compassionately. "Only a mere mortal who happened to be in the neighborhood."

"I'm not dead?"

"Sorry, but if I'm any judge of age, you'll have to wait at least another fifty years."

"I can't move. My legs feel like they're pinned. I think they might be broken. Please . . . please get me out."

"That's why I'm here," said Simon cheerfully. He used his hands to scoop a good foot of ice and snow away from Rubin's upper torso until the trapped arms came free. "There, now you can scratch your nose until I return with a shovel and cutting tools."

Simon reentered the main cabin as Pitt was easing the flight attendant through the door into the waiting arms of Gale's medics, who gently lowered her onto a stretcher.

"Hey, Doc, I've got a live one in the cockpit."

"On my way," replied Gale.

"I could use your help too," Simon said to Pitt.

Pitt nodded. "Give me a couple of minutes to carry another from the aft section."

Hala slid to her knees and leaned over and looked into the mirror. There was enough light to clearly see her reflection. The face that stared back was flat-eyed and expressionless. It was also a disaster. She looked like an over-the-hill street-walker who had been beaten up by her pimp.

She reached out and pulled several paper towels from a rack. She dipped them in the cold water, then wiped clear the clotted blood and lipstick which had smeared around her mouth. Her mascara and eye shadow looked as if they had been applied by Jackson Pollock on a drip painting. She wiped away that mess too. Her hair was still reasonably intact so she patted the loose ends into place.

She still looked awful, she thought despairingly. She forced a smile when Pitt reappeared, hoping she looked more presentable.

He looked at her a long moment and then screwed his face into an expression of awed curiosity. "Excuse me, gorgeous creature, but have you seen an old crone anywhere?"

Tears welled in Hala's eyes and she half-laughed, half-cried. "You're a nice man, Mr. Pitt. Thank you."

"I try, God knows I try," he said humorously.

Pitt had returned with several blankets and he bundled them around her. He placed one arm under her knees and the other around her waist and lifted her without the slightest sign of strain. As he carried her up the aisle his numbed legs began to give out and he stumbled for several steps before recovering.

"Are you all right?" she asked.

"Nothing a shot of Jack Daniel's Tennessee whiskey won't cure."

"As soon as I return home I'll send you a whole case."

"Where's home?"

"At the moment, New York."

"Next time I'm in town, let's have dinner together."

"I'd consider it an honor, Mister Pitt."

"Likewise, Miss Kamil."

Hala raised her eyebrows. "You recognized me, looking horrible like this?"

"I admit it wasn't until after you'd fixed your face a bit."

"Forgive me for putting you to all this trouble. Your legs and feet must be frozen stiff."

"A minor discomfort is a small price for claiming I held the Secretary-General of the U.N. in my arms."

Amazing, truly amazing, thought Pitt. This has to be a red-banner day. Dating the only three women, and attractive ones at that, within two thousand miles of frigid desolation inside of thirty minutes had to be some sort of record. The feat meant more to him than discovering the Russian submarine.

Fifteen minutes later, after Hala, Rubin and the flight attendant were comfortably settled inside the helicopter, Pitt stood in front of the cockpit and waved to Giordino, who acknowledged with a thumbs up sign. The rotors were engaged and the craft rose in the air above a swirling cloud of snow, swung around a hundred and eighty degrees and headed for the *Polar Explorer.* Only when it was safely airborne and on its way did Pitt limp over to the auxiliary heating unit.

He pulled off his waterlogged boots and soggy socks and dangled his feet over the exhaust, soaking up the heat and gratefully accepting the stabbing pain of recirculation. He became vaguely aware of Simon's approach.

Simon stopped and stood, gazing at the wrinkled sides of the aircraft. It did not look forlorn any more. To him, the knowledge of the dead inside gave it a charnel house appearance.

"United Nations delegates," Simon said distantly, "is that who they were?"

"Several were members of the General Assembly," answered Pitt. "The rest were directors and aides of the U.N.'s specialized agencies. According to Kamil, most of them were returning from a tour of their Field Service organizations."

"Who'd gain by murdering them?"

Pitt wrung out his socks and laid them over the heater tube. "I have no idea."

"Middle East terrorists?" Simon persisted.

"News to me they've taken up murder by poison."

"How're your feet?"

"In a state of gradual thaw. How about yours?"

"The Navy issues foul-weather boots. Mine are dry and warm as toast."

"Hooray for considerate admirals," Pitt muttered sardonically.

"I'd say one of the three survivors did the dirty work."

Pitt shook his head. "If in fact it proves to be poison, it probably was introduced into the meal at the food services kitchen before it was loaded on board the aircraft."

"The chief steward or a flight attendant could have done it in the galley."

"Too difficult to poison over fifty meals one at a time without being detected."

"What about the drinks?" Simon tested again.

"You're a persistent bastard."

"Might as well speculate until we're relieved?"

Pitt checked his socks. They were still damp. "Okay, drinks are a possibility, especially coffee and tea."

Simon seemed pleased that one of his theories had been accepted. "Okay, smartass, of the three survivors who's your candidate for most likely suspect?"

"None of the above."

"You saying the culprit knowingly took the poison and committed suicide."

"No, I'm saying it was the fourth survivor."

"I only counted three."

"*After* the plane crashed. *Before* that there were four."

"You don't mean the little Mexican fellow in the copilot's seat?"

"I do."

Simon looked totally skeptical. "What brilliant logic brought you to that conclusion?"

"Elementary," Pitt said with a sly grin. "The killer in the best murder-mystery tradition is always the least obvious suspect."

11

"Who dealt this mess?"

Julius Schiller, Under Secretary for Political Affairs, grimaced good-naturedly as he studied his cards. His teeth clamped on a cold stogie, he looked up and peered over his hand, his intelligent blue eyes moving from player to player.

Four men sat across the poker table from him. None smoked, and Schiller diplomatically refrained from lighting his cigar. A small bundle of cedar logs crackled in an antique mariner's stove, taking the edge off an early fall chill. The burning cedar gave an agreeable aroma to the teak-paneled dining saloon inside Schiller's yacht. The beautifully proportioned 35-meter-motor sailer was moored in the Potomac River near South Island just opposite Alexandria, Virginia.

Soviet Deputy Chief of Mission Aleksey Korolenko, heavy-bodied and composed, wore a fixed jovial expression that had become his trademark in Washington's social circles.

"A pity we're not playing in Moscow," he said in a stern but mocking tone. "I know a nice spot in Siberia where we could send the dealer."

"I second the motion," said Schiller. He looked at the man who had dealt the cards. "Next time, Dale, shuffle them up."

"If your hands are so rotten," growled Dale Nichols, Special Assistant to the President, "why don't you fold?"

Senator George Pitt, who headed up the Senate Foreign Relations Committee, stood and removed a salmon-colored sport jacket. He draped it over the back of the chair and turned to Yuri Vyhousky.

"I don't know what these guys are complaining about. You and I have yet to win a pot."

The Soviet Embassy's Special Adviser on American Affairs nodded. "I haven't seen a good hand since we all began playing five years ago."

The Thursday-night poker sessions had indeed been held on Schiller's boat since 1986, and went far beyond a simple card game between friends who needed one evening out of the week to unwind. It was originally set up as a small crack in the wall separating the opposing superpowers. Alone, without an official setting and inaccessible to

146

the news media, they could informally give and take viewpoints while ignoring bureaucratic red tape and diplomatic protocol. Ideas and information were exchanged that often had a direct bearing on Soviet-American relations.

"I open for fifty cents," announced Schiller.

"I'll raise that a dollar," said Korolenko.

"And they wonder why we don't trust them," Nichols groaned.

The Senator spoke to Korolenko without looking at him. "What's the prediction from your side on open revolt in Egypt, Aleksey?"

"I give President Hasan no more than thirty days before his government is overthrown by Akhmad Yazid."

"You don't see a prolonged fight?"

"No, not if the military throws its weight behind Yazid."

"You in, Senator?" asked Nichols.

"I'll go along for the ride."

"Yuri?"

Vyhousky dropped three fifty-cent pieces in the pot.

"Since Husan took over after Mubarak's resignation," said Schiller, "he's achieved a level of stability. I think he'll hold on."

"You said the same about the Shah of Iran," Korolenko goaded.

"No denying we called the wrong shots." Schiller paused and dropped his throwaway cards on the table. "Let me have two."

Korolenko held up one finger and received his card. "You might as well pour your massive aid into a bottomless pit. The Egyptian masses are on the brink of starvation. A situation that fuels the surge of religious fanaticism sweeping the slums and villages. You stand as little chance of stopping Yazid as you did Khomeini."

"And what is the Kremlin's stance?" asked Senator Pitt.

"We wait," said Korolenko impassively. "We wait until the dust settles."

Schiller eyed his cards and shifted them around. "No matter the outcome, nobody wins."

"True, we all lose. You may be the great Satan in the eyes of Islamic fundamentalists, but as good Communist atheists we're not loved either. I don't have to tell you the biggest loser is Israel. With the disastrous defeat of Iraq by Iran and the assassination of President Saddam Husayn, the road is now open for Iran and Syria to threaten the moderate Arab nations into combining forces for a massive three-front thrust against Israel. The Jews will surely be defeated this time."

The Senator shook his head doubtfully. "The Israelis have the finest fighting machine in the Middle East. They've won before, and they're prepared to do it again."

"Not against 'human wave' attacks by nearly two million Arabs," warned Vyhousky.

"Assad's forces will drive south while Yazid's Egyptians attack north across the Sinai, as they did in 'sixty-seven and 'seventy-three. Only this time Iran's army will sweep over Saudi Arabia and Jordan, crossing the River Jordan from the West. Despite their fighting skills and superior technology, the Israelis will be overwhelmed."

"And when the slaughter finally ends," added Korolenko ominously, "the West will be thrown into a state of economic depression when the united Muslim governments, with total control of fifty-five percent of the world's oil reserves, drive prices to astronomical heights. As they surely will."

"Your bet," Nichols said to Schiller.

"Two bucks."

"Raise you two," came Korolenko.

Vyhousky threw his cards on the table. "I fold."

The Senator contemplated his hand a moment. "I'll match the four and raise another four."

"The sharks are circling," said Nichols with a tight smile. "Count me out."

"Let's not kid ourselves," said the Senator. "It's no secret the Israelis have a small arsenal of nuclear weapons, and they won't hesitate to use them if they're down to the last roll of the dice."

Schiller sighed deeply. "I don't even like to think about the consequences." He looked up as his boat's skipper knocked on the door and hesitantly stepped in.

"Excuse me for interrupting, Mr. Schiller, but there's an important call for you."

Schiller pushed his cards toward Nichols. "No sense in prolonging the agony with this hand. Would you excuse me?"

One of the cardinal rules of the weekly get-together was no phone calls unless it was a matter of urgency that in some way concerned everyone at the table. The game continued, but the four men played automatically, their curiosity mounting.

"Your bet, Aleksey," said the Senator.

"Raise you another four dollars."

"I call."

Korolenko shrugged resignedly and laid down his cards face up. All he had was a pair of fours.

The Senator smiled wryly and turned over his cards. He won with a pair of sixes.

"Oh, good lord," moaned Nichols. "I dropped out with a pair of kings."

"There goes your lunch money, Aleksey." Vyhousky laughed.

"So we bluffed each other," said Korolenko. "Now I know why I won't buy a used car from an American politician."

The Senator leaned back in his chair and ran a hand through a thick mane of silver hair. "As a matter of fact I worked my way through law school selling cars. Best training

I ever had for running for the Senate."

Schiller reentered the room and sat down at the table. "Sorry to leave, but I've just been notified that a chartered United Nations plane crashed on the coast of northern Greenland. Over fifty known dead. No word on survivors."

"Any Soviet representatives on board?" asked Vyhousky.

"The passenger list hasn't come through yet."

"A terrorist bombing?"

"Too early to tell, but first sketchy reports say it was no accident."

"What flight was it?" Nichols asked.

"London to New York."

"Northern Greenland?" Nichols repeated thoughtfully. "They must have strayed over a thousand miles off course."

"Smells of a hijacking," suggested Vyhousky.

"Rescue units are on the site," explained Schiller. "We should know more within the hour."

The expression on Senator Pitt's face darkened. "I have a dire suspicion that Hala Kamil was on that flight. She was due back at United Nations headquarters from Europe for next week's session of the General Assembly."

"I believe George is right," said Vyhousky. "Two of our Soviet delegates were traveling

151

in her party."

"Madness," said Schiller, wearily shaking his head. "Utter madness. Who would gain by murdering a planeload of U.N. people?"

No one answered immediately. There was a long moment's silence. Korolenko stared, expressionless, at the center of the table. Then he spoke in a quiet voice.

"Akhmad Yazid."

The Senator stared the Russian straight in the eye. "You knew."

"I guessed."

"You think Yazid ordered Kamil's death?"

"I can only say our intelligence sources discovered there was an Islamic faction in Cairo that was planning an attempt."

"And you stood by and said nothing while fifty innocent people died."

"A miscalculation," admitted Korolenko. "We did not know how or when the assassination was to take place. It was assumed Kamil's life would be in danger only if she returned to Egypt — not from Yazid himself, but rather his fanatical followers. Yazid has never been tied to any terrorist acts. Your profile of him reads the same as ours: a brilliant man who thinks of himself as a Muslim Gandhi."

"So much for KGB and CIA profiles," said Vyhousky candidly.

"Another classic case of intelligence experts being suckered by a well-conceived public-

152

relations campaign," sighed the Senator. "The man is a bigger psycho case than we figured."

Schiller nodded in agreement. "Yazid has to be responsible for the tragedy. His followers would never have considered it without his blessing."

"He had the motive," said Nichols. "Kamil has immense flair and charm. Her level of popularity with the people and the military far exceeds President Hasan's. She was a strong buffer. If she's dead, Egypt is only hours away from a government led by extremist mullahs."

"And when Hasan falls?" asked Korolenko slyly. "What will be the White House position then?"

Schiller and Nichols exchanged knowing looks. "Why, the same as the Kremlin's," said Schiller. "We're going to wait until the dust settles."

For a moment the fixed smile faded from Korolenko's face. "And if, make that *when,* the combined Arab nations attack the Jewish state?"

"We'll back Israel to the hilt, as we have in the past."

"But will you send in American forces?"

"Probably not."

"Arab leaders might be less cautious if only they knew that."

"Be our guest. Only remember, Aleksey —

this time, we're not going to use our leverage to stop the Israelis from taking Cairo, Beirut and Damascus."

"You're saying the President won't stand in their way if they resort to nuclear weapons?"

"Something like that," Schiller said with studied indifference. He turned to Nichols. "Whose deal?"

"I believe it's mine," said the Senator, trying his best to sound casual. This switch in the President's Middle East policy was news to him. "Shall we ante fifty cents?"

The Russians were not about to let loose.

"I find this most disturbing," said Vyhousky.

"A new posture had to come sometime," Nichols confessed. "The latest projections put United States oil reserves at eighty billion barrels. With prices pushing fifty dollars a barrel, our oil companies can now afford to mount a massive exploration program. And, of course, we can still count on Mexican and South American reserves. The bottom line is that we no longer have to rely on the Middle East for oil. So we're cutting bait. If the Soviet government wants to inherit the Arab mess, take it as a gift."

Korolenko couldn't believe what he was hearing. His ingrained wariness made him skeptical. But he knew the Americans too well to doubt they would bluff or mislead him, on an issue of such magnitude.

Senator Pitt had his doubts, too, about the

game plan the President was leaking to the Soviet representatives. There was a strong possibility oil would not flow over the Rio Grande when America needed it. Mexico was a revolution waiting for the starter's gun.

Egypt was cursed with a Dark Ages fanatic like Yazid. But Mexico had its madman in a Topiltzin, a Benito Juárez/Emilio Zapata messiah who preached a return to a religious state based on Aztec culture. Like Yazid, Topiltzin was supported by millions of his nation's poor, and he was also inches away from sweeping out the existing government.

Where were all the madmen coming from, the Senator wondered? Who was spawning these devils? He made a conscious effort to keep his hands steady as he began to deal.

"Five card stud, gentlemen, jokers wild."

Huge figures rose up in the eerie silence of the night and gazed through empty eyes at the barren landscape as if waiting for some unknown presence to bring them to life. The stark, rigid figures stood as tall as a two-story building, their grim, expressionless faces highlighted by a full moon.

A thousand years ago they had supported a temple roof that sat on top of the five-step pyramid of Quetzalcoatl in the Toltec city of Tula. The temple was gone but the pyramid remained and was reconstructed by archaeologists. The ruins stretched along a low ridge, and during the city's glory sixty-thousand people lived and walked on its streets.

Few visitors found their way to the site, and those who took the trouble were awed by Tula's haunted desolation.

The moon cast ghostly shadows through the dead city as a solitary man climbed the steep steps of the pyramid to the stone statues at the summit. He was dressed in a suit and tie and carried a leather attaché case.

At each of the five terraces he stopped for a few moments and peered at the macabre sculptured friezes decorating the walls. Human faces protruded from the gaping mouths of serpents while eagles shredded human hearts with their beaks. He continued, passing an altar carved with skulls and crossbones, symbols used in later centuries by pirates of the Caribbean.

He was sweating when he finally reached the top of the pyramid and looked around. He was not alone. Two figures stepped forward and roughly searched him. They motioned at his attaché case. He obligingly opened it and the men rummaged through the contents. Finding no weapons, they silently retreated to the edge of the temple platform.

Rivas relaxed and pressed a hidden switch on the handle of the case. A small tape recorder secreted inside the lid began to roll.

After a short minute had passed, a figure emerged from the shadows of the great stone statues. He was dressed in a floor-length robe of white cloth. His hair was long and tied at the base, giving it the look of a rooster tail. His feet were hidden under the robe, but the moon's light revealed circular bands around his arms that were carved from gold and inlaid with turquoise.

157

He was short, and the smooth, oval face suggested Indian ancestry. His dark eyes studied the tall, fair-complexioned man before him, taking in the oddly-out-of-place business suit. He crossed his arms and spoke strange words that sounded almost lyrical.

"I am Topiltzin."

"My name is Guy Rivas, Special Representative for the President of the United States."

Rivas had expected an older man. It was difficult to guess the Mexican messiah's age, but he didn't look a year over thirty.

Topiltzin gestured to a low wall. "Shall we sit while we talk?"

Rivas nodded a "Thank you" and sat down. "You chose a most unusual setting."

"Yes, I thought Tula appropriate." Topiltzin's tone suddenly turned contemptuous. "Your President was afraid for us to confer openly. He did not want to embarrass and anger his friends in Mexico City."

Rivas knew better than to be baited. "The President asked me to express his gratitude for allowing me to talk with you."

"I expected someone with a higher rank of state."

"Your conditions were you'd speak with only one man. We took that to mean no interpreter for our side. And since you do not wish to speak Spanish or English, I am the only ranking government official who has a

158

tongue for Nahuatl, the language of the Aztecs."

"You speak it very well."

"My family immigrated to America from
the town of Escampo. They taught it to me
when I was quite young."

"I know Escampo; a small village with
proud people who barely survive."

"You claim you'll end poverty in Mexico.
The President is most interested in your programs."

"Is that why he sent you?" Topiltzin asked.

Rivas nodded. "He wishes to open a line of
communication."

There was silence as a grim smile crossed
Topiltzin's features. "A shrewd man. Because
of my country's economic collapse he knows
my movement will sweep the ruling Partido
Revolucionario Institucional out of office,
and he fears an upheaval in U.S. and Mexican
relations. So he plays both ends against the
middle."

"I can't read the President's mind."

"He will soon learn the great majority of
Mexican people are finished with being
doormats for the ruling class and wealthy.
They are sick of political fraud and corrup-
tion. They are tired of digging garbage in the
slums. They will suffer no more."

"By building a utopia from the dust of the
Aztecs?"

"Your own nation would do well to return

to the ways of your founding fathers."

"The Aztecs were the biggest butchers in the Americas. To fashion a modern government on ancient barbarian beliefs is . . ." Rivas paused. He almost said "idiotic." Instead, he pulled back and said, "naive."

Topiltzin's round face tensed and his hands worked compulsively. "You forget, it was the Spanish conquistadors who slaughtered our common ancestors."

"Spain could say the same about the Moors, which would hardly justify restoring the Inquisition."

"What does your President want from me?"

"Merely peace and prosperity in Mexico," replied Rivas, holding the line. "And a promise you will not steer a course toward Communism."

"I am not a Marxist. I detest Communists as much as he does. No armed guerrillas exist among my followers."

"He'll be glad to hear it."

"Our new Aztec nation will attain greatness once the criminally wealthy, the corrupt officials, and present government and army leaders are sacrificed."

Rivas wasn't sure he interpreted right. "You're talking about the execution of thousands of people."

"No, Mr. Rivas, I'm talking sacrificial victims for our revered gods, Quetzalcoatl, Huitzilopochtli, Tezcatlipoca."

Rivas looked at him, not comprehending. "Sacrificial victims?"

Topiltzin did not reply.

Rivas, staring at the stoic face, suddenly knew. "No!" he burst out. "You can't be serious."

"Our country will again be known by its Aztec name of Tenochtitlan," Topiltzin continued impassively. "We shall be a religious state. Nahuatl will become our official language. Population will be brought under control by stern measures. Foreign industries will be the property of the state. Only the native born can be allowed to live within our borders. All others will be expelled from the country."

Rivas was stunned. He sat white-faced, listening in silence.

Topiltzin went on without pause. "No more goods are to be purchased from the United States nor will you be allowed to buy our oil. Our debts to world banks will be declared null and void, and all foreign assets confiscated. I also demand the return of our lands in California, Texas, New Mexico and Arizona. To ensure this return I intend to turn loose millions of my people across the border."

Topiltzin's threats were nothing short of frightening. Rivas's distraught mind could not conceive the terrible consequences.

"Pure madness," Rivas said desperately. "The President will never listen to such absurd demands."

"He will not believe what I say?"

"No sane man would."

Rivas in his uneasiness had stepped too far. Topiltzin slowly rose to his feet, eyes unblinking, head lowered, and spoke in a toneless voice. "Then I must send him a message he will understand."

He raised his hands over his head, arms outstretched toward the dark sky. As if on cue four Indians appeared wearing white capes clasped at the neck and nothing else. Approaching from all sides, they quickly subdued Rivas, who froze in astonishment. They carried him to the stone altar sculpted with the skulls and crossbones and threw him on his back, holding him down by the arms and legs.

At first Rivas was too dazed to protest, too incredulous with shock to comprehend Topiltzin's intention. When horror-struck realization came, he cried out.

"Oh, God! No! No!"

Topiltzin coldly ignored the terrified American, the pitiful fright in his eyes, and stepped to the side of the altar. He gave a nod, and one of the men ripped away Rivas's shirt, exposing the chest.

"Don't do this!" Rivas pleaded.

A razor-sharp obsidian knife seemed to materialize in Topiltzin's upraised left hand. The moonlight glinted from the black, glassy

162

blade as it hung poised.

Rivas screamed — the last sound he would ever make.

Then the knife plunged.

The tall column-statues looked down upon the bloody act with stone-cold indifference. They had witnessed the horrible display of inhuman cruelty thousands of times, a thousand years ago. There was no pity in their timeworn chiseled eyes as Rivas's still-beating heart was torn from his chest.

13

Despite the people and activity around him, Pitt was captivated by the dense silence of the cold north. There was an incredible stillness about it that seemed to overwhelm the voices and sounds of machinery. He felt as though he were standing in numbing solitude inside a refrigerator on a desolate world.

Daylight finally appeared, filtered by a peculiar gray mist that permitted no shadows. By midmorning the sun began to burn away the icy haze and the sky turned a soft orange-white. The ethereal light made the rocky peaks overlooking the fjord look like tombstones in a snow-covered cemetery.

The scene surrounding the crash site was beginning to resemble a military invasion. A fleet of five Air Force helicopters had been the first to arrive, ferrying an Army Special Service Force of heavily armed and determined-looking men who immediately cordoned off the fuselage and began patrolling the entire area. An hour later, Federal

Aviation accident investigators landed and set about marking the scattered wreckage for removal. They were followed by a team of pathologists who tagged and removed the bodies to the helicopters, which quickly airlifted them to the morgue at Thule Air Force Base.

The Navy was represented by Commander Knight and the unexpected appearance of the *Polar Explorer.* All halted their grisly chores and turned their eyes toward the sea as a series of loud whoops from the ship's siren echoed off the jagged mountains.

Dodging newly-formed ice calves, floating low and opaque, and the winter's first bergs, which resembled the ruins of Gothic castles, the *Polar Explorer* came about slowly and entered the mouth of the fjord. For a time the ash-blue sea hissed quietly past the scarred bow, and then it turned to white.

The immense prow of the icebreaker effortlessly bulldozed a path through the ice pack, heaving to less than fifty meters from the wreckage. Knight stopped engines, climbed down a ladder to the ice and graciously offered the facilities of the ship to the security and investigation teams as a command post — an offer that was thankfully accepted without a second's hesitation.

Pitt was impressed with the security. The news blackout had not yet been penetrated: the story given out at Kennedy Airport revealed only that the U.N. flight was over-due. It was only a matter of another hour before a shrewd correspondent got wise and blew the whistle.

"I think my eyeballs just froze to their lids," Giordino said gloomily. He was sitting in the pilot's seat of the NUMA helicopter, trying to drink a cup of coffee before it froze. "Must be colder than a Minnesota dairy cow's tit in January."

Pitt gave his friend a dubious look. "How would you know? You haven't been outside your heated cockpit all night."

"I get frostbite by looking at an ice cube in a glass of Scotch." Giordino held up one hand, all five fingers spread. "Look at that. I'm so stiff with cold I can't make a fist."

Pitt happened to glance out the side win-dow and spotted Commander Knight trudg-ing over the ice from the ship. He walked back to the main cabin and opened the cargo door when Knight reached the boarding lad-der. Giordino moaned in self-pity as his pre-cious heat escaped and a frigid breeze en-gulfed the interior of the 'copter.

Knight waved a greeting and climbed on board, his breath exhaling clouds of vapor. He reached inside his parka and produced a leather-covered flask.

"A little something from the sick bay. Cognac. Can't begin to guess the brand. Thought you might find a good use for it."

166

"I think you just sent Giordino to heaven," Pitt said, laughing.

"I'd rather be in hell," Giordino muttered. He tipped the flask and savored the brandy as it trickled into his stomach. Then he raised his hand again and made a fist. "I think I'm cured."

"Might as well settle in," said Knight. "We've been ordered to remain on station for the next twenty-four hours. If you'll pardon the awful pun, they want to keep us on ice until the cleanup is over."

"How are the survivors doing?" inquired Pitt.

"Miss Kamil is resting comfortably. Incidentally, she asked to see you. Something about having dinner together in New York."

"Dinner?" asked Pitt innocently.

"Funny thing," Knight continued. "Just before Doc Gale surgically repaired the flight attendant's torn knee ligaments, she mentioned a dinner date with you too."

Pitt had a pure-as-the-driven-snow expression on his face. "I guess they must be hungry."

Giordino rolled his eyes and tilted the flask again. "I think I've heard this song before."

"And the steward?"

"Rough shape," Knight replied. "But Doc thinks he'll pull through. His name is Rubin. While he was slipping under the anesthetic he babbled some wild story about the pilot murdering the first and second officers and then vanishing in flight."

"Maybe not so wild," said Pitt. "The pilot's body has yet to be found."

"Not my territory," Knight shrugged. "I've got enough to worry about without getting bogged down in an unsolved air mystery."

"Where do we stand on the Russian sub?" asked Giordino.

"We keep the lid on our discovery until we can report face to face with the big brass at the Pentagon. Stupid to fumble away the ball game through a communications leak. A piece of luck, for us at any rate, the plane crashing. Gives us the logical excuse to set a course for home and our dock in Portsmouth as soon as the survivors can be airlifted to a stateside hospital. Let's hope the unexpected diversion will confuse Soviet intelligence analysts enough to get them off our back."

"Don't count on it," Giordino said, his face beginning to glow. "If the Russians had the slightest suspicion we struck pay dirt, *and* they're paranoid enough to think our side caused the plane crash as a diversion, they'll come charging in with salvage ships, a protective fleet of warships, a swarm of covering aircraft and, when they pinpoint the sub, raise and tow it back to their station at Severomorsk on the Kola Peninsula."

"Or blow it into smithereens," Pitt added.

"Destroy it?"

168

"The Soviets don't have major salvage technology. Their prime objective would be to make certain no one else laid hands on it."

Giordino passed the cognac to Pitt. "No sense debating the cold war here. Why don't we return to the ship, where it's nice and warm?"

"Might as well," said Knight. "You two have already done more than your share."

Pitt stretched and began zipping up his parka. "Think I'll take a hike."

"You're not coming back with us?"

"In a bit. Thought I'd look in on the archaeologists and see how they are."

"Wasted trip. Doc sent one of his medics over to their camp. He's already reported back. Except for a few bruises and strains they were all fine."

"Might find it interesting to see what they've dug up," Pitt persisted.

Giordino was an old hand at reading Pitt's mind. "Maybe they've found a few old Greek amphoras lying around."

"Won't hurt to ask."

Knight gave Pitt the benefit of a hard stare. "Mind what you say."

"I have our geological survey story down pat."

"And the aircraft passengers and crew?"

"They were all trapped inside the fuselage and died from hypothermia brought on by exposure to the frigid water."

169

"I think he's ready for the big sting," said Giordino dryly.

"Good," Knight nodded. "You've got the right idea. Just don't suggest anything they have no reason to know."

Pitt opened the cargo door and gave a casual nod. "Don't wait up." Then he stepped into the cold.

"Persistent cuss," Knight muttered. "I didn't know Pitt was interested in antiquities."

Giordino gazed through the cockpit window as Pitt set off across the fjord. Then he sighed.

"Neither did he."

The ice field was firm and flat, and Pitt made good time across the fjord. He scanned the ominous gray cloud ceiling rolling in from the northwest. The weather could change from bright sunshine to a blinding blizzard within minutes and obliterate all landmarks. He wasn't keen on wandering lost without even a compass, and he increased his pace.

A pair of white gyrfalcons soared above him. Seemingly immune to the Arctic cold, they were a select group of birds that remained in the north during the harsh winter.

Moving in a southerly direction, he crossed the shoreline and kept his bearings on the smoke that rose above the archaeologists' hut. The distant and indistinct smudge appeared as though seen through the wrong end of a telescope.

Pitt was only ten minutes away from the camp when the storm struck. One minute he could see nearly twenty kilometers, the next his visibility was cut to less than five meters.

He started jogging, desperately hoping he was traveling in something remotely resembling a straight line. The horizontally driving snow came against his left shoulder and he leaned into it slightly to compensate for his drift.

The wind increased and beat against him until he could barely stand. He shuffled blindly forward, looking down at his feet, counting his strides, his arms huddled about his head. He knew it was impossible to walk sightless without gradually wandering in a circle. He was also aware that he could walk past the archaeolgists' hut, missing it by a few meters, and stumble on until he dropped from exhaustion.

Despite the high wind-chill factor, his heavy clothing kept him reasonably warm, and he could tell by his heartbeat that he was not unduly exerting himself.

Pitt paused when he calculated that he was in the approximate vicinity of the hut. He continued walking another thirty paces before stopping again.

He turned to his right and moved over about three meters until he could still see his footprints trailing off in the blowing snow from the opposite direction. Then he walked parallel to his original path, mowing the lawn as if he was searching for an object beneath the sea. He took about sixty steps before his old footprints faded and disappeared in the snow.

He walked five lanes before he swung to his right again, repeating the pattern until he was sure he had retraced the now obliterated center line. Then he picked up the grid again on the other side. On the third lane he stumbled into a snowdrift and fell against a metal wall.

He followed it around two corners before meeting a rope that led to a door. With a great sigh of relief, Pitt pushed open the door, savoring the knowledge that his life had been in danger and he had won. He stepped inside and tensed.

This was not the living quarters, but rather a large Quonset-like shelter covering a series of excavations in the exposed earth. The interior temperature was not much above freezing, but he was thankful to be safe from the gale-force wind.

The only light came from a Coleman lantern. At first he thought the structure was deserted, but then a head and pair of shoulders seemed to rise up from a trough in the ground. The figure was kneeling, facing away from Pitt, and seeming absorbed in carefully

172

scraping loose gravel from a small shelf in the trough.

Pitt stepped from the shadows and looked down.

"Are you ready?" he asked.

Lily spun around, more puzzled than startled. The light was in her eyes and all she could make out was a vague form.

"Ready for what?"

"To go out on the town."

The voice came back to her. She lifted the lamp and slowly rose to her feet. She stared into his face, captivated once again by Pitt's eyes, while he was taken by her dark red hair that glinted like fire under the bright light of the hissing Coleman.

"Mr. Pitt . . . isn't it?" She slipped off her right glove and extended her hand.

He also removed his glove, reached out and gave her hand a firm squeeze. "I prefer attractive ladies to call me Dirk."

She felt like an embarrassed little girl, mad at herself for not having any makeup on, wondering if he noticed the calluses on her hand. And to make it worse, she could feel herself blushing.

"Lily . . . Sharp," she stammered. "My friends and I were hoping we could thank you for last night. I thought you were joking about dinner. I really didn't think I'd see you again."

"As you can hear —" he paused and tilted

173

his head toward the moaning wind outside
— "a blizzard couldn't keep me away."

"You must be crazy."

"No, just stupid for thinking I could outrun
an Arctic storm."

They both laughed and the tension fell
away. Lily began to climb out of the excavation trough. Pitt took her arm and helped her
up. She winced and he quickly released his
grip.

"You shouldn't be on your feet."

Lily smiled gamely. "Stiff and a little sore
from a sea of black-and-blue marks I can't
show you, but I'll live."

Pitt held up the lantern and peered around
the oddly grouped rocks and excavations.
"Just what is it you have here?"

"An ancient Eskimo village, inhabited one
hundred to five hundred years after Christ."

"Have you a name for it?"

"We call the site Gronquist Bay Village after
Dr. Hiram Gronquist, who discovered it five
years ago."

"One of the three men I met last night?"

"The big man who was knocked unconscious."

"How's he getting along?"

"Despite a large purplish dome on his
forehead, he swears he doesn't suffer from
headaches or dizziness. When I left the hut
he was roasting a turkey."

"Turkey?" Pitt repeated, surprised. "You

must have a first-rate supply system."

"A vertical-lift Minerva aircraft, on loan to the university by a wealthy alumnus, flies in once every two weeks from Thule."

"I thought excavations this far north were limited to mid-summer when above-freezing temperatures thawed the ground."

"Generally speaking that's true. But with the heated prefab shelter over the main section of the village, we can work from April through October."

"Find anything out of the ordinary, like an object that doesn't belong here?"

Lily gave Pitt a queer look. "Why do you ask?"

"Curiosity."

"We've unearthed hundreds of interesting artifacts representing prehistoric Eskimo lifestyles and technology. We have them in the hut, if you care to examine them."

"How's chances of looking at them over the turkey?"

"Good to excellent. Dr. Gronquist cooks gourmet."

"I had hoped to invite you all to the ship's galley for dinner, but the sudden storm messed up my plans."

"We're always happy to see a new face at the table."

"You've discovered something unusual, haven't you?" Pitt asked abruptly.

Lily's eyes widened suspiciously. "How

could you know?"

"Greek or Roman?"

"Roman Empire, Byzantium, actually."

"Byzantium what?" Pitt pushed her, his eyes turned hard. "How old?"

"A gold coin, late fourth century."

He seemed to relax then. He took a deep breath and slowly let it out while she looked at him in confusion and no small degree of irritation.

"Make your point!" Lily snapped at him.

"What if I was to tell you," Pitt began slowly, "there is a trail of amphoras scattered along the seabed that leads into the fjord?"

"Amphoras?" Lily repeated in astonishment.

"I have them on videotape from our underwater cameras."

"They came." She spoke as in a trance. "They really crossed the Atlantic. The Romans set foot on Greenland before the Vikings."

"The evidence points in that direction." Pitt eased his arm around Lily's waist and aimed her toward the door. "Speaking of direction, are we stuck here for the duration of the storm or does that rope outside the door lead to your hut?"

She nodded. "Yes, the line stretches between the two buildings." She paused and stared into the excavation where she had discovered the coin. "Pytheas, the Greek navigator, made an epic voyage in 350 B.C. The legends say he sailed north into the Atlantic and eventually reached Iceland. Strange there are no records or legends telling of a Roman voyage this far north and west, seven hundred and fifty years later."

"Pytheas was lucky: he made it home to tell the tale."

"You think the Romans who came here were lost on the return voyage?"

"No, I think they're still here." Pitt looked down at her with a determined grin. "And you and I, lovely lady, are going to find them."

PART II:
THE *SERAPIS*

14

October 14, 1991
Washington, D.C.

A cold, bleak drizzle shrouded the nation's capital as a taxi pulled to a stop at Seventeenth and Pennsylvania Avenue in front of the old Executive Office Building. A man dressed in a deliveryman's uniform stepped from the rear seat and told the driver to wait. He leaned back in the taxi and retrieved a package wrapped in red silk. He hurried across the sidewalk and down several steps, passing through a doorway into the reception area of the mail room.

"For the President," he said with a Spanish accent.

A postal service employee signed in the package and the time. He looked up and smiled. "Still raining?"

"More like a fine spray."

"Just enough to make life miserable."

"And slow traffic," the deliveryman said with a sour face.

181

"Have a good day anyway."

"You too."

The deliveryman left as the postal worker took the package and ran it under the fluoroscope. He stood back and stared at the screen as the X-rays revealed the object under the wrapping.

He easily identified it as a briefcase, but the picture puzzled him. There was no indication of files or papers inside, no hard object with a distinguishing outline, nothing that looked like explosives. He was an old hand at X-ray identification, but the contents of the case threw him.

He picked up the phone and made a request to the person on the other end. Less than two minutes later a security agent appeared with a dog.

"Got one for Sweetpea?" asked the agent.

The postal worker nodded as he set the package on the floor. "Can't make an I.D. on the scope."

Sweetpea hardly resembled her namesake. She was a mutt, the result of a brief affair between a beagle and a dachshund. Huge brown eyes, a fat little body supported by short spindly legs, Sweetpea was highly trained to sniff out every explosive from the common to the exotic. As the two men watched, she waddled around the package, nose quivering like a plump dowager sniffing at a perfume counter.

Suddenly she stiffened, the hair on her neck and back stood up, and she began backing away. Her face took on an odd, suspicious kind of distasteful expression, and she began to growl.

The agent looked surprised. "That's not her usual reaction."

"There's something weird in there," said the postal worker.

"Who is the package addressed to?"

"The President."

The agent walked over and punched a number on the phone. "We better get Jim Gerhart down here."

Gerhart, Special Agent in Charge of Physical Security for the White House, took the call during a brief lunch at his desk and left immediately for the mail reception room.

He observed the dog's reaction and eyeballed the package under the fluoroscope. "I don't detect any wiring or detonation device," he said in a Georgia drawl.

"Not a bomb," the postal worker agreed.

"Okay, let's open it."

The red silk wrapper was carefully removed, revealing a black leather attaché case. There were no markings, not even a manufacturer's name or model number. Instead of a combination lock, both latches had inserts for a key.

Gerhart tried the latches simultaneously. They both unsnapped.

"The moment of truth," he said with a cautious grin.

He placed his hands on each corner of the upper lid and slowly lifted until the case was open and the contents in view.

"Jesus!" Gerhart gasped.

The security agent's face went white and he turned away. The postal worker made gagging noises and staggered for the lavatory.

Gerhart slammed the lid shut. "Get this thing over to George Washington University Hospital."

The security agent couldn't reply until he swallowed the acid-tasting bile that had risen in his throat. Finally he coughed, "Is that thing real or is this some kind of Halloween trick or treat?"

"It's genuine," said Gerhart grimly. "And believe you me, it ain't no treat."

In his White House office, Dale Nichols settled back in his swivel chair and adjusted his reading glasses. For perhaps the tenth time he began scrutinizing the contents of a thick folder routed to him by Armando López, the President's Senior Director of Latin American Affairs.

Nichols gave off the image of a university professor, which indeed he had been when the President persuaded him to switch his sedate campus classroom at Stanford for the political cesspool of Washington. His initial reluctance had turned to amazement when he discovered he had a hidden talent for manipulating the White House bureaucracy.

His thicket of coffee-brown hair was parted neatly down the middle. His old-style spectacles, with small round lenses and thin wire frames, reflected a plodding temperament, a never-say-die type who was oblivious to everything but his immediate project. And, finally, the ultimate in academic clichés, the bow tie and the pipe.

He lit the pipe without removing his eyes from the articles clipped from Mexican newspapers and magazines dealing with only one subject.

Topiltzin.

Included were interviews granted by the charismatic messiah to officials who represented Central and South American countries. But he had refused to talk to American journalists or government representatives and none had penetrated his army of bodyguards.

Nichols had learned Spanish during a two-year tour in Peru for the Peace Corps, and easily read the stories. He took a legal pad and began making a list of claims and statements that came to light during the interviews.

1. Topiltzin describes himself as a man who came from the poorest of the poor, born in a cardboard shack on the edge of Mexico

185

City's sprawling garbage dump, with no idea of the day, month or year. Somehow he survived and learned what it was to live amid the stink and flies and manure and muck of the hungry and homeless.

2. Admits to no schooling. History from childhood, until his emergence as a self-styled high priest of archaic Toltec/Aztec religion, is blank.

3. Claims to be the reincarnation of To-piltzin, tenth-century ruler of the Toltecs, who was identified with the legendary god Quetzalcoatl.

4. Political philosophy a crazy blend of ancient culture and religion with vague sort of autocratic, one-man, no-party rule. Intends to play benevolent father role to Mexican people. Ignores questions on how he intends to revive shattered economy. Refuses to discuss how he will restructure government if he comes to power.

5. Spellbinding orator. Has uncanny rapport with his audience. Speaks only in old Aztec tongue through interpreters. Language still used by many Indians of Central Mexico.

6. Mainstream supporters are fanatical. His popularity has swept the country like the proverbial tidal wave. Political analysts predict he could win a national election by nearly six percentage points. Yet he refuses to participate in free elections, claiming, and

rightly so, that corrupt leaders would never surrender the government after a losing campaign. Topiltzin expects to take over the country by public acclaim.

Nichols set his pipe in an ashtray, stared at the ceiling thoughtfully for a few moments, and began writing again.

SUMMARY: Topiltzin is either incredibly ignorant or incredibly gifted. Ignorant if he is what he says he is. Gifted if he has a method to his madness, a goal only he can see. *Trouble, trouble, trouble.*

Nichols was going over the articles again, searching for a key to Topiltzin's character, when his phone buzzed. He picked up the receiver.

"The President on one," announced his secretary.

Nichols punched the button. "Yes, Mr. President."

"Any news of Guy Rivas?"

"No, nothing."

There was a pause on the President's end. Then, finally, "He was scheduled to meet with me two hours ago. I'm concerned. If he encountered a problem, his pilot should have sent us word by now."

"He didn't fly to Mexico City in a White House jet," explained Nichols. "In the interests of secrecy he booked passage on a commercial airliner and flew coach class as a tourist on vacation."

"I understand," the President agreed. "If President De Lorenzo learned I sent a personal representative behind his back to make contact with his opposition, he'd take it as an insult and scratch our Arizona conference next week."

"Our primary concern," Nichols assured him.

"Have you been briefed on the U.N. charter crash?" the President asked, suddenly changing tack.

"No, sir," replied Nichols. "My only information is that Hala Kamil survived."

"She and two crew members. The rest died from poison."

"Poison?" Nichols blurted incredulously.

"That's the word from the investigators. They believe the pilot tried to poison everyone on board before parachuting from the plane over Iceland."

"The pilot must have been an imposter."

"We won't know till a body is found, warm or cold."

"Christ, what terrorist movement would have a motive for murdering over fifty U.N. representatives?"

"So far none have claimed credit for the disaster. According to Martin Brogan at CIA, if it is the work of terrorists, they stepped out of character on this one."

"Hala Kamil might have been the target," suggested Nichols. "Akhmad Yazid has sworn to eliminate her."

"We can't ignore the possibility," the President admitted.

"Have the news media gotten wind of it?"

"The story will be all over the papers and TV in the next hour. I saw no reason to hold it back."

"Is there anything you'd like me to do, Mr. President?"

"I'd appreciate it, Dale, if you'd monitor reaction from President De Lorenzo's people. There were eleven delegates and agency representatives from Mexico on the flight. Offer condolences in my name and any co-operation within limits. Oh, yes, you'd better keep Julius Schiller over at the State Department informed so we don't stumble over each other."

"I'll get my staff right on it."

"And let me know the minute you hear from Rivas."

"Yes, Mr. President."

Nichols hung up and forced his attention back to the file. He began to wonder if Topiltzin was somehow connected with the U.N. murder. If only there was a thread he could grasp.

Nichols was not a detective. He had no talent for coldly dissecting a prime suspect layer by layer until he knew what made the man tick. His academic specialty was in systems projections of international political movements.

Topiltzin was an enigma to him. Hitler had a misguided vision of Aryan supremacy. Driven by religious fervor, Khomeini wanted to return the Middle East to the Muslim fundamentals of the Dark Ages. Lenin preached a crusade of world Communism.

What was Topiltzin's objective?

A Mexico of the Aztecs? A return to the past? No modern society could function under such archaic rules. Mexico was not a nation to be run on the fantasies of a Don Quixote. There had to be another driving force behind the man. Nichols was conjecturing in a vacuum. He glimpsed Topiltzin only as a caricature, a villain in a cartoon series.

His secretary entered unannounced and laid a file folder on his desk. "The report you asked for from the CIA — and you have a call on line three."

"Who is it?"

"A James Gerhart," she replied.

"White House security," said Nichols. "Did he say what he wanted?"

"Only that it was urgent."

Nichols became curious. He answered the call. "This is Dale Nichols."

"Jim Gerhart, sir, in charge of —"

"Yes, I know," Nichols interrupted. "What's

the problem?"

"I think you better come down to the pathology lab at George Washington."

"The University Hospital?"

"Yes, sir."

"What in hell for?"

"I'd rather not say too much over the phone."

"I'm very busy, Mr. Gerhart. You'll have to be more specific."

There was a short silence. "This is a matter concerning you and the President. That's all I can say."

"Can't you at least give me a clue?"

Gerhart ignored the probe. "One of my men is waiting outside your office. He will drive you to the lab. I'll meet you in the waiting room."

"Listen to me, Gerhart —" That was as far as Nichols got when the snarl of the dial tone struck his ear.

The drizzle had turned to rain and Nichols's disposition mirrored the dismal weather as he was led through the University Hospital's entrance to the pathology laboratory. He hated the etherlike smells that permeated the halls.

True to his word, Gerhart waited in the anteroom. The two men knew each other by sight and name but had never spoken. Gerhart came forward but made no effort to

191

shake hands.

"Thank you for coming," he said in an official tone.

"Why am I here?" Nichols asked directly.

"For an identification."

Nichols was suddenly flooded with foreboding. "Who?"

"I'd prefer you tell me."

"I don't have the stomach for looking at dead bodies."

"This isn't exactly a body, but you *will* need a strong stomach."

Nichols shrugged. "All right, let's get it over with."

Gerhart held the door open and guided him down a long corridor and into a room with large white tiles inlaid on the walls and floor. The floor was slightly concave with a drain in its center. A stainless steel table stood in stark solitude in the middle of the room. A white, opaque plastic sheet covered a long object that rose no more than an inch above the surface of the table.

Nichols looked at Gerhart in bewilderment. "What am I supposed to identify?"

Without a word Gerhart lifted the sheet and pulled it away, letting it drop in a crumpled wad on the floor.

Nichols stared at the thing on the table, uncomprehending. At first he thought it was a paper outline of a man's figure. Then he shuddered as the gory truth struck him. He leaned over the floor drain and threw up.

Gerhart stepped from the room and quickly returned with a folding chair and a towel.

He steered Nichols to the chair and passed him the towel. "Here," he said without sympathy, "use this."

Nichols sat for nearly two minutes, clutching the towel against his face and dry-retching. At last he recovered enough to look up at Gerhart and stammer.

"Good lord . . . that's nothing but . . ."

"Skin," Gerhart finished for him, "flayed human skin."

Nichols forced himself to stare at the grisly thing stretched out on the table.

He was reminded of a deflated balloon. That was the only way he could describe it. An incision had been made from the back of the head down to the ankles, and the skin peeled away from the body like a pelt from an animal. There was a long vertical slit in the chest that had been crudely sewn. The eyes were missing, but the entire dermis was there, including both shriveled hands and feet.

"Can you tell me who you think he might be?" asked Gerhart softly.

Nichols made a conscious effort, but the grotesque, misshapen facial features made it all but impossible. Only the hair seemed vaguely familiar. Yet he knew.

"Guy Rivas," he murmured.

Gerhart said nothing. He took Nichols by the arm and helped him to another room that was comfortably furnished with soft chairs and a coffee urn. He poured a cup of coffee and handed it to Nichols.

"Drink this. I'll be back in a minute."

Nichols sat there as if in a nightmare, shocked by the sickening sight in the other room. He could not bring himself to grips with the reality of Rivas's horrible death.

Gerhart came back carrying an attaché case. He set it on a low table. "This was dropped off at the mail reception room. The body skin was tightly folded inside. At first I thought it was the work of some psycho. Then I made a thorough search and found a miniature tape recorder mounted beneath the interior lining."

"You played it?"

"Lot of good it did. Sounds like a conversation between two men in some kind of code."

"How did you trace Rivas to me?"

"Rivas's government ID card had been placed inside his flayed skin. Whoever murdered him wanted to make sure we'd put a make on the remains. I went to Rivas's office and interrogated his secretary. I wormed it out of her that he met with you and the President for two hours before leaving for the airport and a flight to an unknown destination. I thought it unusual that his own secretary didn't know his destination, so I

194

reckoned he'd been sent on a classified mission. That's why I contacted you first."

Nichols looked at him narrowly. "You say there's a conversation on the tape?"

Gerhart nodded gravely. "That and Rivas's screams as he was cut apart."

Nichols closed his eyes, trying to force the vision from his mind.

"His next of kin will have to be notified," Gerhart continued. "He have a wife?"

"And four kids."

"You know him well?"

"Guy Rivas was a nice man. One of the few people with integrity I've met since coming to Washington. We worked together on several diplomatic missions."

For the first time Gerhart's stony face went soft. "I'm sorry."

Nichols didn't hear him. His eyes slowly turned bitter and cold. The nightmarelike expression had gone. He no longer tasted the vomit or felt sickened by the horror. The brutal savagery inflicted on someone close to him had triggered a floodgate of anger, anger such as Nichols had never known before.

The professor whose scope of power was limited to the walls of a classroom no longer existed. In his place was a man close to the President, one of a small elite group of Washington power brokers with the muscle to shape events or create havoc around the globe.

By whatever means and power that were his in the White House, with or without Presidential favor or official sanction, Nichols was set on avenging the murder of Rivas. Topiltzin had to die.

15

The small Beechcraft executive jet touched down with a faint squeal from the tires and taxied off the crushed-rock runway of a privately owned airport twenty kilometers south of Alexandria, Egypt. Less than a minute after it rolled to a halt beside a green Volvo with TAXI lettered on the doors in English, the whine from the engines ceased and the passenger door raised open.

The man that stepped to the ground was wearing a white suit with matching tie over a dark blue shirt. Slightly under six feet, with a slim body, he paused a moment and dabbed a handkerchief around a receding hairline, and then smugly brushed a large black moustache with one forefinger. His eyes were hidden by dark glasses and his hands covered by white leather gloves.

Suleiman Aziz Ammar did not resemble in the slightest the pilot who had boarded Flight 106 in London.

He walked over to the Volvo and greeted

the short, muscular driver who emerged from behind the wheel. "Good morning, Ibn. Find any problems on your return?"

"Your affairs are in good order," Ibn replied, opening the rear door and making no effort to conceal a pistolized shotgun in a shoulder holster.

"Take me to Yazid."

Ibn nodded silently as Ammar settled into the rear seat.

The exterior of the taxi was as deceptive as Ammar's many disguises. The darkly tinted windows and body panels were bulletproof. Inside, Ammar sat in a low, comfortable leather chair in front of a compact desk cabinet containing a compact array of electronics that included two telephones, a computer, radio transmitter and TV monitor. There were also a bar and a rack with two automatic rifles.

As the car skirted the crowded central section of Alexandria and turned onto the al-Jaysh Beach road, Ammar busied himself by monitoring his far-flung investment operations. His wealth, known only to him, was enormous. His financial success was accomplished more by ruthlessness than shrewdness. If any corporate executive or government official stood in Ammar's way on a profitable business deal, he was simply eliminated.

At the end of a twenty-kilometer drive, Ibn

slowed the Volvo and stopped at a gate leading up to a small villa squatting on a low hill overlooking a wide sandy beach.

Ammar shut down the computer and stepped from the car. Four guards in desert sand-colored fatigues surrounded him and efficiently searched his clothing. As a backup safeguard he was directed to walk through an airport-type X-ray detector.

He was then led up a stone stairway to the villa past crudely built concrete compounds manned by a small army of Yazid's elite bodyguards. Ammar smiled as they bypassed the ornate front archway, open to honored visitors, and entered through a small side door. He brushed off the insult, knowing it was Yazid's shallow-minded way of humbling those who did his dirty work but were not accepted to his inner circle of fanatic grovelers.

He was ushered into a stark and empty room furnished with only one wooden stool and a large Persian Kashan carpet that hung from one wall. The interior was hot and stuffy. There were no windows and the only illumination came from an overhead skylight. Without a word the guards retreated and closed the door.

Ammar yawned, casually held up his wristwatch as if checking the time. Next he removed his dark glasses and rubbed his eyes. The practiced gestures enabled him to locate the tiny lens of a TV camera within the design of the hanging carpet without giving his discovery away.

He stewed for nearly an hour before the carpet was pulled aside and Akhmad Yazid strutted through a small archway into the room.

The spiritual leader of the Egyptian Muslims was young, no more than thirty-five. He was a small man; he had to look up to meet Ammar's eyes. His face did not have the precise features of most Egyptians, the chin and cheekbones were softer, more rounded. His head was covered by a white lace cloth wound in an abbreviated turban, and his broom handle-thin body was draped in a white silk caftan. When moving from shadow to light, his eyes seemingly altered from black to dark brown.

As a sign of respect, Ammar gave a slight nod without looking Yazid in the eye.

"Ah, my friend," Yazid said warmly. "Good to have you back."

Ammar looked up, smiled and began playing the game. "I'm honored to stand in your presence, Akhmad Yazid."

"Please sit," Yazid said. It was an order rather than an invitation.

Ammar complied, sitting on the small wooden stool so Yazid could look down on him. Yazid also added another form of humiliation. He circled the room as he lectured without prologue, forcing Ammar to twist around the stool to follow him.

"Every week brings a major challenge to President Hasan's fragile authority. All that prevents his fall is the loyalty of the military. He can still rely on the 350,000-strong army for support. For the moment, Defense Minister Abu Hamid straddles the fence. He has assured me he will throw his support to our movement for an Islamic republic, but only if we win a national referendum without bloodshed."

"Is that bad?" asked Ammar with an innocent expression.

Yazid gave him a cold stare. "The man is a pro-Western charlatan, too cowardly to give up American aid. All that matters to him are his precious jets, helicopter gunships and tanks. He fears Egypt will go the way of Iran. The idiot insists on an orderly transition of governments so loans from world banks and financial aid from America will keep pouring in."

He paused, gazing directly into Ammar's eyes, as if daring his prize assassin to contradict him again. Ammar remained silent. The stifling room began to close in on him.

"Abu Hamid also demands my promise that Hala Kamil will remain Secretary-General of the United Nations," Yazid added.

"Yet you ordered me to eliminate her," Ammar said, curious.

Yazid nodded. "Yes, I wanted the bitch dead because she is using her position in the U.N. as a platform to voice her opposition to our movement and turn world opinion against me. Abu Hamid, however, would have slammed the door in my face if she'd been openly assassinated — the reason why I counted on you, Suleiman, to remove her with an unquestionable accident. Regrettably, you failed. You managed to kill everyone on board the aircraft *except* Kamil."

The last words fell like a hammer. Ammar's outward calm disintegrated. He looked up at Yazid in blank confusion.

"She lives?"

Yazid's eyes went cold. "The news broke in Washington less than one hour ago. The plane crashed in Greenland. Every U.N. passenger except Kamil and all but two of the crew were found dead from poison."

"Poison?" Ammar murmured skeptically.

"Our paid sources in the American news media have confirmed the report. What were you thinking of, Suleiman? You assured me the plane was supposed to vanish in the sea."

"Do they say how it reached Greenland?"

"A flight steward discovered the bodies of the flight crew. With help from a Mexican delegate, he took over the controls and managed to crash-land in a fjord on the coast. Kamil might have died from exposure, cutting you off the hook, but an American naval vessel happened to be cruising nearby. They responded almost immediately and saved her life."

Ammar was stunned. He was not used to failure. He could not imagine how his exactingly conceived plan had gone so far off track. He closed his eyes, seeing the plane clear the summit of the glacier. Almost instantly he gleaned the imponderables, focusing on a piece of the puzzle that didn't fit.

Yazid stood quietly for a few moments, then broke Ammar's concentration. "You realize, of course, I will be accused of this mess."

"There is no evidence tying me to the disaster or me to you," Ammar said firmly.

"Perhaps, but call it guilt by motive. Speculation and rumor will convict me in the Western news media. I should have you executed."

Ammar wiped his mind clear and shrugged indifferently. "That would be a sad waste. I'm still the best eliminator in the Middle East."

"And the highest paid."

"I'm not in the habit of charging for unfinished projects."

"I would hope not," said Yazid acidly. He abruptly spun and walked toward the hanging carpet. He reached out and pulled it back with his left hand, paused and turned back to Ammar. "I must prepare my mind for prayer. You may go, Suleiman Aziz Ammar."

"And Hala Kamil? The job is unfinished."

"I am turning her removal over to Muhammad Ismail."

"Ismail," Ammar grunted. "The man is a cretin."

"He can be trusted."

"For what, cleaning sewers?"

Yazid's hard, cold eyes stared at Ammar menacingly. "Kamil is no longer your concern. Remain here in Egypt near my side. My faithful advisers and I have another project to advance our cause. You will have an opportunity to redeem yourself in the eyes of Allah."

Before Yazid could enter the archway, Ammar rose to his feet. "The Mexican delegate who helped fly the aircraft. Was he also poisoned?"

Yazid turned and shook his head. "The report states he was killed in the crash."

Then he was gone and the carpet dropped back.

Ammar settled on the stool again. Slowly the revelation broke through the mists of the enigma. He should have been maddened, but there wasn't the slightest feeling of anger. Instead, an amused smile curled under his moustache.

"So there were two of us," he mused aloud to the empty room. "And the other one poisoned the in-flight meal service." Then he shook his head in wonderment. "Poison in the Beef Wellington. My god, how quaint."

16

At first no one paid any attention to the tiny blur that crept across the outer edge of the sidescan sonar's recording paper.

Six hours into the search they had found several man-made objects. Parts of the downed aircraft that were pinpointed for retrieval, a sunken fishing trawler, bits and pieces of junk thrown over by fishing fleets seeking shelter in the fjord from storms, all were identified by video camera and eliminated.

The last anomaly was not resting on the bottom of the fjord as expected. It sat inside a small inlet encircled by sheer cliffs. Only one end protruded into clear water; the rest was buried under a wall of ice.

Pitt was the first to realize its significance. He was sitting in front of the recorder, surrounded by Giordino, Commander Knight and the archaeologists. He spoke into a transmitter.

"Swing the fish, bearing one-five-zero degrees."

The *Polar Explorer* was still stationary in the icebound fjord. Outside on the pack a team led by Cork Simon had augered through the ice and lowered the sensing unit into the water. Very slowly they swung the fish, as they called it, scanning a 360-degree grid. After searching one area, they unreeled more cable and tried again at another site farther away from the ship.

Simon acknowledged Pitt's command and twisted the cable until the fish's sonar probes were trained at 150 degrees.

"How's this?" he queried.

"You're right on target," Pitt replied from the ship.

Seen from a better angle the target became more distinct. Pitt circled it with a black felt pen.

"I think we've got something."

Gronquist moved in closer and nodded. "Not much showing to identify. What do you make of it?"

"Pretty vague," answered Pitt. "You have to use some imagination since most of the object is covered by ice that has fallen from the surrounding cliffs. But the part that shows underwater suggests a wooden ship. There's a definite angular shape coming together at what might be a high, curving stern-post."

"Yes," said Lily excitedly. "High and graceful. Typical of a fourth-century merchant ship."

"Don't get carried away," cautioned Knight. "She could be an old sail-rigged fisherman."

"Possibly." Giordino looked thoughtful. "But if my memory serves me correctly, the Danes, Icelanders and Norwegians who have fished these waters over the centuries sailed in more narrow beamed double-enders."

"You're right," said Pitt. "The sharp bow and stern were handed down from the Vikings. What we're seeing here might also be a double-ender, but with a broader sweep."

"Can't get a clear picture through the ice-covered section of the hull," said Gronquist. "But we could drop a camera back of the stern in clear water for a better identification."

Giordino looked doubtful. "A camera might confirm the stern section of a wrecked ship, but little else."

"We've plenty of strong male backs on the ship," said Lily. "We could tunnel down through the ice and inspect her at first hand."

Gronquist took a pair of binoculars and walked out of the electronics compartment to the bridge. He returned in half a minute. "I make the ice cover over the wreck to be a good three meters thick. Take at least two days to cut through."

"You'll have to dig without us, I'm afraid,"

said Knight. "My orders are to get under way before 1800 hours. We've no time left for a lengthy excavation."

Gronquist was taken aback. "That's only five hours from now."

Knight made a helpless gesture. "I'm sorry, I have no say in the matter."

Pitt studied the dark spot on the recording paper. Then he turned to Knight. "If I proved positively that's a fourth-century Roman ship out there, could you persuade North Atlantic Command to keep us on station for another day or two?"

Knight's eyes took on a foxy look. "What are you cooking up?"

"Will you go along?" Pitt crowded him.

"Yes," Knight stated firmly. "But only if you prove, without a shadow of a doubt, that's a thousand-year-old shipwreck."

"Then it's a deal."

"How are you going to do it?"

"Simple," said Pitt, reeling Knight in. "I'm going to dive under the ice and come up into the hull."

Cork Simon and his crew worked quickly at cutting an access hole through the one-meter-thick ice sheet with chain saws. They quarried multiple squares until they reached the final layer. They broke through with a sledgehammer mounted on a long pipe and then removed the ice fragments with grappling hooks so Pitt could safely submerge.

When he was satisfied the hole was clear, Simon walked a few steps and entered a small canvas-covered shelter. The interior was heated and warm and crowded with men and diving equipment. An air compressor sat next to the heating unit, chugging away, its exhaust vented to the outside.

Lily and the other archaeologists were sitting at a folding table in one corner of the shelter, making a series of drawings and discussing them with Pitt as he suited up for the dive.

"Ready when you are," Simon announced.

"Another five minutes," Giordino replied while busily checking the valve assemblies and regulator on a Mark I navy diver's mask.

Pitt had slipped a special dry suit over long underwear made of heavy nylon pile for thermal insulation. Next he pulled on a hood and then a quick-release weight belt while trying to absorb a cram course in ancient ship construction.

"In early merchant vessels the shipwrights favored cedar and cypress, and often pine, for the planking," lectured Gronquist. "They mostly used oak for the keel."

"I won't be able to tell one wood from another," Pitt said.

"Then study the hull. The planks were tightly joined by tenons and mortises. Many ships had lead plates laid on their underwater surface. The hardware may be of iron or copper."

"What about the rudder?" asked Pitt. "Anything I should look for in design and fastenings?"

"You won't find a stern-centered rudder," said Sam Hoskins. "They didn't turn up for another eight hundred years. All early Mediterranean merchantmen used twin steering oars that extended from the aft quarters."

"Do you want a reserve 'come home' air bottle?" Giordino interrupted.

Pitt shook his head. "Not necessary for a dive this shallow as long as I'm on a lifeline."

Giordino lifted the Mark I mask and helped Pitt pull it down over his head. He checked the face seal, adjusted the position and cinched up the spider straps. The air supply was on, and when Pitt signaled that he had proper air flow, Giordino secured the communications line to the mask.

While one of the Navy men unreeled and straightened the air-supply hose and communications line, Giordino tied a manila lifeline around Pitt's waist. He performed the pre-dive checkout and then donned a headset with microphone.

"You hear me okay?" he asked.

"Clear but faint," Pitt answered. "Turn up the volume a notch."

"Better?"

"Much."

"How do you feel?"

"Nice and cozy so long as I'm breathing warm air."

"All set?"

Pitt answered by making an okay sign with his thumb and forefinger. He paused to hook an underwater dive light to his belt.

Lily gave him a hug and gazed up through his face mask. "Good hunting, and be careful."

He winked back at her.

He turned and walked through the entryway of the shelter into the cold outside, trailed by two Navy men who tended his lines.

Giordino began to follow when Lily clutched his arm. "Will we be able to hear him?" she asked anxiously.

"Yes, I've connected him into a speaker. You and Dr. Gronquist can stay here where it's warm and listen in. If you have a message for Pitt, simply come and tell me, and I'll pass it on."

Pitt walked stiffly to the edge of the ice hole and sat down. The air temperature had dropped to zero. It was a crystalline November day with a biting edge, courtesy of a ten-mile-an-hour wind.

As he slipped on his fins he looked up at the sheer sides of the mountains that soared above the inlet. The tons of snow and ice clinging to the steep palisades seemed as if they could fall at any moment. He turned to the upper end of the fjord where he could see glacier arms curling and grinding toward the sea. Then he looked down.

The water in the dive hole looked jade, ominous and cold.

Commander Knight approached and put his hand on Pitt's shoulder. All he could see was a pair of intense green eyes through the glass of the mask. He spoke loudly so Pitt could hear.

"One hour, twenty-three minutes left. I thought you ought to know."

Pitt gave him a steel-edged stare but did not reply. He made a "thumbs up" sign and slipped through the narrow hole into the forbidding water.

He slowly settled past the encircling white walls. He felt as if he were diving down a well. Once clear, he was dazzled by the glistening kaleidoscope of color from the sun's rays that penetrated the ice. The underside of the sheet was jagged and uneven and specked with small hanging stalactites formed by brine from the rapidly freezing fresh water carried into the fjord by glaciers.

Underwater visibility was almost eighty meters on a horizontal range. He glanced down and saw a small kelp community grasping the rocky mass carpeting the bottom. Thousands of small shrimplike crustaceans suspended in the still water swirled past his sight.

A huge, three-meter bearded seal eyed him curiously at a distance, tufts of coarse bristles sprouting from its muzzle. Pitt waved his arms, and the big seal shot him a wary look and swam away.

Pitt touched the bottom and paused to equalize his ears. There was a danger in diving with a buoyancy-compensator-type lifejacket under ice and he did not wear one. He was slightly heavy, so he adjusted by removing and dropping a lead weight from his belt. The air that flowed from the compressor through a filter and then an accumulator into his mask tasted bland but pure.

He gazed upward and oriented himself from the eerie glow of the ice hole and checked his compass. He hadn't bothered to carry a depth gauge. He wouldn't be working in water over four meters deep.

"Talk to me," the voice of Al Giordino came through the mask's earphones.

"I'm on the bottom," replied Pitt. "All systems up to par."

Pitt spun and stared through the green void. "She lies about ten meters north of me. I'm going to move toward her. Give me some slack in the lines."

He swam slowly, taking care his lines didn't foul on the rock outcroppings. The intense cold of the frigid water began to seep into his body. He was thankful Giordino had had the foresight to see that his air supply was warm and dry.

The stern of the wreck slowly unveiled before his eyes. The sides were covered with a mat of algae. He brushed away a small area with his gloved hand, stirring up a green cloud. He waited a minute for the cloud to dissipate and then peered at the result.

"Inform Lily and Doc I'm looking at a wooden hull without a stern rudder, but no sign of steering oars."

"Acknowledged," said Giordino.

Pitt pulled a knife from a sheath strapped to one leg and pried at the underside of the hull near the keel. The point revealed soft metal.

"We have a lead-sheathed bottom," he announced.

"Looking good," replied Giordino. "Doc Gronquist wants to know if there is any sign of carving on the sternpost."

"Hold on."

Pitt carefully wiped off the growth over a flat section of the sternpost just before it disappeared upward into the ice, waiting patiently for the resulting algae cloud to drift away.

"There's some kind of a hardwood plaque imbedded into the sternpost. I can make out lettering and a face."

"A face?"

"With a curly head of hair and heavy beard."

"What does it read?"

"Sorry, I can't translate Greek."

"Not Latin?" Giordino asked skeptically.

The raised carving was indistinct in the shimmering light that filtered through the ice. Pitt moved in until his face mask nearly touched the wooden plaque.

"Greek," Pitt stated firmly.

"Certain?"

"I used to go with a girl who was an Alpha Delta Pi."

"Hold on. You've thrown the bone pickers into spasms."

After nearly two minutes, Giordino's voice returned over the earphones. "Gronquist thinks you're hallucinating, but Mike Graham says he studied classical Greek in college and asks if you can describe the lettering."

"First letter resembles an *S* shaped like a lightning strike. Then an *A* with the right leg missing. Next a *P* followed by another handicapped *A* and what looks like an inverted *L* or a gallows. Then an *I*. Last letter is another lightning strike *S*. That's the best I can do."

Listening over the speaker inside the shelter, Graham copied Pitt's meager description on the page of a notebook until he had

ϟΑΡΑΓΙϟ

216

He scrutinized what appeared to be a word for several moments. Something was out of place. He struggled to jog his memory, and then he had it. The letters were Classical but Eastern Greek.

His thoughtful expression slowly turned incredulous. He furiously wrote a short word, tore out the page and held it up. In modern capitals it read,

SARAPIS

Lily stared at Graham questioningly. "Does it mean anything?"

Gronquist said, "I think it's the name of a Greek-Egyptian god."

"A popular deity throughout the Mediterranean," agreed Hoskins. "Modern spelling is usually 'Serapis.' "

"So our ship is the *Serapis*," murmured Lily pensively.

Knight grunted. "So we might have either a Roman, Grecian or Egyptian shipwreck. Which is it?"

"We're over our heads," answered Gronquist. "We'll need the expertise of a marine archaeologist who knows ancient Mediterranean shipping to sort this one out."

Below the ice, Pitt moved across the starboard side of the hull, stopping where the planking vanished into the ice. He swam around the sternpost to the port. The planking looked warped and bowed outward. A few kicks of his fins, and he could see a section that was stove in by the ice.

He eased up to the opening and slipped his head inside. It was like looking in a dark closet. He saw only vague, indiscernible shapes. He reached in and felt something round and hard. He gauged the distance between the broken planks. The gap was too small to squeeze his shoulders through.

He grasped the upper plank, planted a finned foot against the hull and pulled. The well-preserved wood slowly bent but refused to give. Pitt tried both feet and heaved with everything he had. The plank still held firm. When he was just about to call it quits the treenails suddenly tore off the inside ribs and the waterlogged wood peeled away, throwing Pitt backward in awkward slow motion against a large rock.

Any respectable card-carrying marine archaeologist would have gone into cardiac arrest at such irreverent brutality toward an ancient artifact. Pitt felt totally unsympathetic toward academic scruples. He was cold and getting colder, his shoulder began to ache from the impact on the rock, and he knew he couldn't stay down much longer.

"I've found a break in the hull," he said, panting like a marathon runner. "Send down a camera."

"Understood," replied the stolid voice of Giordino. "Come back and I'll pass it to you."

Pitt returned to the dive hole and followed his bubbles to the surface. Giordino lay on his stomach on the ice, reached down and handed Pitt a compact underwater video camera/recorder.

"Take a few meters of tape and get out," said Giordino. "You've accomplished enough."

"What about Commander Knight?"

"Hold tight, I'll put him on."

Knight's voice came over the earphones. "Dirk?"

"Go ahead, Byron."

"Are you one hundred percent certain we've got a thousand-year-old relic in pristine condition?"

"All indications look solid."

"I'll need something tangible if I'm to convince Atlantic Command to keep us on station another forty-eight hours."

"Stand by and I'll seal it with a kiss."

"An identifiable antiquity will suffice," Knight said dourly.

Pitt threw a wave and faded from view.

He did not enter the wreck immediately. How long he floated motionless outside the jagged opening he couldn't be sure. Probably about one minute, certainly no longer then two. Why he hesitated, he didn't know. Maybe he was waiting for an invitation from a skeletal hand beckoning from within, maybe he was afraid of finding nothing more than debris from an eighty-year-old Icelandic fishing schooner, or maybe he was just leery of entering what might be a tomb.

Finally he lowered his head, tightened his shoulders and cautiously kicked his fins.

The black unknown opened up and he swam in.

17

Once Pitt squeezed inside, he paused and hung motionless, slowly settling on his knees, listening to his pounding heart and his breath escaping from the exhaust valve, waiting until his eyes eventually became accustomed to the fluid gloom.

He didn't know what he'd expected to find: what he found was an array of terra-cotta jars, pitchers, cups and plates neatly stacked in shelves set in the bulkheads. One was a large copper pot he had touched when groping through the hull; its walls had turned a deep patina green.

At first he thought his knees were resting on the hard surface of the deck. He felt about with his hands and discovered he was kneeling on the tiled surface of a hearth. He glanced up and saw his bubbles rise up and spread in a wavering cover. He stood and surfaced into clear air, his head and shoulders having risen above the water level of the fjord.

"I'm inside the ship's galley," he notified

the spellbound party on the ice. "The upper half is dry. Camera is rolling."

"Acknowledged," Giordino said briefly.

Pitt used the next few minutes to video-record the galley's interior above and below the water level, while keeping a running dialogue on the inventory. He found an open cupboard stocked with several elegant glass vessels. He lifted one and peered inside. It held coins. He picked one out, rubbed away the algae with his gloved fingers, and shot tape with one hand. The coin's surface revealed a golden color.

A sense of awe and apprehension flooded over Pitt. He looked quickly around as if expecting a ghostly crew, or at least their skeletal apparitions, to come bursting through the hatchway to accuse him of theft. Only there was no crew. He was alone and touching objects that belonged to men who had walked the same deck, prepared food and eaten here — men who had been dead for sixteen centuries.

He began to wonder what had happened to them. How had they come to be in the frozen north when there were no records of such a historic voyage? They must have died of exposure, but where did their bodies lie?

"You'd better come up," said Giordino. "You've been down almost thirty minutes."

"Not yet," replied Pitt. Thirty minutes, he thought. It seemed more like five. Time was

222

slipping away from him. The cold was beginning to affect his brain. He dropped the coin back in the glass vessel and continued his inspection.

The galley's ceiling rose half a meter above the main deck overhead, and small arched windows that normally allowed ventilation were battened down on the upper side of the forward bulkhead. Pitt pried one partially open only to confront a solid wall of ice.

He made a rough measurement and found the water level was deeper toward the aft end of the galley. Pitt took this to indicate that the bow and central section of the hull were aground on the raised slope of the ice-buried shoreline.

"Come up with anything else?" Giordino inquired with burning curiosity.

"Like what?"

"Remains of the crew?"

"Sorry, no bones to be seen." Pitt ducked under the water and scanned the deck to make certain. It was free and clean of litter.

"They probably panicked and abandoned ship at sea," Giordino theorized.

"Nothing points to a panic," said Pitt. "The galley could pass a general inspection."

"Can you penetrate the rest of the ship?"

"There's a hatchway in the forward bulkhead. I'm going to see what's on the other side."

He leaned down and ducked through the

low and narrow opening, carefully pulling his lifeline and air hose after him. The darkness was oppressive. He unhooked the dive light from his weight belt and swept its beam around a small compartment.

"I'm now in some kind of storeroom. The water is shallower here, rising just short of my knees. I can see tools, yes, the ship's carpenter's tools, spare anchors, a large steelyard —"

"Steelyard?" Giordino broke in.

"A balance scale that hangs from a hook."

"Got you."

"There's also an assortment of axes, lead weights and fish netting. Hold on while I document."

A narrow wooden ladder led upward through an opening in the main deck. After shooting tape, he cautiously tested it, surprised to find it still stout enough to support his weight.

Pitt slowly climbed the rungs and poked his head into the shattered remains of a deck cabin. Little was visible except a few buried bits of debris. The cabin had been nearly crushed flat by the build up of ice.

He dropped down and waded through another hatch that opened into the cargo hold. He swung the dive light's beam from starboard to port and instantly went numb from shock.

It was not only a cargo hold.

It was also a crypt.

The extreme cold had transformed the dry hold into a cryogenic chamber. Eight bodies in a state of near-perfect preservation were grouped around a small iron stove toward the bow. Each was covered by a shroud of ice, making them look as though they had been individually wrapped in a thick, clear plastic.

Their facial expressions appeared peaceful and their eyes were locked open. Like mannikins in a shop window, they were posed in different positions as if placed and adjusted for the correct attitude. Four sat around a table eating, plates in hand, cups raised to mouth. Two reclined side by side against the hull, reading what Pitt guessed were scrolls. One was bent over a wooden chest, while the last was seated in the act of writing.

Pitt felt as if he had entered a time machine. He could not believe he was staring at men who had been citizens of Imperial Rome. Ancient mariners who sailed into ports long buried under the debris of later civilizations, ancestors over sixty generations from the past.

They had not been prepared for the Arctic cold. None wore heavy clothing; all were bundled in coarse blankets. They seemed small in size compared to Pitt; all would have measured a good head shorter. One little man was bald, with gray woolly side hair. Another had shaggy red hair and was heavily bearded.

225

Most were clean-shaven. From what he could read through their icy covering, the youngest was around eighteen and the oldest close to forty years of age.

The mariner who had died while writing had a leather cap pulled tight around his head and long strips of wool wrapped around his legs and feet. He was bent over a small stack of wax tablets resting on the scarred surface of a small folding table. A stylus was still gripped in his right hand.

The crew did not look as if they had starved or died slowly from the cold. Death had come suddenly and unexpectedly.

Pitt guessed the cause. All hatch covers had been tightly sealed to keep out the cold, and the only opening for ventilation had frozen over. The pots containing the last meal were sitting on the small oil stove. There was no way for the heat and smoke to escape to the outside. Lethal carbon monoxide had built up within the cargo hold. Unconsciousness had struck without warning, and each man died where he sat.

Almost as if he was afraid to awaken the long-dead seaman, Pitt very carefully chipped the ice away from the wax tablets until they came free. Then he unzipped the front of his dry suit and slipped them inside.

Pitt no longer noticed the agony of the cold, the nervous sweat that was trickling from his pores, or the shivering. His mind was so absorbed in the morbid scene that he failed to hear Giordino's repeated demands for a reply.

"Are you still with us?" asked Giordino. "Answer, dammit!"

Pitt mumbled a few unintelligible words.

"Say again. Are you in trouble?"

Giordino's concerned tone finally shook Pitt out of his trance-like state.

"Inform Commander Knight his worst fear is confirmed," Pitt answered. "The antique status of the ship is genuine. And by the way," he added in a monotonous, laconic voice, "you might also mention that if he needs witnesses, I can produce the crew."

18

"You're wanted on the phone," Julius Schiller's wife called through the kitchen window.

Schiller looked up from the barbecue in the backyard of his tree-shaded home in Chevy Chase. "They give a name?"

"No, but it sounds like Dale Nichols."

He sighed and held up a pair of tongs. "Come mind the steaks so they won't burn."

Mrs. Schiller gave her husband a brief kiss as they passed each other on the porch. He entered his study, closed the door and picked up the receiver.

"Yes?"

"Julius, Dale."

"What's on your mind?"

"Sorry to call on a Sunday," said Nichols. "Did I interrupt anything?"

"Only a family barbecue."

"You must be a diehard. It's only forty-five degrees outside."

"Beats smoking up the garage."

"Steak and scrambled eggs, that's my favorite."

Schiller caught Nichols's drift on the eggs and switched his phone onto a secure line that entered a computerized scramble mode. "Okay, Dale, what have you got?"

"Hala Kamil. The exchange came off smoothly."

"Her look-alike is at Walter Reed Hospital?" Schiller asked.

"Under tight security to go along with the act."

"Who doubled for her?"

"Teri Rooney, the actress. She did a superb makeup job. You couldn't tell her apart from the real Secretary-General unless you were nose to nose. As a backup, we arranged a press conference by hospital doctors. They gave out a story describing her serious condition."

"And Kamil?"

"She remained on the Air Force plane that brought her from Greenland. After refueling, it flew to Buckley Field near Denver. From there she was flown by helicopter to Breckenridge."

"The ski resort in Colorado?"

"Yes, she's resting comfortably at Senator Pitt's chalet just outside of town. No injuries except a few bruises and a mild case of frostbite."

"How is she taking her forced convalescence?"

"No word yet. Hala was heavily sedated when she was carried from the hospital at Thule. But she'll go along when she learns of our operation to safeguard her arrival at the U.N. headquarters to address the opening session of the General Assembly. A reliable source close to her says she plans on making a scathing indictment of Yazid, exposing him as a religious charlatan and offering proof of his underground terrorist activities."

"I've read a report from the same source," Schiller admitted.

"Five days until the opening session," said Nichols. "Yazid will pull out all stops to blow her away."

"She's got to be kept on ice until she steps to the podium," Schiller said, deadly serious.

"She's safe," said Nichols. "Any word from the Egyptian government on your end?"

"President Hasan is giving us his full cooperation regarding Kamil. He's scratching every hour he can buy or steal to launch his new economic reforms and replace military leaders with men he can trust. Hala Kamil is the only thread preventing Yazid from attempting a quick grab for the Egyptian government. If Yazid's assassins stop her before her speech goes out over world news satellite channels, there is a real danger of Egypt becoming another Iran before the month is out."

"Relax, Yazid won't get wise to the scam until it's too late," said Nichols confidentially.

"I assume she is under heavy guard?"

"By a top team of Secret Service agents. The President is personally keeping a tight grip on the operation."

Schiller's wife knocked on the door and spoke loudly from the other side. "Steaks are ready, Julius."

"In a minute," he answered.

Nichols picked up on the exchange. "That's all I have for now. I'll let you get back to your steaks."

"I'd feel better if the FBI was lending a hand," said Schiller.

"The White House security staff has considered every contingency. The President thought it best to keep all intelligence within a tight circle."

Schiller paused pensively for a moment. Then he said, "Don't screw it up, Dale."

"Not to worry. I promise, Hala Kamil will arrive at the U.N. building in New York in pristine condition and full of fire."

"She'd better."

"Does the sun set in the west?"

Schiller set down the phone. He had an uneasy feeling. He hoped to God the White House knew what it was doing.

Across the street three men sat in the back of

a Ford van with "Capitol Plumbing, 24-hour emergency service" painted on the panels. The cramped interior was crowded with electronic eavesdropping equipment.

Tedium had set in five hours ago. Surveillance is perhaps the most boring job since watching rails rust. Irritation was in the air. One man smoked and the other two didn't and couldn't stand the stale air. All were stiff and cold. Former counterespionage agents, they had resigned to become independent contractors.

Most retired agents occasionally take on an outside job for the government, but these three were among the very few who respected money more than patriotic duty, and they sold whatever classified information they could ferret out to the highest bidder.

One of them, a blond, scarecrow type, peered through binoculars out a tinted window at Schiller's house. "He's leaving the study."

The fat man hunched over a recording machine with earphones nodded in agreement. "All talk has ceased."

The third, who had a great waxed handlebar moustache, operated a laser parabolic, a sensitive microphone that received voice sounds inside a room from the vibrations on a windowpane, and then magnified them through fiber optics onto a sound channel.

"Anything interesting?" asked the skinny blond.

The fat man removed the earphones and wiped his sweating forehead. "I think my share from this gig will pay off my fishing boat."

"I love a marketable commodity."

"This information is worth big bucks to the right party."

"Who've you got in mind?" asked the one with the moustache.

The fat man grinned like a glutted coyote. "A wealthy, highly placed raghead who wants to make points with Akhmad Yazid."

19

The President rose from behind his desk and gave a brief nod as CIA Director Martin Brogan was ushered into the Oval Office for the morning intelligence briefing.

The formality of a handshake between the two men had fallen by the wayside soon after their daily meetings began. The slim, urbane Brogan didn't mind in the least. He had narrow, long-fingered violinist's hands, while the tall, two-hundred-pound President had massive paws and a bone-crushing grip.

Brogan waited until the President sat down before settling in a leather chair. Almost as if it were a ritual, the President poured a cup of coffee, ladled in a teaspoon of sugar and graciously handed a large mug to Brogan.

The President brushed a hand over his head of silver hair and fixed Brogan with a limpid pair of gray eyes. "Well, what secrets does the world hold this morning?"

Brogan shrugged and passed a leather-bound file across the desk. "At 0900 Moscow time, Soviet President Georgi Antonov balled his mistress in the backseat of his limousine on the way to the Kremlin."

"I envy his method for starting the day," the President said with a broad smile.

"He also made two calls from his car phone. One to Sergei Kornilov, head of the Soviet space program, the other to his son, who works in the commercial section of the embassy in Mexico City. You'll find the transcript of the conversations on pages four and five."

The President opened the file, slipped on a pair of reading glasses and scanned the transcript, amazed, as always, at the penetration of intelligence gathering.

"And how was the rest of Georgi's day?"

"He spent most of his time on domestic affairs. You wouldn't want to be in his shoes. The outlook on the Soviet economy grows worse by the day. His reforms in the fields and factories have gone down the toilet. The old guard in the Politburo is trying to undermine him. The military isn't happy with his arms proposals and has gone public with its opposition. Soviet citizens are getting more vocal as the lines get longer. With a little prodding by our operatives, graffiti knocking the government are appearing throughout the cities. Overall economic growth has flattened out at two percent. There is a strong possibility Antonov may be forced from power before next summer."

"If our deficit doesn't level off I may wind up in the same boat," the President said grimly.

Brogan made no comment. He wasn't expected to.

"What's the latest intelligence from Egypt?" the President asked, moving on.

"President Hasan is also hanging by the skin of his teeth. The air force remains loyal, but the army generals are close to throwing in with Yazid. Defense Minister Abu Hamid held a secret meeting with Yazid in Port Said. Our informants say Hamid won't swing his support without assurances of a solid power position. He does not want to be dictated to by Yazid's circle of fanatical mullahs."

"Think Yazid will give in?"

Brogan shook his head. "No, he has no intention of sharing power. Hamid has under-estimated Yazid's ruthlessness. We've already uncovered a conspiracy to place a bomb in Hamid's private plane."

"Have you alerted Hamid?"

"I'll need your authority."

"You have it," said the President. "Hamid is cagey. He may think we're pulling a ploy to keep him out of Yazid's camp."

"We can supply the names of Yazid's assassin team. Hamid can take it from there if he insists on proof."

The President leaned back and stared at

the ceiling for a moment. "Can we tie Yazid to the crash of the U.N. plane carrying Hala Kamil?"

"Circumstantial evidence at best," Brogan admitted. "We won't have any concrete conclusions until the investigators wrap up and make their report. For now, the disaster is a real puzzle. Only a few facts have been uncovered. We do know the genuine pilot was murdered; his body was found in the trunk of a car parked at Heathrow airport."

"Sounds like a mafia hit."

"Almost, except the killer did a masterful job of disguising himself well enough to double as the pilot. After actually taking off the plane, he killed the flight crew by injecting them with a toxic nerve agent known as sarin, turned off course and abandoned the aircraft over Iceland."

"He must have worked with a team of highly trained professionals," the President said admiringly.

"We have reason to think he acted alone," said Brogan.

"Alone?" The President's expression turned incredulous. "This guy has to be one canny son of a bitch."

"The finesse and intricacy are trademarks of an Arab whose name is Suleiman Aziz Ammar."

"A terrorist?"

"Not in the crude sense. Ammar is one of

the cleverest assassins in the game. I wish he was on our side."

"Never let the liberals in Congress hear you say that," the President said wryly.

"Or the news media," Brogan added.

"Do you have a file on Ammar?"

"About a meter thick. He's what the trade used to call a master of disguise. A good, practicing Muslim who has little interest in politics, a mercenary with no known association with fanatical Islamic diehards. Ammar charges enormous fees, and gets them. A shrewd businessman. His wealth is estimated at over sixty million dollars. He seldom goes by the book. His hits are ingeniously planned and carried out. All are planned to look like accidents. None can be laid on his doorstep with certainty. Innocent victims mean nothing to him so long as his target is taken out. We suspect he is responsible for over a hundred deaths in the past ten years. His attempt, if proven, to kill Hala Kamil would mark his first recorded failure."

The President adjusted his glasses and turned to the report on the air crash. "I must have missed something. If he meant for the plane to vanish in the ocean, why did he bother poisoning the passengers? What possible reason could he have for killing them twice?"

"There's the catch," explained Brogan. "My analysts don't think Ammar was responsible for murdering the passengers."

The President's eyes took on a look of surprise. "You've switched me on a sidetrack, Martin. What in hell are you talking about?"

"Pathologists from the FBI labs flew up to Thule and performed autopsies on the victims. They found fifty times the sarin required to kill inside the flight crew's bodies, but their tests showed the passengers died from ingesting manchineel in the flight meal."

Brogan paused to sip his coffee.

The President waited, impatiently tapping a pen against a desk calendar.

"Manchineel, or poison guava as it's called, is native to the Caribbean and gulf coast of Mexico," Brogan continued. "It comes from a tree that bears a deadly, sweet-tasting, apple-shaped fruit. Carib indians used the sap to tip their arrows. Any number of early shipwrecked sailors and modern tourists have died after eating the manchineel's poisonous juices."

"And your people believe an assassin of Ammar's caliber wouldn't stoop to using manchineel?"

"Something like that." Brogan nodded. "Ammar's connections would have no trouble buying or stealing sarin from a European chemical-supply company. Manchineel is something else. You can't find it on a shelf. It also works too slowly for a quick kill. I find it doubtful Ammar would even consider using it."

"If not the Arab, then who?"

"We don't know," answered Brogan. "Certainly none of the three survivors. The only trail, and a faint one, leads to a Mexican delegate by the name of Eduardo Ybarra. He's the only other passenger besides Hala Kamil who didn't eat the meal."

"It says here he died in the crash." The President looked up from the briefing file. "How could he insert poison in the flight meals without being seen?"

"That was done in the kitchen of the company that caters for the airline. British investigators are checking out that lead now."

"Maybe Ybarra is innocent. Maybe for some simple reason he didn't eat."

"According to the surviving flight attendant, Hala slept through the meal, but Ybarra feigned an upset stomach."

"It's possible."

"The surviving flight attendant saw him eating a sandwich from his briefcase."

"Then he knew."

"Looks that way."

"Why did he risk coming on board if he knew everyone was going to die except him?"

"As a backup, in case the main target, or targets, probably the entire contingent of Mexicans, didn't take the poison."

The President leaned back in his chair and

studied the ceiling. "Okay, Kamil is a thorn in the side of Yazid. He pays Ammar to erase her. The job is botched and the plane doesn't disappear in the middle of the Arctic Ocean as planned but comes down in Greenland. So much for mystery number one. Solid facts for a good case. We'll call it the Egyptian connection. Mystery number two, the Mexican connection, is far more cloudy. There is no obvious motive for a mass murder, and the only suspect is dead. If I were a judge I'd order the case dismissed for lack of evidence."

"I'd have to go along," said Brogan. "There has been no evidence of terrorist movements operating out of Mexico."

"You forget Topiltzin," the President said unexpectedly.

Brogan was surprised at the cold, furious look of pure anger that spread across the President's face.

"The agency has not forgotten Topiltzin," Brogan assured him, "or what he did to Guy Rivas. I'll have him taken out whenever you say the word."

The President suddenly sighed and sagged in his chair. "If only it was that simple. Snap my fingers and the CIA obliterates a foreign opposition leader. The risk is too great. Kennedy found that out when he condoned the mafia's attempt to kill Castro."

"Reagan made no objections to the attempts to get Muammar Qaddafi."

241

"Yes," the President said wearily. "If only he had known Qaddafi would fool everyone and die of cancer!"

"No such luck with Topiltzin. Medical reports say he's as strong as a Missouri mule."

"The man is a bloody lunatic. If he takes over Mexico, we'll have a disaster on our hands."

"You played the tape made by Rivas?" Brogan asked, knowing the answer.

"Four times," the President said bitterly. "It's enough to provoke nightmares."

"And if Topiltzin topples the present government and makes good his threat by sending millions of his people flooding across our border in a mad attempt to recover the American Southwest . . . ?" Brogan let the question hang.

The President replied in a strangely mild tone. "Then I will have no choice but to order our armed forces to treat any horde of illegal aliens as foreign invaders."

Brogan arrived back in his office at the CIA headquarters in Langley and found the Assistant Secretary of the Navy, Elmer Shaw, waiting for him.

"Sorry to foul up your busy schedule," said Shaw, "but I have some interesting news that might make your day."

"Must be important to warrant your personal visit."

"It is."

"Come in and sit down. Is the news good or bad?"

"Very good."

"Nothing else is going right lately," said Brogan solemnly. "I'll be glad to hear something decent for a change."

"Our survey ship, the *Polar Explorer,* has been searching for the Soviet Alfa-class submarine that went missing —"

"I'm familiar with the mission," Brogan interrupted.

"Well, they've found it."

Brogan's eyes widened slightly, and he rapped his desk in a rare display of pleasure. "Congratulations. The Alfa class is the finest sub in both navies. Your people have pulled off a master stroke."

"We haven't got our hands on it yet," said Shaw.

Brogan's eyes suddenly narrowed. "What about the Russians? Are they aware of the discovery?"

"We don't think so. Shortly after instruments detected the sunken sub, which, by the way, includes videotape of the wreckage, our ship pulled off the search track and assisted in the rescue operations of the downed U.N. aircraft. A heaven-sent smoke screen. Our best intelligence from inside the Soviet navy confirms business as usual. Nothing from the KGB either. And our space surveillance of their North Atlantic fleet shows no indication of dramatic course changes toward the search area."

"Odd they didn't have a spy trawler shadow the *Polar Explorer*."

"They did," explained Shaw. "They also kept a close eye on our operations all right, monitoring our ship's course and communications by satellite. They left it alone, sitting back and hoping our more advanced underwater search technology would get lucky where theirs failed. Then they banked their expectations on the clear possibility our crew would give away the location through the tiniest of errors."

"But they didn't."

"No," answered Shaw firmly. "Ship security was airtight. Except for the captain and two NUMA underwater search experts, the entire crew was briefed to think they were on an iceberg-tracking and sea-bottom geology survey. My report on the success of the discovery was hand-carried from Greenland by the *Polar Explorer*'s executive officer so there was no chance of communications penetration."

"Okay, where do we go from here?" inquired Brogan. "Obviously the Soviets would never allow another *Glomar Explorer* snatch. And they still have a ship patrolling the area where they lost that missile sub off the East Coast in 'eighty-six."

"We have an underwater salvage job in mind," said Shaw.

"When?"

"If we began putting together the operation now, redesigning and modifying existing submersibles and equipment, we should be ready for salvage in ten months."

"So we ignore the sub, or act like it until then?"

"Correct," replied Shaw. "In the meantime, another event has fallen into our laps that will confuse the Soviets. The Navy needs your agency's cooperation to carry it out."

"I'm listening."

"During rescue and subsequent investigation of the air crash, the NUMA people working with us in the search accidentally stumbled on what looks like an ancient Roman shipwreck buried in ice."

Brogan stared at Shaw skeptically. "In Greenland?"

Shaw nodded. "The word from experts is it's genuine."

"What can the CIA do to help the Navy with an old shipwreck?"

"A little disinformation. We'd like the Russians to think the *Polar Explorer* was looking for the Roman ship all along."

Brogan noted a flashing light on his intercom. "A sound concept. While the Navy prepares to grab their newest sub, we scatter bread crumbs down the wrong path."

"Something like that."

"How will you handle the Roman wreck from your end?"

"We set up an archaeological project as a cover for an on-site base of operations. The *Polar Explorer* will remain on station so the crew can give a hand in the excavation."

"Is the sub close by?"

"Less than ten miles away."

"Any idea of her condition?"

"Some structural damage from a collision with a rise on the seafloor, but otherwise intact."

"And the Roman ship?"

"Our men on the scene claim they've found the frozen bodies of the crew in an excellent state of preservation."

Brogan rose from his desk and walked with Shaw to the door. "Incredible," he said, fascinated. Then he grinned impishly. "I wonder if any ancient state secrets will be found too?"

Shaw grinned back. "Better a hoard of treasure."

Neither man would have bet a dime their humorous exchange was to return to haunt them within the next forty-eight hours.

20

Under the direction of the archaeologists the crew of the *Polar Explorer* cut their way down to the ice-locked ship, layer by layer, until the top deck was laid bare from bow stem to stern-post.

Everyone in the fjord was drawn to the site, hypnotized by curiosity. Only Pitt and Lily were missing. They remained on board the icebreaker to study the wax tablets.

A compelling silence gripped the crowd of seamen and archaeologists, joined by the air-crash investigating team, as they stood on the edge of the excavation. They stared down at the partially cleared vessel as though it were a hidden tomb of ancient royalty.

Hoskins and Graham measured the hull, arriving at an overall length of just under twenty meters, with a beam of seven meters. The mast had broken two meters above its step and was missing. The remains of the hemp rigging snaked over the weather deck and sides as if wadded up and dropped by a giant bird. A few shredded pieces of canvas were all that remained of the once broad, square sail.

The deck planking was tested for strength and found to be as solid as the day the ship was launched from some long-forgotten Mediterranean shipyard. The artifacts strewn about the deck were photographed, tagged and carefully lifted to the surface and carried to the *Polar Explorer,* where they were cleaned and catalogued. Then each object was stored in the ship's ice locker to prevent decay during the voyage to a nation that was not in existence when the old merchant vessel sailed on her final voyage.

Gronquist, Hoskins and Graham did not touch the collapsed deckhouse or enter the galley. Slowly, almost tenderly, the three of them lifted one end of the cargo hatch and propped it half-open.

Gronquist stretched out on his stomach and leaned his head and shoulders into the gap until his vision ranged beneath the deck beams.

"Are they there?" Graham asked excitedly. "Are they as Pitt described them?"

Gronquist stared at the ghastly white faces, the frozen masklike expressions. It seemed to him that if he scraped away the ice and shook them, their eyes would blink and they'd come alive.

He hesitated before answering. The bright

daylight above gave him a clear view of the entire hold, and he glimpsed two forms huddled together in the extreme angle of the bow that Pitt had missed.

"They're just as Pitt described," he said soberly, "except for the dog and the girl."

Pitt stood in the shelter of a deck crane and watched as Giordino jockeyed the NUMA helicopter over the stern of the *Polar Explorer.* Fifteen seconds later the landing skids kissed the painted bull's-eye on the deck, the turbine's shrill whine died away and the rotor blades beat to a slow stop.

The right-hand cockpit door opened and a tall man wearing a green turtleneck sweater under a brown corduroy sport jacket jumped to the deck. He looked around for a moment as though getting his bearings and then spied Pitt, who threw a wave of greeting. He walked swiftly, shoulders huddled, hands shoved deeply into pockets to shield them from the cold.

Pitt stepped forward and quickly ushered the visitor through a hatch into the warmth of the ship.

"Dr. Redfern?"

"You Dirk Pitt?"

"Yes, I'm Pitt."

"I've read of your exploits."

"Thank you for taking time from your busy schedule to come."

"Are you kidding?" blurted Redfern, eyes wide with enthusiasm. "I jumped at your invitation. There isn't an archaeologist in the world who wouldn't give an eyetooth to be in on this find. When can I take a look?"

"Be dark in another ten minutes. I think it will be practical if you're briefed by Doctor Gronquist, the archaeologist who supervised the excavation. He'll also show you the artifacts he's recovered off the main deck. Then at first light you set foot on the vessel and take charge of the project."

"Sounds good."

"Have any luggage?" Pitt asked.

"I traveled light. Only a briefcase and a small tote bag."

"Al Giordino —"

"The helicopter pilot?"

"Yes, Al will see that your gear is taken to your quarters. Now if you'll follow me, I'll see you get something warm in your stomach and pick your brain on an intriguing puzzle."

"After you."

Dr. Mel Redfern towered over Pitt and had to duck halfway to his navel when he passed through a hatch. His blond hair had receded to a widow's peak and he wore designer glasses in front of gray-blue eyes. His long body was still reasonably trim for a man of forty with a slight but noticeable paunch.

A former college basketball star who passed on playing for the pros to earn his doctorate

250

in anthropology, Redfern later turned his considerable talents to underwater exploration and became one of the world's leading experts in classical marine archaeology.

"Did you have a good flight from Athens to Reykjavik?" asked Pitt.

"Slept through most of that one," answered Redfern. "It was the ride in the navy patrol plane from Iceland to the Eskimo settlement a hundred miles to the south of here that damned near turned me into an ice cube. I hope I can borrow some cold-weather clothing. I packed for the sunny islands of Greece and didn't plan for a rush trip to the Arctic Circle."

"Commander Knight, the ship's skipper, can fix you up. What were you working on?"

"A second-century B.C. Greek merchant ship that sank with a cargo of marble sculptures." Redfern could not contain his curiosity and began to grill Pitt. "You didn't state in your radio message what the ship was carrying."

"Except for the bodies of the crew, I found the cargo hold empty."

"Can't have it all your way," Redfern said philosophically. "But you did say the ship was basically intact."

"Yes, that's true. If we repair a hole in the hull, restore the mast and the rigging and hang new steering oars, you could sail her into New York harbor."

"God, that's astounding. Has Dr. Gronquist been able to determine an approximate date on her?"

"Yes, by coins minted around A.D. 390. We even know her name. *Serapis.* It was carved in Greek on the sternpost."

"A completely preserved fourth-century Byzantine merchant ship," Redfern murmured in wonder. "This has to be the archaeological find of the century. I can't wait to lay my hands on her."

Pitt led him into the officers' wardroom, where Lily sat at a dining table copying the wording from the wax tablets onto paper. Pitt made the introductions.

"Dr. Lily Sharp, Dr. Mel Redfern."

Lily rose and extended her hand. "This is an honor, Doctor. Although my field is land science, I've been a fan of your underwater work since grad school."

"The honor is mine," said Redfern politely. "Let's cut the fancy titles and stick with first names."

"What can we get you?" asked Pitt.

"A gallon of hot chocolate and a bowl of soup should thaw me out just fine."

Pitt relayed the order to a steward.

"Well, where's this puzzle you mentioned?" asked Redfern with the anxiousness of a kid leaping out of bed on Christmas Day.

Pitt stared at him and smiled. "How's your Latin, Mel?"

"Passable. I thought you said the ship was Greek."

"It is," answered Lily, "but the Captain wrote out his log on wax tablets in Latin. Six were inscribed with wording. The seventh has lines like a map. Dirk recovered them during his initial entry into the ship. I've transposed the writing into more readable form on paper so it can be run off on a copy machine. I drew an enlarged scale of the tablet depicting a chart of some kind. So far we haven't been able to pin down a geographical location because it lacks labels."

Redfern sat down and held one of the tablets in his hand. He studied it almost reverently for several moments before setting it aside. Then he picked up Lily's pages and began to read.

The steward brought a mug of hot chocolate and a large bowl of Boston clam chowder. Redfern became so engrossed in the translation that he lost his appetite. Like a robot, he raised the cup and sipped the chocolate without taking his eyes from the handwritten pages. After nearly ten minutes, he stood up and paced the deck between the officers' dining tables, muttering Latin phrases to himself, oblivious to his rapt audience.

Pitt and Lily sat in utter silence, careful not to interrupt his thoughts, curiously watching his reactions. Redfern stopped as if mentally placing a problem into proper perspective.

He returned to the table and examined the pages again. The air fairly crackled with expectancy.

Several more minutes dragged by before Redfern finally laid the pages on the table with trembling hands. Then he stared vacantly into the distance, his eyes strangely blurred.

Redfern had been rocked right down to his toenails.

"You look like you just found the Holy Grail," said Pitt.

"What is it?" asked Lily. "What did you find?"

They could barely hear Redfern's answer. His head was down.

He said, "It's possible, just possible, your chance discovery may unlock the door to the greatest collection of art and literary treasures the world has ever known."

21

"Now that you have our undivided attention," Pitt said dryly, "you mind sharing your revelation?"

Redfern shook his head as if to clear it. "The story — saga is a better definition — is overwhelming. I can't quite comprehend it all."

Lily asked, "Do the tablets tell why a Graeco-Roman ship sailed far beyond her home waters?"

"Not Graeco-Roman, but Byzantine," Redfern corrected her. "When the *Serapis* sailed the ancient world, the seat of the Empire had been moved by Constantine the Great from Rome to the Bosporus, where the Greek city of Byzantium once stood."

"Which became Constantinople," said Pitt.

"And then Istanbul." Redfern turned to Lily. "Sorry for not giving you a direct answer. But, yes, the tablets reveal how and why the ship came here. To fully explain, we have to set the stage, beginning with 323

B.C., the year Alexander the Great died in Babylon. His empire was split up by his generals. One of them, Ptolemy, carved out Egypt and became king. A canny guy, Ptolemy. He also managed to get his hands on Alexander's corpse, encasing it in a gold-and-crystal coffin. He later enshrined the body in an elegant mausoleum and built a magnificent city around it that surpassed Athens. In honor of his former king, Ptolemy called it Alexandria."

"What does all this have to do with the *Serapis*?" asked Lily.

"Please bear with me," replied Redfern genially. "Ptolemy founded a massive museum and library from scratch. The inventory became monumental. His descendants, through Cleopatra, and later successors all continued to acquire manuscripts and art objects until the museum, and especially the library, became one of the largest storehouses of art, science and literature that has ever existed. This vast collection of knowledge lasted until A.D. 391. In that year, Emperor Theodosius and the patriarch of Alexandria, Theophilos, who was a religious nut case, decided all reference to anything except newly formed Christian principles was paganism. They masterminded the destruction of the library's contents. Statues, fabulous works of art in marble, bronze, gold and ivory, incredible paintings and tapestries, countless numbers of books inscribed on lambskin or papyrus scrolls, even Alexander's corpse: all were to be smashed into dust or burned to ashes."

"What kind of numbers are we talking about?" Pitt asked.

"The books alone numbered in the hundreds of thousands."

Lily shook her head sadly. "What a terrible waste."

"Only Biblical and church writings were left," continued Redfern. "The entire library and museum was finally leveled after Arab and Islamic armies swept Egypt sometime around A.D. 646."

"The earlier masterworks that took centuries to collect were lost, gone forever," Pitt summed up.

"Lost," Redfern agreed. "So historians have thought until now. But if what I just read rings true, the cream of the collection is not gone forever. It lies hidden somewhere."

Lily was confused. "It exists to this day? Smuggled out of Alexandria by the *Serapis* before the burning?"

"According to the inscriptions on the tablets."

Pitt looked doubtful. "No way the *Serapis* sneaked off with more than a tiny fraction of the collection. It won't wash. The ship is too small. Less than forty tons burden. The crew might have crammed a few thousand scrolls and a couple of statues into the cargo hold, but nothing like the quantity you're talking about."

Redfern gave Pitt a respectful gaze. "You're very astute. You have a good knowledge of early ships."

"Let's get back to the *Serapis* washing up in Greenland," Pitt urged, as Redfern picked up the appropriate pages of Lily's text and shuffled them into order.

"I won't give you a literal translation of fourth-century Latin. Too stiff and formal. Instead, I'll try and relate the text in English vernacular. The first entry is under the Julian calendar date of April third, A.D. 391. The report begins:

"I, Cuccius Rufinus, captain of the *Serapis,* in the employ of Nicias, Greek shipping merchant of the port city of Rhodes, have agreed to transport a cargo for Junius Venator of Alexandria. The voyage is said to be long and arduous, and Venator will not disclose our destination. My daughter, Hypatia, sailed with me this trip and her mother will be very concerned at our lengthy separation. But Venator is paying twenty times the usual rate, a good fortune that will greatly benefit Nicias as well as myself and the crew.

"The cargo was put on board at night under heavy guard, and quite mysteriously, as I was ordered to remain at the docks with my crew during the loading. Four soldiers under the command of the centurion Domitius Severus have been commanded to stay on the ship and sail with us.

"I do not like the look of it, but Venator has paid me for the voyage in full, and I cannot go back on my contract."

"An honest man," said Pitt. "Hard to believe he didn't discover the nature of his cargo."

"He comes to that later. The next few lines are a log of the voyage. He also makes mention of his ship's namesake. I'll skip to where they make their first port.

"I thank our god Serapis for providing us with a smooth and fast passage of fourteen days to Carthago Nova where we rested for five days and took on four times our normal supply of provisions. Here we joined Junius Venator's other ships. Most are over two hundred tons burden, some close to three hundred. We total sixteen with Venator's flagship. Our sturdy *Serapis* is the smallest vessel in the fleet."

"A fleet!" Lily cried. Her eyes gleamed, her whole body taut. "They did save the collection."

Redfern nodded delightedly. "A damned

good chunk of it anyway. Two-to-three-hundred-ton-ships were representative of large merchantmen of that era. Allowing for two ships to carry men and provisions, and taking an average tonnage of two hundred for the other fourteen ships, you have a gross tonnage for the fleet of 2,800 tons. Enough to transport a third of the Library's books and a fair share of the museum's art treasures."

Pitt called for a break. He went to the galley counter and brought back two cups of coffee. He set one in front of Lily and returned for a plate of doughnuts. He remained standing. He thought and concentrated better on his feet.

"So far the great Library snatch is theory," he said. "I've heard nothing that proves the goods were actually spirited away."

"Rufinus nails it down further on," said Redfern. "The description of the *Serapis*'s cargo comes near the end of the log."

Pitt gave the marine archaeologist an impatient look and sat back, waiting.

"On the next tablet Rufinus mentions minor repairs to the ship, dockside gossip, and a tourist's eye of Carthago Nova, now Cartagena, Spain. Oddly, he doesn't express any further uneasiness about the coming voyage. He even failed to note the date the fleet left port. But the really offbeat part is the censorship. Listen to the next paragraph.

"We sailed today toward great sea. The faster ships towing the slower ones. I can write no more. The soldiers are watching. Under strict orders of Junius Venator there can be no record of the voyage."

"Just when we set the straight pieces of the puzzle together," Pitt muttered, "the center section is missing."

"There must be more," Lily insisted. "I know I copied beyond that part of the report."

"You did," acknowledged Redfern, shuffling the pages. "Rufinus takes up the tale eleven months later.

"I am free now to record our cruel voyage without fear of punishment. Venator and his small army of slaves, Severus and his legionaries, all the ship's crews, have all been slain by the barbarians and the fleet burned. The *Serapis* escaped because my fear of Venator made me cautious.

"I learned the source and contents of the fleet's cargo and know its hiding place in the hills. Secrets such as these must be kept from mortal men. I suspected Venator and Severus meant to murder all but a few of their trusted soldiers and the crew of one ship to insure their return home.

"I feared for the life of my daughter so I armed my crew and ordered them to remain close to the ship so we could cast off at the first sign of treachery. But the barbarians struck first, slaughtering Venator's slaves and Severus's legion. Our guards died in the battle, and we cut the lines and heaved our ship from the beach. Venator tried to save himself by running into the water. He shouted for rescue. I could not risk the lives of Hypatia and the crew to save him and refused to turn back. To do so against the current would have been suicidal."

Redfern paused in the translation before continuing. "At this point Rufinus jumps around and flashes back to the fleet's departure from Cartagena.

"The voyage from Hispania to our destination in the strange land took fifty-eight days. The weather was favorable with winds at our backs. For this good fortune, Serapis demanded a sacrifice. Two of our crew died from a malady unknown to me."

"He must mean scurvy," said Lily.
"Ancient seamen rarely sailed more than a week or two without touching land," Pitt clarified. "Scurvy did not become common until the long voyages of the Spanish. Could be they died from any number of reasons."
Lily nodded at Redfern. "Sorry for interrupting. Please go on."

"We first stepped ashore on a large island inhabited by barbarians who resembled Scythians, but with darker skins. They proved friendly and willingly helped the fleet replenish our food and fresh water supplies.

"We sighted more islands, but the flagship sailed on. Only Venator knew where the fleet was to land. At last we sighted a barren shore and came to the wide mouth of a river. We stood off for five days and nights until the winds blew to our advantage. Then we set sail up the river, rowing at times, until we reached the hills of Rome."

"The hills of Rome?" Lili repeated absently. "That's a twist."

"He must have meant it as a comparison," said Pitt.

"A tough riddle to crack," Redfern admitted.

"The slaves under the overseer Latinius Macer dug into the hills above the river. Eight months later the fleet's cargo was carried from the ships to the hiding ground."

"Did he describe the 'hiding ground'?" asked Pitt.

Redfern picked up a tablet and compared it to Lily's copy. "Parts of the wording are indistinct. I'll have to fill in as best I can.

"Thus, the secret of the secrets lies within the hill inside a chamber dug by the slaves. The place cannot be seen because of the palisade. After all was stored, the barbarian horde swarmed from the hills. I do not know if the chamber was sealed in time as I was busy helping my crew push the boat from the sand."

"Rufinus fails to record distances," said Pitt, disillusioned, "and never gives directions. Now we have an odds-on chance the barbarians, whoever the hell they were, robbed the store."

Redfern's expression turned grim. "We can't ignore the possibility."

"I don't think the worst happened," said Lily optimistically. "An immense collection can't be erased as though it never existed. A few pieces would have eventually turned up."

"Depends on the area where the action took place," said Pitt. "Fifty-eight days at an average speed of — say three and a half knots, a vessel designed along the ancient lines of the *Serapis* — might have sailed over four thousand nautical miles."

"Providing they sailed in a straight line," said Redfern. "Not a likely prospect. Rufinus merely states they sailed fifty-eight days before stepping ashore. Traveling in unknown waters, they probably hugged the coastlines."

"But traveling to where?" Lily asked.

"The southern coast of Western Africa is the most logical destination," answered Redfern. "A crew of Phoenicians sailed around Africa clockwise in the fifth century B.C. Quite a bit of it was charted by Rufinus's time. Stands to reason Venator would have turned his fleet south after passing through the Straits of Gibraltar."

"Never sell a jury," said Pitt. "Rufinus described islands."

"Could be the Madeira, Canary or Cape Verde Islands."

"Still won't sell. You can't explain how the *Serapis* ended up halfway across the globe from the tip of Africa to Greenland. You're talking a distance of eight thousand miles."

"That's true. I'm confused on that count."

"My vote goes for a northern course," said Lily. "The islands also might be the Shetlands or the Faroes. That would put the excavation site along the Norwegian coast or, better yet, Iceland."

"She makes a good case," Pitt agreed. "Her theory would explain how the *Serapis* came to be stranded in Greenland."

"What does Rufinus tell us after he escaped the barbarians?" she asked.

Redfern paused to finish off his hot chocolate. "He goes on to say:

"We reached the open sea. Navigating was difficult. The stars are in different positions.

265

The sun is not the same also. Violent storms struck us from the south. One crewman was swept overboard on the tenth day, a Gaul. We continued to be driven toward the north. On the thirty-first day our god led us to a safe bay where we made repairs and took what provisions we could find from the land. We also added extra ballast stone. Some distance beyond the beach there is a great sea of dwarf-like pines. Fresh water seeps from sand with the jab of a stick.

"Six days of good sailing and then another tempest, worse than the last. Our sails are split and useless. The great gale shattered the mast, and the steering oars were swept away. We drifted helplessly under the merciless wind for many days. I lost record of days. Sleep became impossible. The weather turned very cold. Ice formed on the deck. The ship became very unstable. I ordered my frozen and exhausted crew to throw our water and wine jars over the side."

"The amphoras you found on the bottom outside the fjord." Redfern paused, nodding at Pitt. Then he continued reading.

"Shortly after we were driven into this long bay, we managed to beach the ship and fall into a dead sleep for two days and nights.

"The god Serapis is unkind. Winter has set in and ice has bound the ship. We have

266

no choice but to brave out the winter until the days warm. A barbarian village lies across the bay and we have found them open to trade. We barter with them for food. They use our gold coins as trinkets, having no idea of their value. They have showed us how to keep warm by burning oil from a monstrous fish. Our stomachs are full, and I think we shall survive.

"While I am comfortable with much time on my hands I will write a few words each day. This entry I shall recall the amount and type of cargo that Venator's slaves unloaded from the hold of the *Serapis* as I watched unseen from the galley and made an accounting. At the sight of the great object, everyone sank to their knees in proper reverence."

"What does he mean?" asked Lily.
"Patience," said Redfern. "Listen.

"Three hundred twenty copper tubes marked *Geologic Charts*. Sixty-three large tapestries. These were packed around the grand gold-and-glass casket of Alexander. My knees trembled. I could see his face through . . ."

"Rufinus wrote no more," Redfern said sadly. "He didn't finish the sentence. The last tablet is a drawing showing the general configuration of the shoreline and the course of the river."

"The lost coffin of Alexander the Great," Lily said, slightly above a whisper. "Can he still lie buried in a cavern somewhere?"

"Along with treasures from the Alexandria Library?" Redfern added to Lily's question. "We can do little else but hope."

Pitt's reaction was quite different; it was one of profound confidence. "Hope is for spectators. I figure I can find your antiques in thirty . . . make that twenty days."

Lily's and Redfern's eyes opened wide. They regarded Pitt with the suspicion usually awarded a politician promising to lower taxes. They flatly didn't believe him.

They should have.

"You sound pretty cocky," said Lily.

Pitt's green eyes glowed with a look of utter sincerity. "Let's have a look at the map."

Redfern handed him a rendering Lily had made from the tablet and then enlarged. There was little to examine except a series of wavy lines.

"Won't tell us much," he said. "Rufinus didn't label anything."

"It's enough," said Pitt, his tone dry and unperturbed. "Enough to lead us to the front door."

It was four in the morning when Pitt awoke. He automatically rolled over to return to sleep but realized through the cobwebs that someone had turned on the light and was talking to him.

"Sorry, pal, but you've got to rise and shine."

Pitt groggily squinted into the serious face of Commander Knight. "What gives?"

"Orders from the top. You're to shove off for Washington immediately."

"They say why?"

"*They* is the Pentagon, and, no, *they* didn't grace me with an explanation."

Pitt sat up and swung his bare feet onto the deck. "I was hoping to hang around a bit longer and watch the excavation."

"No such luck," said Knight. "You, Giordino and Dr. Sharp have to be on your way within the hour."

"Lily?" Pitt stood and made his way to the head. "I can understand the big brass wanting to question Al and me about the Soviet sub, but why are they interested in Lily?"

"The Joint Chiefs don't confide in the serfs." Knight smiled wryly. "I haven't a clue."

"What about transportation?"

"Same way Redfern came in. Helicopter to the Eskimo village and weather station, a Navy plane to Iceland, where you transfer to an Air Force B-52 bomber that's rotating back to the States for overhaul."

"Not the way it's done," mumbled Pitt with a toothbrush in his mouth. "If they want my wholehearted cooperation, it's private jet or nothing."

"You're pretty heady for this early in the morning."

"When I'm kicked out of bed before dawn I'm not shy about telling the Joint Chiefs to insert it among their hemorrhoids."

"There goes my next promotion," moaned Knight. "Guilt by association."

"Stick with me and you'll wind up Fleet Admiral."

"I bet."

Pitt tapped his head with the toothbrush. "Genius has struck. Fire off a message. Say we'll meet them halfway. Giordino and I will fly our NUMA 'copter direct to Thule Air Force Base. *They* can damn well have a government jet waiting to zap us to the Capital."

"You might as well tease a Doberman when he's eating."

Pitt threw up his hands. "Why is it nobody around here has any faith in my creative smarts?"

22

Washington closed down after a dazzling clear day. The crisp fall weather sharpened the air as the setting sun glazed the white granite of the government buildings into a goldlike porcelain. The sky was sprinkled with cotton-ball clouds that looked solid enough for the Gulfstream IV jetliner to land on.

The plane could carry up to nineteen passengers, but Pitt, Giordino and Lily had the main cabin all to themselves. Giordino had promptly fallen asleep before the plane's wheels lifted from the U.S. Air Force Base at Thule and hadn't opened an eye since. Lily had dozed on and off or read Marlys Millhiser's *The Threshold.*

Pitt stayed awake, lost in his thoughts, occasionally making entries in a small notebook. He turned and stared out the small window at the homeward-bound traffic slowly beating its way from the core of the Capital.

His thoughts wandered back to the frozen crew of the *Serapis,* its skipper, Rufinus, and

271

his daughter, Hypatia. Pitt was sorry his eyes had failed to find the girl in the darkness of the cargo hold even though the video camera had recorded her quite clearly, arms circled around a small long-haired dog.

Gronquist almost cried when he described her. Pitt wondered if she would end up as a frozen display in a museum, viewed in hushed astonishment by endless lines of the curious.

Gazing down at the Washington mall as the Gulfstream circled for its approach, Pitt put off his thoughts of the *Serapis* and focused on the search for the Alexandria Library treasures. He knew exactly how he was going about it. The part of his plan that didn't thrill him was putting all his eggs in one basket. He had to bank his entire search on a few lines crudely scratched in wax by the freezing hand of a dying man. Murphy's Law — Whatever can go wrong, will go wrong — was already erecting the barricades against him.

The lines in the map might not fit a known geographical location for any number of reasons: distortion in the wax from rapid temperature changes during the initial freeze on the *Serapis* and later thaw on board the *Polar Explorer;* or perhaps Rufinus erred in the scale and misplaced the curves and angles of the shoreline and river; or the worst and most probable scenario — great changes in the landscape due to soil buildup or erosion, earthquakes or extreme changes in climate during the past 1,600 years. No river in the world had maintained an unvarying course over a thousand years.

Pitt smelled the intoxicating scent of challenge. To restless men it is a real scent that wafts somewhere between a sexually aroused woman and newly cut grass after a rain. It tempts and addicts until the challenger is oblivious to any thought of failure or danger. The excitement of the chase meant as much to Pitt as actual success. And yet, when he did achieve the near-impossible, there was always the inevitable letdown afterward.

His first obstacle was lack of time to conduct a search. The second was the Soviet sub. He and Giordino were the front-running candidates to oversee the underwater salvage operation.

Pitt's reverie was interrupted by the pilot's voice over the speakers to fasten seat belts. He watched the plane's tiny shadow enlarge against the leafless trees below. The brown grass flashed past and turned to concrete. The pilot taxied off the main runway at Andrews Air Force Base and braked to a stop beside a Ford Taurus station wagon.

Pitt helped Lily step from the plane. Then he and Giordino unloaded the luggage and stacked it in the rear of the Taurus. The driver, a young athletic prep-school type, stood back as if afraid to interfere with the two hard-core types who handled the heavy suitcases and duffel bags as lightly as pillows.

"What's the plan?" Pitt asked the driver.

"Dinner with Admiral Sandecker at his club."

"Admiral who?" asked Lily.

"Sandecker," answered Giordino. "Our boss at NUMA. We must have done something right. It's a rare treat when he pops for a meal."

"Not to mention an invitation to the John Paul Jones Club," added Pitt.

"Exclusive?"

Giordino nodded. "A depository for rusty old naval officers with bilge water in their bladders."

It was dark when the driver finally turned into a quiet residential street in Georgetown. Five blocks later he eased the car onto a gravel drive and stopped beneath the portico of a red-brick Victorian mansion.

In the entrance hall a short gamecock of a man strode across the carpet dressed in a tailored silk suit with a vest. He moved in rapid, energetic steps like a cat sneaking through a door crack. His features were sharp and always reminded Pitt of a griffin. The deep red hair on his head connected to a meticulously trimmed Van Dyke beard. His eyes seemed filled with spit and vinegar.

Admiral James Sandecker was not the kind to creep into a room; he took it by storm.

"Good to see you boys back," he snapped

in a tone more official than friendly. "I hear your ancient ship discovery may change the history books. The news media is giving it a big play."

"We had a few lucky breaks," said Pitt. "May I present Dr. Lily Sharp. Lily, Admiral James Sandecker."

Sandecker beamed like a lighthouse when he was in the presence of an attractive woman, and he went luminous for Lily. "Doctor, you have to be the loveliest lady to ever grace these walls."

"I'm happy to see your club shows no discrimination toward females."

"Not because the membership is open-minded," said Giordino slyly. "Most women would rather get a tetanus shot than come here and hear old derelicts rehash the wars."

Sandecker shot Giordino a withering stare.

Lily looked at the two men, puzzled. She thought perhaps she was caught in the middle of a long-standing feud.

Pitt forced back a laugh, but couldn't suppress a smile. He'd witnessed the give-and-take for ten years. Everyone close to them knew Giordino and Sandecker were the warmest of friends.

Lily decided to make a tactical retreat. "If one of you gentlemen will point out the ladies room, I'll freshen up."

Sandecker gestured up a hallway. "First door on the right. Please take your time." As soon as she had left, the admiral motioned Pitt and Giordino into a small sitting room and closed the door. "I have to leave for a meeting with the Secretary of the Navy in an hour. This will be our only chance to talk in private so I'll have to make it quick before Dr. Sharp returns. Let me begin by saying you did a damned fine job finding the Soviet sub and then clamping a lid on it. The President was most pleased when he received the news and asked me to thank you."

"When do we start?" asked Giordino.

"Start what?"

"A covert underwater salvage operation on the sub."

"Our intelligence people insist it be put on hold. Their scheme is to feed Soviet agents misleading information. Make it appear any further search is a waste of taxpayers' money, and we've written it off as a lost cause."

"For how long?" Pitt asked.

"Maybe a year. Whatever time it takes for the mission project people to draw up plans and construct the equipment for the project."

Pitt stared at the admiral suspiciously. "I get the feeling we won't be included."

"Dead on," Sandecker said flatly. "As they say at the police precinct, you're off the case."

"Can I ask why?"

"I have a more important job for you two characters."

"What could be more important than stealing the secrets of the Soviet Navy's deadliest submarine?" Pitt asked guardedly.

"A skiing holiday," Sandecker replied. "Nothing like the invigorating air and the powder snow of the Rockies. You're booked on a commercial flight to Denver tomorrow morning at ten forty-five. Dr. Sharp will accompany you."

Pitt looked at Giordino, who merely shrugged. He turned back to Sandecker. "Is this a reward or exile?"

"Call it a working vacation. Senator Pitt will explain the details."

"My dad?"

"He's expecting you later this evening at his home." Sandecker pulled a large gold pocket watch from his vest pocket and read the ivory face. "We must not keep a pretty lady waiting."

Sandecker started for the door while Pitt and Giordino stood dumbly rooted to the room's faded carpet.

"Don't hold back, Admiral!" Pitt's voice was sharp. "Unless you play it straight, there's no way in hell I'll be on that plane tomorrow."

"Accept my regrets too," Giordino said. "I feel an attack of Borneo jungle fungus coming on."

Sandecker paused in mid-stride, turned, lifted an eyebrow and stared directly at Pitt. "You don't fool me for a minute, mister. You don't give a damn about the Soviet sub. You want to find the relics of the Alexandria Library so bad you'd give up sex."

Pitt said with forbearance, "Your insight is flawless, as usual. So is your underground grapevine. I intended to turn over the transcription of the *Serapis*'s log to you on our return to Washington. Apparently someone beat me to it."

"Commander Knight. He radioed Dr. Redfern's translation in code to the Navy Department, who turned it over to the National Security Council and the President. I read a copy before you left Iceland. You opened Pandora's box and didn't know it. If the cache exists and can be found, it will cause a political upheaval. But I'm not about to go into it. That job was given to your father for reasons he's better qualified to explain."

"How does Lily fit in the picture?"

"She's part of your cover. A backup in the event there's a leak or the KGB suspects their sub was actually found. Martin Brogan wants to make it clear you're working on a legitimate archaeological project. That's why I'm meeting you at the club, and your father will brief you at home. Your movements must look routine should you be tailed."

"Sounds like an overkill to me."

"The bureaucracy works in mysterious ways," said Giordino resignedly. "I wonder if I can get tickets to a Denver Bronco game."

"I'm glad we see eye to eye," Sandecker said with some satisfaction. "Now let's find our table. I'm starved."

They dropped Lily off at the Jefferson Hotel. She gave them both a hug and entered the lobby, followed by a porter with her bags. Pitt and Giordino directed the driver to the ten-story solar-glass building that was the headquarters for the National Underwater & Marine Agency.

Giordino went directly to his office on the fourth floor while Pitt remained on the elevator and rode up to the communication-and-information network on the top level. He left an attaché case with the receptionist and removed an envelope, slipping it in his coat pocket.

He wandered around the seemingly endless rows of electronic equipment and computer hardware until he found a man sitting cross-legged on the tiled floor contemplating a miniature tape recorder dissected from a large kangaroo doll.

"Does it sing 'Waltzing Matilda' off-key?" Pitt asked.

"How'd you know?"

"A lucky guess."

Hiram Yaeger looked up and grinned. He had a droll face with straight blond hair tied in a ponytail. His beard, curled in long ringlets, looked as if he had borrowed it from

279

a costume rental. He peered through a pair of granny spectacles and was dressed like a down-and-out rodeo performer in old Levi's and boots a bag lady would throw away.

Sandecker had pirated Yaeger away from a computer-design company in California's Silicon Valley and had given him free reign to create NUMA's data complex from scratch. It was a perfect marriage between human genius and central processing unit. Yaeger supervised a vast library of information containing every known report and book written about the world's oceans.

Yaeger studied the doll's recording and speaker unit with a critical eye. "I could have designed a better system than this with kitchen utensils."

"Can you fix it?"

"Probably not."

Pitt shook his head and gestured around the computer complex. "You set up all this but can't repair a simple cassette player?"

"My heart isn't in it." Yaeger rose, walked into an office and stood the stuffed kangaroo on one corner of his desk. "Maybe someday when I'm inspired I'll modify it into a talking lamp."

Pitt followed him and closed the door. "Feel in the mood for a more exotic project?"

"Along what lines?"

"Research."

"Lay it on me."

Pitt removed the envelope from his pocket and gave it to Yaeger. NUMA's computer wizard slouched in a chair, opened the envelope flap and withdrew the contents. He rapidly scanned the typed transcript, then read through it again more slowly. After a long silence, he peered over his spectacles at Pitt.

"This from that old ship you found?"

"You know of it?"

"Have to be blind and deaf not to. The story has been all over the newspapers and TV."

Pitt nodded at the papers in Yaeger's hand. "A translation from Latin of the ship's log."

"What do you want from me?"

"Take a look at the page with the map."

Yaeger held it up and studied the unlabeled lines. "You want me to make a match with a known geographical location?"

"If you can," Pitt acknowledged.

"Not a hell of a lot to go on. What is it?"

"An ocean shoreline and a river."

"When was it drawn?"

"A.D. 391."

Yaeger gave Pitt a bemused look. "You might as well ask me to name the streets of Atlantis."

"Program your electronic playmates for a projection of the ship's course after the fleet left Cartagena. You might also try working backwards from the shipwreck site in Greenland. I've included the position."

"You realize this river may not exist any more."

"The thought entered my mind."

"I'll need authorization from the Admiral."

"You'll get it first thing in the morning."

"All right," Yaeger said glumly. "I'll give it my best shot. What's my deadline?"

"Just stay with it until you have something," Pitt replied. "I've got to go out of town for a while. I'll check in with you the day after tomorrow to see how you're doing."

"Can I ask a question?"

"Sure."

"Is this really important?"

"Yes," Pitt said slowly, "I think it is. Maybe more important than you and I can ever imagine."

23

When Pitt's father opened the door to his colonial home on Massachusetts Avenue in Bethesda, Maryland, he wore a faded pair of khaki pants and a well-snagged pullover sweater. The Socrates of the Senate was noted for his expensive and fashionable suits, always embellished with a California golden poppy in the lapel. But out of the public eye he dressed like a rancher camped out on the range.

"Dirk!" he said with pleasure, giving his son a warm bear hug. "I see you too infrequently these days."

Pitt put his arm around the Senator's shoulder, and they walked side by side into a paneled den with filled bookshelves stretching from floor to ceiling. A fire flickered under an ornate mantel carved from teak.

The Senator motioned his son to a chair and walked behind a wet bar.

"Bombay gin martini with a twist, isn't it?"

"A bit cool for gin. How about a Jack

Daniel's straight up."

"Every man to his own poison."

"How's Mom?"

"She's at some highfalutin spa, a fat farm in California on her annual crusade to lose weight. She'll be back day after tomorrow, two pounds heavier."

"She never gives up."

"It keeps her happy."

The Senator passed Pitt a bourbon and then poured himself a port. He raised the glass. "Here's to a fruitful trip to Colorado."

Pitt didn't drink. "Whose bright idea was it to send me skiing?"

"Mine."

Pitt calmly took a swallow of Jack Daniel's and gave his father a hard stare. "What is your involvement with the Alexandria Library artifacts?"

"Very heavy if they truly exist."

"Are you speaking as a private citizen or a bureaucrat?"

"A patriot."

"All right," Pitt said with a deep sigh. "Fill me in. Why are classical art and literary works and the coffin of Alexander so vital to United States interests?"

"None of the above," said the Senator. "The prime meat of the inventory is maps showing geological resources of the ancient world. The lost gold mines of the Pharaohs, the forgotten emerald mines of Cleopatra, the fabled but mystic land of Punt that was famous for its riches of silver, antimony and unusual greenish gold; locations known two and three thousand years ago but buried in the oblivion of time. There was also the fabulous land of Ophir and its recorded wealth of precious minerals. Its location still remains a tantalizing mystery. The mines of King Solomon, Nebuchadnezzar of Babylon, and Sheba, the queen of Saba, whose fabled land today is only a biblical memory. The legendary wealth of the ages still lies hidden under the sands of the Middle East."

"So it's found, so what? How can precious-mineral deposits belonging to other countries concern our government?"

"As bargaining chips," answered the Senator. "If we're able to point the way, negotiations can be opened for joint ventures in the exploitation. We can also make points with national leaders and spread a little badly needed goodwill."

Pitt shook his head and considered. "News to me Congress has turned to prospecting for good foreign relations. Must be more to this than meets the eye."

The Senator nodded, marveling at his son's insight. "There is. Are you familiar with the term 'stratigraphic trap'?"

"I should be." Pitt smiled. "I found one in the Labrador Sea off Quebec Province a few years ago."

"Yes, the Doodlebug project. I remember."

"A stratigraphic trap is one of the toughest oil deposits to discover. Normal seismic exploration won't detect it. Yet they often prove out to have incredibly high yields."

"Which leads us to bitumen, a hydrocarbon-like tar or asphalt that was used in Mesopotamia as long as five thousand years ago for waterproofing buildings, canals, clay drainage pipes and caulking boats. Other uses included roads, treatment of wounds, and adhesives. Much later the Greeks mention springs along the North African coast that bubble with oil. The Romans recorded a site in the Sinai they called Petrol Mountain. And the Bible tells of God ordering Jacob to suck oil out of flintlike rock, and describes the vale of Siddim being full of slime pits, which can be interpreted as tar pits."

"None of these areas has been relocated or drilled?" Pitt asked.

"There has been drilling, yes, but no significant strikes to date. Geologists claim there's a ninety percent probability of finding five hundred million barrels of crude petroleum under Israel alone. Unfortunately, the ancient sites have been lost and covered over through the centuries due to land upheavals and earthquakes."

"Then the main goal is to find a massive oil bonanza in Israel."

"You have to admit it would solve a multi-

286

tude of problems."

"Yes, I guess it would."

The Senator and Pitt sat in silence for the next minute, staring into the fire. If Yaeger and his computer banks didn't pick up a lead, the chances were, at best, hopeless. Pitt was suddenly angered that the power brokers in the White House and Congress were more interested in oil and gold than in the art and literature that could fill in the missing gaps of history.

It was, he thought, a sad commentary on the affairs of state.

The silence was broken by the ring of the telephone. The Senator walked over to a desk and picked up the receiver. He said nothing, merely listened for a moment. Then he hung up.

"I doubt if I'll find the lost Library in Colorado," Pitt said dryly.

"Everyone concerned would be surprised if you did," the Senator came back. "My staff has arranged a briefing for you by the leading authority on the subject. Dr. Bertram Rothberg, a professor of classical history at the University of Colorado, has made the study of the Alexandria Library his life's work. He'll fill you in on background data that could help your search."

"Why do I have to go to him? Seems to me it would be more practical to bring him to Washington."

"You met with Admiral Sandecker?"

"Yes."

"Then you know it's vital to distance yourself and Al Giordino from the discovery of the Soviet submarine. That phone call a minute ago was from an FBI agent who is tailing a KGB agent who is tailing you."

"Nice to know I'm popular."

"You're to make no move that would cause suspicion."

Pitt nodded approvingly. "Fine and dandy, but suppose the Russians get wise to the mission? They have as much to gain by laying their hands on the Library data as we do."

"The possibility exists but is extremely remote," the Senator said guardedly. "We've taken every precaution to keep the wax tablets secret."

"Next question."

"Shoot."

"I'm under surveillance," said Pitt. "What's to stop the KGB from following me to Dr. Rothberg's doorstep?"

"Nothing," the Senator answered. "We have every intention of sitting on the sidelines and cheering them on."

"So we put on a show of status quo."

"Exactly."

"Why me?"

"Because of your L-29 Cord."

"My Cord?"

"The classic car you had restored in Denver. The man you hired called here last week and said to tell you the job is finished and she looks beautiful."

"So I travel to Colorado under a spotlight to pick up my collector car, get in a little ski time on the slopes, and party with Dr. Sharp."

"Exactly," the Senator repeated. "You're to check into the Hotel Breckenridge. A message will be waiting explaining where and when you'll make contact with Dr. Rothberg."

"Remind me never to trade horses with you."

The Senator laughed. "You've been involved with some pretty devious schemes yourself."

Pitt finished the bourbon, stood, and placed his glass on the mantel. "Mind if I borrow the family lodge?"

"I'd prefer you stay away from it."

"But my boots and skis are stored in the garage."

"You can rent your equipment."

"That's ridiculous."

"Not so ridiculous," the Senator said in an even voice, "when you consider that the instant you open the front door, you'll be shot."

"You sure you want to get out here, buddy?" the cabdriver inquired as he stopped beside what looked like an abandoned hangar on one corner of Washington's International Airport.

"This is the place," replied Pitt.

The driver glanced warily around at the deserted unlit area. This had all the earmarks of a mugging, he thought. He reached under the front seat for a length of pipe he hid for such an occasion. He kept an apprehensive eye on the rearview mirror as Pitt pulled a wallet from his inside coat pocket. The driver relaxed slightly. His fare wasn't acting like a mugger.

"What do I owe you?"

"I got eight-sixty on the meter," the driver replied.

Pitt paid the fare plus tip and exited the cab, waiting for the driver to open the trunk and remove the luggage.

"Hell of a place for a drop," the driver muttered.

"Someone is meeting me."

Pitt stood and watched the cab's taillights dim in the distance before he turned off the hangar's alarm system with a pocket transmitter and entered through a side door. He pressed a code on the transmitter and the interior became bathed in bright fluorescent light.

The hangar was Pitt's home. The main floor was lined with a glittering collection of classic and milestone automobiles. There were also an old Pullman railroad car and a Ford tri-motor airplane. The most bizarre oddity was a cast-iron bathtub with an outboard motor attached to it.

He walked toward his living quarters, which stretched across an upper level against the far wall. Reached by an ornate iron spiral staircase, the door at the top opened onto a living room flanked by a large bedroom and a study on one side and a dining area and kitchen on the other.

He unpacked and entered a shower stall, turning up the hot water and aiming the nozzle against a tiled wall. He lay on his back with his feet stretched upward just below the faucets so he could control the spray temperature with his toes. Then he promptly dozed off.

Forty-five minutes later, Pitt slipped on a robe and turned on the TV set. He was about to reheat a pot of Texas chili when the buzzer on the intercom sounded. He pressed the door speaker button, half-expecting Al Giordino to answer.

"Yes?"

"Greenland catering," a feminine voice answered.

He laughed and pressed a switch that unlocked the side door. He stepped onto the balcony and stared down.

Lily walked in carrying a large picnic basket. She stopped and gazed in astonishment for several moments, her eyes dazzled by the light reflecting off the sea of chrome and highly polished lacquer paint.

"Admiral Sandecker tried to describe your place to me," she said admiringly, "but he didn't do it justice."

Pitt came down the stairs to meet her. He took the picnic basket and nearly dropped it. "This thing weighs a ton. What's in it?"

"Our late dinner. I stopped off at a delicatessen and picked up a few goodies."

"Smells like a tasty menu."

"We begin with smoked salmon followed by wild mushroom soup, spinach salad with pheasant and walnuts, linguine in oyster sauce and white wine, all washed down with a bottle of Principessa Gavi. For dessert we have coffee chocolate trifle."

Pitt looked down at Lily and smiled in genuine admiration. Her face was alive and her eyes sparkling. There was a vibrancy he had not noticed before. Her hair was brushed long and straight. She wore a tight-fitting tank dress with a revealing back and black sequins that flashed as she walked. Free of the heavy coat she had worn since Greenland, her breasts loomed larger and her hips more slender than he had pictured them in his imagination. Her legs were long and angled provocatively, and she moved with a sensual vivacity.

After they entered his living room, Pitt dropped the food basket in a chair and reached out and took her hand. "We can eat later," he said softly.

In automatic shyness she dropped her gaze downward, then slowly, as if drawn by an irresistible force, her eyes slowly rose to meet his. Pitt's green eyes were so piercing that her legs grew weak and her hands trembled. She began to flush.

This was stupid, Lily thought. She had calmly planned the seduction, down to the right wine, the dress and the alluring black lace bra and panties beneath. And now she was swept by confusion and doubt. She didn't dream things would move so quickly.

Without a word Pitt peeled the straps from Lily's shoulders, allowing the sequined dress to fall in a pool of shimmering light around her high heels. He slipped his hands around her bare waist and under her knees, lifting her body in one flowing motion.

As he carried her into the bedroom she buried her face against his chest. "I feel like a brazen harlot," she whispered.

Pitt tenderly laid her on the bed and looked down. The sight of her body made the fire burn within him.

"Better," he said in a husky voice, "that you act like one."

24

Yazid entered the dining hall of his villa. He paused and gave a brief nod at the long table covered with plates, serving dishes, eating utensils and goblets, all cast in bronze.

"I trust my friends enjoyed their dinner."

Mohammed al-Hakim, a scholarly mullah who was Yazid's shadow, pushed back his chair and stood. "Excellent as always, Akhmad. But we missed your enlightened presence."

"Allah does not reveal his wishes to me when my stomach is full," Yazid said with a faint smile. He looked around the room at the five men who had risen to their feet and were acknowledging his authority with varied degrees of respect.

No two were dressed alike. Colonel Naguib Bashir, leader of a clandestine organization of pro-Yazid officers, had worn a loose flowing djellaba with long sleeves and hood to conceal his identity since leaving Cairo. A turban sat like a grotesque lump on the head of al-Hakim, and his frail body was covered from shoulders to feet in a drab robe of black cotton worn smooth. Mussa Moheidin, a journalist who was Yazid's chief propagandist, was dressed casually in slacks and a sports shirt open at the neck, while the young Turk of the group, Khaled Fawzy, the ramrod of the revolutionary council, wore battle fatigues. Only Suleiman Ammar was impeccably dressed in a tailored safari suit.

"You must all be wondering why I called this emergency meeting," Yazid announced, "so I won't waste time. Allah has provided me with a plan to rid ourselves of President Hasan and his den of corrupt thieves in one master stroke. Now please be seated and finish your coffee."

He walked over to one wall and pushed a switch. A large colored map slowly dropped toward the floor. Ammar recognized it as a standard Egyptian school map of South America. A blowup of the coastal city of Punta del Este, Uruguay, was circled in red. Taped to the lower half of the map was an enlarged photo of a luxury cruise ship.

The men around the table sat down again, their faces expressionless. Their interest was hooked. They waited patiently to hear the revelation Allah had bestowed on their religious leader.

Only Ammar veiled his skepticism. He was too much the realist to believe in pious concoctions.

"In six days," Yazid began, "the international economic summit meetings, brought on by the world monetary crisis, will be held in the resort city of Punta del Este, former scene of the Inter-American Economic and Social Council conference which proclaimed the Alliance for Progress. The debtor nations, except Egypt, have banded together to repudiate all loans and erase foreign debt. This act will force hundreds of banks in the United States and Europe to fail. Western bankers and their national financial experts have called for round-the-clock talks in a last-ditch attempt to stall the coming economic catastrophe. Our imperialist bootlicking President is the only holdout. Hasan is scheduled to attend the talks and undermine our Islamic brothers and Third World friends by begging the Western money changers for more loans to keep his eroding grip on Egypt. This we will not permit. *Bis millah,** we will take advantage of this moment to establish a true Islamic government for our people."

"I say we kill the tyrant and be done with it," Khaled Fawzy said harshly. He was young and arrogant and tactless. Already his impatience had resulted in a failed coup by his student revolutionaries that had cost thirty lives. His dark eyes darted back and forth

_____

* With God's Help.

around the table. "One well-placed ground-to-air missile as Hasan's plane takes off for Uruguay, and we will be rid of his corrupt regime for good."

"And open the door for Defense Minister Abu Hamid to set himself up as dictator before we are ready," finished Mussa Moheidin. The famous Egyptian writer was in his mid-sixties. He was a witty, urbane and articulate man, with a slow and gracious manner. Moheidin was the only man at the table Ammar truly respected.

Yazid turned to Bashir. "Is that a valid prediction, Colonel?"

Bashir nodded. A vain and shallow man, he was quick to display his narrow vision of military affairs. "Mussa is right. Abu Hamid dangles the prospect of his support for you, using the excuse that he is waiting for you to produce a mandate from the people. This is merely a stalling tactic. Hamid is ambitious. He is banking on an opportunity to use the army to set himself up as President."

"All too true," said Fawzy. "One of his close aides is a member of our movement. He revealed that Hamid plans to install himself as President and consolidate his position by marrying Hala Kamil because of her popularity with the people."

Yazid smiled. "He has built a castle of sand. Hala Kamil will not be available for the marriage ceremony."

"Is that a certainty?" asked Ammar.

"Yes," Yazid answered smoothly. "Allah has willed that she not live beyond the next sun."

"Please share your revelation, Akhmad," begged al-Hakim. Unlike the other dark-skinned men around him, al-Hakim had the face of a man who had spent half his life in a dungeon. His pale skin seemed almost transparent. Yet the eyes, which were magnified by thick-lensed glasses, were set in unshakable determination.

Yazid nodded. "I have been informed by my well-placed sources in Mexico that because of an unexpected heavy invasion of tourists there is a shortage of luxury hotel rooms and palatial residences in Punta del Este. To keep their nation from losing the summit talks and the international limelight, Uruguayan officials have arranged for the foreign leaders and their statesmen to be hosted on board chartered luxury cruise ships moored in the port. Hasan and the Egyptian delegation will be staying on a British liner called the *Lady Flamborough*. President De Lorenzo of Mexico and his staff will also be on board."

Yazid paused and looked from one man to the next. Then he said, "Allah came to me in a vision and commanded me to seize the ship."

"Praise be to Allah!" Fawzy burst out.

The other men glanced at each other,

incredulous. Then they turned their attention back to Yazid, expectantly, without voicing a question.

"I see by the look in your eyes, my friends, you doubt my vision."

"Never," said al-Hakim solemnly. "But perhaps you misinterpreted Allah's command."

"No, it was quite clear. The ship with President Hasan and his ministers must be seized."

"For what purpose?" asked Mussa Moheidin.

"To seal off Hasan and prevent his return to Cairo while our Islamic forces sweep into power."

"Abu Hamid will call out the army to foil any overthrow other than his," cautioned Colonel Bashir. "I know this for a fact."

"Hamid cannot stop a tidal wave of revolutionary fervor," said Yazid. "Civil unrest is at a peak. The masses are fed up with harsh austerity brought on by payment demands on foreign loans. He and Hasan are cutting their own throats by not denouncing the godless moneylenders. Egypt can only be saved by embracing the purity of Islamic law."

Khaled Fawzy leaped to his feet and raised a fist. "You have only to give me the order, Akhmad, and I will have a million people in the streets."

Yazid paused, breathing heavily with religious zeal. Then he said, "The people will lead. I will follow."

The expression on al-Hakim's face was grave. "I must confess — I have dark misgivings."

"You are a coward!" Fawzy snapped in rash defiance.

"Mohammed al-Hakim is wiser than you," said Moheidin patiently. "I know his mind. He does not wish a repeat of the *Achille Lauro* fiasco in nineteen eighty-five, when Palestinians commandeered the Italian cruise liner and murdered an old Jew invalid in a wheelchair."

Bashir spoke up. "Terrorist slaughter will not help our cause."

"You wish to go against the will of Allah?" said Yazid, annoyed.

Everyone began talking at once. The room went sour with vehemence as they argued back and forth.

Only Ammar remained detached. They're idiots, he thought, goddamned idiots. He tuned out of the debate and stared at the photo of the cruise ship. The wheels inside his head began to shift through the gears.

"We are not only Egyptians," argued Bashir, "we are Arabs. The other Arab nations will turn against us if we murder our officials and any of theirs who get in the way. They won't see it as a gift from Allah, but rather as a political terrorist plot."

Moheidin gestured toward Fawzy. "Khaled made a point. Better to kill Hasan on home territory than launch a bloodbath on board a ship holding the leader of Mexico and his delegation as well."

"We cannot condone an act of mass terrorism," said al-Hakim. "The negative consequences for our new government would be disastrous."

"You are all worms who belong in Hasan's camp," Fawzy spat. "I say attack the ship and show the world our power."

Nobody paid any attention to the militant fanatic who was viciously anti-Jew and anti-Christian.

"Don't you see, Akhmad," pleaded Bashir, "security in Punta del Este will be impossible to penetrate? Uruguayan patrol boats will be thick as locusts. Every ship housing summit leaders will be heavily guarded. You're talking a suicide assault by an army of commandos. It simply can't be done."

"We will have help from a source that must remain confidential," said Yazid. He turned and studied Ammar. "You, Suleiman — You're our expert on undercover operations. If a team of our best fighters can be smuggled on board the *Lady Flamborough* without detection, can the ship be taken and held until we can form a republic in the name of Islam?"

"Yes," replied Ammar, without taking his

eyes off the cruise ship's photo. The voice was quiet, but it carried total conviction. "Six days is cutting it slim, but the ship can be carried with ten experienced fighting men and five experienced seamen, with no blood-shed providing we have the element of sur-prise."

Yazid's eyes gleamed. "Ah, I knew I could count on you."

"Impossible," Bashir roared. "You could never smuggle that many men into Uruguay without arousing suspicion. And even if through some miracle you captured the ship and subdued the crew, every special assault team in the West would be swarming over your hide inside of twenty-four hours. Threats to kill the hostages won't stop them. You'd be lucky to hold out more than a few hours."

"I can take and hold the *Lady Flamborough* for two weeks."

Bashir shook his head. "You're lost in a dream world."

"How is that possible?" asked Moheidin. "I'm interested in learning how you expect to outwit an army of highly trained international security forces without a pitched battle."

"I don't intend to fight."

"This is nonsense!" Yazid said, shocked.

"Not really," said Ammar. "It's all in know-ing the trick."

"Trick?"

"Precisely." Ammar smiled benignly. "You

302

see, I plan on making the *Lady Flamborough,* her crew and passengers, all disappear."

25

"My visit is strictly unofficial," Julius Schiller advised Hala Kamil as they stepped into the log-beamed sitting room of Senator Pitt's ski lodge. "My aides are covering for me, saying I'm fishing in Key West."

"I understand," said Hala. "I'm grateful for the chance to talk to someone other than the cook and Secret Service guards."

She greeted him dressed fashionably in an Icelandic brown wool sweater-jacket with matching pants, looking even younger than Schiller remembered.

He looked out of place at a ski resort in a business suit, polished wing-tip shoes, and carrying an attaché case. "Is there anything I can arrange to make your safety more bearable?"

"No, thank you. Nothing can relieve the frustration of inactivity when there is so much I must do."

"A few more days and it will be over," Schiller said consolingly.

"I hardly expected to see you here, Julius."

"Something has come up that concerns Egypt. Our President thought it prudent you be consulted on a recent event."

Hala curled her legs under her and sipped at the tea. "Should I be flattered?"

"Let's say he'd be grateful for your co-operation."

"Regarding what?"

Schiller opened the attaché case, gave Hala a bound folder and sat back with his tea. He watched as the soft features of her angelic face slowly tightened as she realized the scope of what she read. Finally she finished the last page and closed the folder. She gave Schiller a penetrating stare.

"Is the public aware of this?"

He nodded. "The discovery of the ship will be announced this afternoon. But we're holding off any reference to the Alexandria Library treasures."

Hala gazed out the window. "Our loss of the Library sixteen centuries ago would compare to your President suddenly ordering the burning of the Washington archives, the Smithsonian Institution and the National Art Gallery."

Schiller nodded. "A fair comparison."

"Is there hope the ancient books can be recovered?"

"We don't know yet. The wax tables from

the ship only provided a few tantalizing clues. The hiding place could be anywhere between Iceland and South Africa."

"But you do intend to search," she said, her interest growing.

"The discovery project is underway."

"Who else knows about this?"

"Only the President, myself and a few trusted members of our government, and now you."

"Why have you included me and not President Hasan?"

Schiller got up and walked across the room. Then he turned back to Hala. "Your nation's leader may not be in control much longer. We feel the information is too far-reaching to fall into the wrong hands."

"Akhmad Yazid."

"Frankly, yes."

"Your government will have to deal with him sooner or later," said Hala. "If the Library treasures and their valuable geological data can be located, Yazid will demand they be returned to Egypt."

"We understand," said Schiller. "That's the purpose behind our meeting here in Breckinridge. The President wishes you to announce the imminent discovery in your address to the United Nations."

Hala looked at Schiller thoughtfully for a moment. Then her eyes turned and anger came into her voice.

"How can I say the discovery is just around the corner when a search may take years and never be successful? I find it most distasteful that the President and his advisers insist on creating a lie and using me to speak it. Is this another one of your stupid Middle East foreign policy games, Julius? A last-ditch gamble to keep President Hasan in power and erode Akhmad Yazid's influence? Am I the tool to mislead the Egyptian people into believing rich mineral deposits are about to be found in their country that will turn around our depressed economy and eliminate the terrible poverty?"

Schiller sat silently and made no denials.

"You have come to the wrong woman, Julius. I'll see my government fall, and face death from Yazid's executioners, before I deceive my people with false hope."

"Noble sentiments," Schiller said quietly. "I admire your principles; however, I firmly believe the plan is sound."

"The risk is too great. If the President fails to provide the Library's great knowledge, he will be inviting a political disaster. Yazid will take advantage with a propaganda campaign that will broaden his power base and make him stronger than your experts on Egypt can ever conceive. For the tenth time in as many years, United States foreign policy experts will look like amateurish clowns in the eyes of the world."

"Mistakes have been made," Schiller admitted.

"If only you hadn't interfered in our affairs."

"I didn't come here to debate Middle Eastern policy, Hala. I came to ask your help."

She shook her head and turned away. "I'm sorry. I can't go on record with a lie."

Schiller looked at her with compassion in his eyes. He didn't push her, but thought it better to back off.

"I'll tell the President of your response," he said, picking up his attaché case and making for the doorway. "He'll be most disappointed."

"Wait!"

He turned expectantly.

Hala rose and came to him. "Prove to me that your people have a positive lead to the location of the Library artifacts and not a foggy clue, and I'll do as the White House wishes."

"You'll make the announcement?"

"Yes."

"Four days until your address is not much time."

"Those are my terms," Hala said bluntly.

Schiller nodded gravely. "Accepted."

Then he turned and walked out the door.

Muhammad Ismail watched Schiller's limousine come off the private road leading to Senator Pitt's lodge and turn onto Highway 9 toward the ski town of Breckenridge. He did not see who was seated in the rear seat, and he did not care.

The sight of the official car, men patrolling the grounds who spoke into radio transmitters at regular intervals, and the two armed guards inside a Dodge van at the road's entrance were all he needed to confirm the information purchased by Yazid's agents in Washington.

Ismail leaned casually against a large Mercedes-Benz diesel sedan, shielding a man sitting inside peering out an open window through a pair of binoculars. A rack on the roof held several sets of skis. Ismail was dressed in a white ski suit. A matching ski mask hid his perpetually scowling face.

"Seen enough?" he asked while seemingly adjusting the ski rack.

"Another minute," answered the observer. He was staring at the lodge, which was partially visible through the trees. All that could be seen around the binoculars was a heavy black beard and a mass of uncombed hair.

"Make it quick. I'm freezing out here just standing around."

"Bear with me another minute."

"How does it look?" asked Ismail.

"No more than a five-man detail. Three in

the house. Two in the van. Only one man patrols around the grounds at a time, not a second more than thirty minutes. They don't dally. The cold gets to them too. They walk the same trail through the snow. No sign of TV cameras, but they probably have one mounted in the van that is monitored inside the house."

"We'll move in two groups," said Ismail. "One takes the house, the other kills the guard patrolling outside and destroys the van from the rear, where they least expect an attack."

The observer dropped the glasses. "Do you plan to move in tonight, Muhammad?"

"No," answered Ismail. "Tomorrow, when the American pigs are stuffing their mouths with their morning meal."

"A daylight raid will be dangerous."

"We will not sneak around in the dark like women."

"But our only escape route to the airport is through the center of town," the observer protested. "The streets will be crowded with traffic and hundreds of skiers. Suleiman Ammar would not risk such an adventure."

Ismail suddenly spun and slapped the observer with his gloved hand. "I am in charge here!" he snapped. "Suleiman is an overrated jackal. Do not speak his name in my presence."

The observer did not cower. His dark eyes

flashed with hostility. "You'll kill us all," he said quietly.

"So be it," Ismail hissed, his voice as cold as the snow. "If we die so Hala Kamil can die, the price will be cheap."

26

"Magnificent," said Pitt.

"Gorgeous, simply gorgeous," Lily murmured.

Giordino nodded in agreement. "A real winner."

They were standing in an antique and classic automobile restoration shop, and their admiring stares were directed toward a 1930 L-29 Cord town car, a model with an open front for the chauffeur. The body was painted burgundy while the fenders were a buff that was matched by the leather-covered roof over the passenger's compartment. Elegantly styled, long and graceful, the car had front-wheel drive that helped to give it a low silhouette. The original coachmaker had stretched the chassis until it measured nearly five-and-a-half meters from front to rear bumper. Almost half the length was hood, beginning with a race-car-type grill and ending with a sharply raked windshield.

It was big and sleek, a thing of beauty that

belonged to an era fondly revered by older generations but unknown to those who followed.

The man who had found Pitt's car stored in an old garage, hidden under forty years of trash, and had restored it from a mangled hulk, was proud of his handiwork. Robert Esbenson, a tall man with a pixie face and limpid blue eyes, gave the hood a final, loving wipe with a dust cloth and turned the car over to Pitt.

"I hate to see this one go."

"You've done a remarkable job," said Pitt.

"Are you going to ship it home?"

"Not just yet. I'd like to drive it for a few days."

Esbenson nodded. "Okay, let me adjust the carburetor and distributor for our mile-high altitude. Then, when you return to the shop, I'll have it detailed and arrange for an auto transporter to ship it to Washington."

"Can I ride in it?" Lily asked anxiously.

"All the way to Breckenridge," Pitt replied. He turned to Giordino. "Coming with us, Al?"

"Why not? We can leave the rental car outside in the parking lot."

They switched the luggage, and ten minutes later Pitt turned the Cord onto Interstate 70 and aimed the long hood toward the foothills leading into the snow-peaked Rocky Mountains.

Lily and Al sat warmly in the luxurious passenger compartment separated from Pitt by the divider window. Pitt did not pull out the transformable top that protected the chauffeur's seat, but sat in the open bundled up in a heavy sheepskin coat, savoring the cold air on his face.

For the moment his mind was on his driving, scanning the instruments to make sure the sixty-year-old car was performing as it was designed to do. He held to the right lane, allowing most of the traffic to pass and gawk.

Pitt felt exhilarated and content behind the wheel, listening to the smooth purr of the eight-cylinder engine and the mellow tone of the exhaust. It was as though he had control over a living thing.

If he had had any inkling of the mess he was driving into, he would have turned around and headed straight back to Denver.

Darkness had fallen over the Continental Divide when the Cord rolled into the legendary Colorado mining town turned ski resort. Pitt drove up the main street, whose old buildings retained their historic western flavor. The sidewalks were crowded with people coming from the slopes, carrying their skis and poles over one shoulder.

Pitt parked near the entrance of the Hotel Breckenridge. He signed the register and took two phone messages from the desk clerk. He read both slips of paper and slipped them into a pocket.

"From Dr. Rothberg?" asked Lily.

"Yes, he's invited us for dinner at his condo. It's just across the street from the hotel."

"What time?" Giordino queried.

"Seven-thirty."

Lily glanced at her watch. "Only forty minutes to shower and do my hair. I'd better get with it."

Pitt gave her the room key. "You're in two twenty-one. Al and I have rooms adjoining yours on each side."

As soon as Lily disappeared with the porter into an elevator, Pitt motioned Giordino into the cocktail lounge. He waited until the barmaid took their drink order before passing the second message across the table.

Giordino read it aloud softly. " 'Your library project takes top priority. Most urgent you find a permanent address for Alex in the next four days. Luck, Dad.' " He looked up, utterly confused. "Do I read this right? We have only four days to identify the location?"

Pitt nodded positively. "I read panic between the lines and smell something rumbling in Washington power circles."

"They might as well ask us to invent a common cure for herpes, AIDS and acne," Giordino grumbled. "We can kiss off our skiing trip."

"We'll stay," said Pitt resolutely. "Nothing

we can do until Yaeger gets lucky." Pitt rose from his chair. "And speaking of Yaeger, I'd better give him a call."

He found a public telephone in the hotel lobby and made a call on his credit card. After four rings a voice answered in what sounded like the middle of a yawn.

"Yaeger here."

"Hiram, this is Dirk. How's your search going?"

"It's going."

"Run onto anything?"

"My babies sifted through every piece of geological data in their little banks from Casablanca around the horn to Zanzibar. They failed to find a hot spot along the coast of Africa that matched your drawing. There were three vague possibilities. But when I programmed profiles on land-mass transformations that might have occurred over the past sixteen hundred years, none proved encouraging. Sorry."

"What's your next step?"

"I'm already in the process of heading north. This will take more time because of the extensive shoreline encompassing the British Isles, the Baltic Sea and the Scandinavian countries as far as Siberia."

"Can you cover it in four days?"

"Only if you insist I put the hired help on a twenty-four-hour schedule."

"I insist," said Pitt sternly. "Word has just

come down that the project has become an urgent priority."

"We'll hit it hard," Yaeger said, his voice more jovial than serious.

"I'm in Breckenridge, Colorado. If you strike on something, call me at the Breckenridge Hotel." Pitt gave Yaeger the hotel phone and his room number.

Yaeger dutifully repeated the digits. "Okay, got it."

"You sound like you're in a good mood," said Pitt.

"Why not? We accomplished quite a lot."

"Like what? You still don't know where our river lies."

"True," replied Yaeger cheerfully. "But we sure as hell know where it ain't."

Snowflakes the size of cornflakes were falling as the three trudged across the street from the hotel to a two-story cedar-sided condominium. A flood-lighted sign read SKIQUEEN. They climbed a stairway and knocked on the door to unit 22B.

Bertram Rothberg greeted them with a jolly smile beneath a splendid gray beard and sparkling blue eyes. His ears rose in full sail through a swirling sea of gray hair. A red plaid shirt and corduroy trousers clad his beefy body. Put an ax in one hand and a crosscut saw in the other, and he could have reported for duty as a lumberjack.

He shook hands warmly and without introductions as if he'd known everyone for years. He led them up a narrow stairwell to a combination living-dining room beneath a high-peaked ceiling with skylights.

"How does a gallon bottle of cheap burgundy sound before dinner," he asked with a sly grin.

Lily laughed. "I'm game."

Giordino shrugged. "Makes no difference as long as it's wet."

"And you, Dirk?"

"Sounds good."

Pitt didn't bother asking Rothberg how he recognized each of them. His father would have provided descriptions. The performance was nearly flawless. Pitt suspected the historian had worked for one of the government's many intelligence agencies at some time in the past.

Rothberg retired to the kitchen to pour the wine. Lily followed.

"Can I help you with anything — ?" She suddenly stopped and peered at the empty counters and the cold stove.

Rothberg caught her curious look. "I'm a lousy cook so our dinner will be catered. It should show up around eight." He pointed at the sectional couch in the living room. "Please get comfortable around the fire."

He passed the glasses and then lowered his rotund figure into a leather easy chair. He raised his glass.

"Here's to a successful search."

"Hear, hear," said Lily.

Pitt got off the mark. "Dad tells me you've made the Alexandria Library a life study."

"Thirty-two years. Probably been better off to have taken a wife all that time instead of rummaging around dusty bookshelves and straining my eyes over old manuscripts. The subject has been like a mistress to me. Never asking, only giving. I've never fallen out of love with her."

Lily said, "I can understand your attraction."

Rothberg smiled at her. "As an archaeologist, you would."

He rose and jabbed in the fireplace with a poker. Satisfied that the logs were burning evenly, he sat down again and continued.

"Yes, the Library was not only a glorious edifice of learning, but it was the chief wonder of the ancient world, containing vast accumulations of entire civilizations." Rothberg spoke almost as if he was in a trance, his mind seeing shadows from the past. "The great art and literature of the Greeks, the Egyptians, the Romans, the sacred writings of the Jews, the wisdom and knowledge of the most gifted men the world has ever known, the divine works of philosophy, music of incredible beauty, the ancient best-sellers, the masterworks of medicine and science, it was the finest storehouse of materials and knowledge ever assembled in antiquity."

"Was it open to the public?" asked Giordino.

"Certainly not to every beggar off the street," answered Rothberg. "But researchers and scholars pretty much had the run of the place to examine, catalog, translate and edit, and to publish their findings. You see, the Library and its adjoining museum went far beyond being mere depositories. Their halls launched the true science of creative scholarship. The Library became the first true reference library, as we think of today, where books were systematized and catalogued. In fact the complex was known as the Place of the Muses."

Rothberg paused and checked his guests' glasses. "You look like you can use another shot of wine, Al."

Giordino smiled. "I never turn down a free drink."

"Lily, Dirk?"

"I've hardly touched mine," said Lily.

Pitt shook his head. "I'm fine."

Rothberg refilled Giordino's glass and poured his own before continuing.

"Later empires and nations owe a staggering debt to the Alexandria Library. Few institutions of knowledge have produced so much. Pliny, a celebrated Roman of the first century A.D., invented and wrote the world's first encyclopedia. Aristophanes, head of the Library two hundred years before Christ, was the father of the dictionary. Callimachus, a famous writer and authority on Greek tragedy, compiled the earliest Who's Who. The great mathematician Euclid devised the first known textbook on geometry. Dionysius organized grammar into a coherent system and published his 'Art of Grammar,' which became the model text for all languages, written and spoken. These men, and thousands of others, labored and produced their epoch achievements while working at the Library."

"You're describing a university," said Pitt.

"Quite right. Together the library and museum were considered the university of the Hellenistic world. The immense structures of white marble contained picture galleries, statuary halls, theaters for poetry reading and lectures on everything from astronomy to geology. There were also dormitories, a dining hall, cloisters along colonnades for contemplation, and an animal park and botanical garden. Ten great halls housed different categories of manuscripts and books. Hundreds of thousands of them were handwritten on either papyrus or parchment, and then rolled into scrolls and stored in bronze tubes."

"What's the difference between the two?" asked Giordino.

"Papyrus is a tropical plant. The Egyptians

made a paper-like writing material out of its stems. Parchment, also called vellum, was produced from the skins of animals, especially young calves, kids or lambs."

"Is it possible they could have survived the centuries?" Pitt asked.

"Parchment should last longer than papyrus," answered Rothberg. Then he looked at Pitt. "Their condition after sixteen hundred years would depend on where they've been stored. Papyrus scrolls from Egyptian tombs are still readable after three thousand years."

"A hot and dry atmosphere."

"Yes."

"Suppose the scrolls were buried somewhere along the northern coast of Sweden or Russia?"

Rothberg bent his head thoughtfully. "I suppose the winter freeze would preserve them, but during the summer thaw they would rot from the dampness."

Pitt could smell defeat looming down the road. This was one more nail in the coffin. Hope of finding the Library manuscripts intact seemed dimmer than ever.

Lily did not share Pitt's pessimism. She had the glow of excitement on her face. "If you had been Junius Venator, Dr. Rothberg, what books would you have saved?"

"Hard question," Rothberg said, winking at her. "I can only guess he might have attempted to save the complete works of

Sophocles, Euripides, Aristotle and Plato for a start. And of course, Homer. He wrote twenty-four books, but only a very few have come down to us. I think Venator would have saved as many of the fifty thousand volumes on Greek, Etruscan, Roman and Egyptian history as his fleet of ships could carry. The latter would be extremely interesting, since the Library's monumental store of Egyptian literature and religious and scientific material has all been lost. We know practically nothing about the Etruscans, yet Claudius wrote an extensive history on them that must have sat on the Library's shelves. I'd certainly have taken religious works on Hebrew and Christian laws and traditions. The revelations of these scrolls would probably knock the socks off modern biblical scholars."

"Books of the sciences?" added Giordino.

"That goes without saying."

"Don't forget cookbooks," said Lily.

Rothberg laughed. "Venator was a shrewd operator. He'd have saved a general spread of knowledge and material, including books on cooking and household hints. Something for everyone, you might say."

"Especially the ancient geological data," said Pitt.

"Especially that," Rothberg agreed.

"Has anything come down on what kind of a man he was?" inquired Lily.

"Venator?"

"Yes."

"He was the leading intellectual of his time. A renowned scholar and teacher who was hired away from one of the great learning centers of Athens to become the last of the Alexandria Library's prominent curators. He was the great chronicler of his age. We know he wrote over a hundred books of political and social commentary that covered the known world going back four thousand years. None of which has survived."

"Archaeological researchers would have a field day with data compiled by someone who was two thousand years closer to our past," said Lily.

"What else do we know about him?" Pitt asked.

"Not much. Venator attracted a large number of pupils who went on to become recognized men of letters and science. One student, Diocles of Antioch, mentioned him briefly in one of his essays. He described Venator as a daring innovator who struck out into areas other scholars feared to tread. Though a Christian, he saw religion more as a social science. This was the main cause behind the friction that existed between Venator and the Christian zealot Theophilos, Bishop of Alexandria. Theophilos went after Venator with a vengeance, claiming the museum and Library were hotbeds of paganism. He finally persuaded the Emperor Theodosius, a devout Christian, to burn the place. In the uproar and riots that occurred between Christians and non-Christians during the destruction, it was supposed Junius Venator was murdered by fanatical followers of Theophilos."

"But now we know he escaped with the pick of the collection," said Lily.

"When Senator Pitt called with the news of your discovery in Greenland," said Rothberg, "I felt as excited as a street sweeper who'd won a million-dollar lottery."

"Can you give us any thoughts on where you think Venator hid the artifacts?" asked Pitt.

Rothberg considered for a long moment. Finally he said quietly, "Junius Venator was not an ordinary man. He followed his own path. He had access to a mountain of knowledge. His route would have been scientifically planned, only the unknowns were left to chance. He certainly did an efficient job when you consider the relics have remained hidden for sixteen hundred years." Rothberg threw up his hands in defeat. "I can't offer a clue. Venator is too tough a customer to second-guess."

"You must have some idea," Pitt persisted.

Rothberg looked long and deeply into the flames wavering in the fireplace. "All I can say is, Venator's burial place must be where no man would think to look."

27

0758, read Ismail's watch. He flattened himself behind a small blue spruce and peered at the lodge. Wood smoke was curling from one of two chimneys while steam issued from the heater vents. Kamil, he knew, was an early riser and a good cook. He rightly reasoned that she was up and making breakfast for her guards.

He was a man of the desert and not used to the icy cold that gripped him. He wished he could stand, flail his arms and stamp his feet. His toes ached and his fingers were becoming numb inside the gloves. The agony of the cold was filling his mind and slowing his reaction time. A creeping fear fell over him, a fear that he might botch the job and die for no purpose.

Ismail's inexperience was showing through. At the crucial stage of the mission he was coming unstrung. He suddenly wondered if the hated Americans somehow knew or suspected his presence. Nervous and afraid, his mind began to lose its ability to make hard-and-fast decisions.

0759. One quick glance at the van just above the entrance to the road. Shifts were alternated every four hours between the guards in the warm lodge and those huddled inside the van. Two relief men were due to make the hundred-meter walk from the lodge at any time.

He turned his attention to the guard walking a well-beaten path through the snow around the grounds. He was slowly approaching Ismail's tree, his breath coming in clouds of vapor, his gaze alert for any sign out of the ordinary.

The monotony and the bitter cold had not slackened the Secret Service agent's vigilance. His eyes swept back and forth over the area like radar. Less than a minute remained before he would see Ismail's trail in the snow.

Ismail swore softly under his breath and pressed more deeply into the snow. He was, he knew, terribly exposed. The pine needles shielding him from view would not stop bullets.

0800. Almost on the dot, the front door of the lodge opened and two men stepped out. They wore stocking caps and down-filled ski coats. They automatically scanned the snowy landscape as they moved down the road in quiet conversation.

Ismail's plan was to wait until the relief

party reached the van and then take out all four guards at the same time. But he had misjudged and moved into position too early. The two men had only walked fifty meters down the road when the guard circling the lodge spotted Ismail's footprints.

He stopped and raised the transmitter to his lips. His words were cut off by a loud series of cracks from Ismail's Heckler & Koch MP5 submachine gun.

Ismail's amateurish plan had gotten off to a bad start. A pro would have snuffed the guard with a single shot between the eyes from a silenced semiautomatic. Ismail stitched the guard's coat in the chest area with ten rounds; a good twenty others sprayed the woods beyond.

One of the Arabs frantically began lobbing grenades at the van while another pumped bullets through the sides. Sophisticated assault was beyond the scope of most terrorists. Finesse was as foreign to them as liquid soap. Their only salvation was luck. One of the grenades found its way through the windshield, bursting with a loud thud. The explosion bore no similarity to motion-picture special effects. The gas tank did not go up in a fiery ball. The body of the van bulged and split as if a cherry bomb had gone off inside a tin can.

Both occupants were killed instantly.

Excited with blood lust, the two assassins,

neither older than twenty, kept up their attack on the mangled van until the magazines of their rifles were empty, instead of concentrating on the Secret Service agents on the road, who took cover behind trees and unleashed an accurate fire from their Uzis that quickly cut them down.

Correctly figuring their fellow agents inside the van were beyond help, they began retreating toward the lodge, running in a sideways motion back to back, one of them exchanging fire with Ismail, who had found cover behind a large mossy rock.

Ismail's strategy was blown away by the confusion.

The other ten men of the terrorist team were supposed to rush the rear door at the sound of Ismail's gunfire, but they lost valuable time wading through knee-deep snow. Their assault came late and they were effectively pinned down by the agents inside.

One Arab managed to gain temporary safety under the north wall of the lodge. He pulled the pin on a grenade and flipped it at a large sliding window. He misjudged the thickness of the double panes, and the grenade bounced back. His face had only time for an expression of horror before the blast blew him apart.

The two agents scrambled up the steps and leapt through the front door. The Arabs laid down a barrage of fire that caught one of the men in the back, dropping him with only his feet showing across the threshold. He was quickly dragged inside and the door slammed shut at the exact instant three dozen shots and a grenade blasted it into splinters.

The windows disintegrated in showers of glass but the heavy log walls easily withstood the onslaught. The agents dropped two more of Ismail's men, but the rest dodged in closer, using the pines and rocks for cover. When they had moved within twenty meters of the lodge, they began hurling grenades through the windows.

Inside the lodge, an agent roughly shoved Hala into a cold fireplace. He was in the act of pushing a writing desk over the hearth to shield her when a hail of fire through a window ricocheted off the stone mantel, three of the bullets smashing into his neck and shoulder. Hala could not see, but she heard his body thump as it made contact with the wood floor.

The grenades were taking deadly effect now. At close range the shrapnel was far more damaging to human tissue than a rifle bullet. The agents' only defense was a sharp and precise fire, but they had not counted on a heavy assault and their small stockpile of ammunition was down to the last few clips.

A call for assistance had been transmitted immediately after Ismail's opening shots, but the emergency plea went to the Secret Service office in Denver and precious time was lost before the local sheriff's department was notified and their units organized.

A grenade exploded in a storeroom, igniting a can of paint thinner. A gas can used for filling the tank of a snowblower went next, and one entire side of the lodge soon crawled with flames.

The gunfire died as the fire spread. The Arabs cautiously tightened the net. They formed a loose circle around the lodge; every automatic rifle was trained on the doors and windows. They waited patiently for the survivors to be flushed out by the blaze.

Only two Secret Service agents were still on their feet. The rest were sprawled in bloody heaps among the mutilated pieces of furniture. The full fury of the fire raced into the kitchen and up a rear staircase, spreading to the upstairs bedrooms. Already it was far beyond any hope of extinction. The heat swiftly became unbearable to the defenders on the lower floor.

The sound of sirens echoed up the valley from the direction of town and drew closer.

One agent pushed away the desk protecting Hala in the fireplace and led her on hands and knees to a low window.

"The local sheriff's deputies are arriving," he said quickly. "As soon as they draw off the terrorist fire, we'll make a run for it before we're barbecued to death."

Hala could only nod. She could hardly hear him. Her eardrums hurt from the roar of the grenades. Her eyes were filled with tears, and she pressed a handkerchief tightly against her nose and mouth to filter out the thickening blanket of smoke.

Outside, Ismail lay prone, clutching his H & K automatic, torn by indecision. The lodge had swiftly become a blazing inferno, smoke and flame were rolling through the windows. Anyone still living had to escape in the next few seconds or die.

But Ismail could not wait it out. Already he could see red and blue lights flashing through the trees as a sheriff's car sped up the highway.

Of his original team of twelve men, seven were left, including himself. Any wounded were to be killed rather than left behind to be interrogated by American intelligence officials. He shouted a command to his men and they pulled away from the lodge and hurried off toward the entrance road.

The first deputies to arrive slid to a stop and blocked the road to the lodge. While one reported on the radio, his partner cautiously eased open his door and studied the van and burning lodge, holding his drawn revolver. They were only to observe, report and wait for backup.

It was a sound tactic when facing armed and dangerous criminals. Unfortunately, it didn't work with a small army of unseen terrorists who suddenly opened fire with a storm of bullets that shredded the patrol car and killed the two deputies before they had a chance to react.

At a signal from one of the agents peering around the window, Hala was lifted and brusquely flung out onto the ground. The Secret Service men followed and quickly took her by the arms and began running, stumbling through the snow on an angle toward the highway.

They had covered only thirty paces when one of Ismail's men spotted them and shouted the alarm. Shots struck the trees and branches fell around the fleeing survivors. One of the agents suddenly threw up his hands, clawing at the sky, stumbled forward a few steps and then fell face downward in the snow.

"They're trying to cut us off from the highway!" the other agent snapped. "You try to make it. I'll make a stand and delay them."

Hala started to say something, but the agent spun her around and gave her a not-too-gentle shove that sent her on her way.

"Run, dammit, run!" he yelled.

But he could see it was already too late. Any hope of escape was dealt a death blow. They had taken the wrong angle away from the burning lodge and were headed on a direct line toward two Mercedes-Benz sedans parked in woods beside the road. In dazed defeat he realized the cars belonged to the terrorists. He had no alternative. If he couldn't stop them, he would at least slow them down long enough for Hala to hail a passing car. In a suicide gamble, the agent ran at the Arabs, finger locked on the trigger of his Uzi, shouting every obscenity he'd ever learned.

Ismail and his men were momentarily stunned into immobility by what they saw as a charging demon. For two incredulous seconds they hesitated, then recovered and let loose a long burst at the courageous Secret Service agent, cutting him down in mid-stride.

But not before he took out three of them.

Hala saw the cars too. She also saw the terrorists rushing for them. Behind her she heard the thunderous fusillade of shots. Choking and gasping for breath, her clothes and hair singed, she staggered into a small ditch and up the other side before sprawling on a hard surface.

She raised her head slightly and found herself staring at black asphalt. She pushed herself to her feet and began running, knowing she was only delaying the inevitable, knowing with dread certainty she would be lying dead in the next few minutes.

28

The Cord rolled majestically along the high-way from Breckenridge, the morning sun gleaming on the bright chrome and new paint. Skiers walking to the lifts waved as the elegant sixty-year-old classic swept past. Giordino dozed in the enclosed rear seat while Lily sat up front in the open with Pitt.

Pitt had awakened in a stubborn mood that morning. He saw no reason to ski on rental skies when his own American-made Olin 921s were in a closet only three miles up the road from the hotel. Besides, he reasoned, he could drive to the family lodge, pick up his gear and be sitting on a chair lift in half the time it took waiting his turn to be fitted in a rental shop.

Pitt shrugged off his father's unexplained warning to stay clear of the lodge. He simply wrote it off as bureaucratic overplay. The Senator would have made the same impression on Hulk Hogan by telling the wrestler to turn the other cheek after an opponent had kicked him in the groin.

"Who's shooting off fireworks so early in the morning?" Lily wondered aloud.

"Not fireworks," Pitt said, tuning in the sharp crack of gunfire and the explosive thump from grenades echoing off the mountainsides of the valley. "Sounds like an infantry firefight."

"It's coming from the woods up ahead —" Lily pointed — "to the right of the road."

The smile wrinkles around Pitt's eyes tightened. He increased the Cord's speed and rapped on the divider window. Giordino came awake and cranked the glass down.

"You woke me just as the orgy was getting started," he said between yawns.

"Listen up," ordered Pitt.

Giordino winced as the cold air flew into the passengers' compartment. He cupped his ears. Slowly an expression of bewilderment crossed his face.

"Have the Russians landed?"

"Look!" said Lily excitedly. "A forest fire."

Giordino made a quick study of the black smoke that abruptly billowed above the treetops, chased by columns of flame. "Too concentrated," he stated briefly. "I'd say it was a burning structure, probably a house or condominium."

Pitt knew Giordino was on target. He swore and pounded the steering wheel, knowing with sickening certainty it was his family's lodge that was feeding the growing mushroom of fire and smoke.

He said, "No sense asking for trouble by stopping. We'll drive past and check out the action. Al, you come up front. Lily, climb in the rear and keep your head down. I don't want you hurt."

"What about me?" Giordino asked in resigned indignation. "Don't I rate a little concern? Give me one good reason why I should sit up there exposed with you?"

"To protect your trusty chauffeur from harm, evil and unsavory felons."

"Definitely not a good reason."

Pitt tried another tack. "Of course, there's that fifty bucks I borrowed from you in Panama and never paid back."

"Plus interest."

"Plus interest," Pitt repeated.

"What I won't go through to protect my meager assets." Giordino's weary despair sounded almost genuine as he scrambled through the open divider window and changed places with Lily.

Farther down the highway, a half-mile before the entrance to the lodge, people were stopping and crouching behind their parked cars, gawking at the swirling smoke and listening to the rattle of automatic rifles. Pitt thought it odd that the sheriff's department hadn't put in an appearance, and then he saw the bullet-riddled patrol car barricading the

337

road to the lodge.

His attention was focused to his right and the inferno beyond when suddenly, at the very edge of his peripheral vision, he caught a vague form running down the road on a collision course with the Cord.

He stomped on the brakes, hard, and cramped the steering wheel to the right, whipping the Cord into a ninety-degree angle and sending it on a broadside skid. The high, narrow tires shrieked from their treads' friction against the pavement. The Cord ended up sideways, blocking both lanes of the highway, the driver's side not more than a meter from a woman standing stock-still.

Pitt's heart had doubled its beat. He let out a deep breath and looked at the woman he'd come within a hair of mashing like a bug. He saw the fear and shock in her eyes slowly transform into an expression of incredulity.

"You!" she gasped. "Is it really you?"

Pitt stared at her blankly. "Ms. Kamil?"

"I believe in *déjà vu*," Giordino mumbled. "I do, I do, I do."

"Oh, thank God," she whispered. "Please help me. Everyone is dead. They're coming to kill me."

Pitt climbed from behind the wheel at the same time Lily stepped from the passengers' compartment. They helped Hala inside and lowered her on the rear seat.

"Who's they?" Pitt asked.

"Yazid's paid assassins. They murdered the Secret Service men guarding me. We must get away quickly. They'll be here any second."

"Rest easy," Lily said soothingly, noticing Hala's smoke-blackened skin and singed hair for the first time. "We'll take you to a hospital."

"No time," Hala gasped, making a trembling gesture through the window. "Please hurry or they'll kill all of you too."

Pitt turned just in time to see two black Mercedes sedans burst from the woods and veer onto the highway. He studied them for no more than a second before jumping into the driver's seat. He shifted into first gear and jammed the accelerator to the floor. He twisted the wheel and turned the Cord in the only direction open to him — back toward downtown Breckenridge.

He looked briefly into the mirror strapped to the side mount spare tire. He estimated the distance between the Cord and the terrorists' cars at no more than three hundred meters. That brief glimpse was all he had time for. His rear view was suddenly cut off as a bullet drilled through the mirror and shattered the reflection.

"Down on the floor!" he yelled at the two women in back.

There was no drive shaft on the Cord, and the women were able to curl up and press themselves against the flat floor. Hala stared into Lily's face and began trembling uncontrollably. Lily put an arm around her and forced a brave smile.

"Not to panic," she said encouragingly. "Once we make it to town we'll be safe."

"No," Hala murmured as shock began to set in. "We won't be safe anywhere."

In the front seat Giordino hunched low to get what shelter he could from the gunfire and frigid wind whistling around the windshield. "How fast will this thing go?" he asked conversationally.

"The best top speed ever recorded for an L-29 was seventy-seven," answered Pitt.

"Miles or kilometers?"

"Miles."

"I have a sinking feeling we're outclassed." Giordino had to shout in Pitt's ear to be heard above the howl of the Cord's second gear.

"What are we up against?"

Giordino swung around, leaned over the door and cast a wary eye backward. "Hard to tell what model a Mercedes is from the front, but I'd say the hounds are driving three hundred SDLs."

"Diesels?"

"Turbocharged diesels to be exact, capable of 220 kilometers per hour."

"They gaining?"

"Like tigers after a three-toed sloth," Giordino replied dismally. "They'll chew our ass long before we reach the local sheriff's coffee hangout."

Pitt jammed the clutch to the floor, grasped the end of the gearshift arm that extended from the dashboard and shoved it into third. "Better we save lives by staying away. Those kill-crazy bastards are liable to slaughter a hundred innocent bystanders just to assassinate Kamil."

Giordino peered to the rear again. "I think I can see the whites of their eyes."

Ismail screamed a dozen curses as his gun jammed. In a rage, he heaved it out of the Mercedes onto the highway and snatched another from the hands of his follower in the backseat. He reached out the window and squeezed off a burst at the Cord. Only five shells spat from the muzzle before the ammo clip emptied. He cursed again as he fished in his pocket for another clip, wrestled it free and pushed it in the slide.

"Do not excite yourself," said the driver calmly. "We'll catch them in the next kilometer. I'll come around on the left while Omar and his men in the other car take the right. We can snare them in a cross fire at close range."

"I want to kill the scum who interfered," Ismail snarled.

"You'll get your chance. Patience."

Almost like a sullen child who can't have

his way, Ismail slumped in the seat and stared vengefully through the windshield at the fleeing car ahead.

Ismail was the worst kind of killer. He was utterly incapable of remorse. He would have celebrated after blowing up a maternity ward. First-class hit men recorded their kills and studied ways to improve their craft. He never bothered to reexamine or count the bodies. His planning was sloppy, and on two occasions he had wiped out the wrong quarry, which made a fanatic like Ismail all the more dangerous. Unpredictable as a shark, he struck indiscriminately and without mercy at any innocent victim who was unlucky enough to step in his way. He justified his bloody deeds by killing for a religious cause, but in another time, another place, he'd have been a serial murderer, leaving a trail of dead for the fun of it. Ismail would have sickened John Dillinger and Bonnie and Clyde.

He sat there moving his fingers over the rifle as if it were a sensual object, waiting, waiting to pump its lethal fire through the thin walls of the old car and into the flesh that had temporarily cheated him of his prey.

"They must be saving their ammunition," said Giordino thankfully.

"Only until they box us in and can't miss," Pitt replied. His eyes were on the road, but his mind was desperately turning over escape schemes.

"My kingdom for a rocket launcher."

"Which reminds me. When I got in the car this morning, I accidentally kicked something under the seat."

Giordino bent down and probed the floorboard under Pitt. His hand touched a cold, hard object. He held it aloft. "Only a socket wrench," he announced sadly. "Might as well be a hambone for all the good it'll do."

"There's a Jeep trail just ahead that leads up to the top of the ski runs. Maintenance vehicles sometimes use it to carry supplies and equipment to the peak. Might give us a slim chance to lose them in the woods or a ravine. We're dead if we stick to the highway."

"How far?"

"Around the next bend in the road."

"Can we make it?"

"You tell me."

Giordino looked back for the third time. "Seventy-five meters and hauling ass."

"Close, too close," said Pitt. "We'll have to slow them down."

"I could show my ugly face and make obscene gestures," Giordino said dryly.

"Only make them madder. We have to go to plan one."

"I missed the briefing," Giordino said sarcastically.

"How's your throwing arm?"

Giordino nodded in understanding. "Keep

this old barge in a straight line and fireball Giordino will retire the opposing team."

The open town car made a perfect platform. Giordino planted his knees on the seat facing backward, his head and shoulders exposed above the roof. He took aim, raised his arm and hurled the socket wrench in a high arc toward the leading Mercedes.

For an instant his heart seized. He thought he had underthrown as the wrench dropped low and landed on the hood of the car. But it took a bounce and smashed neatly through the windshield.

The Arab driver had spotted Giordino in the act of heaving the wrench. His reaction time was good but not good enough. He hit the brakes and cramped the wheel to swerve out of the way just as the glass burst in a thousand tiny pieces and sprayed into his face. The wrench caromed off the steering wheel and dropped into Ismail's lap.

The driver in the second Mercedes was hanging close to the rear bumper of Ismail's car, and he didn't see the socket wrench sailing through the air. He was caught completely off guard when the taillights in front of his eyes suddenly flashed red. He stared helplessly as he rammed the first Mercedes, sending it spinning out of control until it came to a halt facing in the opposite direction.

"That what you had in mind?" asked Giordino cheerfully.

"Right on the money. Hold on, we're approaching our turn." Pitt slowed and swung the Cord onto a narrow, snow-packed road leading in a series of switchbacks up the mountainside.

The straight-eight engine with its 115-horsepower strained to pull the heavy car over the slippery, uneven surface. The stiff chassis springs jolted everyone like tennis balls in a washing machine as the lighter rear end slewed back and forth. Pitt compensated with a deft touch on the accelerator and steering wheel, using the pulling power of the front-wheel drive to keep the long hood pointed up the middle of a road that had all the qualifications of a vague hiking trail.

Lily and Hala had picked themselves up off the floor and were sitting in the seat, feet braced against the divider partition, hanging onto the overhead straps for dear life.

Six minutes later they left the trees behind and were climbing above timberline. The road now ran between steep inclines carpeted with massive rocks and deep snow. It had been Pitt's original idea to abandon the Cord and make a run for it, using the woods and craggy landscape for cover, but the depth of Colorado's famous powdery snow sharply increased at the higher altitudes, making any passage on foot nearly impossible. He was left with no alternative but to reach the summit with enough time to take a chair lift down the mountain to the town and become lost in the crowds.

"We're boiling," Giordino observed.

Pitt didn't need to see the steam starting to issue around the base of the radiator cap; he'd been watching the needle on the temperature gauge creep upward until it was pegged on HOT.

"The engine was rebuilt with close tolerances," he explained. "We've given it too much of a beating before it had a chance to break in."

"What do we do when the road ends?" asked Giordino.

"Plan two," answered Pitt. "We take a leisurely ride down a chair lift to the nearest saloon."

"I like your style, but the war's not over." Giordino nodded over his shoulder. "Our friends are back."

Pitt had been too busy to keep track of his pursuers. They had recovered from the accident and charged up the mountain after the Cord. Before he could look behind, bullets shattered the rear window between Lily's and Hala's heads, traversed the car and passed cleanly through the windshield, leaving three small, starred holes. The women didn't have to be told to crouch on the floor again. This time they tried to melt into it.

"I think they're mad about the wrench," said Giordino.

"Not half as mad as I am over the way they're trashing my car."

Pitt hauled the car around a steep switchback, and when he straightened out again, he turned and stole a quick look at the chasing cars. The rearward view was not lacking in menace.

The twin Mercedeses were violently slewing all over the snow-covered road. Their superior speed was partially offset by the Cord's front-wheel traction. Pitt pulled away in the tight turns, but the Arabs narrowed the gap in the straight-aways.

Pitt caught a glimpse of the lead driver twisting and turning his wheel like a maniac, ignoring caution and keeping the rear-drive wheels in a constant state of spin. At every switchback he came within a hair of sliding into heavy snow and becoming hopelessly stuck.

Pitt was surprised that the Mercedeses showed no signs of wearing snow tires. He couldn't have known the Arabs had driven the cars over the border from Mexico to muddy their trail. Registered to a nonexistent textile company in Matamoros, they were to be abandoned at the Breckenridge airport after Hala's assassination was completed.

Pitt didn't like what he saw. The Mercedeses were moving relentlessly closer. They were only fifty meters behind. He also didn't like the sight of a man sticking an automatic rifle through the smashed windshield.

"Here comes the mail!" he shouted, slipping under the wheel until his eyes barely peered over the top of the dashboard. "Everyone down!"

The words were barely out of his mouth when bullets began thumping into the Cord. One burst ripped the right fender-mounted spare tire and wheel. The next tore through the roof, shredding the leather padding and mangling the metal skin underneath.

Pitt tensed and tried to duck even lower as the left side of the car was cut open as if attacked by an army of can openers. The hinges flew off a rear door and it fell open, hanging grotesquely for a few moments until it was torn away as the Cord brushed a tree. Glass fragments flew like rain. One of the women screamed, he didn't know which one. He became aware of a fine spray of blood on the dashboard. A bullet had ploughed a furrow through one of Giordino's ears, but the gritty little Italian made no sound.

Giordino probed the wound indifferently, almost as though it belonged to someone else. Then he tilted his head and gave Pitt a slanted grin. "I fear last night's wine is leaking out."

"Is it bad?" Pitt asked.

"Nothing a plastic surgeon can't fix for two thousand dollars. What about the women?"

Pitt shouted without turning. "Lily, are you

and Hala all right?"

"A few scratches from flying glass," Lily replied gamely. "Otherwise we're unhurt." She was good and scared but not anywhere near the edge of panic.

The steam from the Cord's radiator was escaping like a high-pressure jet now. Pitt could feel the engine lose revolutions as it slowly began to seize up. Like a jockey riding a tired old nag long overdue for the pasture, he pushed the car as hard as he dared.

He worked coolly, concentrating on hurling the Cord around the last switchback before the summit. He had gambled and failed to elude the assassins. They clung to his rear bumper as if chained there.

The engine bearings began to rattle in protest from the excessive heat and strain. Another volley of bullets peppered the left rear fender and flattened the tire. Pitt fought the wheel to keep the rear end from careening off the side of the road and dragging the car down a 60-percent grade filled with large jagged boulders.

The Cord was dying. Ominous blue smoke filtered through the hood louvers. Beneath the engine, oil seeped through a gouge torn in the oil pan by a rock Pitt could not avoid. The oil pressure gauge quickly registered zero. Any chance of making the temporary safety of the summit became more remote with each knock of the piston rods.

The lead Mercedes charged around the switchback in a wild skid. Pitt clutched the wheel despairingly. He could picture the look of triumph on his pursuers' faces as they sensed they were seconds away from running their prey to the ground.

He saw no place for a desperation escape on foot. They were trapped on the narrow road between a steep drop on one side and a sharp rocky rise on the other. There was nowhere to go but ahead until the Cord's engine gave up and froze.

Pitt jammed the accelerator pedal against the floorboard with all the strength in his leg and uttered a fast prayer.

Incredibly, the battle-weary old classic had something more to give. As though a mechanical thing had a mind of its own, it reached down into its iron and steel for one final, magnificent effort. The engine revolutions suddenly increased, the front tires dug in, and the Cord struggled up the final grade to the summit. A minute later, trailing clouds of blue smoke and white steam, it broke out onto the open crest of a ski run.

Not one hundred meters away stood the upper end of a triple-chair ski lift. At first Pitt thought it strange that no one was skiing on the slope directly below the Cord. People were dropping off the chairs and turning toward the opposite side of the lift before starting down a parallel ski trail.

350

Then he observed his section of the slope was roped off. Several signs hung on a line festooned with bright orange streamers warning skiers not to ski this run because of dangerous, icy conditions.

"The end of the trail," Giordino said solemnly.

Pitt nodded in frustration. "We can't make a break for the lift. They'd shoot us down before we ran ten meters."

"It's either fight them with snowballs or take our chances and surrender."

"Or we can try plan three."

Giordino peered at Pitt curiously. "Can't be any worse than the first two." Then his eyes widened and he groaned, "You're not — oh, God, no!"

The two Mercedeses were almost within spitting distance. They had pulled side by side to box in the Cord when Pitt twisted the wheel and sent the car plummeting down the ski run.

29

"Allah help us," muttered Ismail's driver. "The crazy idiots. We can't stop them."

"Keep after them!" Ismail shouted hysterically. "Don't let them escape."

"They'll die anyway. No one can survive a runaway car down a mountainside."

Ismail swung his gun barrel and roughly pushed the muzzle into his driver's ear. "Catch those pigs," he snarled viciously, "or you'll see Allah sooner than you planned."

The driver hesitated, seeing death no matter which move he made. Then he gave in and turned the Mercedes down the steep incline after the Cord.

"Allah guide my actions," he uttered in sudden fear.

Ismail pulled the gun away and pointed through the broken windshield. "Be still and mind your driving."

Ismail's henchmen in the second Mercedes didn't pause. Dutifully they plunged after their leader.

The Cord hurtled across the hard-packed snow like a runaway freight train, gaining speed at a terrifying rate. There was no slowing the heavy car. Pitt steered with a light touch and feathered the brakes, cautious not to lock them and send the Cord into an uncontrollable spin. A sideways slide down the steep incline would only result in the car's overturning and ending up at the base of the mountain in a scattered trail of metal and broken bodies.

"Is this a good time to raise the question of seat belts?" asked Giordino with his feet raised and wedged against the dashboard.

Pitt shook his head. "Not optional equipment in nineteen thirty."

Pitt sensed a tiny bit of luck as the bullet-shredded rubber tore off the rear wheel. Free of the deflated tire, the double edges of the rim gave him a small measure of control as they bit into the icy surface, throwing up fan-like sheets of ice particles.

The speedometer was hovering at sixty when Pitt saw a field of moguls coming up. Expert skiers found the rounded snow bumps a favorite obstacle course. So did Pitt when he schussed down a slope at high speed. But not now, not playing downhill racer with a weighty 2,120 kilograms of automobile.

With a deft touch, he gently nudged the car off to the side of the trail where the path ran smooth. He felt as though he were trying to thread a needle with an Olympic bobsled. Subconsciously Pitt tensed himself for the violent shock and crushing impact should he make the slightest wrong move and hurl the car into a tree, smashing everyone to bloody pulp.

But there was no crushing impact. The Cord somehow shot through the narrow slot, the moguls on one side and the trees on the other flashing by like blurred stage sets.

As soon as Pitt was on a wide, unobstructed run, he snapped his head around to check the status of his pursuers.

The driver of the lead Mercedes was savvy. He'd followed in the Cord's tire tracks around the moguls. The second driver either didn't see them or didn't consider them dangerous. He realized his mistake too late and compounded it by throwing the Mercedes wildly from side to side in a desperate effort to dodge the meter-high humps.

The Arab actually slipped past three or four before he took one head-on. The front end dug in and the rear rose up and appeared to hang on a ninety-degree angle. The car stood poised there for an instant, and then it flipped end over end as if a child had flipped a short stick. It struck the hard snowpack again and again with the splitting sound of crashing metal and glass.

The occupants might have survived if they'd been thrown clear, but the jarring series of impacts had jammed the doors. The car began to disintegrate. The engine tore from its mountings and tumbled crazily into the woods. Wheels, front suspension, rear-drive train, none of it was built to take this destructive torture. It all wrenched away from the chassis, bouncing in mad gyrations down the hill.

Pitt could not spare the time to watch the Mercedes cartwheel and crumple into an indistinguishable heap before finally grinding to a halt on its squashed roof in a small ravine.

"Would it sound gauche," said Giordino for the first time since they plunged off the crest, "if I said, One down?"

"I wish you wouldn't use that term," Pitt muttered through gritted teeth. "The score is about to escalate." He briefly took one hand from the wheel and motioned ahead.

Giordino tensed as he observed the ski run fork and merge with another trail crowded with people in vividly colored ski suits. He jerked himself to a standing position by grabbing the remains of the windshield frame, shouting and waving frantically as Pitt laid on the Cord's twin horns.

The startled skiers turned at the honking and saw the two speeding cars barreling down the ski trail. With seconds to spare, they traversed to the sides and gaped in astonishment as the Cord, with the Mercedes right behind, sped past.

A ski jump rose from the trail and dropped off a hundred meters away. Pitt hardly had time to distinguish the snowy ramp blending in with the hillside. Without hesitation he aimed the radiator ornament at the starting drop-off.

"You wouldn't?" blurted Giordino.

"Plan four," Pitt assured him. "Brace yourself. I may lose control."

"I thought you've been doing that right along."

Far smaller than the structures built for Olympic competition, the jump was used only for acrobatic and hot-dog skiing exhibitions. The ramp was wide enough to take the Cord and then some. It extended thirty meters into a concave dip before abruptly ending twenty meters above the ground.

Pitt lined up on the starting gate, using the Cord's wide body to hide the ski jump from the view of the Mercedes. The tricky part depended on exact timing and a nimble twist of the steering wheel.

At the last instant, before the front wheels rolled across the starting line, Pitt flicked the steering wheel and spun the Cord's rear end, whipping the car away from the ramp down the ski jump. Alert to the sudden antics of the Cord, Ismail's driver swung to avoid a collision and made a perfect entry through the starting gate.

As Pitt wrestled the Cord back on a straight path, Giordino looked back at the Mercedes and stared into a face masked with a weird expression of frightened rage. Then it was gone as the car shot down the steep slant out of all control. It should have soared into the sky like a fat bird with no wings. But the rear end broke loose and it slipped on a slight angle, dropping the right wheels off the ramp's side a few meters before the final edge and sending the car spiraling through the air like a well-thrown football.

The Mercedes must have been hitting close to 120 kilometers when it lifted off. Impelled by tremendous momentum, it twirled through sky for an incredible distance before curving earthward and striking the snowpack with a tremendous impact on its four wheels. As if in slow motion, it bounced and sailed into a tall ponderosa pine, smashing against the thick trunk. The grinding screech of mangled metal split the thin air as the chassis and body wrapped around the tree until the front and rear bumpers met like a pitched horseshoe against a steel stake. Glass exploded like confetti and the bodies inside were twisted and mashed like flies under a swatter.

Giordino shook his head in wonder. "That's the damnedest sight I've ever seen."

"More to come," said Pitt. He had straightened out the Cord's wild slide, but there was no slowing its velocity. The brakes had burned out halfway down the slope and the steering tie rod was bent and hanging by a thread. The Cord's path was unmistakable. It was heading toward the large ski facility and restaurant building at the base of the chair lifts. All Pitt could do was keep blowing the horns and struggle to avoid skiers too dumb to scramble out of the way.

The women had watched the destruction of the last Mercedes with morbid curiosity and vast relief. The relief was short-lived. They turned and stared aghast at the rapidly approaching building.

"Can't we do something?" Hala demanded.

"I'm open for suggestions," Pitt fired back. He became quiet as he managed to dodge a ski class made up of young children by careening up a snowbank and curling around them. The main mass of skiers had either heard or witnessed the crash of the Mercedes and were galvanized into action at the sight and sound of the Cord. They quickly moved to the side of the trail and stared in utter incomprehension as the Cord rocketed by.

Warnings of the runaway vehicles had been phoned from the upper end of the chair lift, and ski instructors had cleared most of the crowd away from the base area. There was a shallow, frozen pond to the right of the ski center. Pitt hoped to angle in that direction and run onto the ice until it cracked open sinking the car to the running boards and bringing it to an abrupt halt. The only problem was, the onlookers had unwittingly formed a corridor leading to the restaurant.

"I don't suppose there's a plan five," said Giordino, bracing himself for the collision.

"Sorry," said Pitt. "We're all sold out."

Lily and Hala watched, helpless and horror-stricken. Then they dived behind the division behind the chauffeur's seat, closed their eyes and clutched each other.

Pitt stiffened as they struck several long racks holding skis and poles. The skis seemed to explode as they were sent flying through the air like toothpicks. For an instant the Cord seemed buried, but then it burst clear and bored up the concrete stairway, missing the restaurant but splintering through the wooden wall of the cocktail lounge.

The room had been emptied except for the piano player, who sat paralyzed at his keyboard, and a bartender, who elected discretion and frantically took refuge behind the bar just as the Cord exploded into the room and bulldozed its way through a sea of chairs and tables.

The Cord almost broke through the far wall and down a two-story drop. Miraculously, its momentum finally spent, the mutilated car stopped short, leaving only its badly distorted front bumper protruding through the wall. The cocktail lounge looked like the recipient of an artillery barrage.

Except for the hiss of the radiator and the crackling of the overheated engine, an eerie silence filled the room. Pitt had banged his head against the windshield frame and blood was streaming down his face from a cut above the hairline. He looked over at Giordino, who sat staring at the wall as if turned to stone. Pitt turned and stared down at the women behind. They were wearing their best "are we still alive?" look, but seemed none the worse for wear.

The bartender was still huddled out of sight behind the bar, so Pitt turned to the piano player, who sat in a daze on a three-legged stool. He was wearing a derby hat and the cigarette that dangled from the side of his mouth hadn't even lost its ash. His hands were poised above the keys, his body rigid as if he was locked in suspended animation. He stared, shaken, at the bloody apparition who insanely smiled back.

"Pardon me," said Pitt politely. "Can you play 'Fly Me to the Moon'?"

■ ■ ■ ■

PART III:
THE *LADY*
FLAMBOROUGH

■ ■ ■ ■

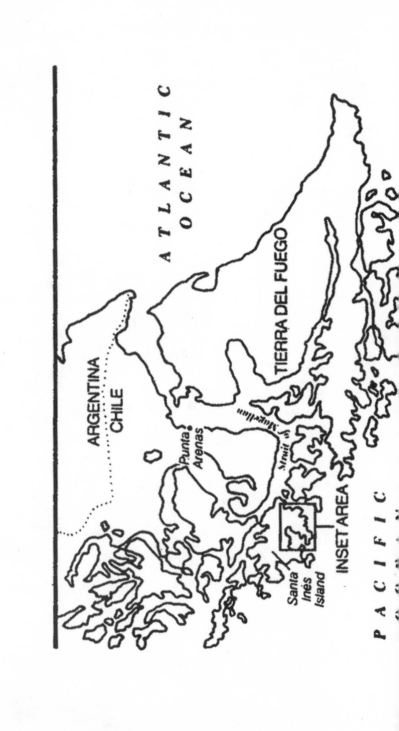

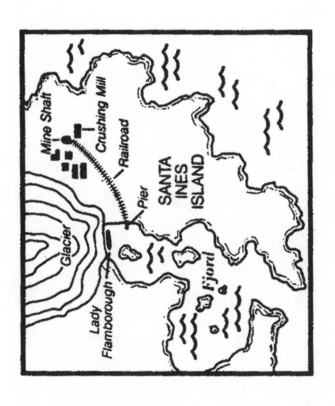

30

October 19, 1991
Uxmal, Yucatán

The stonework on the massive structure reflected an unearthly glow under the battery of multicolored floodlights. Blue dyed the walls of the great pyramid, while orange highlighted the Temple of the Magician on the top. Red spotlights swept up and down the wide staircase, giving the effect of cascading blood. Above, on the roof of the temple, a slender figure stood haloed in white.

Topiltzin spread his arms and open hands in a divine gesture and stared down at the hundred thousand upraised faces surrounding the temple/pyramid in the ancient Mayan city of Uxmal on the Yucatán peninsula. He ended his speech, as he always did, with a chant in the lilting Aztec tongue. The vast audience picked up the phrases and repeated them in unison.

"The strength and courage of our nation lies in us who will never be great or wealthy.

365

We starve, we toil for leaders who are less noble and honest than ourselves. There can be no glory or greatness in Mexico until the false government is dead. No longer will we endure slavery. The gods are gathering again to sacrifice the corrupt for the decent. Their gift is a new civilization. We must accept it."

As the words died away, the colored lights slowly dimmed until only Topiltzin remained brightly lit. Then the white spotlights blinked out and he was gone.

Great bonfires were lit, and a truck caravan began handing out boxes of food to the grateful mass of people. Each container held the same amount of flour and canned goods, and a cartoonlike booklet, heavy on illustrations, light on captions. President De Lorenzo and his cabinet ministers were drawn to resemble demons being driven out of Mexico and into the open arms of an evil-looking Uncle Sam by Topiltzin and four major Aztec gods.

A list of instructions was also included, describing peaceful but effective methods of eroding government influence.

During the food handout, men and women worked the crowd, recruiting new followers for Topiltzin. The event was staged and oiled with the professionalism of a rock concert organization. Uxmal was only one stop on Topiltzin's campaign to subvert the government in Mexico City.

He preached to the masses only at the great

stone centers of the past — Teotihuacán, Monte Albán, Tula and Chichén Itzá. He never appeared in Mexico's modern cities.

The people cheered Topiltzin and shouted his name. But he no longer heard them. The instant the spotlights went off, his bodyguards hustled him down a ladder on the backside of the pyramid and into a large truck and semitrailer. The engine was started and the truck, led by one car and followed by another, slowly wound its way through the crowd until it met the highway. Then it turned toward the Yucatán state capital of Mérida and picked up speed.

The interior of the trailer was expensively decorated and divided between a conference room and Topiltzin's private living quarters.

Topiltzin briefly discussed the next day's schedule with his close worshipers. When the meeting broke up, the truck was stopped, and everyone bid him a good night. The two cars collected the weary followers and drove them to hotels in Mérida.

Once Topiltzin closed the door and shut off one world, he entered another.

He removed a feathered headdress and stripped off his white robe, revealing a pair of expensive slacks and a sports shirt underneath. He opened a hidden cabinet, removed a chilled bottle of Schramsberg Blanc de Blanc sparkling wine and swiftly extracted the cork. The first glass was downed for thirst, but the second was slowly savored.

Relaxed, Topiltzin entered a small cubicle containing communications equipment, punched in a numbered code on a holographic telephone and turned to face the center of the room. He sipped at the California champagne and waited. Slowly an indistinct figure began to materialize in three dimensions. At the same time, Topiltzin was visible thousands of miles away.

When the details cleared, another man sat on an ottoman couch and stared back at Topiltzin. His complexion was dark, and the thin brushed-back hair gleamed with oil. His eyes had a hard-jeweled gleam. The visitor was dressed in a silk paisley robe over pajamas. He studied Topiltzin's shirt and slacks for a moment and frowned when he noticed the glass in one hand.

"You live dangerously," he said sternly in American English. "Designer clothing, champagne — next it will be women."

Topiltzin laughed. "Don't tempt me. Acting like the Pope and wearing a bizarre costume eighteen hours a day is bad enough without practicing celibacy."

"I endure the same inconvenience."

"We both have our own cross to bear," Topiltzin said in a bored tone.

"Do not get careless so close to success."

"I don't intend to. None of my people would dare disturb my privacy. Whenever I'm alone, they think I'm communicating with the gods."

The other man smiled. "The routine sounds familiar."

"Shall we get down to business?" said Topiltzin.

"All right, what's the status?"

"The arrangements are sealed. Everyone will be in his place at the right moment. I paid out over ten million pesos in bribes to set up the rendezvous. Once the fools on the take did their job, they were sacrificed, not only to guarantee their silence but also as a warning to those who are waiting to carry out our instructions."

"My congratulations. You're very thorough."

"I leave the cleverness to you."

There was a friendly silence after this remark, which lasted several moments while both men rested on their thoughts. At last the caller smiled craftily and produced a small brandy snifter from beneath a fold of his gown.

"Your health."

Topiltzin gave a satiric laugh and raised his champagne glass. "To a successful venture."

The ethereal visitor paused. "A successful venture," he repeated, and then added, "with no snags." After an even longer pause he said pensively, "It will be interesting to see how our efforts alter the future."

31

The roar of the engines lessened as the unmarked Beechcraft jet lifted away from Buckley Field outside Denver and rose toward its cruising altitude. The snow-capped Rockies fell away behind as the aircraft set its nose across the great plains.

"The President sends his best wishes for a speedy recovery," said Dale Nichols. "He was quite angered when briefed on your ordeal —"

"Madder than hell is a better description," Schiller cut in.

"Let's say he wasn't happy," Nichols continued. "He asked me to express his apologies for not providing stronger security measures and promised he will do everything within his power to ensure your safety while you remain in the United States."

"Tell him I'm grateful," Hala replied, "and please beg him for me to give every consideration to the families of the men who died saving my life."

"They'll be well taken care of," Nichols assured her.

Hala was lying propped in a bed, wearing a white velour sweatsuit striped in jade with a knit polo collar. Her right ankle was in a plaster cast. She looked at Nichols, then toward Julius Schiller and Senator Pitt, who were all seated opposite her bed. "I'm honored that three such distinguished gentlemen took time from their busy schedules to fly to Colorado and accompany me back to New York."

"If we can do anything —"

"You've done much more than any foreigner on your soil could expect."

"You have the lives of a cat," said Senator Pitt.

Her lips parted in a slight smile. "I owe two of them to your son. He has a capacity for appearing in the right place when you least expect him."

"I saw Dirk's old car. It's a miracle you all survived."

"A truly beautiful machine," Hala sighed. "A pity it was destroyed."

Nichols cleared his throat. "If we may touch on the subject of your address to the U.N. tomorrow . . ."

"Have your people turned up any solid data leading to the Alexandria Library artifacts?" Hala asked sharply.

Nichols glanced at the Senator and Schiller

with the look of a man who suddenly stepped in quicksand. The Senator threw him a rope and gave the reply.

"We haven't had time to launch a massive search," he said honestly. "We know little more than we did four days ago."

Nichols began hesitantly. "The President . . . he hoped . . ."

"I'll save you time, Mr. Nichols." Hala's eyes turned to Schiller. "You may rest easy, Julius, my speech will include a brief report on the *imminent discovery* of the Alexandria Library antiquities."

"I'm glad to hear you've changed your mind."

"Considering recent events, I owe your government that much."

Nichols was visibly relieved. "Your announcement will give President Hasan a sharp political advantage over Akhmad Yazid, and a golden opportunity to boost Egyptian nationalism over religious fundamentalism."

"Don't expect too much," said the Senator. "We're only filling cracks on a crumbling fort."

Schiller's lips parted in a cold smile. "I'd give a month's salary to see Yazid's face when he realizes he's been had."

"I'm afraid he'll really come after Hala with a vengeance," said Schiller.

"I don't think so," said Nichols. "If the FBI can link a chain from the dead terrorists to

Yazid and then to the assassin responsible for the plane crash with the death of sixty people, many moderate Egyptians who do not condone terrorism will withdraw their support from his movement. With an internationally publicized terrorist mission laid on his doorstep, he'd have to think twice before ordering another attempt on Ms. Kamil's life."

"Mr. Nichols is correct on one point," said Hala. "Most Egyptians are Sunni Moslems who do not follow the bloody revolutionary drumbeat of the Iranian Shiites. They prefer an evolutionary approach that slowly changes the people's loyalty from a democratic government to a religious leadership. They will not accept Yazid's bloodlust methods." Hala paused a moment. "I disagree on the second point. Yazid won't rest until I'm dead. He is too fanatical to give up. He's probably planning another attempt on my life this minute."

"She may be right; we must keep a sharp intelligence eye on Yazid," cautioned the Senator.

"What are your plans after your U.N. address?" asked Schiller.

"This morning, before we left the hospital, I was given a letter from President Hasan by an attaché from our embassy in Washington. President Hasan wishes me to meet with him."

"Once you leave our boundaries we can't

guarantee your protection," Nichols warned her.

"I understand," she replied. "But there is little cause for concern. Since President Sadat's assassination, Egyptian security people have become quite efficient."

"May I ask where this meeting will be held?" queried Schiller. "Or is it none of my business?"

"No secret; in fact it will be covered by the world news media," Hala answered nonchalantly. "President Hasan and I will confer during the coming economic meetings in Punta del Este, Uruguay."

The mangled and bullet-holed Cord sat forlornly in the middle of the shop floor. Esbenson slowly circled the car and shook his head sadly.

"This is the first time I've ever had to restore a classic car two days after I finished it."

"We had a bad day," Giordino explained. He was wearing a neck brace, one arm was in a sling, and his nicked ear was heavily bandaged.

"It's a wonder any of you are standing here."

Except for six stitches, mostly hidden by his hair, Pitt was unmarked. He patted the buckled chrome radiator shell as if the car was an injured pet.

"Lucky for us they used to build them to last," he said quietly.

Lily limped painfully from the shop office. Her left cheek was bruised and the opposite eye was blackened.

"I have Hiram Yaeger on the phone," she announced.

Pitt nodded. He put a hand on Esbenson's shoulder. "Make her even better than she was before."

"We're looking at six months and heavy bucks," said Esbenson.

"Time is no problem and neither is money." Pitt paused and broke into a grin. "The government is going to foot the bill this time around." He turned, walked into the office and picked up the phone. "Hiram, you got something for me?"

"Just a status report," Yaeger replied from Washington. "I've eliminated the Baltic Sea and the coastline of Norway."

"And nothing showed."

"Nothing worth celebrating. No matching of geologic contours or geographic descriptions from the *Serapis* log. The barbarians Rufinus mentioned don't come close to fitting the early Vikings. He wrote of people who resembled Scythians, but with darker skins."

"That bothered me too," Pitt agreed. "The Scythians came from Central Asia. Not damned likely they'd have been fair-skinned and blond."

"I see no sense in continuing the computer search around Norway into the northern waters of Russia."

"I agree. What about Iceland? The Vikings didn't settle there for another five hundred years. Maybe Rufinus meant Eskimos."

"No go," said Yaeger. "I checked. Eskimos never migrated to Iceland. Rufinus also threw in the mystery of the 'great sea of dwarflike pines.' He couldn't have found them on Iceland. And don't forget, you're talking about a six-hundred-mile voyage across some of the worst seas in the world. Historical marine records are quite precise: Roman ship captains rarely sailed out of sight of land for more than two days. The voyage from the nearest European land mass would have taken a fourth-century ship four and a half days under ideal conditions."

"So where do we go from here?"

"I'll run the West African coast by again. We might have missed something. Dark-skinned Africans and a warmer climate seem more logical than the cold northern countries, especially to men from the Mediterranean."

"You still have to explain how the *Serapis* came to be in Greenland."

"A projection of wind and currents could give us a clue."

"I'm flying back to Washington tonight,"

said Pitt. "I'll look in on you tomorrow."

"Maybe I'll have something," said Yaeger, but his tone did not sound optimistic.

Pitt hung up and stepped from the office. Lily looked at him with an expression of hope. Then she read the disappointment in his eyes.

"No good news?" she asked.

He shrugged negatively. "Seems we haven't left square one."

She took his arm. "Yaeger will come through," she said encouragingly.

"He can't work miracles."

Giordino held up a watch on his good arm. "We don't have much time to make our flight. We'd better get rolling."

Pitt walked over, shook Esbenson's hand and smiled. "Make her well again. She saved our lives."

Esbenson looked at him. "Only if you promise me you'll keep her away from flying bullets and ski slopes."

"Done."

After they left for the airport, Esbenson opened a rear door of the Cord. The door handle came off in his hand.

"God," he said mournfully, "what a mess."

377

32

A loud roar of applause erupted in the public galleries and swept over the delegates on the main floor below as Hala refused all assistance and slowly made her way to the podium on crutches. She stood behind the podium, poised and serene, speaking in a strong, convincing voice. Her theatrics were low-key and subtle. She moved the audience with an emotional appeal to stop the useless killing of innocent people in the name of religion. Only when she called for a censure of governments that turned a blind eye toward terrorist organizations did a few delegates shift in their seats and stare into space.

An undercurrent of murmurs trailed her news of the forthcoming Alexandria Library discovery as the immense potential took time to sink in. Then Akhmad Yazid came in for a scathing attack, as she accused him directly of the attempts on her life.

Hala concluded by firmly stating she would

not be driven out of her position as Secretary-General by threats of future harm, but would remain until her fellow delegates asked for her resignation.

The response was a standing ovation that became thunderous as she stood off to one side of the podium and displayed the cast on her ankle.

"She's some lady," said the President admiringly. "What I wouldn't give to have her sit in my cabinet." He pressed the off button on a remote control and the television screen went black.

"An excellent speech," said Senator Pitt. "She tore Yazid apart — and made a good pitch on the Library search project."

The President nodded. "Yes, she came through for us on both counts."

"You know, of course, she's leaving for Uruguay to confer with President Hasan."

"Dale Nichols briefed me on the conversation you had with her on the plane," the President acknowledged. He was seated behind his desk in the Oval Office. "How do we stand on the search?"

"NUMA's computer facility is working on a location," answered the Senator.

"Are they close?"

The Senator shook his head. "No closer now to a breakthrough than they were four days ago."

"Can't we speed up the process? Bring in a think tank, university people, other government agencies?"

Senator Pitt looked doubtful. "NUMA has the finest computer library in the world on oceans, lakes and rivers. If they can't find the destination of the Egyptian fleet, no one can."

"What about archaeological and historical records?" the President suggested. "Maybe something's been uncovered in the past that could offer a clue."

"Might be worth a try. I know a good man at Penn State University who's a triple-A researcher. He can have thirty people digging the archives here and in Europe by this time tomorrow."

"Good, give him a crack at it."

"Now that the news media and Hala have spread the word," said the Senator, "half the governments and most of the fortune hunters of the world will be on the hunt for the Library collection."

"I considered that probability going in," the President said. "But propping up President Hasan's government takes top priority. If we make the discovery first and then pretend to back down after Hasan makes a dramatic show of demanding the artifacts be returned to Egypt, his domestic popularity will take a big jump, and make him a hero in the eyes of the Egyptian people."

"While stalling off the threat of a takeover

by Yazid and his followers," added the Senator. "The only problem is Yazid himself. The man is extremely unpredictable. Our best Middle East experts can't read him. He's liable to pull a rabbit out of the hat and steal the scene."

The President looked at him steadily. "I see no problem in cutting him out of the limelight when the artifacts are turned over to President Hasan."

"I'm on your side, Mr. President, but it's dangerous to underestimate Yazid."

"He's far from perfect."

"Yes, but unlike the Ayatollah Khomeini, Akhmad Yazid is a brilliant intellect. He's what the advertising agencies call a good concept man."

"In political areas perhaps, but hardly in assassinations."

The Senator shrugged and smiled knowingly. "His plans were, no doubt, screwed up by his henchmen. As President, you know better than anyone how easily an aide or adviser can botch a simple project."

The President smiled back without humor. He leaned back in his chair and toyed with a pen. "We know damned little about Yazid, where he came from, what makes him tick."

"He claims to have spent the first thirty years of his life wandering the Sinai desert talking to Allah."

"So he's lifted a page from Jesus Christ.

What else do we have on him?"

"You might ask Dale Nichols," answered the Senator. "I understand he's working with the CIA on building a biographical and psychological profile."

"Let's see if they've come up with anything." The President pressed a button on his intercom. "Dale, can you come in for a minute?"

"Be right there," came Nichols's voice over the speaker.

Neither of the men in the Oval Office spoke during the fifteen seconds Nichols took to walk from his office. He knocked, then opened the door and stepped in.

"We were discussing Akhmad Yazid," the President informed him. "Have Brogan's people turned up any data on his background?"

"I talked to Martin only an hour ago," replied Nichols. "He said his analysts should have a file put together in another day or two."

"I want to see it the minute it's completed," said the President.

"Not to change the subject," said Senator Pitt, "but shouldn't someone brief President Hasan on what we've got in mind in case the Library collection can be pinpointed in the next few weeks?"

The President nodded. "Definitely." He stared directly at the Senator. "Think you could sneak off for forty-eight hours and do the honors, George?"

"You want me to meet with Hasan in Uruguay." It was more a statement than question.

"Do you mind?"

"This is really a matter for Doug Oates over at the State Department. He and Joe Arnold from Treasury are already in Kingston holding preliminary meetings with foreign economic leaders. Do you think it wise to go behind his back?"

"Ordinarily, no. But you're better informed on the search project. You've also met with President Hasan on four different occasions, and you're close to Hala Kamil. Simply put, you're the best man for the job."

The Senator lifted his hands in resignation. "No heavy votes coming up in the Senate. My staff can cover for me. If you arrange for a government plane, I can leave here early Tuesday, meet with Hasan that evening and report back to you the following afternoon."

"Thank you, George, you're a good scout." The President paused, and then sprang the trap. "There is one other thing."

"There always is." The Senator sighed.

"I'd like you to inform President Hasan in private, under the strictest secrecy, that I will fully cooperate with him in the event he decides to remove Yazid."

The Senator's voice was shocked. "Since

when does the White House deal in political assassination? I implore you, Mr. President, do not lower your office into the slime with Yazid and other terrorists."

"If someone had had the foresight to take Khomeini for a ride twelve years ago, the Middle East would be a far more peaceful place."

"King George might have said the same about George Washington and the colonies in 1778."

"Come now, George, we could spend all day making comparisons. The final decision is up to Hasan. He has to give the go-ahead."

"A bad idea," said the Senator resolutely. "I have grave doubts about such an offer. If this leaked out it could shatter your Presidency."

"I respect your advice and honesty. That's why you're the only man I can trust to deliver the message."

The Senator caved in. "I'll do as you ask and gladly brief Hasan on the Library proposal, but don't expect me to sell him on Yazid's murder even if it's deserved."

"I'll see that Hasan's staff is alerted to your arrival," said Nichols, stepping in diplomatically.

The President rose from behind his desk, signaling the end of the conference. He shook hands with the Senator.

"I'm grateful, old friend. I'll look forward to your report Wednesday afternoon. We'll have an early supper together."

"See you then, Mr. President."

"Have a good flight."

As Senator Pitt left the Oval Office he had a dire sense that the President might very well be dining alone Wednesday evening.

33

The *Lady Flamborough* slipped smoothly into the tiny harbor of Punta del Este just minutes before the sun fell over the western interior of the mainland. A soft breeze drifted in from the south that barely fluttered the Union Jack on her stern.

She was a beautiful cruise ship, trim and handsomely designed, with a streamlined superstructure. She broke with the traditional British black hull and more common white on her upper works. She was painted entirely in a soft slate blue with a sharply raked funnel banded in royal purple and burgundy.

One of the new breed of sleek, small cruise ships, the *Lady Flamborough* looked more like a posh motor yacht. Her trim 101-meter-long hull contained the most sumptuous luxuries afloat. With only fifty large suites, she carried just one hundred passengers, who were catered to by an equal number of crew members.

On this voyage, however, from her home

port in San Juan, Puerto Rico, she sailed without passengers.

"Two degrees port," said the dark-skinned pilot.

"Two degrees port," acknowledged the helmsman.

The pilot stood in loose khaki shirt and shorts and kept a calculating eye on the finger of land that sheltered the bay until it slipped behind the *Lady Flamborough*'s stern.

"Begin coming around to starboard and hold steady at zero eight zero."

The helmsman dutifully repeated the command and the ship very slowly swung on its new course.

The harbor was crowded with yachts and other cruise ships flying flocks of colorful pointed and swallowtail pennants. Some vessels were chartered as floating hotels for the economic conference, others were filled with their usual complement of vacationing passengers.

Half a kilometer from the mooring site the pilot ordered the engines on "dead stop." The luxurious ship slipped through the calm water on her momentum, eating up the distance and gradually easing to a halt.

Satisfied, the pilot spoke into a portable transmitter. "We're in position. Slow aft and drop the hook."

The order was relayed to the bow, and the anchor payed out as the ship very slightly moved astern. When the flukes dug into the harbor silt, the slack was taken up and the order was given to ring the engines to "off."

Captain Oliver Collins, a slim man standing straight as a plumb line in an impeccably tailored white uniform, nodded at the pilot in respect and offered his hand.

"Neatly done as always, Mr. Campos." Captain Collins had known the pilot for almost twenty years, yet he never referred to anyone, even his closest friends, by his Christian name.

"If her length stretched another thirty meters I couldn't squeeze her in." Harry Campos smiled, revealing an array of tobacco-stained teeth. His accent was more Irish than Spanish. "Sorry we can't slip her into a berth, Captain, but I was told to moor you in the harbor."

"For security reasons, I should imagine," said Collins.

Campos lit the stub of a cigar. "The bigwig meetings have the whole island turned upside down. You'd think there was a sniper behind every palm the way security police are acting."

Collins stared through the bridge windows at the popular playground of South America. "I'll not complain. This ship will be hosting the presidents of Mexico and Egypt during the conference."

"That a fact?" muttered Campos. "No

wonder they wanted to keep your vessel off-shore."

"May I offer you a drink in my cabin, or better yet, considering the hour, would you do the honor of dining with me?"

Campos shook his head. "My thanks for the invite, Captain." He paused and motioned at the mass of ships filling the harbor. "But she's a busy time. Maybe a rain check for your next layover."

Campos filled out his document for payment and handed it to Captain Collins, who signed. Campos looked through the aft bridge windows at the immaculate decks of the ship.

"One of these days I'll take a holiday and sail with you as a passenger."

"Let me know," said Collins. "I'll see the company covers all your expenses."

"A mighty kind offer. If I tell my wife, she'll never let up till I take advantage of it."

"A pleasure, Mr. Campos. Any time you say the word."

The pilot boat came alongside and Campos jumped onto the deck from the boarding ladder. He gave a final wave as the boat pulled away and headed out to sea to pilot the next incoming vessel.

"Most enjoyable voyage I ever sailed." This from Collins's first officer, Michael Finney. "A full crew and no passengers. For six days I thought I'd died and gone to heaven."

Company orders required ship's officers to

spend almost as much time entertaining the passengers as sailing the ship, a duty Finney hated with a passion. A fine seaman, he stayed away from the main dining salon as much as possible, preferring to eat with his fellow officers, or making constant inspections of the ship.

Finney didn't exactly look the part of a party mixer. He was big, with a barrel chest that fought to explode from the tight confines of his uniform.

"I don't imagine you missed the joy of mingling and small talk," said Collins sarcastically.

Finney made a disagreeable face. "Wouldn't be so bad if they didn't ask the same stupid questions all the time."

"Courtesy and respect when dealing with passengers, Mr. Finney," Collins admonished. "It goes with the waters. Mind your manners in the next few days. We'll be entertaining some rather important foreign leaders and statesmen."

Finney did not reply. He gazed at the modern high-rise buildings towering over the beachside chalets.

"Everytime I see the old town," he said wistfully, "they've added another hotel."

"Yes, you're from Uruguay."

"Born just west in Montevideo. My father was a sales rep for a Belfast machinery company."

"You must enjoy coming home," said Collins.

"Not really. I signed aboard a Panamanian ore carrier when I was sixteen. Mum and dad are gone. Nobody left I grew up with." He paused and pointed through the bridge window at an approaching boat. "Here come the bloody customs and immigration inspectors."

"Since we have no passengers, and the crew won't be going ashore," said Collins, "the vessel should be cleared with a rubber stamp."

"The health inspectors are the worst nuisance."

"Notify the purser, Mr. Finney. Then show them to my cabin."

"Begging your pardon, sir, but isn't that a bit much? I mean, greeting mere customs inspectors in the Captain's cabin."

"Perhaps, but I want everything to run smoothly with the bureaucracy while we're in harbor. You never know when we might require a favor."

"Aye, sir."

It was dusk as the customs and immigration officials brought their boat alongside the *Lady Flamborough* and mounted the boarding ladder. The ship's lights suddenly blazed on and illuminated her upper decks and superstructure. Moored amid the lights of the city and the other cruise ships, she sparkled like a diamond in a jewelry box.

The Uruguayan officials, led by Finney, approached the open doorway to the Captain's cabin. Collins studied the five men trailing his first officer. He was a man who missed very little, and he quickly noticed something odd about one of them. One man had on a wide-brimmed straw hat pulled low over his eyes and was wearing a jumpsuit, while the rest were dressed properly enough in the casual uniforms worn by most officials throughout the Caribbean islands.

The fellow who stood out walked without looking up, keeping his eyes on the feet of the man in front of him. When they reached the doorway, Finney politely stood aside and allowed them to enter first.

Collins stepped forward. "Good evening, gentlemen. Welcome aboard the *Lady Flamborough.* I'm Captain Oliver Collins."

The visiting officials stood strangely silent and Collins and Finney exchanged curious glances. Then the man in the jumpsuit stepped forward and slowly peeled it off, revealing a white uniform with gold braid that was an exact copy of the one Collins wore. Next he removed the straw hat and replaced it with a cap that matched the uniform.

The normally unperturbed Collins was momentarily caught off balance. He felt as though he was staring into a mirror. The stranger could easily have passed for a twin brother.

"Who are you?" Collins demanded. "What's going on here?"

"No name is necessary," said Suleiman Aziz Ammar with a disarming smile. "I am taking command of your ship."

34

Surprise is the key for any successful clandestine operation. And the surprise takeover of the *Lady Flamborough* was total. Except for Captain Collins, First Officer Finney and a stunned purser, who were bound, gagged and closely guarded in Finney's cabin, none of the other officers or crew had the vaguest idea their ship had been hijacked.

Ammar cut his timing to a fine edge. The bona fide Uruguayan customs inspectors showed up only twelve minutes later. He greeted them as if they were old acquaintances in his makeup and near-perfect disguise as Collins. The men he had handpicked to play the roles of Finney and the purser kept to the shadows. They were both experienced ship's officers and bore a remarkable resemblance to their counterparts. Few crew members would have noticed the facial differences outside of three meters.

The Uruguayan officials cleared the vessel and were soon on their way. Ammar called

Collins's second and third officers to the captain's cabin. This would be his first and most crucial test. If he passed their inspection without arousing suspicion, they would become invaluable to him as innocent accomplices to carry out the complicated plot in the next twenty-four hours.

Making himself up to look like Dale Lemke, the pilot of Nebula Flight 106, was not a difficult process. Ammar had easily cast a plaster mold from Lemke's face after he'd murdered him. Disguising himself to pass as the captain of the *Lady Flamborough* was another matter. He was forced to work from only eight photographs of Collins obtained on short notice by one of his agents in Britain. He also had to inject himself with a compound that raised his voice to an identical level with recordings of Collins's voice.

He hired a skilled artist to sculpt a likeness of Collins's face from the photos. Male and female molds were cast from the sculpture. Next, a natural latex, dyed to match Captain Collins's skin coloring, was pressed between the molds and set aside until gelation occurred, and then baked. He trimmed and carefully fitted the latex mask, using a resin-wax mixture to match minor changes in facial structure.

Then Ammar applied foamed ear and nose prosthetics and added makeup. Finally, a correctly dyed, barbered and parted hairpiece, contact lenses to match the color of Collins's eyes, tooth caps, and Ammar became the spitting image of the cruise liner's Captain.

Ammar did not have the time to study Oliver Collins's personality profile in depth or study the Captain's mannerisms. He just managed to take a cram course on shipboard duties and memorize the names and faces of the ship's officers. He had no choice but to bluff it out, relying correctly on the assumption the crew did not have the slightest reason to be skeptical. As soon as the two officers stepped into the Captain's cabin, Ammar immediately acted to tip the scales in his favor.

"Pardon me, gentlemen, for sounding and looking a bit under the weather, but I've picked up a case of the flu."

"Shall I send for the ship's doctor?" asked Second Officer Herbert Parker, physically fit, suntanned, with a smooth boyish face that seemed as if it saw a razor only on Saturday evenings.

A near-mistake, thought Ammar. A doctor familiar with Collins would have spotted the masquerade in a flash.

"He's already given me enough pills to choke an elephant. I feel fit enough to muddle through my duties."

The third officer, a Scot with the unlikely name of Isaac Jones, pushed aside a shag of red hair from his high forehead. "Anything we can do, sir?"

"Yes, Mr. Jones, there is," answered Ammar. "Our VIP passengers will be arriving tomorrow afternoon. You will be in charge of the welcoming party. We don't often have the honor of entertaining two presidents, and I should think the company will expect us to carry out a first-rate ceremony."

"Yes, sir," snapped Jones. "Depend on it."

"Mr. Parker."

"Captain."

"A landing craft will arrive within the hour to transship a cargo for the company. You will be in charge of the loading operations. A team of security people will also be coming aboard this evening. Please see they are provided with suitable quarters."

"Rather short notice, isn't it, sir, taking on cargo? And I thought the Egyptian and Mexican security agents weren't due until early morning."

"Our company directors work in mysterious ways," Ammar said philosophically. "As to our armed guests, company orders again. They want their own security personnel on board in case of a problem."

"A matter of one security team overseeing another."

"Something like that. I believe Lloyds demanded extra precautions or they threatened to raise our insurance rate to some astronomical height."

"I understand."

"Any questions, gentlemen?"

There were none and the two officers turned to leave.

"Herbert, there is one more thing," said Ammar. "Please load the cargo as quietly and quickly as possible."

"I will, sir."

Once they were out of earshot on the deck, Parker turned to Jones. "Did you hear that? He called me by my first name. Don't you think that jolly queer?"

Jones shrugged indifferently. "He must be sicker than we thought."

The landing craft came alongside and a small cargo boom was run out. The loading operation went smoothly. The rest of Ammar's men, dressed in business suits, also came on board and were assigned to four empty suites.

By midnight the landing craft slipped into the darkness and was gone. The *Lady Flamborough*'s cargo boom was pulled into the hold out of sight and the large double loading doors were closed.

Ammar rapped five times on Finney's door and waited. The door was cracked slightly and the guard stood back. Ammar took a quick look up and down the carpeted passageway and entered.

He nodded toward the Captain. The guard moved forward and stripped the tape from Collins's mouth. "I regret the inconvenience,

Captain. But I suppose it would be a waste of words to ask you to give me your word you won't attempt to escape and warn your crew."

Collins sat stiffly in a chair, his arms and legs chained together, and glared at Ammar with murder in his eyes. "You sordid sewer filth."

"You British have a literary quality to your insults that is quite amusing. An American would have simply used a four-letter word meaning the same thing."

"You'll get no cooperation from me or my officers."

"Not even if I order my men to slit the throats of your female crew members one by one and throw their bodies to the sharks?"

Finney lunged at Ammar but the guard swiftly thrust the butt end of his automatic rifle into the first officer's groin. Finney fell back into his chair with a muffled groan, his eyes glazed in pain.

Collins's eyes never left Ammar. "I'd expect as much from a band of subhuman terrorists."

"We are not ignorant juveniles out to butcher infidels," Ammar explained patiently. "We are top-line professionals. This is not a repeat of the unfortunate *Achille Lauro* episode of a few years back. We do not intend to murder anyone. Our purpose is simply to hold Presidents Hasan and De Lorenzo and

399

their staffs for ransom. If you do not stand in our way, we shall make our deal with their respective governments and be on our way."

Collins studied Ammar's mirrored face, searching for the lie, but the Arab's eyes reflected genuine honesty. He could not know Ammar was a master at theatrical deception.

"But you wouldn't hesitate to butcher my crew otherwise."

"And you too, of course."

"What do you want from me?"

"You, actually nothing. Mr. Parker and Mr. Jones have accepted me as Oliver Collins. It's First Officer Finney whose services I require. You will order him to obey my commands."

"Why Finney?" asked Collins.

"I opened the desk file in your cabin and read the officers' personal records. Finney knows these waters."

"I don't see what you're getting at."

"We cannot afford the risk of calling for a pilot," explained Ammar. "Tomorrow after dark, Finney will take the helm and steer the ship through the channel into the open sea."

Collins calmly considered that. Then he slowly shook his head. "Once the port authorities get on to you they'll block the harbor entrance whether you threaten to kill everyone on board or not."

"A darkened ship can slip out on a dark night," Ammar assured him.

"How far do you expect to go? Every patrol

boat within a hundred miles will have you boxed in by daylight."

"They won't find us."

Collins looked slightly dazed. "That's crazy. You can't hide a ship like the *Lady Flamborough*."

"Quite true," said Ammar, a cold, knowing smile forming on his lips. "But I *can* make her invisible."

Jones was bent over a desk in his cabin making notes for the morning's welcoming ceremonies when Parker knocked on the door and entered. He looked tired and his uniform was damp with sweat.

Jones turned and looked at him. "Loading duty finished?"

"Yes, thank God."

"How about a nightcap?"

"A glass of your good Scottish malt whiskey?"

Jones rose and lifted a bottle from a dresser drawer. He poured two glasses and handed one to Parker.

"Look at it this way," he said. "You were relieved of standing early-morning anchor watch."

"I'd have preferred that to cargo loading," said Parker tiredly. "What about you?"

"Just got off duty."

"I wouldn't have bothered you if I hadn't seen a light through your port."

401

"Burning the midnight oil, making sure everything runs tick-tock smooth tomorrow."

"Finney isn't about and I felt I had to talk to someone."

For the first time Jones noticed the confused expression in Parker's eyes. "What's bothering you?"

Parker downed the Scotch and stared at the empty glass.

"We've just taken on the damnedest cargo I've ever seen come on board a cruise liner."

"What did you load?" asked Jones, his curiosity aroused.

Parker sat quite still, shaking his head. "Painting gear. Air compressors, brushes, rollers and fifty drums of what I assumed was paint."

Jones couldn't resist asking, "What color?"

Parker shook his head. "Can't say. The drums were marked in Spanish."

"Nothing odd about that. The company must want it on hand when the *Lady Flamborough* goes in for a refit."

"That's only the half of it. We transshipped huge rolls of plastic."

"Plastic?"

"And great sheets of fiberboard," Parker continued. "We must have loaded kilometers of the stuff. We barely squeezed it through the loading doors. Mucked around a good three hours just trying to stow it."

Jones stared at his glass through half-open

eyes. "What do you suppose the company plans to do with it?"

Parker looked up at Jones with a puzzled frown. "I haven't the foggiest idea."

35

The Egyptian and Mexican security agents came on board soon after sunup and proceeded to inspect the ship for hidden explosives and make cursory checks of the crew members' records for any hint of a possible assassin. Except for a sprinkling of Indians and Pakistanis, the members of the crew were British, and had no quarrel with the governments of either Egypt or Mexico.

Ammar's terrorist team all spoke fluent English and acted very cooperative, showing their counterfeit British passports and insurance-security documents when asked, and offering their assistance in the ship's inspection.

President De Lorenzo came on board later in the morning. He was a short man in his early sixties, physically robust, with wind-blown gray hair, mournful dark eyes, and the suffering look of an intellectual condemned to a mental institution.

He was welcomed by Ammar impersonating Captain Collins in an award-winning performance. The ship's orchestra played the Mexican national anthem, and then the Mexican leader and his staff were escorted to their suites on the starboard side of the *Lady Flamborough.*

In the middle of the afternoon a yacht belonging to a wealthy Egyptian exporter came alongside and President Hasan climbed onto the ship. The Egyptian leader was the complete opposite of his Mexican counterpart. He was younger, just past his fifty-fourth birthday, with thinning, black hair. He stood slim and tall, yet he moved with the halting movements of a man who was ill. His dusky eyes were watery and seemed to stare through a filter of suspicion.

The ceremony was repeated and President Hasan along with his staff were quartered in the suites running the length of the port side.

Over fifty Third World heads of state had arrived in Punta del Este for the economic summit. Some chose to stay in palatial estates owned by their nation's citizens or at the exclusive Cantegril Country Club. Others preferred the offshore quiet of the cruise ships.

Visiting diplomats and journalists soon crowded the streets and restaurants. Uruguayan officials worried whether they could cope with the sudden mass of important foreigners combined with the routine influx of tourists. The nation's military force and police units did their best to control the situation, but they were soon overwhelmed by the human tidal wave sweeping the streets, and they gave up all attempts at traffic control, concentrating their efforts on guarding the summit meeting leaders.

Ammar stood on the starboard bridge wing and surveyed the teeming city through binoculars. He lowered them for a moment and checked his watch for the time.

His close friend Ibn studied him carefully. "Are you counting the minutes until nightfall, Suleiman Aziz?"

"Sunset in forty-three minutes," said Ammar without turning.

"The water is busy," said Ibn, nodding at the fleet of small boats darting around the harbor, their decks crowded with journalists demanding interviews and tourists hoping to spot international celebrities.

"Allow no one to board except Egyptian and Mexican delegates who belong on De Lorenzo and Hasan's staffs."

"And if any wish to go ashore before we leave port?"

"Permit them to do so," said Ammar. "Ship's routine must appear normal. The confusion in the city works to our advantage. We won't be missed until it's too late."

"The port authorities are no fools. When our lights fail to come on after dark, they will investigate."

"They'll be notified that our main generator is under repair." Ammar pointed toward another cruise liner that was anchored farther offshore between the *Lady Flamborough* and the encircling peninsula. "From shore her lights will seem like ours."

"Unless someone looks closely enough."

Ammar shrugged. "One hour is all we need to make the open sea. The Uruguayan security will not consider a search outside the harbor before daylight."

"If the Egyptian and Mexican security agents are to be removed in time," said Ibn, "we must begin now."

"Your weapons are heavily silenced?"

"Our fire will sound no louder than the clap of hands."

Ammar gave Ibn a piercing stare. "Stealth and quiet, my friend. Use whatever deception necessary to isolate and take them out one at a time. No hue or cry. If any escape overboard and alert the security forces on shore, we all die. Make sure your men understand."

"We'll need every strong back and pair of hands we can muster for this night's work."

"Then it's time to earn our fee and make Yazid ruler of Egypt."

The Egyptian guards were the first to be eliminated. Having no reason to distrust Ammar's fake insurance-security agents, they

407

were easily lured into vacant passenger suites that quickly became killing grounds.

Any ruse that rang with a grain of truth was used to decoy the security men. The lie that worked best was deceiving them into believing one of their high-ranking officials was stricken with food poisoning and the ship's captain required their presence.

Once the Egyptian agents crossed the threshold, the door was closed and a hijacker coldly shot them pointblank in the heart. While the blood was quickly cleaned away, the bodies were stacked in an adjoining bedroom.

When the Mexicans' turn arrived, two of De Lorenzo's guards became suspicious, refusing to enter the suite. But they were swiftly overpowered and knifed in an empty passageway before they could sound the alarm.

One by one the security agents went to their deaths, twelve in all, until only two Egyptians and three Mexicans, standing guard outside their leaders' suites, were left.

Dusk was closing in from the east as Ammar shed his ship's captain's uniform and donned a black cotton jumpsuit. Next he peeled off the latex disguise and slipped a small jester's mask over his face.

He was in the act of tightening a heavy belt containing two automatic pistols and a portable radio around his waist when Ibn knocked and entered the cabin.

"Five remain," he reported. "They can only be taken by direct assault."

"Good work," said Ammar. He gave Ibn a steady stare. "We're past the need for subterfuge. Rush them, but warn your men to be cautious. I don't want Hasan and De Lorenzo accidentally killed."

Ibn nodded and gave the order to one of his men waiting outside the door. Then he turned and again faced Ammar with a confident smile. "Consider the ship secure."

Ammar motioned toward a large brass chronometer above Captain Collins's desk. "We shove off in thirty-seven minutes. Collect all passengers and crew members, except the ship's engineers. See that the engine-room crew is prepared to get underway when I give the command. Assemble the rest in the main dining salon. It's time to reveal ourselves and deliver our demands."

Ibn did not respond but stood without moving, the smile spreading until every tooth showed. "Allah has blessed us with great fortune," he said at last.

Ammar looked at him. "We'll know better whether he's blessed us five days from now."

"He's already sent a good omen. She is here."

"She? Who are you talking about?"

"Hala Kamil."

At first Ammar could not comprehend.

Then he could not believe. "Kamil, she's here on this ship?"

"She stepped on board less than ten minutes ago," announced Ibn, beaming. "I've placed her under guard in one of the female crew members' quarters."

"Allah is indeed kind," said Ammar incredulously.

"Yes, he has sent the fly to the spider," Ibn said darkly, "and given you a second chance to kill her in the name of Akhmad Yazid."

Just as darkness was approaching, a light tropical rain cleared the sky and passed northward. Lights were blinking to life along Punta del Este's streets and on board the ships in the harbor, casting flickering reflections across the water.

Senator Pitt thought it strange that nothing showed of the *Lady Flamborough* except her outline against the brightly lit glow of the ship moored behind her. She looked dark and deserted as the launch swung past her bow and came alongside the boarding stairs.

Carrying only a briefcase, the Senator jumped lightly onto the narrow platform. He had hardly climbed two steps before the launch turned away and headed back to the dock area. He reached the deck and found himself standing alone. Something was terribly wrong. His first thought was that he'd boarded the wrong ship.

The only sounds, the only sounds of life were a voice somewhere within the super-structure coming through a speaker system, and the generators humming deep in the bowels of the hull.

He turned to hail the launch but it had already traveled too far for him to be heard above the exhaust of its tired old diesel engine. Then a figure in a black jumpsuit stepped out of the shadows, holding an automatic rifle leveled at the Senator's stomach.

"Is this the *Lady Flamborough*?" the Senator demanded.

"Who are you?" the voice came back in little more than a whisper. "What is your business here?" The guard stood there, gun held rock-steady, staring with his head cocked at an angle while the Senator explained his presence.

"Senator George Pitt, you say. An American. You were not expected."

"President Hasan was informed of my arrival," said the Senator impatiently. "Please lower your weapon and take me to his quarters."

The guard's eyes glinted suspiciously from the glare of the lights on shore. "Anyone else come with you?"

"No, I'm quite alone."

"You must return ashore."

The Senator tilted his head at the retreating launch. "My transportation has left."

The guard seemed to be thinking it over. Finally he lowered the gun and silently walked a few steps down the deck and stopped beside a doorway. He held out a free hand and nodded toward the briefcase.

"In here," he said softly as though it was some kind of secret. "Give me your case."

"These are official documents," said the Senator flatly. He clutched his briefcase in both hands and brushed past the guard.

He walked into a heavy black curtain, slapped it to one side and found himself standing in a 2,000-square-meter ballroom/dining salon. The vast room was paneled in oak and styled after an English manor. A small army of people, some standing, some sitting, wearing either business suits or crew uniforms turned and gazed at him in unison as though he were a ball in a tennis match.

There were nine men spread around the walls, silent, deadly serious men dressed alike in the black jumpsuits and matching jogging shoes; each slowly swept the muzzle of a shoulder-slung automatic weapon back and forth over their captive audience.

"Welcome," came the amplified voice of a figure standing on a stage in front of a microphone, a man indistinguishable from the others except for a comical mask covering his face — but with that any sign of humor quickly came to a halt. "Please state

412

your identity."

Senator Pitt stared in confusion. "What's going on here?"

"You will please answer my question," said Ammar with icy politeness.

"Senator George Pitt, United States Congress. I'm here to confer with President Hasan of Egypt. I was told he was staying on board this ship."

"You'll find President Hasan seated in the front row."

"Why are these men holding guns on everyone?"

Ammar feigned weary patience. "Why, Senator, I thought it obvious. You've blindly walked into the middle of a hijacking."

A growing incomprehension and the tentative beginnings of a dazed fear mushroomed inside Senator Pitt. He moved forward as if hypnotized, past Captain Collins and his officers, and stared at the pale, familiar faces of Presidents Hasan and De Lorenzo. He stopped short and looked down into the stricken eyes of Hala Kamil.

At that moment he realized people were going to die.

He silently put his arm around Hala's shoulder and was swept with sudden anger. "In God's name, do you know what you're doing?"

"I know very well what I'm doing," said Ammar. "Allah has worked with me every

413

step of the way. In your poker idiom, he has sweetened the pot by raising the stakes with the unexpected arrivals of the Secretary-General of the United Nations, and now a distinguished Senator from the United States."

"You've made a grave mistake," the Senator snarled defiantly. "You'll never live to get away with this and brag about it."

"Ah, but I can and I will."

"Impossible!"

"Not impossible at all," said Ammar with an ominous finality in his voice. "As you shall soon see."

36

Nichols had donned his overcoat and was stuffing papers inside his attaché case before departing for home when his secretary leaned through his open door.

"A gentleman from Langley is here with a drop."

"Have him come in."

A CIA agent whom Nichols recognized entered carrying an old-fashioned leather accountant's-style briefcase.

"You caught me just in time, Keith," said Nichols. "I was on my way home."

Keith Farquar had a bushy moustache, thick brown hair, and wore horn-rimmed glasses. A large, no-nonsense type of man with contemplative eyes, he was, Nichols thought, the kind of agent who made up the solid bulwark of the Central Intelligence Agency.

Without an invitation Farquar sat down in a chair, placed the case on his lap and set the correct numbers on a combination lock that released the catch and switched off the circuit of a small incendiary explosive inside. He lifted out a thin file and placed it on the desk in front of Nichols.

"Mr. Brogan instructed me to tell you that hard data on Akhmad Yazid is extremely sparse. Biographical records regarding birth, parents and ancestors, schooling, marriage, children, or any mention in legal proceedings either criminal or civil, are virtually nonexistent. Most of what our Middle East section was able to put together comes from descriptions of people who have known him. Unfortunately, most of them, for one reason or another, became enemies of Yazid. So their accounts are somewhat biased."

"Did your psychological section make up a profile?" asked Nichols.

"They put together a rough projection. Yazid is as hard to penetrate as a desert sandstorm. A shroud of security has covered him in mystery. Journalists' interviews with people around him are met with ambiguity and vague shrugs."

"Which adds to the mirage," commented Nichols.

Farquar smiled. "Mr. Brogan's exact description of Yazid. 'An elusive mirage.' "

"Thank you for bringing the file by," said Nichols. "And thank everyone involved with assembling the information for me."

"Anything for a client." Farquar snapped

the catches closed on his briefcase and ambled toward the door. "Have a nice evening."

"You too."

Nichols buzzed for his secretary. She appeared wearing a coat and holding a purse. "Anything I can do before I leave?" she asked apprehensively, afraid she would be asked to work overtime for the third night in a row.

"Could you please call my wife on your way out?" asked Nichols. "And tell her not to worry. I'll make the dinner party, but will be delayed for about half an hour."

His secretary sighed thankfully. "Yes, sir, I'll tell her. Good night."

"Good night."

Nichols slipped his pipe between his teeth but didn't pack or light the bowl. He set his attaché case off to the side of his desk, and, still wearing his overcoat, he sat down and examined Yazid's file.

Farquar had not exaggerated. It was slim pickings. Although the last six years were heavily reported, Yazid's life before his rapid rise from obscurity took up little more than a paragraph. His debut in the news media began with his arrest by Egyptian police during a sit-in demonstration for Cairo's starving masses inside the lobby of a luxury tourist hotel. He had distinguished himself by preaching in the worst slum areas of the country.

Akhmad Yazid stated he was born in squalid poverty in a mud hut among the decaying mausoleums of the City of the Dead that spilled into the garbage dumps of Cairo. His family lived on the thin margin between survival and death until his two sisters and father died from disease brought on by hunger and filthy living conditions.

He had no formal schooling except what was given during his adolescent years by Islamic holy men, none of whom were found to back up this assertion. Yazid claimed Muhammad the Prophet spoke through him, uttering divine revelations to the faithful and urging them to return Egypt to a utopian Islamic state.

Yazid possessed a resonant speaking voice. He had the skilled mannerisms and delivery to enrapture a crowd of listeners, slowly building them to a fever pitch at the finish. He insisted Western philosophy was incapable of resolving Egypt's social/economic problems. He preached that all Egyptians are members of a lost generation who must find themselves through his moral vision.

Though he vehemently claimed otherwise, evidence indicated he was not above using terrorism to achieve his goals. Five separate incidents, including the murder of a high-ranking Air Force general, a truck explosion outside the Soviet Embassy, and the execution-style killing of four university teachers who spoke out in favor of Western ways, were traced to Yazid's doorstep. Nothing was proven but through sketchy information gained from Muslim informants, CIA analysts felt certain Yazid was planning a masterstroke to eliminate President Hasan and sweep into power on a rising wave of public acclaim.

Nichols laid down the file and finally filled and lit his pipe. A tiny, indefinable thought tugged at him from the far reaches of his mind.

Something about the report struck him as vaguely familiar. He laid aside a glossy photo of Yazid glaring malevolently at the camera.

The answer suddenly struck Nichols. It was simple and it was shocking.

He picked up his telephone and punched the coded number of a direct line, impatiently drumming the desk top with his fingers until a voice answered on the other end.

"This is Brogan."

"Martin, thank heavens you're working late. This is Dale Nichols."

"What can I do for you, Dale?" asked the Director of the CIA. "Did you get the packet on Akhmad Yazid?"

"Yes, thank you," replied Nichols. "I've gone through it and found something you can help me with."

"Sure, what is it?"

"I need two sets of blood types and finger-prints."

"Fingerprints?"

"That's right."

"We use genetic codes and DNA tracing nowadays," Brogan answered indulgently. "Any particular reason in mind?"

Nichols paused to collect his thoughts. "If I tell you, I swear to God you'll think I should be fitted for a straitjacket."

Yaeger pulled off his granny reading glasses, tucked them into the pocket of a denim jacket, shuffled and stacked a pile of computer reports, then settled back in his chair and sipped from a can of diet soda.

"Zilch," he said almost sadly. "A wasted effort up and down the line. A 1,600-year-old trail is too cold to follow without solid data. A computer can't go back in time and tell you exactly how it was."

"Maybe Dr. Gronquist can determine where the *Serapis* made landfall after he's had a chance to study the artifacts," Lily said optimistically.

Pitt sat two rows below and off to one side from the others in NUMA's small amphitheater. "I talked to him by radio an hour ago. He's found nothing that isn't Mediterranean in origin."

A three-dimensional projection of the Atlantic Ocean showing land folds and the irregular geology of the sea bottom filled a screen above the stage. Everyone seemed obsessed by it. Their eyes were drawn to the contoured imagery even as they spoke.

Everyone, that is, except Admiral James Sandecker. His eyes suspiciously observed Al Giordino, particularly the large cigar sprouting from one side of the Assistant Project Director's mouth as if it had grown from a seedling.

"When did you start buying Hoyo de Monterrey Excaliburs?"

Giordino looked at the Admiral with an innocent expression. "You talking to me, Admiral?"

"Since you and I are the only ones in the theater smoking Excaliburs, and I'm not in the habit of talking to myself, yes."

"Great, full flavor," said Giordino, holding up the fat cigar and expelling a gush of blue smoke. "I commend your discriminating taste."

"Where did you get it?"

"A little shop in Baltimore. I forget the name."

Sandecker wasn't fooled for an instant. Giordino had been stealing his expensive cigars for years. What drove the Admiral up the wall was that he never discovered how. No matter how well he hid or locked them away, his inventory count always showed two missing every week.

Giordino kept the secret from Pitt so his best friend would never have to lie if asked how it was done. Only Giordino and an old buddy from the Air Force who was a professional burglar for an intelligence agency knew the technicalities of Operation Stogie.

"I've a good notion to ask to see a receipt," growled Sandecker.

"We've been attacking this thing from the wrong angle," Pitt said, steering the meeting back on course.

"There's another angle?" asked Yaeger. "We took the only logical approach open to us."

"Without any reference to direction, it was an impossible job," Lily backed him.

"A pity Rufinus didn't log his daily positions and distance traveled," mused Sandecker.

"He was under strict orders not to record anything."

"Could they determine a position back then?" asked Giordino.

Lily nodded. "Hipparchus the Greek determined the positions of earth landmarks by figuring their latitude and longitude a hundred and thirty years before Christ."

Sandecker laced his hands across his trim stomach and gazed at Pitt over his reading glasses. "I know that lost look in your eyes. Something's nagging at you."

Pitt slouched in his seat. "We've been judging facts and using guesswork without considering the man who conceived the smuggling plan."

"Junius Venator?"

"A brilliant guy," Pitt continued, "who was described by a contemporary as 'a daring innovator who struck out into areas other scholars feared to tread.' The question we've overlooked is, if we were in Venator's shoes, where would we have taken and hidden the great art and literary treasures of our time?"

"I still say Africa," volunteered Yaeger. "Preferably around the Cape somewhere up a river along the eastern coastline."

"Yet your computers couldn't make a marriage."

"They never came close," Yaeger admitted. "But God only knows how land formations have changed since Venator's day."

"Could Venator have taken the fleet northeast into the Black Sea?" Lily queried.

"Rufinus was specific about a voyage of fifty-eight days," said Giordino.

Sandecker, puffing his cigar, nodded. "Yes, but if the fleet was hit by foul weather or adverse winds, they could have traveled less than a thousand miles in that time."

"The Admiral has a point," Yaeger conceded. "Ancient ships of the period were constructed to run with the sea and before the wind. Their rigging was not efficient for windward sailing. Heavy-weather conditions

could have cut their progress by eighty percent."

"Except," Pitt said, hanging on the word,
"Venator loaded his ships 'with four times
their normal supply of provisions.' "

"He planned for an extended voyage," said
Lily, suddenly intrigued. "Venator never
intended to land every few days and resupply
his fleet."

"All that that proves to me," said Sandecker, "is that Venator wanted to keep the
entire voyage as secret as possible by never
coming ashore and leaving a trail."

Pitt shook his head. "As soon as the ships
cleared the Straits of Gibraltar, any need for
secrecy evaporated. Venator was free and in
the clear. Byzantine warships sent to stop him
would be as much in the dark as we are of
his next course heading."

Yaeger looked quizzically at Pitt. "So we
put ourselves in Venator's shoes or sandals or
whatever they wore then. What's our plan?"

"Dr. Rothberg unknowingly came up with
the key to the mystery," Pitt explained. "He
thought Venator buried the artifacts where no
one of his day would think to look."

Yaeger looked at him blankly. "That could
be anywhere in the ancient world."

"Or outside of the world as the Romans
knew it."

"Charted geography didn't extend very far
below North Africa or east of the Black Sea

and Persian Gulf," said Lily. "Nothing was explored beyond."

"We don't know that," Pitt disagreed. "Junius Venator had access to four thousand years of man's knowledge. He knew of the existence of the African continent and the great steppes of Russia. He must have known of trade with India, which in turn imported and exported goods from China. And he'd have studied the records of voyages that sailed far beyond the usual Roman/Byzantine trade routes."

"We're certain the Alexandria Library had an entire section devoted to geographical records," said Lily. "Venator could have worked from source maps compiled from much earlier times."

"What do you think he discovered that influenced him?" asked Sandecker.

"A direction," Pitt answered.

All had focused their curiosity on Pitt, and he did not disappoint them. He walked down to the stage and picked up a flashlight that shone a small arrow on the three-dimensional projection.

"The only question in my mind," said Giordino, "is whether the fleet turned north or south."

"Neither." Pitt moved the lighted arrow through the Gibraltar Straits and across the Atlantic. "Venator led his fleet west to the Americas."

His statement was greeted with stunned disbelief.

"There is no archaeological evidence supporting pre-Columbian contact in the Americas," Lily stated firmly.

"The *Serapis* is a pretty good indicator they could have made such a voyage," said Sandecker.

"It's a heated controversy," admitted Pitt. "But there are too many similarities in Mayan art and culture that cannot be ignored. Ancient America may not have been as isolated from European and Asian influence as we once thought."

"Frankly, I buy it," said Yaeger, his enthusiasm restored. "I'd bet my Willie Nelson record collection the Phoenicians, the Egyptians, Greeks, Romans and Vikings all landed on North and South American soil before Columbus."

"No self-respecting archaeologist would take you up on it," said Lily.

Giordino grinned at her. "That's because they won't stake their precious reputations on it."

Sandecker looked at Yaeger. "Let's give the project another try."

Yaeger looked at Pitt. "What shorelines do you want me to cover?"

Pitt scratched his chin. He realized he badly needed a shave. "Begin at the fjord in Greenland and work south down to Panama." He paused to stare at the chart projection with thoughtful curiosity. "It has to be along there somewhere."

37

Captain Oliver Collins rapped a knuckle against the bridge barometer. He squinted at the needle barely visible from the lights on shore and cursed under his breath at the fair-weather reading. If only there was a storm, he thought, the ship could not have left the harbor. Captain Collins was a first-rate seaman, but a poor judge of human nature.

Suleiman Aziz Ammar would have ordered the *Lady Flamborough* to sea in the middle of a hurricane with ninety-knot winds. He sat tensely in the captain's seat behind the bridge windows and wiped away the sweat from around his neck that had trickled from his chin.

The mask was a torture in the humid climate, and so were the gloves he wore constantly. He suffered the discomfort stoically. If the hijacking failed and he escaped, international intelligence services could never identify him with witnesses or fingerprints.

One of his men had taken the helm and

was looking at him expectantly across the darkened bridge. Two more were guarding the bridge doorways, their guns aimed at Collins and First Officer Finney, who was standing next to Ammar's helmsman.

The tide had come in and swung the ship on her anchor until her bow was pointing toward the harbor entrance. Ammar made one final sweep of the harbor and dock area with a pair of binoculars and then motioned at Finney with his hand while speaking into a small radio.

"Now," he ordered, "get her underway and launch the labor crews."

Finney, his face twisted in anger, looked at Collins imploringly for a sign of defiance. But the Captain gave a subdued shrug and the first officer reluctantly gave the command to raise the anchor.

Two minutes later, dripping silt from the harbor bottom, the anchor rose out of the black water and was pulled tight against the hawsehole. The helmsman stood by the wheel but made no move to grasp the spokes. On modern ships manual steering is used mostly during heavy weather and while under the command of pilots upon entering and departing port. It was Finney who steered the ship and regulated the speed from a panel tied through fiber optics to the ship's automated control system. He also kept a sharp eye on the radar screen.

Once the ship was free of port the helm was placed on automatic pilot, and ringing the chief engineer down below for "Slow Ahead" on the bridge telegraph was quickly becoming more of a tradition than a necessity.

Moving wraithlike in the evening darkness, her outline visible only when she blocked off lights from the opposite shore, the *Lady Flamborough* slipped through the crowded harbor indistinct and unnoticed. Her diesels murmured faintly as the big bronze screws bit through the water.

Like a ghost feeling its way through the tombstones of a cemetery, the ship wove its way around the other moored ships and turned into the narrow channel for the open sea.

Ammar picked up the bridge phone and called the communications room.

"Anything?" he asked tersely.

"Nothing yet," answered his man who monitored the radio frequencies of the Uruguayan navy patrol boats.

"Patch any signal through to the bridge speakers."

"Affirmative."

"A small boat crossing our bow dead ahead," announced Finney. "We have to give way."

Ammar placed the muzzle of an automatic pistol against the base of Finney's skull.

"Maintain course and speed."

"We're on a collision course," Finney protested. "The ship has no lights. They can't see us."

Ammar's only reply was to increase the pressure of the gun muzzle.

They could clearly see the approaching boat now. She was a large custom-designed motor yacht. Collins guessed her dimensions at forty meters in length with a beam of eight meters. She was beautiful and elegant, and she blazed with lights. There was a party on board and people were grouped in conversation or dancing on her spacious sun decks. Collins was stricken to see the radar antenna wasn't turning.

"Give them a blast of the horn," he implored. "Warn them while they still have a chance to give way."

Ammar ignored him.

The seconds ticked away under a cloud of dread until the collision was inevitable. The people partying on the yacht and the man at its helm were completely oblivious to the steel monster bearing down on them out of the dark.

"Inhuman!" Collins gasped. "This is inhuman."

The *Lady Flamborough* crashed bow-on into the starboard side of the big yacht. There was no heavy jar or shriek of metal against metal. The men on the bridge of the cruise liner felt

431

only a very slight tremor as the four-story bow crushed the smaller boat nearly under the water before slicing its hull in two.

The destruction was as devastating as a sledgehammer smashing a child's toy.

Collins's fists were clenched on the forward bridge railing as he gazed in horror at the disaster. He clearly heard the panicked screams of women as the yacht's shattered bow and stern sections scraped along the sides of the *Lady Flamborough* before they sank less than fifty meters astern. The dark surface of the liner's wake was littered with wreckage and bodies.

A few of the unfortunate passengers were thrown clear and were trying to swim clear while the injured grasped anything that would keep them afloat. Then they were lost in the night.

The bitterness and rage welled up in Finney's throat. "You murdering bastard!" He spat at Ammar.

"Only Allah knows the unforeseen," said Ammar, his voice remote and indifferent. He slowly pulled the automatic away from Finney's skull. "As soon as we clear the channel, bear on a heading of one-five-five degrees magnetic and engage the automatic pilot."

Gray-faced beneath his tropic tan, Collins turned and faced Ammar. "For God's sake, radio the Uruguayan sea-rescue service and give them a chance to save those poor people."

"No communications."

"They don't have to know who sent the transmission."

Ammar shook his head, "Less than an hour after the local authorities are alerted to the accident, an investigation will be underway by security forces. Our absence will quickly be discovered and a pursuit launched. I'm sorry, Captain, every nautical mile we put between our stern and Punta del Este is critical. The answer is no."

Collins stared into Ammar's eyes, stared without speaking while his stunned mind fought to orient itself. Then he said, "What price must be paid before you release my ship?"

"If you and your crew do what I command, no harm will come to any of you."

"And the passengers, Presidents De Lorenzo and Hasan and their staffs? What are your plans for them?"

"Eventually they will be ransomed. But for the next ten hours they're all going to get their hands dirty."

Bitter helplessness was sharp in Collins's mouth, but his voice was impassive. "You have no intention of holding them as hostages for money."

"Are you a mind reader as well as a sea captain?" asked Ammar with detached interest.

"It doesn't take an anthropologist to see your men were born in the Middle East. My guess is you intend to assassinate the Egyptians."

Ammar smiled emptily. "Allah decides man's fate. I only carry out my instructions."

"Instructions from what source?"

Before Ammar could reply, a voice broke over the bridge speakers. "Rendezvous at approximately zero two-thirty, Commander."

Ammar acknowledged on his portable transmitter. Then he looked at Collins. "There is no more time for conversation, Captain. We have a great deal to accomplish before daylight."

"What are your plans for my ship?" demanded Collins. "You owe me the answer to that question."

"Yes, of course, I owe you that," Ammar muttered automatically, his mind already training on another subject. "By this time tomorrow evening, international news services will report that the *Lady Flamborough* has been posted missing and presumed lost with all passengers and crew in two hundred fathoms of water."

38

"Did you hear something, Carlos?" the old fisherman asked as he gripped the worn spokes on the wheel of an ancient fishing boat.

The younger man, who was his son, cupped his ears and peered into the darkness beyond the bow. "You have better ears than mine, Papa. All I hear is our engine."

"I thought I heard someone, like a woman screaming for help."

The son paused, listened again and then shrugged. "Sorry, I still hear nothing."

"It was there." Luiz Chavez rubbed his grizzled beard on a sleeve and then pulled the throttle on idle. "I wasn't dreaming."

Chavez was in a hearty mood. The fish catch had been good. The holds were only half-full, but the nets had pulled in a quality and variety that would bring top prices from the chefs of the hotel and resort restaurants. The six bottles of beer that were sloshing in his stomach didn't hurt his jolly disposition either.

"Papa, I see something in the water."

"Where?"

Carlos pointed. "Off the port bow. Looks like pieces of a boat."

The old fisherman's eyes were not so sharp at night any more. He squinted and gazed in the direction his son was pointing. Then the running lights began to pick out scattered bits of wreckage. He recognized the bright white paint and varnished debris as coming from a yacht. An explosion, or perhaps a collision, he thought. He settled on a collision. The nearest lights of the port were only two kilometers away. An explosion would have been seen and heard. He saw no sign of navigation lights from rescue boats converging in the channel.

The boat was entering the debris field when his ears caught it again. What he had thought was a scream now sounded like sobbing. And it came from close by.

"Get Raul, Justino and Manuel from the galley. Quickly. Tell them to make ready to go in the water after survivors."

The boy rushed off as Chavez set the gear lever to "Stop." He stepped out of the wheelhouse and snapped on a spotlight and slowly swept its beam across the water.

He spotted two huddled shapes lying half across a small splintered section of teak decking and half in the water less than twenty meters away. One, a man, appeared inert. The other, a woman, her face like chalk, stared into the light and frantically waved. Then suddenly, she began yelling hysterically and thrashing at the water.

"Hold on!" Chavez shouted. "Don't panic. We're coming for you."

Chavez turned at the sound of running feet behind him. His crew had rushed out of the deckhouse and quickly crowded around him.

"Can you make anything out?" asked Luis.

"Two survivors floating on some wreckage. Get ready to pull them on board. One of you might have to go in the water and give them a hand."

"No one is going in the water tonight," said one of the crew, his face turning pale.

Chavez turned back to the survivors just as the woman let out a terrified shriek. His heart turned to ice as he saw the tall fin, the ugly head with the ink-spot eye, whipping back and forth with its jaws locked around the woman's lower legs.

"Adored Mary, Mother of Jesus!" muttered Luis, crossing himself as fast as his hand could move.

Chavez shuddered but could not pull his eyes away as the shark dragged the woman off farther into the water. Other sharks circled, drawn by the blood, bumping against the shattered deck until the body of the man rolled off. One of the fishermen turned and vomited over the side as the scream turned to an ungodly gurgling noise.

Then the night fell silent.

Less than an hour later, Colonel José Rojas, Uruguayan Chief Coordinator for Special Security, stood ramrod straight in front of a group of officers in battle dress. He had trained with the British Grenadier Guards after graduating from his country's military school, and he had taken up their antiquated habit of carrying a swagger stick.

He stood over a table containing a model diorama of the Punta del Este waterfront and addressed the assembled men. "We will organize into three roving teams to patrol the docks on rotating eight-hour shifts," he began while dramatically slapping the stick in the palm of one hand. "Our mission is to stand on constant alert as a backup force in the event of a terrorist attack. I realize it's difficult for you to look inconspicuous, but try anyway. Stay in the shadows at night and off the main thoroughfares by day. We don't want to frighten the tourists into thinking Uruguay is an armed state. Any questions?"

Lieutenant Eduardo Vazquez raised a hand. "Colonel?"

"Vazquez?"

"If we see someone who looks suspicious, what should we do?"

"You do nothing except report him. He'll

438

probably turn out to be one of the international security agents."

"What if he appears to be armed?"

Rojas sighed. "Then you'll *know* he's a security agent. Leave international incidents to the diplomats. Is everyone clear?"

No hands went up.

Rojas dismissed the men and walked to his temporary office in the Harbor Master's building. He stopped at a coffee machine to pour a cup when his aide approached.

"Captain Flores in Naval Affairs asked if you could meet him downstairs."

"Did he say why?"

"Only that it was urgent."

Rojas didn't want to spill his coffee, so he took the elevator instead of the stairs. Flores, impeccable in a white navy dress uniform, greeted him on the first floor but offered no explanations as he escorted Rojas across the street to a large shed that housed the coastal rescue boats. Inside, a group of men were examining several mangled fragments that looked to the Colonel as if they came from a boat.

Captain Flores introduced him to Chavez and his son. "These fishermen have just brought in this wreckage, which they discovered in the channel," he explained. "They say it looked to them like a yacht had been crushed in a collision with a large ship."

"Why should a yachting accident concern

special security?" asked Rojas.

The Harbor Master, a man with cropped hair and a bristling moustache, spoke up. "It may well be a disaster that could cast a cloud on the economic summit." He paused and added, "Rescue craft are on the scene now. So far no survivors have been found."

"Have you identified the yacht?"

"One of the scraps Mr. Chavez and his crew fished out of the water bears a nameplate. The craft was called the *Lola*."

Rojas shook his head. "I'm a soldier. Pleasure boats are not familiar. Is the name supposed to mean something to me?"

"The yacht was named for the wife of Victor Rivera," answered Flores. "You know him?"

Rojas stiffened. "I am acquainted with the Speaker of our Chamber of Deputies. The yacht was his?"

"Registered in his name," Flores nodded. "We've already contacted his secretary at her home. Gave her no information, of course. Merely inquired as to Mr. Rivera's whereabouts. She said he was on board his yacht hosting a party for Argentinean and Brazilian diplomats."

"How many?" Rojas inquired, a fear growing within him.

"Rivera and his wife, twenty-three guests and five crew members. Thirty in all."

440

"Names?"

"The secretary did not have the guest list in front of her. I've taken the liberty of sending my aide to Rivera's headquarters for a copy."

"I think it best if I take command of the investigation from this point," stated Rojas officially.

"The Navy stands ready to offer every assistance," said Flores, happy to wash his hands of any authority.

Rojas turned to the Harbor Master. "What ship was involved with the collision?"

"A mystery. No ship has arrived or departed the harbor in the last ten hours."

"Is it possible for a ship to enter port without you knowing?"

"A captain would be stupid to try it without calling for a pilot."

"Is it possible?" Rojas persisted.

"No," stated the Harbor Master firmly. "No oceangoing ship could dock or moor in the harbor without my being aware of it."

Rojas accepted that. "Suppose one sailed out?"

The Harbor Master considered the question for a few moments. Then he gave a slight nod. "One could not cast off from a dock without my knowledge. But if the vessel was anchored offshore, if her skipper or his officers knew the channel, and if she ran without lights, she might make it out to sea unnoticed. But I must say it would be close to a miracle."

"Can you furnish Captain Flores with a list of moored ships?"

"I'll have a copy in his hands within ten minutes."

"Captain Flores?"

"Colonel?"

"Since a missing ship is a naval operation, I'd like you to take command of the search."

"Gladly, Colonel. I'll begin immediately."

Rojas stared thoughtfully at the wreckage littering the concrete floor. "There'll be hell to pay before this night is through," he muttered.

Shortly before midnight, after Captain Flores had conducted a thorough search of the harbor and the waters outside the channel, he notified Rojas that the only ship he could not account for was the *Lady Flamborough.*

Colonel Rojas was stunned when he examined the cruise liner's VIP passenger list. He demanded a follow-up investigation in the false hope that the Egyptian and Mexican Presidents had disembarked for quarters on shore. Not until it was confirmed that they were missing along with the ship did the horrible specter of a terrorist hijacking become evident.

An extensive air search was launched at dawn. Every aircraft the combined air forces of Uruguay, Argentina and Brazil could put in the air scoured over 400,000 square kilometers of the South Atlantic.

No sign of the *Lady Flamborough* was found.

It was as though she had been swallowed by the sea.

39

Two hands were running under his shirt and up his back. He struggled to wake from a sound sleep, dreaming he was deep in the water swimming upward toward the shimmering surface, but never able to reach it. He rubbed his eyes, saw he was still on the couch in his office, and rolled over, his gaze blocked by a pair of shapely legs.

Pitt came to a sitting position and stared into Lily's beguiling eyes. He held up his wrist, but he had taken his watch off and placed it on the desk with his keys, change and wallet.

"What time is it?" he asked.

"Five-thirty," she replied sweetly, moving her hands across his shoulders and massaging his neck.

"Night or day?"

"Late afternoon. You only dozed off for three hours."

"Don't you ever drop off?"

"I can get by with only four hours' sleep

out of every twenty-four."

He yawned. "Your next husband has my deepest sympathy."

"Here's some coffee." She set a cup on an end table near his head.

Pitt slipped on his shoes and tucked in his shirttails. "Yaeger found anything?"

"Yes."

"The river?"

"No, not yet. Hiram is very mysterious about it, but he claims you were right. Venator sailed across the Atlantic before either the Vikings or Columbus."

He took a sip of the coffee and made a face. "This is almost solid sugar."

Lily looked surprised. "Al said you always take four spoonfuls."

"Al lied. I prefer it pure black with grounds on the bottom of the cup."

"I'm sorry," she said with an unremorseful smile. "I guess I was taken in by a practical joker."

"You're not the first," he said, staring out the door of his office.

Giordino was seated with his feet on Yaeger's desk, devouring the last slice of a pizza while he studied a detailed topographic map of a shoreline.

Yaeger sat with bloodshot eyes aimed at a computer monitor while jotting notes on a pad. He did not have to turn as Pitt and Lily entered the room. He could see their reflections in the screen.

"We've made a breakthrough," he said with some satisfaction.

Pitt asked, "What have you got?"

"Instead of concentrating on every nook and cranny south from the *Serapis*'s grave in Greenland, I leapfrogged down to Maine and began looking for a match-up of his landing description."

"And it paid off," Pitt said in anticipation.

"Yes. If you recall, Rufinus wrote that after they deserted Venator, they were battered by storms from the south for thirty-one days before finding a safe bay where they could make repairs to the ship. On the next leg of the voyage more storms blew away the sails and tore off the steering oars. Then the ship drifted for an unspecified number of days before ending up in the Greenland fjord."

Yaeger stopped and called up a chart of the American side of the North Atlantic on the monitor. Next his fingers nimbly punched out a series of codes. A small line formed and began traveling southward from the east coast of Greenland south in a broken, zig-zagged path around Newfoundland, past Nova Scotia and New England, ending at a point slightly above Atlantic City.

"New Jersey?" muttered Pitt, puzzled.

"Barnegat Bay, to be exact," said Giordino. He brought over the topographic map and laid it on a table. Then he circled a section of the coast with a red marker.

"Barnegat Bay, New Jersey?" Pitt repeated.

"The shape of the land was quite different back in three ninety-one," Yaeger lectured matter-of-factly. "The beach strand was more broken and the bay was deeper and more sheltered."

"How did you arrive at this exact spot?" asked Pitt.

"In describing the bay, Rufinus mentioned a great sea of dwarflike pines where fresh water seeped from the sand with the jab of a stick. New Jersey has a forest of dwarf pines that fits the description. It's called the Pine Barrens, and it spreads across the southern center of the state bordering on the coast to the east. The water level is just under the surface. During spring runoff or after heavy rains you can literally poke a hole in the sandy soil and strike water."

"Looks promising," said Pitt. "But didn't Rufinus also say they added ballast stone?"

"I admit that had me baffled. So I put in a call to a geologist at the Army Corps of Engineers. He came up with a stone quarry that pinpointed almost the exact site where I believe the *Serapis*'s crew landed."

"Nice job," said Pitt gratefully. "You've put the show on the right track."

"Where do we go from here?" asked Lily.

"I'll continue working south," answered

Yaeger. "At the same time I'll have my people compute an approximate trace of Venator's course west from Spain. With hindsight, it seems obvious the islands that made up the fleet's first landfall after leaving the Mediterranean were the West Indies. By continuing the *Serapis*'s path from New Jersey and projecting Venator's track to the Americas, we should arrive at an approximate intersect within five hundred miles of a river that fits the bill."

Lily looked skeptical. "I fail to see how you expect to trace Venator's track when he censored all accounts of heading, currents, winds and distances."

"No great flash," Yaeger replied dryly. "I'll lift the log data from the voyages of Columbus to the New World, taking his computed course and adjusting it for differences in hull design and water friction, rigging, and sail area between his ships and the Byzantine fleet a thousand years earlier."

"You make it sound simple."

"Believe me, it's not. We may be homing in on the target, but it's going to take another solid four days of study to get us there."

The weariness and long hours of tedious study seemed forgotten. Yaeger's reddened eyes blazed with determination. Lily appeared to be galvanized with excess energy. They were poised for the starter's gun.

"Do it," said Pitt. "Find the Library."

Pitt thought Sandecker sent for him for a status report on the search, but the instant he saw the somber expression on the Admiral's face, he knew there was a problem. What really bothered Pitt was the soft look in the Admiral's eyes; they were usually as hard as flint.

Then when Sandecker came over and took him by the arm and led him to a couch and sat down alongside, Pitt *knew* there was a problem.

"I've just received some disturbing news from the White House," Sandecker began. "The cruise ship that was hosting Presidents De Lorenzo and Hasan at the economic summit in Uruguay is suspected of being hijacked."

"I'm sorry to hear it," said Pitt, "but how does that affect NUMA?"

"Hala Kamil was on board."

"Damn!"

"And so was the Senator."

"My father?" Pitt muttered in surprise. "I talked to him by phone the night before last. How did he come to be in Uruguay?"

"He was on a mission for the President."

Pitt stood up, paced back and forth and then sat down again. "What's the situation?"

"The *Lady Flamborough* — the name of the

449

British cruise liner — disappeared from the port of Punta del Este last night."

"Where is the ship now?"

"An extensive air search has yet to turn up a trace of her. The general consensus of the officials on the scene is that the *Lady Flamborough* lies at the bottom of the sea."

"Without absolute proof, I can't accept that."

"I'm with you."

"Weather conditions?"

"I gather from the report the area was fair with calm seas."

"Ships vanish in storms," said Pitt. "Seldom in calm seas."

Sandecker made an empty gesture with his hands. "Until more details come in we can only speculate."

Pitt could not believe his father was dead. What he heard was too inconclusive. "What is the White House doing about it?"

"The President's hands are tied."

"That's ridiculous," Pitt said sharply. "He could order all naval units in the area to assist in the search."

"That's the catch," said Sandecker. "Except for an occasional training exercise, none of which is occurring now, there are no United States naval units on station in the South Atlantic."

Pitt stood again and stared out the window at the lights of Washington. Then he fixed

Sandecker with a penetrating stare. "You're telling me the United States government is in no way involved with the search?"

"It looks that way."

"What's to stop NUMA from searching?"

"Nothing except we lack a fleet of Coast Guard vessels and an aircraft carrier."

"We have the *Sounder.*"

Sandecker stared back thoughtfully for a moment. Then his face took on a questioning expression. "One of our research vessels?"

"She's on a sonar mapping project of the continental slope off southern Brazil."

Sandecker nodded. "All right, I get your drift, but the *Sounder* is too slow to be of any help on an extensive sea search. What do you expect to accomplish with her?"

"If my father's ship can't be found on the surface, I'll hunt for her below."

"You could be looking at a thousand square miles, maybe more."

"The *Sounder's* sonar gear can cut a swath two miles wide, and she carries a submersible. All I need is your permission to take command of her."

"You'll need someone to back you up."

"Giordino and Rudi Gunn. We make a good team."

"Rudi is on a deep-sea mining operation off the Canary Islands."

"He could be in Uruguay in eighteen hours."

Sandecker clasped his hands behind his head and stared at the ceiling. Deep down he felt Pitt was chasing shadows, but he never doubted for an instant what his answer would be.

"Write your own ticket," he said in a level tone. "I'll back you."

"Thank you, Admiral," Pitt said. "I'm grateful."

"How does the Alexandria Library project stand?"

"Yaeger and Dr. Sharp are close to a solution. They don't need Al and me getting in the way."

Sandecker rose and placed both his hands on Pitt's shoulders. "He may not be dead, you know."

"Dad better *not* be dead," Pitt said with a grim smile. "I'd never forgive him."

40

"Dammit, Martin!" the President said abruptly. "Didn't your Middle East people smell a plot to hijack the *Lady Flamborough*?"

Martin Brogan, the CIA director, shrugged wearily. He was well insulated for taking the blame for every terrorist act that killed Americans or took them hostage. The CIA's successes were rarely heralded, but their mistakes were the stuff of Congressional investigations and hype from the news media.

"The ship, along with its entire passenger list and crew, was snatched from under the noses of the finest security agents in the world," he replied. "Whoever dreamed up the venture and executed it is one shrewd operator. The mere scope is far beyond any terrorist activity we've seen in the past. In light of this, I find it hardly surprising our counterterrorist network was not tipped off in advance."

Alan Mercier, the National Security Adviser, removed his glasses and idly wiped the lenses with a handkerchief. "My end struck out too," he said, backing up Brogan. "Analysis of our eavesdropping monitoring systems failed to reveal any hint of a potential cruise-liner hijacking and abduction of two foreign leaders."

"By sending George Pitt to meet with President Hasan, I sentenced an old friend to death," the President said regretfully.

"Not your fault," Mercier consoled him.

The President angrily pounded the desk with one fist. "The Senator, Hala Kamil, De Lorenzo and Hasan. I can't believe they're all gone."

"We don't know that for sure," said Mercier.

The President stared at him. "You can't hide a cruise liner and all the people on board, Alan. Even a dumb politician like me knows that."

"There is still a chance —"

"Chance, hell. It was a suicide mission plain and simple. All those poor people were probably locked up while the ship was scuttled. The terrorists never meant to escape. They went down too."

"All the facts aren't in yet," Mercier argued.

"Just what do we know?" demanded the President.

"Our experts are already in Punta del Este working with the Uruguayan security people," explained Brogan. "So far, we only have preliminary conclusions. First, the hijacking has been tied to an Arab group. Two witnesses came forward who were in a passing launch when they saw the *Lady Flamborough* taking on cargo from a landing barge. They heard crewmen on both vessels speaking Arabic. The landing barge has not been found and is assumed to be scuttled somewhere in the harbor."

"Any idea on the cargo?" asked Mercier.

"All the witnesses could recall seeing were some drums," answered Brogan. "Second, a phony report was given to the Harbor Master's office from the cruise liner saying its main generator had broken down, and the vessel would only run navigation lights until repairs were carried out. Then, as soon as it became dark, the unlit ship pulled up its anchor and slipped out of the harbor, colliding with a private yacht carrying important South American businessmen and diplomats. The only fumble in an otherwise flawless execution. Then it disappeared."

"Hardly a slop job," said Mercier, "unlike the botched second assassination attempt on Hala Kamil."

"A different group entirely," Brogan added.

Dale Nichols spoke up for the first time in the meeting. "Which you linked directly to Akhmad Yazid."

"Yes, the assassins were not very careful. Egyptian passports were found on the bodies. One, the leader, we identified as a mullah and fanatical follower of Yazid."

"Do you think Yazid's responsible for the hijacking?"

"He certainly had the motive," answered Brogan. "With President Hasan out of the way, he has a clear shot at taking over the Egyptian government."

"The same goes for President De Lorenzo, Topiltzin and Mexico," Nichols stated flatly.

"An interesting tie-in," said Mercier.

"What can we do besides send a few CIA terrorist investigators to Uruguay?" asked the President. "What are our options in helping with the search for the *Lady Flamborough*?"

"To answer the first part of your question," said Brogan, "very little. The investigation is in good hands. Uruguayan police and security intelligence chiefs were trained here and in Britain. They know the score and are most cooperative in working with our experts." He paused and avoided the President's eyes. "As to the second, again, very little. The Navy Department has no ships patrolling the ocean off South America. The nearest vessel to the area is a nuclear sub on a training exercise off Antarctica. Our Latin friends are doing fine without us. Over eighty military and commercial aircraft and at least fourteen ships from Argentina, Brazil and Uruguay have been combing the sea off Punta del Este since dawn."

"And they haven't found a clue to the *Lady Flamborough's* fate," said the President. What little optimism he had before was rapidly eroding into despondency.

"They will," said Mercier tersely.

"Wreckage and bodies most certainly will turn up," said Brogan candidly. "No ship that size can vanish without leaving some trace behind."

"Has the story broken in the press yet?" asked the President.

"I was informed it came over the wire services an hour ago," Nichols answered.

The President folded his hands and clenched them tightly. "Holy hell will cut loose in Congress when they find out one of their members is a victim of a terrorist act. No telling what kind of revenge they'll demand."

"The purpose of the Senator's mission alone is enough to cause a major scandal if it leaks out," said Nichols.

"Strange that terrorists can murder international leaders and diplomats, with an army of innocent victims thrown in, and get off with a few years in prison," mused the President. "But if we play their game and go after them with guns blasting, we're branded immoral, blood-thirsty avengers. The news media get on our case and Congress demands investigations."

"It hurts being the good guys," said Brogan.

He was beginning to sound tired.

Nichols stood up and stretched. "I don't think we have to worry. Nothing was put down on paper or recorded on tape. And only the men in this room know why Senator Pitt flew down to Punta del Este to confer with President Hasan."

"Dale's right," said Mercier. "We can come up with any number of excuses to explain away his mission."

The President unclasped his hands and rubbed his eyes tiredly. "George Pitt hasn't been dead a day and already we're trying to cover our asses."

"That problem is minor compared to the political disasters we're facing in Egypt and Mexico," said Nichols. "With Hasan and De Lorenzo dead too, Egypt will go the way of Iran and be irretrievably lost for the West. Then with Mexico . . ." He hesitated. "We'll have a time bomb ready to go off along our own border."

"As my Chief of Staff and closest adviser, what measures do you suggest we take?"

Nichols's stomach was attacked by a cramp and his heartbeat quickened. The President and the two intelligence advisers seemed to be studying his eyes. He wondered if the stress that was twisting his guts came from being put on the spot or the thought of a looming foreign catastrophe.

"I propose we wait for proof the *Lady Flam-*

borough and everybody on her lies on the bottom of the ocean."

"And if no evidence is forthcoming?" asked the President. "Do we go on waiting until Egypt and Mexico, their leaders missing and presumed dead, are taken over by Topiltzin and Akhmad Yazid, a pair of crazed megalomaniacs? What then? What course of action is left to stop them before it's too late?"

"Short of assassination, none." Nichols's hand nervously massaged his aching stomach. "We can only prepare for the worst."

"Which is . . . ?"

"We write off Egypt," Nichols said gravely, "and invade Mexico."

41

A heavy rain soaked Uruguay's capital city of Montevideo as the small jet dropped from the clouds and lined up on the runway. Soon after touchdown it swung away from the commercial terminal and rolled onto a taxi strip toward a cluster of hangars flanked by rows of fighter jets. A Ford sedan with military markings appeared and led the pilot to a parking area reserved for visiting VIP aircraft.

Colonel Rojas stood inside a hangar office and peered out a water-streaked window. As the aircraft rolled closer he could see the letters NUMA across the aquamarine color scheme running down the fuselage. The sound of the engines died away, and a minute later three men climbed out. They quickly piled into the Ford to escape the deluge and were driven inside the hangar where Rojas waited.

The Colonel stepped to the office door and studied them as they were ushered across the vast concrete floor by a young lieutenant who was his aide.

The short one with a curly jungle of black hair and a battleship chest strutted with an easy vigor. His hands and arms might have been grafted from a bear. His eyes scowled, but his lips showed white, even teeth in a satirical smile.

The slim man with the horn-rimmed glasses, narrow hips and shoulders looked like an accountant who had come to audit the company ledgers. He carried a briefcase and two books under one arm. He also wore a smile, but it seemed more mischievous than plain humorous. Rojas pegged him as a pleasant sort, easily amused yet highly competent.

The tall man who brought up the rear had black wavy hair and heavy eyebrows, his face craggy and tanned. There was an air of indifference about him as though he would have enjoyed a prison sentence with the same expectation as a Tahitian holiday. Rojas was not fooled. The man's penetrating eyes gave him away. While the other two gazed around the hangar as they walked, this man fixed Rojas with a burning stare like the sun through twin magnifying glasses.

Rojas stepped forward and saluted. "Welcome to Uruguay, gentlemen. Colonel Jose Rojas at your service." Then he addressed himself to the tall man, speaking in perfect English with a slight trace of cockney he'd

461

picked up from the British. "I've looked forward to meeting you since our phone conversation, Mr. Pitt."

Pitt stepped between his friends and shook Rojas's hand. "Thank you for taking the time to see us." He turned and introduced the man with the glasses. "This is Rudi Gunn and the criminal type on my right is Al Giordino."

Rojas gave a slight bow of the head and idly tapped his swagger stick against a neatly pressed pants leg. "Please forgive the Spartan surroundings, but an army of world journalists have invaded our country like the plague since the hijacking. I thought it more convenient to confer away from the horde."

"A sound idea," Pitt agreed.

"Would you care to relax a bit after your long flight and dine at our Air Force officers' club?"

"Thank you for the invitation, Colonel," said Pitt graciously, "but if you don't mind, we'd like to get to it."

"Then, if you'll step this way, I'll brief you on our search operations."

Inside the office Rojas introduced Captain Ignacio Flores, who had coordinated the air/sea hunt. Then he motioned the three Americans to gather around a large table covered with nautical charts and satellite-imagery photos.

Before he launched the briefing, Rojas looked at Pitt solemnly. "I am sorry to hear

462

your father was a passenger on board the ship. When we spoke on the phone you didn't mention your relationship."

"You're well informed," said Pitt.

"I've been in hourly communication with your President's security adviser."

"You'll be happy to know that the intelligence people in Washington who briefed me on the situation praised your efficiency."

Rojas's official bearing crumbled. He had not expected such a compliment. He began to loosen up. "I regret I can't give you encouraging news. No new evidence has turned up since you departed the United States. I can, however, offer you a drink of our fine Uruguayan brandy."

"Sounds good to me," Giordino said without hesitation. "Especially on a rainy day."

Rojas nodded to his aide. "Lieutenant, if you will do us the honors." Then the Colonel leaned over the table and pieced together several enlarged black-and-white satellite images until he had a mosaic of the waters stretching three hundred kilometers off the coast. "I take it you're all familiar with satellite imagery?"

Rudi Gunn nodded. "NUMA currently has three satellite oceanography programs in progress to study currents, eddys, surface winds and sea ice."

"But none are focusing on this section of the South Atlantic," said Rojas. "Most geo-

463

graphic information systems are aimed north."

"Yes, you're quite right." Gunn adjusted his glasses and examined the photo blowups on the table. "I see you've used the Earth Resources Tech Satellite."

"Yes, the Landsat."

"And you used a powerful graphic system to show ships at sea."

"We had a piece of luck," Rojas continued. "The polar orbit of the satellite takes it over the sea off Uruguay only once every sixteen days. It arrived at a most opportune time."

"The Landsat's primary use is for geological survey," said Gunn. "The cameras are usually shut down when it orbits over the oceans to conserve energy. How did you get the images?"

"Immediately after the search was ordered," explained Rojas, "our meteorological defense section was alerted to provide weather forecasts for the patrol boats and aircraft. One of the meteorologists had an inspiration and checked the Landsat's orbit and found it would pass over the search area. He sent an urgent request to your government to turn it on. The cameras were engaged with an hour to spare and the signals sent to a receiving station in Buenos Aires."

"Could a target the size of the *Lady Flamborough* show up on a Landsat image?" asked Giordino.

"You won't see detail like you would in a high-resolution photo from a defense intelligence satellite," replied Pitt, "but she should be as visible as a pinprick."

"You described her perfectly," said Rojas. "See for yourselves."

He set a large magnified viewing lens with an interior light over a tiny section of the satellite photo mosaic. Then he stood back.

Pitt was the first to look. "I can make out two, no, three vessels."

"We have identified all three."

Rojas turned and nodded to Captain Flores, who began to read aloud from a sheet of paper, struggling with his English as if reciting in front of a class. "The largest ship is a Chilean ore carrier, the *Cabo Gallegos,* bound from Punta Arenas to Dakar with a load of coal."

"The northbound vessel, just coming into view on the bottom edge of the image?" asked Pitt.

"Yes," Flores agreed. "That is the *Cabo Gallegos.* The one opposite on the top is southbound. She's of Mexican registry. A container ship, the *General Bravo,* carrying supplies and oil-drilling equipment to San Pablo."

"Where's San Pablo?" asked Giordino.

"A small port city on the tip of Argentina," replied Rojas. "There was an oil strike there last year."

"The vessel between them and closer toward shore is the *Lady Flamborough.*" Flores spoke the cruise liner's name as if he were giving a eulogy.

Rojas's aide appeared with the bottle of brandy and five glasses. The Colonel raised his and said, *"Saludos."*

"Salute," the Americans acknowledged.

Pitt took a large sip that he swore later incinerated his tonsils and resumed his study of the tiny dot for several seconds before giving up the viewing glass to Gunn. "I can't make out her heading."

"After sneaking out of Punta del Este she sailed due east without a course change."

"You've been in contact with the other ships?"

Flores nodded. "Neither one reported seeing her."

"What time did the satellite pass over?"

"The exact time was 03:10 hours."

"The imagery was infrared."

"Yes."

"The guy who thought of using the Landsat ought to get a medal," said Giordino as he took his turn at the viewer.

"A promotion is already in channels," Rojas said, smiling.

Pitt looked at the Colonel. "What time did your aerial reconnaissance get off the ground?"

"Our aircraft began searching at first light. By noon we had received and analyzed the

Landsat imagery. We then could calculate the speed and course of the *Lady Flamborough* and direct our ships and planes to an interception point."

"But they found an empty sea."

"Quite right."

"No wreckage?"

Captain Flores spoke up. "Our patrol boats did run on several pieces of debris."

"Was it identified?"

"Some was pulled on board and examined but quickly discarded. It appeared to have come from a cargo ship rather than a luxury cruise liner."

"What sort of debris?"

Flores checked through a briefcase and removed a thin file. "I have a short inventory received from the Captain of the search vessel. He lists one worn overstuffed chair; two faded life-jackets, at least fifteen years old, with operation instructions stenciled in almost illegible Spanish; several unmarked wooden crates; a bunk mattress; food containers; three newspapers, one from Veracruz, Mexico, the other two from Recife, Brazil —"

"Dates?" Pitt interrupted.

Flores looked questioningly at Pitt for a moment and then he averted his gaze. "The Captain did not give them."

"An oversight that will be corrected," said Rojas sternly, immediately picking up on Pitt's thoughts.

"If it isn't already too late," Flores came back uneasily. "You must admit, Colonel, the debris appears to be trash, not ship's wreckage."

"Could you plot the coordinates of the ships as they're shown on the satellite photo?" asked Pitt.

Flores nodded and began plotting the positions on to a nautical chart.

"Another brandy, gentlemen?" Rojas offered.

"It's quite vibrant," said Gunn, holding out his glass to the lieutenant. "I detect a very slight coffee flavor."

Rojas smiled. "I can see you're a connoisseur, Mr. Gunn. Quite right. My uncle distills it on his coffee plantation."

"Too sweet," said Giordino. "Reminds me of licorice."

"It also contains anisette." Rojas turned to Pitt. "And you Mr. Pitt. How do you taste it?"

Pitt held up the glass and studied it under the light. "I'd say about two hundred proof."

North Americans never ceased to amaze Rojas. All business one moment, complete jesters the next. He often wondered how they built such a superpower.

Then Pitt laughed his infectious laugh. "Only kidding. Tell your uncle if he ever exports it to the U.S., I'll be the first in line to distribute it."

Flores threw down his dividers and tapped a penciled box on the chart. "They were here at 03:10 yesterday morning."

Everyone moved back to the table and hovered over the chart.

"All three were on converging courses all right," observed Gunn. He took a small calculator from his pocket and began punching its buttons. "If I make a rough estimate of speeds, say about thirty knots for the *Lady Flamborough,* eighteen for the *Cabo Gallegos,* and twenty-two for the *General Bravo . . ."* his voice trailed off as he made notations on the edge of the chart. After several moments he stood back and tapped the figures with a pencil. "Not surprising the Chilean coal carrier didn't make visual contact. She would have crossed the cruise liner's bow a good sixty-four kilometers to the east."

Pitt stared thoughtfully at the lines across the chart. "The Mexican container ship, on the other hand, looks as if she missed the *Lady Flamborough* by no more than three or four kilometers."

"Not surprising," said Rojas, "when you consider the cruise liner was running without lights."

Pitt looked at Flores. "Do you recall the phase of the moon, Captain?"

"Yes, between new moon and first quarter, a crescent."

Giordino shook his head. "Not bright

enough if the bridge watch wasn't looking in the right direction."

"I assume you launched the search from this point," said Pitt.

Flores nodded, "Yes, the aircraft flew grids two hundred miles to the east, north and south."

"And found no sign of her."

"Only the container ship and the ore carrier."

"She might have doubled back and then cut north or south," suggested Gunn.

"We thought of that, too," said Flores. "The aircraft cleared all western approaches toward land when they returned for fuel and went out again."

"Considering the facts," said Gunn ominously, "I fear the only place the *Lady Flamborough* could have gone is down."

"Take her last position, Rudi, and figure how far she might have sailed before the search planes arrived."

Rojas stared at Pitt with interest. "May I ask what you intend to do? Further search would be useless. The entire surface where she vanished has been swept."

Pitt seemed to stare through Rojas as though the Colonel were transparent. "Like the man just said, 'The only place she could have gone is down.' And that's precisely where we're going to look."

"How can I be of service?"

"The *Sounder,* a NUMA deep-water research ship, should arrive in the general search area sometime this evening. We'd be grateful if you could spare a helicopter to shuttle us out to her."

Rojas nodded. "I will arrange to have one standing by." Then he added, "You realize you might as well be hunting one particular fish in ten thousand square kilometers of sea. It could take you a lifetime."

"No," said Pitt confidently. "Twenty hours on the outside."

Rojas was a pragmatic man. Wishful thinking was foreign to him. He looked at Giordino and Gunn, expecting to see skepticism mirrored in their eyes. Instead, he saw only complete agreement.

"Surely, you can't believe such a fanciful time schedule?" he asked.

Giordino held up a hand and casually studied his fingernails. "If experience is any judge," he replied placidly, "Dirk has overestimated."

42

Exactly fourteen hours and forty-two minutes after the Uruguayan army helicopter set them on the landing pad of the *Sounder,* they found a shipwreck matching the *Lady Flamborough*'s dimensions in 1,020 meters of water.

On the discovery pass the target showed up as a tiny dark speck on a flat plain below the continental slope. As the *Sounder* moved in closer, the sonar operator decreased the recording range until the shadowy image of a ship became a discernible shape.

The *Sounder* did not carry the five-million-dollar viewing system Pitt and Giordino had enjoyed on the *Polar Explorer.* No color video cameras were mounted on the trailing sonar sensor. The mission of her oceanographic scientists was purely to map large sections of the sea bottom. Her electronic gear was designed for distance and not close-up detail of man-made sunken objects.

"Same configuration all right," said Gunn. "Pretty vague. Could be my imagination but she appears to have a swept-back funnel on her stern superstructure. Her sides look high and straight. She's sitting upright, no more than a ten-degree list."

Giordino held back. "We'll have to get cameras on her to make a positive ID."

Pitt said nothing. He kept watching the sonar recording long after the target slipped behind the *Sounder's* stern. Any hope of finding his father alive was draining away. He felt as though he was staring at a coffin as dirt was being thrown on the lid.

"Nice going, pal," Giordino said to him. "You laid us right on the dime."

"How did you know where to look?" asked Frank Stewart, skipper of the *Sounder.*

"I gambled the *Lady Flamborough* didn't change her heading after crossing the inside path of the *General Bravo,*" Pitt explained. "And since she wasn't spotted by search aircraft beyond the outside course of the *Cabo Gallegos,* I decided the best place to concentrate our search was on a track extending east from her last-known heading as shown by the Landsat."

"In short, a narrow corridor running between the *General Bravo* and the *Cabo Gallegos,*" said Giordino.

"That about sums it up," Pitt acknowledged.

Gunn looked at him. "I'm sorry it's not an

occasion to celebrate."

"Do you want to send down an ROV?"* asked Stewart.

"We can save time," answered Pitt, "by skipping a remote camera survey and going direct to a manned probe. Also, the submersible's manipulator arms may be useful if we need to lift anything from the wreck."

"The crew can have the *Deep Rover* ready to descend in half an hour," said Stewart. "You going to act as operator?"

Pitt nodded. "I'll take her down."

"At a thousand meters, you'll be right at the edge of its depth rating."

"Not to worry," said Rudi Gunn. "The *Deep Rover* has a four-to-one safety factor at that depth."

"I'd sooner go over Niagara Falls in a Volkswagen," said the Captain, "than go down a thousand meters in a plastic bubble."

Stewart, narrow-shouldered, with slicked-down long, burnt-toast-brown hair, looked like a small-town feed-store merchant and scoutmaster. A seasoned seaman, he could swim but was leery of the deep and refused to learn to dive. He catered to the scientists' requests and whims concerning their oceanographic projects as in any business/client relationship. But the ship operation was his

* Remote Operated Vehicle; tethered, underwater viewing system.

domain, and any academic type who played Long John Silver with his crew was cut off at the knees in short order.

"That plastic bubble," said Pitt, "is an acrylic sphere over twelve centimeters thick."

"I'm happy to sit on deck in the sunshine and wave goodbye to anyone who takes the plunge in that contraption," Stewart muttered as he walked through the door.

"I like him," said Giordino moodily. "Utterly lacking in savoir faire, but I like him."

"You two have something in common," Pitt said, grinning.

Gunn froze an image of the wreck on videotape from the sonar recording and studied it thoughtfully. He slid his glasses over his forehead and refocused his eyes. "The hull looks intact. No sign of breakup. Why in hell did she sink?"

"Better yet," mused Giordino, "why no flotsam?"

Pitt stared at the blurred image too. "Remember the *Cyclops*? She was lost without a trace too."

"How can we forget her?" Giordino groaned. "We still carry the scars."

Gunn looked up at him. "In all fairness, you can't compare a poorly laden ship built around the turn of the century with a modern cruise liner carrying a thousand built-in safety features."

"No storm put her down there," said Pitt.

"Maybe a rogue wave?"

"Or maybe some sand kicker blew her bottom out," said Giordino.

"We'll know soon enough," Pitt said quietly. "In another two hours we'll be sitting on her main deck."

The *Deep Rover* looked like she'd be more at home orbiting space than cruising the depths of the ocean. She had a shape only a Martian could love. The 240-centimeter sphere was divided by a large O-ring and sat on rectangular pods that held the 120-volt batteries. All sorts of strange appendages sprouted from behind the sphere: thrusters and motors, oxygen cylinders, carbon dioxide removal canisters, docking mechanism, camera systems, scanning sonar unit. But it was the manipulators that extended in the front that would have made any self-respecting robot green with envy. Simply described they were mechanical arms and hands with a canny way of doing everything flesh and bone could do, and then some. A sensory feedback system made it possible to control the hand and arm movements to within thousandths of a centimeter, while force feedback allowed the hands to delicately hold a cup and saucer or grab and lift an iron stove.

Pitt and Giordino patiently circled the *Deep Rover* while she was fussed over by a pair of engineers. She sat on a cradle inside a cavernous chamber called the "moon pool." The platform holding her cradle was part of the *Sounder*'s hull and could be lowered twenty feet into the sea.

One of the engineers finally nodded. "She's ready when you are."

Pitt slapped Giordino on the back. "After you."

"Okay, I'll handle the manipulators and cameras," he said jovially. "You drive, only mind the rush-hour traffic."

"You tell him," yelled Stewart from an overhead balcony, his voice echoing inside the chamber. "Bring it back in one piece and I'll give you a great big kiss."

"Me too?" Giordino yelled back, going along with the joke.

"You too."

"Can I take out my dentures?"

"Take out anything you want."

"You call that an incentive?" Pitt said dryly. He was grateful to the Captain for trying to take his mind off what they might find. "I may make a beeline for Africa rather than come back here."

"You'll need an extra truckload of oxygen," said Stewart.

Gunn walked up, oblivious to the good-natured exchange, a pair of earphones clamped to his head with the cable dangling at his leg.

He tried to keep his instructions business-like, but compassion crept into his voice. "I'll be monitoring your audio locator beacon and communications. Soon as you see bottom, make a three-hundred-and-sixty-degree sweep until your sonar picks out the wreck. Then give me your heading. I expect you to keep me informed every step of the way."

Pitt shook Gunn's hand. "We'll stay in touch."

Gunn stared up at his old friend bleakly. "You sure you wouldn't rather stay topside and let me go down?"

"I've got to see for myself."

"Good luck," Gunn murmured, and then he quickly turned away and mounted a ladder leading from the moon pool.

Pitt and Giordino settled into the side-by-side, aircraft-style armchairs. The engineers swung the top half of the sphere closed against the watertight O-ring and tightened the clamps.

Giordino began running through the pre-dive checklist. "Power?"

"Power on," affirmed Pitt.

"Radio?"

"Are we coming in, Rudi?"

"Loud and clear," Gunn answered.

"Oxygen?"

"Twenty-one-point-five percent."

When they finished, Giordino said, "Ready when you are, *Sounder.*"

"You're cleared for takeoff, *Deep Rover,*"

Stewart replied in his usual ironic tone. "Bring back a lobster for dinner."

Two divers stood by in full gear as the platform was slowly lowered into the sea. The water surged around the *Deep Rover* and soon enveloped the sphere. Pitt looked up into the shimmering lights of the moon pool and saw the wavering figures leaning over the balconies. The entire company of oceanographers and crew turned out for the dive, hovering around Gunn and listening to the reports from the sub. Pitt felt like a fish on display in an aquarium.

When they were fully submerged, the divers moved in and unhitched the submersible from its cradle. One of them held up a hand and gave an "Okay" sign. Pitt smiled and answered with a "Thumbs up," and then pointed ahead.

The handgrips on the end of the armrests guided the manipulators, while the armrests themselves controlled the four thrusters. Pitt flew the *Deep Rover* as if it were an underwater helicopter. A slight pressure on his elbows and she rose off the cradle. Then he pushed his arms forward and the horizontal thrusters eased her ahead.

Pitt moved the little craft off the platform about thirty meters and stopped to assess his compass bearing. Then he engaged the vertical thrusters and began the descent.

Down, down the *Deep Rover* fell through

the dimensionless void, the darkening water burying her in its depths. The vibrant blue-green of the surface soon turned to a soft gray. A small, one-meter blue shark swam effortlessly toward the sub, circled once and, finding nothing inviting, continued its lonely journey into the fluid haze.

They felt no sense of movement. The only sound came from the soft crackle of the radio and the pinging of the locator beacon. The water became a curtain of black surrounding their small circle of light.

"Passing four hundred meters," Pitt reported as calmly as a pilot announcing his flight altitude.

"Four hundred meters," Gunn repeated.

Ordinarily the wit and the sarcasm would have bounced off the interior of the submersible to pass the time, but this trip Pitt and Giordino were strangely silent. Seldom during the descent did their conversation run more than a few words.

"There's a real sweetheart," said Giordino, pointing.

Pitt saw it at the same time. One of the ugliest of the deep's resident citizens. Long, eel-shaped body, outlined by luminescence like a neon sign. The frozen, gaping jaws were never fully closed, kept apart by long, jagged teeth that were used more for entrapping prey than for chewing them. One eye gleamed nastily while a tube that was attached to a luminated beard dangled from its lower jaw to lure the next meal.

"How'd you like to stick your arm in that thing?" asked Pitt.

Before Giordino could answer, Gunn broke in. "One of the scientists wants to know what you saw."

"A dragonfish," Pitt replied.

"He wants a description," said Giordino.

"Tell him we'll draw a picture when we come home," Pitt grunted.

"I'll pass the word."

"Passing eight hundred meters," Pitt reported.

"Mind you don't smack the bottom," Gunn warned him.

"We'll keep an eye peeled. Neither of us is keen on making a one-way trip."

"Never hurts to have a worrywart on your side. How's your oxygen?"

"On the money."

"You should be getting close."

Pitt slowed the *Deep Rover*'s descent with a light touch of the sliding armrest. Giordino peered downward, his eyes watchful for a sign of rocks. Pitt could have sworn his friend never blinked in the next eight minutes it took for the seabed to gradually materialize below.

"We're down," Giordino announced. "Depth one thousand fifteen meters."

Pitt applied extra power to the vertical

thrusters, bringing the submersible to a hovering stop three meters above the gray silt. Due to the water pressure, the weight of the craft had increased during the descent. Pitt turned one of the ballast tank valves, keeping an eye on the pressure gauge, and filled it with just enough air to achieve neutral buoyancy.

"Making our sweep," he notified Gunn.

"The wreck should bear approximately one one zero degrees," Gunn's voice crackled back.

"Affirmative, I read you," said Pitt. "We have a sonar target two hundred twenty meters, bearing one one two degrees."

"I copy, *Deep Rover.*"

Pitt turned to Giordino. "Well, let us see what we shall see."

He increased the power on the horizontal thrusters and executed a sweeping bank, studying the barren seascape ahead as Giordino kept him on track by reading off the compass heading.

"Come left a couple of points. Too much. Okay, you've got it. Keep her straight."

There was not a flicker of emotion in Pitt's eyes. His face was strangely still. He wondered with a growing fear what he might find.

He recalled the haunting story of a diver salvaging a ferry that had sunk after a collision. The diver was working the wreck at thirty meters when he felt a tap on his shoulder. He swung around and was confronted by the body of a beautiful girl who was staring at him through sightless eyes, one arm extended and touching him as if asking to take her hand. The diver had nightmares for years afterward.

Pitt had seen bodies before, frozen as the crew of the *Serapis;* bloated and grotesque as the crew of the Presidential yacht *Eagle;* decayed and half-dissolved in sunken airplanes off Iceland and a lake in the Colorado Rockies. He could still close his eyes and visualize them all.

He hoped to God he wouldn't see his father as a floating corpse. He shut his eyes for a few moments and almost ran the *Deep Rover* into the bottom. Pitt wanted to remember the Senator as alive and vibrant — not as a ghostly thing in the sea or a ridiculously made up stiff in a casket.

"Object in the silt to the right," Giordino said, jolting Pitt from his morbid thoughts.

Pitt leaned forward. "A two-hundred-liter drum. Three more off to the left."

"They're all over the place," said Giordino. "Looks like a junkyard down here."

"See any markings?"

"Only some stenciled lettering in Spanish. Probably weight and volume information."

"I'll move closer to the one dead ahead. A trace of whatever was in them is still rising to the surface."

Pitt edged the *Deep Rover*'s sphere to within a few inches of the sunken drum. The lights showed a dark substance curling from the drain hole.

"Oil?" said Giordino.

Pitt shook his head. "The color is more rustlike. No, wait, it's red. By God, it's an oil-base red paint."

"There's another cylindrical object next to it."

"What do you make of it?"

"I'd say it's a big roll of plastic sheeting."

"I'd say you're right."

"Might not be a bad idea to take it aboard the *Sounder* for examination. Hold position. I'll grab it with the manipulators."

Pitt nodded silently and held the *Deep Rover* steady against the gentle bottom current. Giordino clutched the handgrip controls and curled the arm assemblies around the plastic roll, much like a human would bend both elbows to embrace a friend. Next he positioned the four-function hands so they gripped the bottom edge.

"She's secure," he announced. "Give us a little vertical thrust to pull it out of the silt."

Pitt complied, and the *Deep Rover* slowly rose, carrying the roll with her, followed by a swirling cloud of fine silt. For a few moments they couldn't see. Then Pitt eased the submersible ahead until they broke into clear water again.

"We should be coming up on her," said Giordino. "Sonar shows a massive target in front and slightly to the right."

"We show you to be practically on top of her," said Gunn.

Like a ghostly image in a darkened mirror, the ship rose out of the gloom. Magnified by the water distortion, she seemed a staggering sight.

"We have visual contact," Giordino reported.

Pitt slowed the *Deep Rover* to a stop seven meters from the hull. Then he maneuvered the sub up and alongside the derelict's foredeck.

"What the hell —" Pitt broke off suddenly. Then, "Rudi, what colors were on the *Lady Flamborough*?"

"Hold on." No more than ten seconds elapsed before Gunn answered. "Light blue hull and superstructure."

"This ship has a red hull with white upperworks."

Gunn did not reply immediately. When he did, his voice sounded old and tired. "I'm sorry, Dirk. We must have stumbled on a missing World War Two ship that was torpedoed by a U-boat."

"Can't be," muttered Giordino distantly. "This wreck is pristine. No sign of growth or corrosion. I can see oil and air bubbles escaping. She can't be more than a week old."

485

"Negative," Stewart's voice came over the radio. "The only ship reported missing during the last six months in this part of the Atlantic is your cruise liner."

"This ain't no cruise ship," Giordino shot back.

"Hold for a minute," said Pitt. "I'm going to come around the stern and see if we can make an identification."

He threw the *Deep Rover* into a steep bank and glided parallel to the ship's side. When they reached the stern, he spun sideways to a halt. The sub hung there motionless only one meter from the name of the ship painted on beaded welding.

"Oh, my God," Giordino whispered in incredulous awe. "We've been conned."

Pitt did not sit there in stunned disbelief. He grinned like a madman. The puzzle was far from complete, but the vital pieces had fallen into place. The white raised letters on the red steel plates did not read *Lady Flamborough*.

They read *General Bravo.*

486

43

From four hundred meters her designers and shipbuilders would not have recognized the *Lady Flamborough*. Her funnel had been recontoured and every square inch of her repainted. To complete the facade, the hull was streaked with simulated rust.

Her once-beautiful superstructure, stateroom windows and promenade deck were now hidden by great sheets of fiber-board assembled to look like cargo containers.

Where the cruise liner's modern, rounded bridge features were impossible to remove or hide, they were squared with wooden framework and canvas and painted with fake hatches and portholes.

Before the lights of Punta del Este had dropped astern, every crew member and passenger was drafted into forced-labor parties and driven to the point of exhaustion by Ammar's armed hijackers. The ship's officers, cruise directors, the stewards, chefs and waiters, and ordinary deckhands — they all hammered and slaved at assembling the prefabricated containers through the night.

None of the VIP guests was spared. Senator Pitt and Hala Kamil, Presidents Hasan and De Lorenzo, along with their cabinet members and staff aides, were all pressed into service as carpenters and painters.

By the time the cruise liner rendezvoused with the *General Bravo,* the counterfeit cargo containers were in place and the ship sported a nearly identical configuration and color scheme.

From the waterline up, the newly disguised *Lady Flamborough* could have easily passed as the container ship. An overhead inspection from the air would have revealed few discrepancies. Only a close examination from the sea might have detected obvious differences.

Captain Juan Machado and eighteen crewmen from the *General Bravo* transferred to the cruise liner after opening all seacocks and cargo doors and detonating strategically placed charges throughout the hull. With a series of muffled explosions the container ship slipped beneath the sea with only a few faint gurgles of protest.

When the eastern sky began to brighten with a new sun, the disguised *Lady Flamborough* was steaming south toward the advertised destination of the *General Bravo.* But when the port of San Pablo, Argentina, was forty kilometers off the starboard beam, the liner bypassed the port and continued due south.

Ammar's ingenious scheme had worked. Three days had passed, and the world was still fooled into believing the *Lady Flamborough* and her distinguished passengers were lying somewhere on the bottom of the sea.

Ammar sat at a chart table and marked the ship's latest position. Then he drew a straight line to his final destination and marked it with an X. Smugly complacent, he dropped the pencil and lit a long Dunhill cigarette, exhaling the smoke across the chart like a bank of mist.

Sixteen hours, he reckoned. Sixteen more hours of sailing time without pursuit and the ship would be securely hidden without the slightest chance of detection.

Captain Machado stepped into the chart room from the bridge, balancing a small tray on one hand. "Would you like a cup of tea and a croissant?" he asked in fluent English.

"Thank you, Captain. Come to think of it, I haven't eaten since we departed Punta del Este."

Machado set the tray on the table and poured the tea. "I know you haven't slept since my crew and I came on board."

"There is still much to do."

"Perhaps we should begin by formally introducing ourselves."

"I know who you are, or at least the name

you go by," said Ammar indifferently. "I'm not interested in lengthy biographies."

"That's how it is?"

"Yes."

"Mind letting me in on your plans?" said Machado. "I was informed of nothing beyond our transfer to your ship after scuttling the *General Bravo.* I'd be most interested in hearing about the next step of the mission, especially the part on how our combined crews intend to abandon the ship and evade arrest by international military forces."

"Sorry, I've been too busy to enlighten you."

"Now might be a good time," Machado pressed.

Characteristically, Ammar calmly sipped at his tea and finished off the croissant beneath his mask before answering. Then he looked across the chart table at Machado without expression.

"I don't intend to abandon the ship just yet," he said evenly. "My instructions from your leader and mine are to mark time and delay the final destruction of the *Lady Flamborough* until they both have time to assess the situation and turn it to their advantage."

Slowly Machado relaxed, looked through the mask into the cold, dark eyes of the Egyptian, and he knew this was a man solidly in control. "I have no problem with that." He held up the pot. "More tea?"

Ammar passed his cup. "What do you do when you're not sinking ships?"

"I specialize in political assassinations," said Machado conversationally. "The same as you, Suleiman Aziz Ammar."

Machado could not see the wary frown behind Ammar's mask, but he knew it was there.

"You were sent to kill me?" Ammar asked, casually flicking an ash from his cigarette while lining up a tiny automatic pistol that suddenly appeared in his palm like a magic trick.

Machado smiled and crossed his arms, keeping his hands in open view. "You can relax. My orders were to work in total harmony with you."

Ammar replaced the gun in a spring-operated device under his right sleeve. "How do you know me?"

"Our leaders have few secrets between them."

Damn Yazid, Ammar thought angrily. Yazid had betrayed him by giving away his identity. He wasn't taken in for an instant by Machado's lie. Once President Hasan was out of the way, the reincarnated Muhammad had no further use for his hired killer. Ammar was not about to reveal his escape plans to the Mexican hit man. He clearly realized his counterpart had no option but to form an alliance of expediency. Ammar was quite

491

comfortable in knowing he could kill Machado at any time, while the Mexican had to wait until survival was assured.

Ammar knew exactly where he stood.

He raised his teacup. "To Akhmad Yazid."

Machado stiffly raised his. "To Topiltzin."

Hala and Senator Pitt had been locked in a suite along with President Hasan. They were grimy and splattered with paint, too exhausted to sleep. Their hands were blistered and their muscles ached from physical labor none had been conditioned for. And they were hungry.

After the frenzied remodeling of the cruise liner's outer structure since leaving Uruguay, the hijackers had not allowed them any food. Their only liquid intake came from the faucet in the bathroom. And to make their condition worse, the temperature had been steadily dropping and no heat was coming through the ventilators.

President Hasan was stretched out on one of the beds in abject misery. He suffered from a chronic back problem, and the strain from ten hours of uninterrupted bending and stretching had left him in a torrent of pain which he endured stoically.

For all the movement they made, Hala and the Senator might have been carved from wood. Hala sat at a table with her head lowered in her hands. Even in her disheveled state, she still looked serene and beautiful.

Senator Pitt reclined on a couch, staring pensively at a light fixture in the ceiling. Only his blinking eyes showed that he was alive.

Finally Hala raised her head and looked at him. "If only we could do something," she said, barely above a whisper.

The Senator rose stiffly to a sitting position. For his age, he was still in good physical shape. He was sore from neck to feet, but his heart beat as soundly as if he was twenty years younger.

"That devil with the mask doesn't miss a trick," he said. "He won't feed us so we'll stay weak; everyone is locked away separately so we can't communicate or cooperate in a counter-takeover; and, he and his terrorists have not made any contact with us for two days. All calculated to keep us on edge and in a state of helplessness."

"Can't we at least try to get out of here?"

"There's probably a guard at the end of the hallway waiting to blast the first body that breaks through a door. And even if we somehow got past him, where could we go?"

"Maybe we could steal a lifeboat," Hala suggested wildly.

The Senator shook his head and smiled. "Too late for any attempt now. Not with the hijacker's force doubled by the crew from that Mexican cargo ship."

"Suppose we break out the window and

leave a trail with furniture, bed linen or whatever else we could throw out," Hala persisted.

"Might as well toss bottles with notes inside. The currents would carry them a hundred kilometers from our wake by morning." He paused to shake his head. "Searchers would never find them in time."

"You know as well as I, Senator, no one is looking for us. The outside world thinks our ship sank and everyone died. Search efforts would have been called off by now."

"I know one man who will never give up."

She looked at him questioningly. "Who?"

"My son, Dirk."

Hala rose and limped over to the window and stared vacantly at the outside fiberboard that hid her view of the sea. "You must be very proud of him. He's a brave and resourceful man, but only human. He'll never see through the deception —" She paused suddenly and peered down through a tiny crack that showed a brief span of water. "There's something drifting past the ship."

The Senator came over and stood beside her. He could just make out several white objects against the blue of the sea. "Ice," he said, stunned. "That explains the cold. We must be heading into the Antarctic."

Hala sagged against him and buried her face in his chest. "We'll never be rescued now," she murmured in helpless resignation. "No one will think to look for us there."

44

No one knew the *Sounder* could drive so hard. Her decks trembled with the straining throb of her engines and the hull shuddered as it pounded into the swells.

Launched at a shipyard in Boston during the summer of 1961, she had spent almost three decades chartering out to oceanographic schools for deep-water research projects in every sea of the world. After her purchase by NUMA in 1990, she had been completely overhauled and refitted. Her new 4,000-horsepower diesel engine was designed to push her at a maximum of fourteen knots, but Stewart and his engineers somehow coaxed seventeen out of her.

The *Sounder* was the only ship on the trail of the *Lady Flamborough,* and she stood as much chance of closing the gap as a basset hound after a leopard. Warships of the Argentine Navy and British naval units stationed in the Falkland Islands might have intercepted the fleeing cruise ship, but they were not alerted.

After Pitt's coded message to Admiral San-decker announcing the astonishing discovery of the *General Bravo* instead of the *Lady Flamborough,* the Joint Chiefs of Staff and the White House intelligence chiefs strongly advised the President to order a tight security lid on the revelation until U.S. Special Operations Forces could reach the area and coordinate a rescue.

So the old *Sounder* surged through the sea, alone and without any high official authority, her crew of seamen and scientists caught up in the mad excitement of the chase.

Pitt and Giordino sat in the ship's dining room, studying a chart of the extreme South Atlantic Ocean that Gunn had laid out on the table and pinned down with coffee cups.

"You're convinced they headed south?" Gunn said to Pitt.

"A U-turn to the north would have put the liner back in the search grid," explained Pitt. "And there's no way they would have swung west toward the coastline of Argentina."

"They might have made a run for the open sea."

"With a three-day lead they could be halfway to Africa by now," added Giordino.

"Too risky," said Pitt. "Whoever is running the show doesn't lack for gray matter. Turning east across the ocean would have laid the ship open to exposure by search aircraft and any passing vessels. No, his only option to avoid undue suspicion was to continue on the *General Bravo's* advertised course to San Pablo on Tierra del Fuego."

"But the port authorities would have blown the whistle when the container ship was overdue," insisted Giordino.

"Don't underestimate this guy. What do you want to bet he signaled the San Pablo Harbor Master and said the *General Bravo* was running late due to engine breakdown?"

"A neat touch," agreed Giordino. "He could easily gain another forty-eight hours."

"Okay," said Gunn. "What's left? Where does he go? There are a thousand uninhabited islands he could get lost in around the Straits of Magellan."

"Or —" Giordino hung on the "or" — "he might sail to the Antarctic, where he figures no one will search."

"We're all talking in the present tense," said Pitt. "For all we know, he's already moored in some deserted cove."

"We're on to his tricks now," said Gunn. "The Landsat cameras will be activated on its next pass over, and the *Lady Flamborough,* alias *General Bravo,* will be revealed in all her glory."

Giordino looked at Pitt for comment, but his old friend was staring off into space. He had picked up on Pitt's habit of tuning out and knew the signs all too well.

Pitt was no longer on the *Sounder,* he was on the bridge of the *Lady Flamborough,* attempting to get inside the head of his adversary. It wasn't an easy chore. The man who ramrodded the hijacking had to be the shrewdest customer Pitt had ever come up against.

"He's aware of that," Pitt said finally.

"Aware of what?" Gunn asked curiously.

"The fact he can be detected by satellite photographs."

"Then he knows he can run, but he can't hide."

"I think he can."

"I'd like to know how."

Pitt stood and stretched. "I'm going to take a little walk."

"You didn't answer my question." Gunn was anxious now, impatient.

Pitt swayed and balanced his body with the rock of the ship and looked down at Gunn with a half grin. "If I were him," he said as if talking about a man he knew well, "I'd make the ship disappear a second time."

Gunn's mouth dropped open as Giordino gave him an "I told you so" look. But before he could probe further, Pitt had exited the dining room.

Pitt made his way aft and dropped down a ladder to the moon pool. He walked around the *Deep Rover* and stopped in front of the large roll of plastic sheeting they had pulled up from the bottom. It stood on end nearly as tall as Pitt and was secured by ropes against a stanchion.

He stared at it for nearly five minutes before he rose and patted it with one hand. Intuition, an intuition that grew into a certainty, put a look that could be best described as pure Machiavellian in his eyes.

He spoke a single word, uttered under his breath so softly that an engineer standing only a few meters away at a workbench didn't hear him.

"Gotcha!"

45

A flood of information on what became known as the *Flamborough* crisis poured through teletype and computer into the Pentagon's Military Command Center, the State Department's seventh floor Operations Center, and the War Games room in the old Executive Office Building.

From each of these strategy tanks, the data were assembled and analyzed with almost lightning speed. Then the condensed version, fused with recommendations, was rushed to the Situation Room located in the White House basement for final assessment.

The President, dressed casually in slacks and a woolen turtleneck, entered the room and sat at one end of the long conference table. After being updated on the situation, he would ask for options from his advisers for appropriate action. Though final decisions were his alone, he was heavily reinforced by crisis-management veterans who labored in search of a policy consensus and stood ready to carry it out once he gave it his stamp of approval despite dissenting opinions.

The intelligence reports from Egypt were mostly all bad. A state of anarchy was in full swing; the situation was deteriorating by the hour. The police and military forces remained in their barracks while thousands of Akhmad Yazid's followers staged strikes and boycotts throughout the country. The only shred of good news was that the demonstrations were not marked by violence.

Secretary of State Douglas Oates briefly examined a report that was placed in front of him by an aide. "That's all we need," he muttered.

The President looked at him expectantly in silence.

"The Muslim rebels have just stormed and taken Cairo's major TV station."

"Any appearance by Yazid?"

"Still a no-show." CIA chief Brogan walked over from one of the computer monitors. "The latest intelligence says he's still holed up in his villa outside Alexandria, waiting to form a new government by acclamation."

"Shouldn't be long now." The President sighed wearily. "What stance are the Israeli ministers taking?"

Oates neatly stacked some papers as he spoke. "Strictly a wait-and-see attitude. They don't picture Yazid as an immediate threat."

"They'll change their tune when he tears

up the Camp David Peace Accord." The President turned and coldly stared into Brogan's eyes. "Can we take him out?"

"Yes." Brogan's answer was flat, emphatic.

"How?"

"In the event it comes back to haunt your administration, Mr. President, I respectfully suggest you don't know."

The President bowed his head slightly in agreement. "You're probably right. Still, you can't do the job unless I give the order."

"I strongly urge you not to resort to assassination," said Oates.

"Doug Oates is right," said Julius Schiller. "It could boomerang. If word leaked out, you'd be considered fair game by Middle East terrorist leaders."

"Not to mention the uproar from Congress," added Dale Nichols, who sat midway down the table. "And the press would murder you."

The President thoughtfully weighed the consequences. Then he finally nodded. "All right, so long as Yazid hates Soviet Premier Antonov as much as he does me, we'll put his demise on the back burner for now. But bear this in mind, gentlemen, I'm not about to take half the crap from this nut that Khomeini dished out to my predecessors."

Brogan scowled, but an expression of relief was exchanged between Oates and Schiller.

Nichols merely puffed contentedly on his pipe.

The actors in the drama were strong men with definite and often conflicting viewpoints. Victory came easy, but defeat smoldered.

The President shifted the agenda. "Any late word on Mexico?"

"The situation is uncomfortably quiet," answered Brogan. "No demonstrations, no rioting. Topiltzin appears to be playing the same waiting game as his brother."

The President looked up, puzzled. "Did I hear you correctly? You said 'brother'?"

Brogan tilted his head toward Nichols. "Dale made a good call. Yazid and Topiltzin are brothers who are neither Egyptian nor Mexican by birth."

"You've definitely proven a family connection?" Schiller interrupted in astonishment. "You have proof?"

"Our operatives obtained and matched their genetic codes."

"This is the first I've heard about it," said a stunned President. "You should have informed me sooner."

"The final documentation is still being evaluated and will be sent over from Langley shortly. I'm sorry, Mr. President. At the risk of sounding overly cautious, I didn't want to throw out such a shocking discovery until we had gathered solid evidence."

"How in hell did you get their genetic

codes?" asked Nichols.

"Both those guys are vain promoters," explained Brogan. "Our forgery department sent a Koran to Yazid, and a photograph to Topiltzin showing him in full Aztec regalia, along with requests begging them in each to inscribe a short prayer on both items and return them. Actually, it was a bit more complicated, writing the requests in the handwriting of known adoring followers — influential followers with financial and political clout, I might add. Both fell for it. The tricky part was intercepting the return mail before it reached the correct addresses. The next problem was sifting out the several sets of fingerprints which accompanied each object. Aides, secretaries, whoever. One thumbprint on the Koran matched with a known set of Yazid's prints that were on file with Egyptian police when he was arrested several years ago. We then traced his DNA from his fingerprint oils.

"Topiltzin was not so easy. He had no record in Mexico, but the lab matched his code to his brother's from prints pulled from the photo. Then a chance find in the international criminal records at Interpol's Paris headquarters dealt us a straight flush. It all came together. What we'd stumbled on was a family organization, a crime dynasty that arose after World War Two. A billion-dollar empire ruled by a mother and father, three brothers and a sister, who spearhead the operations, and run by a network of uncles, aunts, cousins, or whoever is related by blood or marriage. This tight association has made it nearly impossible for international investigators to penetrate."

Except for the click of the teletype machines and the hushed murmur of aides, a stunned silence settled over the table. Brogan looked from Nichols to Schiller to Oates to the President.

"Their name?" the President asked softly.

"Capesterre," answered Brogan. "Roland and Josephine Capesterre are the father and mother. Their eldest son is Robert, or, as we know him, Topiltzin. The next brother in line is Paul."

"He's Yazid?"

"Yes."

"I think we'd be interested in hearing all you know," said the President.

"As I've stated," said Brogan, "I don't have all the facts at my fingertips, such as the whereabouts of Karl and Marie, the younger brother and sister, or the names of associate relatives. We've only scratched the surface. From what I recall, the Capesterres are a tradition-bound criminal family that began almost eighty years ago when the grandfather emigrated from France to the Caribbean and launched a smuggling business, moving stolen goods and bootleg booze to the U.S.

during Prohibition. At first he operated out of Port of Spain, Trinidad, but as he prospered he bought a small nearby island and set up business there. Roland took over when the old man died, and along with his wife, Josephine — some claim she's the brain behind the throne — lost no time in expanding into drug traffic. First they built their island into a legitimate banana plantation, making a nice, honest profit. Next they turned inventive and made a real killing by harvesting two crops. The second, marijuana, was cultivated under the banana trees, to avoid detection. They also set up a refining lab on the island. Have I painted a clear picture?"

"Yes . . ." the President said slowly. "We all see it clearly. Thank you, Martin."

"They had it all worked out," murmured Schiller. "The Capesterres produced, manufactured and smuggled in one efficient operation."

"And distributed," Brogan continued. "But interestingly, not in the U.S. They sold the drugs only in Europe and the Far East."

"Are they still into narcotics?" asked Nichols.

"No." Brogan shook his head. "Through contacts, they received a tip their private island was about to be raided by the joint West Indies security forces. The family burned the marijuana crop, kept the banana plantation and began buying controlling interests in financially shaky corporations. They became extremely successful in turning businesses around and showing staggering profits. Of course, their unusual method of management might have had something to do with it."

Nichols took the hook. "What was their system?"

Brogan grinned. "The Capesterres relied on blackmail, extortion and murder. Any time a competing company got in the way, the corporate executive officers, for some strange reason, initiated merger negotiations with the Capesterre interests, losing their collective asses on the deal, naturally. Developers who hindered projects, opposing lawyers with lawsuits, unfriendly politicians, they all came to know and love the Capesterres, or one sunny day their wives and kids had accidents, their houses burned to the ground or they just up and vanished."

"Kind of like the Mafia managing General Motors or Gulf and Western," said the President sardonically.

"A fair comparison." Brogan nodded politely and continued. "Now the family controls a vast worldwide conglomeration of financial and industrial enterprises worth an estimated twelve billion dollars."

"Billion, as spelled with a 'b'?" Oates mumbled incredulously. "I may never attend church services again."

Schiller shrugged wonderingly. "Who said crime doesn't pay?"

"No wonder they're pulling the strings in Egypt and Mexico," said Oates. "They must have bought, blackmailed or strong-armed their way into every department of the government and military."

"I begin to see how their scheme is coming together," said the President. "But what I can't understand is how can the sons pass themselves off as native-born Egyptians or Mexicans? No one can fool millions of people without somebody getting wise."

"Their mother was descended from black slaves, which accounts for their dark skin," Brogan said in a patiently explaining tone. "We can only speculate about their past. Roland and Josephine must have laid the groundwork forty or more years ago. As their children were born, they began a vigorous program of making over the boys into foreign nationals. Paul was no doubt tutored in Arabic before he could walk, while Robert learned to speak in ancient Aztec. When the boys became older they probably attended private schools in both Mexico and Egypt under assumed names."

"A grand plan," muttered Oates admiringly. "Nothing so mundane as burying intelligence moles, but infiltration at the very highest levels, and with the image of a messiah thrown in for good measure."

"Sounds pretty diabolical to me," said Nichols.

"I agree with Doug," said the President, nodding at Oates. "A grand plan. Training children from birth, using untold wealth and power to set up a national takeover. What we're really looking at here is an incredible display of unbending doggedness and patience."

"You have to give the bastards credit," Schiller admitted. "They stuck to their script until events swung in their favor. Now they're within centimeters of ruling two of the Third World's leading countries."

"We can't allow it to happen," the President said bluntly. "If the brother in Mexico becomes head of state and makes good his threat by driving two million of his countrymen across our borders, I see no choice but to send in our armed forces."

"I must caution against aggressive action," said Oates, speaking like a Secretary of State. "Recent history has shown that invaders do not fare well. Assassinating Yazid and Topiltzin, or whatever their names, and launching an assault on Mexico won't solve the long-range problem."

"Maybe not," grunted the President, "but it will damn well give us time to ease the situation."

"There may be another solution," said

Nichols. "Use the Capesterres against themselves."

"I'm tired," said the President, stress showing in the lines around his eyes. "Please skip the riddles."

Nichols looked at Brogan for support. "These men were drug traffickers. They must be wanted criminals. Is that right?"

"Yes on the first, no on the second," answered Brogan. "They're no petty street crooks. The entire family has been under investigation for years. No arrests. No convictions. They've got a staff of corporate and criminal lawyers that would put Washington's biggest law office to shame. They've got friends and connections that go straight to the top of ten major governments. You want to pick up this bunch and put them on trial? You'd do better tearing down the pyramids with an ice pick."

"Then expose them to the world for the scum they are," pursued Nichols.

"No good," said the President. "Any attempt will surely backlash as a lie and propaganda ploy."

"Nichols might have a direction," said Schiller quietly. He was a man who listened more than he spoke. "All we need is a base that can't be cracked or shattered."

The President looked speculatively at Schiller. "Where are you leading, Julius?"

"The *Lady Flamborough*," replied Schiller,

his face carefully pensive. "Come up with indisputable proof that Yazid is behind the ship's hijacking and we can crack the Capesterre wall."

Brogan nodded heavily. "The ensuing scandal would certainly be a step in stripping away Yazid's and Topiltzin's mystiques and opening the door to the family's countless criminal activities."

"Don't forget the world news media. They'd have a shark feeding frenzy once they bit into the Capesterres' bloody past." Nichols belatedly winced at his unthinking pun.

"You're all overlooking one important fact," Schiller said with a long sigh. "At the moment, any tie between the ship's disappearance and the Capesterres is strictly circumstantial."

Nichols frowned. "Who else has motives for getting rid of Presidents De Lorenzo and Hasan, and Hala Kamil?"

"No one!" Brogan said heatedly.

"Wait up," the President said patiently. "Julius has a sound point. The hijackers are not acting like typical Middle East terrorists. They have yet to identify themselves. They've made no demands or threats. Nor have they used the crew and passengers as hostages for international blackmail. I'm not ashamed to admit I find the silence nightmarish."

"We're faced with a different breed this time," admitted Brogan. "The Capesterres are playing a waiting game, hoping De Lorenzo's and Hasan's governments will fall in their absence."

"Any word on the cruise ship since George Pitt's son discovered the switch?" asked Oates, coolly steering the discussion clear of an impending confrontation.

"Somewhere off the east coast of Tierra del Fuego," replied Schiller. "Sailing like hell to the south. We're tracking by satellite and should have her cornered by this time tomorrow."

The President didn't look happy. "The hijackers could have murdered everyone on board by then."

"If they haven't already," said Brogan.

"What forces do we have in the area?"

"Virtually none, Mr. President," answered Nichols. "We have no call to maintain a presence that far south. Except for a few Air Force transport planes ferrying supplies to polar research stations, the only U.S. vessel anywhere near the *Lady Flamborough* is the *Sounder,* a NUMA deep-water survey ship."

"The one carrying Dirk Pitt?"

"Yes, sir."

"What about our Special Forces people?"

"I was on the phone with General Keith at the Pentagon twenty minutes ago," Schiller volunteered. "An elite team, along with their equipment, boarded C-140 cargo jets and took off about an hour ago. They were accompanied by a wing of Osprey assault aircraft."

The President sat back in the chair and folded his hands. "Where will they set up their command post?"

Brogan called up a map displaying the tip of South America on a giant wall monitor. He used a flashlight arrow to indicate a particular spot.

"Unless we receive new information that will alter the tentative plan," he explained, "they'll land at an airport outside the small Chilean city of Punta Arenas on the Brunswick Peninsula and use it as a base for operations."

"A long flight," said the President quietly. "When will they arrive?"

"Inside fifteen hours."

The President looked at Oates. "Doug, I leave it to you to handle any sovereignty issues with the Chilean and Argentine governments."

"I'll see to it."

"The *Lady Flamborough* will have to be found before the Special Forces can launch a rescue attempt," said Schiller with remorseless logic.

"We're up the creek on this one." There was a curious acceptance in Brogan's voice. "The closest carrier fleet is almost five thousand miles away. No way a full-scale air and sea search can be mounted."

Schiller stared at the table thoughtfully. "Any rescue attempt could take weeks if the hijackers slip the *Lady Flamborough* in among the barren bays and coves along the Antarctic coast line. Fog, mist and low overcast wouldn't help matters either."

"Satellite surveillance is our only tool," said Nichols. "The predicament is that we have no spy satellites eyeballing that region of the earth."

"Dale is right," Schiller agreed. "The far southern seas are not high on the strategic surveillance list. If we were talking northern hemisphere, we could focus a whole array of listening and imagery gear to tune in conversations on board the ship and read a newspaper on deck."

"What's available?" the President asked.

"The Landsat," answered Brogan, "a few Defense meteorological satellites, and a Seasat used by NUMA for Antarctic ice and sea current surveys. But our best bet is the SR-90 Casper."

"Do we have SR-90 reconnaissance aircraft in Latin America?"

"A tight security airfield in Texas is as close as we come."

"How long to fly one down and back?"

"A Casper is capable of reaching mach five, or just under five thousand kilometers per hour. One can fly to the tip of Antarctica, make a photo run and have the film back in

515

five hours."

The President slowly shook his head in dismay. "Will someone please tell me why the United States government is always caught with our pants down? I swear to God, nobody screws up like we do. We build the most sophisticated detection systems the world has ever known, and when we need them, they're all concentrated in the wrong place at the wrong time."

Nobody spoke, nobody moved. The President's men avoided his eyes and stared uncomfortably at the table, papers, wall, anything but another face.

At last Nichols spoke in a quiet, confident voice. "We'll find the ship, Mr. President. If anyone can get them out alive, the Special Forces will."

"Yes," the President drawled softly. "They're highly trained for such a mission. The only question in my mind is whether the crew and passengers will be there to be rescued. Or will the Special Forces find a silent ship filled with corpses?"

46

Colonel Morton Hollis wasn't overjoyed at leaving his family in the middle of his wife's birthday party. The understanding look in her eyes wrenched his gut. The cost would hit him dearly, he knew. The red coral necklace was about to be enhanced by the five-day cruise to the Bahamas she'd always pestered him about.

He sat at a desk in a specially designed office compartment inside the C-140 transport, flying south over Venezuela. He puffed away deeply on a large Havana cigar he had purchased at the base store, now that the embargo on Cuban imports had been lifted.

Hollis studied the latest weather reports on the Antarctic peninsula and peered at photographs showing the ragged, icy coastline. He'd already run over the difficulties in his mind a dozen times since takeoff. During their brief history the newly formed Special Operations Forces had already achieved a notable record, but they had yet to tackle a major rescue of the magnitude of the *Lady Flamborough* hijacking.

The orphan child of the Pentagon, the Special Operations Forces were not molded into a single command until the fall of 1989. At that time the Army's Delta Force, whose fighters were drawn from the elite Ranger and Green Beret units and a secret aviation unit known as Task Force 160, merged with the top-of-the-line Navy SEAL Team Six and the Air Force's Special Operations Wing.

The unified forces cut across service rivalries and boundaries and became a separate command, numbering twelve thousand men, headquartered at a tightly restricted base in southeast Virginia. The crack fighters were heavily trained in guerrilla tactics, parachuting, wilderness survival and scuba diving, with special emphasis on storming buildings, ships and aircraft for rescue missions.

Hollis was short — he'd barely met the height requirements of the Special Forces — and almost as wide in the shoulders as he was tall. Forty years old but immensely tough, he had survived a rigorous simulated guerrilla war in the swamps of Florida for three weeks, and parachuted right back in for another exercise. His closely cropped brown hair was thin and graying early. His eyes were a blue-green, the whites slightly yellowed from too much time in the sun without proper glasses.

An astute man who always looked over the next hill and planned accordingly, he left very little to chance. He blew a smoke ring from the cigar with a degree of elation. He couldn't be leading a better team if he'd picked the medal winners of a military Olympics. They were the elite of the elite for fighting low-intensity conflicts. The eighty men of his team, who called themselves the Demon Stalkers, were selected for the *Lady Flamborough* rescue because they actually had engaged in winter assault exercises against mock terrorists who had held a ship and crew hostages off the coast of Norway. Forty were "shooters" while the other half acted as logistical and support fighters.

His second in command, Major John Dillinger, rapped on the door and stuck his head in. "You busy, Mort?" he asked in a decided Texas twang.

Hollis waved a casual hand. "My office is your office," he assured Dillinger jovially. "Squeeze in and sit yourself in my new French leather designer couch."

Dillinger, a lean, stringy man with a pinched face, but hard as an anvil, stared dubiously at the canvas seat bolted to the floor and sat down. Forever kidded about being saddled with the same name as the famous bank robber, he was a master of the art of tactical planning and the penetration of almost impossible defenses.

"Covering the bases?" he asked Hollis.

"Going over meteorological forecasts, ice and terrain conditions."

"See any jazz in your crystal ball?"

"Too early." Hollis raised an eyebrow. "What plans are forming in your perverted mind?"

"I can recite and draw pictures of six different ways to board a ship by stealth. I've already familiarized myself with the design and deck layout of the *Lady Flamborough*, but until we learn whether we're coming in by parachute, by scuba, or by foot from hard beach or ice, I can only plot an outline."

Hollis nodded solemnly. "Over a hundred innocent people are on that ship. Two Presidents and the Secretary-General of the United Nations. God help us if one steps in our line of fire."

"We can't go in with blanks," Dillinger said caustically.

"No, and we can't drop from noisy helicopters with all weapons blasting. We've got to infiltrate before the hijackers know we're there. Complete surprise is crucial."

"Then we hit 'em by 'stealth parachute' at night."

"Could be," Hollis acknowledged tersely.

Dillinger shifted uncomfortably in the canvas seat. "A night landing is dangerous enough, but dropping blindly on a darkened ship can mean slaughter. You know it, and I know it, Mort. Out of forty men, fifteen will miss the target and fall in the sea. Twenty will sustain injuries impacting on hard, protruding surfaces of the ship. I'll be lucky to have five men in fighting trim."

"We can't rule it out."

"Let's wait until more info comes in," suggested Dillinger. "Everything hinges on where the ship is found. Whether she's moored or sailing across the sea makes all the difference in the world. As soon as we receive word on her final status, I'll formulate a tight assault plan and lay it in your hands for final approval."

"Fair enough," said Hollis agreeably. "How are the men?"

"Doing their homework. By the time we land at Punta Arenas, they'll have memorized the *Lady Flamborough* well enough to run around her decks blindfolded."

"A lot is riding on them this time out."

"They'll do the job. The trick is to get them on board in one piece."

"There is one thing," Hollis said, a deep apprehension on his face. "The latest estimate from intelligence sources on the strength of the hijackers . . . it just came in from the Pentagon."

"How many are we talking about, five, ten, maybe twelve?"

Hollis hesitated. "Assuming the crew of the Mexican ore carrier that boarded the cruise ship are also armed . . . we could be looking at a total of forty."

Dillinger gaped. "Oh, my gawd. We're going up against an equal number of terrorists?"

"Looks that way." Hollis nodded grimly.

Dillinger shook his head in shocked disapproval and drew a hand across his forehead. Then his eyes burned into Hollis's.

"Some people," he said disgustedly, "are going to get their butts stomped before this caper is over."

Deep in a concrete bunker tunneled into a hill outside Washington, D.C., Lieutenant Samuel T. Jones came rushing into a large office, panting as though he'd just run a two-hundred-meter dash, which indeed he had — only two steps shy of the exact distance from the communications room to the photo-analysis office.

His face was flushed with excitement, and he held a huge photograph spread between his upraised hands.

Jones had often rushed along the corridors during crisis exercise drills, but he, and the other three hundred men and women who worked in the Special Operations Forces Readiness Command, hadn't really put their hearts into it until now. Practice did not make the adrenaline pump like the real thing. After waiting like hibernating groundhogs, they had erupted into life when the alert on the *Lady Flamborough* hijacking came in from the Pentagon.

Major General Frank Dodge headed up the SOF. He and several members of his staff were tensely awaiting the arrival of the latest satellite image depicting the waters south of Tierra del Fuego when Jones burst into the room.

"Got it!"

Dodge gave the young officer a stern look for unmilitary enthusiasm. "Should have been here eight minutes ago," he grunted.

"My fault, General. I took the liberty of trimming the outer perimeters and enlarging the immediate search area before having it computer-enhanced."

Dodge's stern expression softened and he nodded approvingly.

"Good thinking, Lieutenant."

Jones gave a short sigh and quickly clipped the newest satellite image on a long wallboard under a row of hooded spotlights. An earlier image hung nearby, showing the *Lady Flamborough*'s last known position circled in red, her previous course marked in green, and predicted course in orange.

Jones stepped back as General Dodge and his officers crowded around the image, peering anxiously for the tiny dot indicating the cruise ship.

"The last satellite sighting put the ship about one hundred kilometers south of Cape Horn," said a major, tracing the course from the previous chart. "She should be well out into Drake's Passage by now, approaching the islands off the Antarctic peninsula."

After nearly a full minute of appraisal, General Dodge turned to Jones. "Did you study the photo, Lieutenant?"

"No, sir. I didn't take the time. I rushed it over as quickly as possible."

"You're certain this is the latest transmission?"

Jones looked puzzled. "Yes, sir."

"No mistake?"

"None," Jones replied unhesitatingly. "The NUMA Seasat satellite recorded the area with digital electronic impulses that were sent to ground stations instantaneously. You're seeing an image no more than six minutes old."

"When will the next photo come in?"

"The Landsat should orbit the region in forty minutes."

"And the Casper?"

Jones glanced at his watch. "If she returns on schedule, we should be looking at film in four hours."

"Get it to me the instant it arrives."

"Yes, sir."

Dodge turned to his subordinates. "Well, gentlemen, the White House *ain't* going to like this."

He went over and picked up a phone. "Put me through to Alan Mercier."

The National Security Adviser's voice came over the line within twenty seconds. "I hope you've got some good news, Frank."

"Sorry, no," Dodge answered flatly. "It appears the cruise ship —"

"She sank?" Mercier cut him off.

"We can't say with any certainty."

"What *are* you saying?"

Dodge took a breath. "Please inform the President the *Lady Flamborough* has vanished again."

47

By the early 1990s equipment for sending photographs or graphics around the world by microwave via satellite or across town by fiber optics became as common in business and government offices as copy machines. Scanned by laser and then transmitted to a laser receiver, the image could be reproduced almost instantly in living color with extraordinary detail.

So it was that within ten minutes of General Dodge's call, the President and Dale Nichols were hunched over the desk in the Oval Office scrutinizing the Seasat image of waters off the tip of South America.

"She may really be on the bottom this time," said Nichols. He felt tired and confused.

"I don't believe it," the President said, his face a mask of repressed fury. "The hijackers had their chance to destroy the ship off Punta del Este and make a clean getaway on the *General Bravo*. Why sink her now?"

"Escape by submarine is a possibility."

The President seemed not to hear. "Our inability to deal with this crisis is frightening. Our whole response seems mired in inertia."

"We were caught unprepared and un-equipped," Nichols offered lamely.

"An event that occurs too frequently around here," the President muttered. He looked up, fire in his eyes. "I refuse to write those people off. I owe George Pitt. Without his support, I wouldn't be sitting in the Oval Office." He paused for effect. "We're not going to snap at a red herring again."

Sid Green was scrutinizing the satellite images too. A photo-intelligence specialist with the National Security Agency at its headquarters in Fort Meyer, he had projected the last two satellite pictures on one screen. Intrigued, he ignored the most recent photo, the one that failed to reveal the ship, and concentrated on the earlier one. He zoomed in on the tiny blip that represented the *Lady Flamborough* with a computerized lens.

The outline was fuzzy, too indistinct to make out little more than the ship's profile. He turned to the computer at his left and entered a series of instructions. A few details that were hidden to his eye became apparent now. He could discern the funnel and shape of the superstructure and blurred sections of the upper decks.

He played with the computer keyboard, trying to sharpen the cruise ship's features. He spent nearly an hour at it before he finally sat back, put his arms behind his head and rested his eyes.

The door to the darkened room opened and Green's supervisor, Vic Patton, entered. He stood behind Green for a moment looking at the projections.

"It's like trying to read a newspaper on the street from the roof of the World Trade Center," he observed.

Green spoke without turning. "A 70-by-130 kilometer swath doesn't offer us much resolution, even after enlarged enhancement."

"Any sign of the ship on the last image?"

"Not a hint."

"Too bad we can't drop our KH spy birds that low."

"A KH-15 might get a picture."

"The situation in the Middle East is heating up again. I can't pull one out of orbit until the dust settles."

"Then send in a Casper."

"One is on the way," said Patton. "You should be reading the color of the hijackers' eyes by lunch."

Green motioned at the computer lens. "Take a look and tell me if something looks out of place."

Patton pressed his face against the rubber eyepiece and peered at the speck that was the

Lady Flamborough. "Too damned blurred to discern incidentals. What am I missing?"

"Check the bow section."

"How can you tell the back from the front?"

"By the wake behind the stern," Green answered patiently.

"Okay, I've got it. The deck behind the bow looks obscured, almost as if it was covered."

"You win first prize at the fair," said Green.

"What are they up to?" Patton mused.

"We'll know when the film from the Casper comes in."

On board the C-140, now cruising over Bolivia, there was an atmosphere of bitter disappointment. The photo minus the cruise ship came over the aircraft's laser receiver and caused as much agitation inside the cramped command center as in Washington's power circles.

"Where in hell did it go?" Hollis demanded.

Dillinger could only mutter blankly, "She can't be gone."

"Well, she sure is. See for yourself."

"I did. I can't spot her any more than you can."

"This makes three times in a row we've been shut out at the gate by bad information, lousy weather or equipment breakdown. Now our target ups and plays hide-and-seek."

"She must have sunk," mumbled Dillinger. "I don't see any other explanation."

"I can't see forty hijackers all agreeing on a suicide pact."

"What now?"

"Beyond requesting instructions from Readiness Command, I see little else I can do."

"Shall we abort the mission?" asked Dillinger.

"Not unless we're ordered to turn back."

"So we keep going."

Hollis nodded dejectedly. "We fly south until ordered otherwise."

The last to know was Pitt. He was sleeping like the dead when Rudi Gunn entered his cabin and shook him awake.

"Come alive," said Gunn briskly. "We've got a big problem."

Pitt popped his eyes open and checked the dial of his watch. "Did we get a speeding ticket coming into Punta Arenas?"

Gunn looked at Pitt in weary despair. Anyone who awoke from a sound sleep in a cheerful mood and instantly made bad jokes had to have come from a broken branch of evolution.

"The ship won't enter the harbor for another hour yet."

"Good, I can doze a while longer."

"Get serious!" Gunn said bluntly. "The latest satellite photo just rolled out of the ship's receiver. The *Lady Flamborough* has gone missing for the second time."

"She's really dropped out?"

"Enhanced magnification can't find a sign of her. I've just talked to Admiral Sandecker. The White House and Pentagon are spitting out orders like slot machines gone mad. A Special Operations Force rescue team is on the way, steamed and primed for action, but with no place to go. They're also sending a spy plane to produce some decent aerial pictures."

"Ask the Admiral if he can arrange a meeting between the SOF team leader and me as soon as they land."

"Why don't *you* tell him?"

"Because I'm going back to sleep," Pitt replied with a loud yawn.

Gunn was at a loss. "Your father's on that boat. Don't you give a damn?"

"Yes," said Pitt, his eyes flashing a caution light, "I give a damn. But I don't see what I can do about it at the moment."

Gunn backed off. "Anything else the Admiral should know?"

Pitt pulled the blanket under his armpits, rolled over and faced the bulkhead. "Yes, as a matter of fact. You can tell him I know how the *Lady Flamborough* vanished. And I can make a pretty good guess as to where she hides."

If any other man had spoken those words, Gunn would have called him a liar. But Pitt he didn't doubt for a second.

"Mind giving me a clue?"

Pitt half-turned. "You're an art collector of sorts, aren't you, Rudy?"

"My small collection of abstracts won't match the New York Museum of Modern Art, but it's respectable." He looked at Pitt in uncomprehending curiosity. "What has this got to do with anything?"

"If I'm right, we may be getting into art in a big way."

"Are we on the same frequency?"

"Christo," said Pitt as he turned and re-faced the bulkhead. "We're about to review a Christo-inspired sculpture."

48

A light snow had turned to a miserable, wind-driven sleet over the southernmost large city in the world. Punta Arenas had flourished as a port of call before the Panama Canal was built, and died afterward. The city gradually returned as a sheep-raising center and was now booming after productive oil fields were discovered close by.

Hollis and Dillinger stood on a harbor pier, waiting anxiously to board the *Sounder*. The temperature had dropped several degrees below freezing; it was a damp, harsh cold that bit at their exposed faces. They felt like camels in the Arctic. Through the cooperation of Chilean authorities, they had gone under-cover and exchanged their battle dress for the uniforms of immigration officials.

As scheduled, their aircraft had landed at a nearby military airport while it was still dark. The storm came as an added bonus, holding visibility to a few hundred meters and keeping their arrival unobserved. The Chilean military command was most generous in their hospitality and provided hangar space for Hollis's small flight of C-140s and Ospreys to park out of sight.

They moved from the shelter of a warehouse as the research ship's mooring lines were dropped over the dock bollards and the gangway lowered. Both men flinched as the full force of the icy wind struck them.

A tall man with a craggy face and a friendly grin, wearing a ski jacket, appeared on the bridge wing. He cupped his hands around his mouth.

"Señor López?" he shouted through the sleet.

"*Sí!*" Hollis yelled back.

"Who's your friend?"

"*Mi amigo es* Señor Jones," Hollis answered, nodding at Dillinger.

"I've heard better Spanish in a Chinese restaurant," Dillinger muttered.

"Please come on board. After you reach the main deck, take the ladder to your right and come up to the bridge."

"*Gracias.*"

The two leaders of America's elite fighting force dutifully walked up the slanted gangway and climbed the ladder as directed. Hollis's curiosity was eating him up. An hour before reaching Punta Arenas, he'd received an urgent coded communication from General Dodge ordering him to covertly meet the

Sounder when she docked in port. No explanation, no further instructions. He knew only from a hurried briefing in Virginia that the survey ship and its crew were responsible for discovering the deception between the Mexican container ship and the *Lady Flamborough*. Nothing else. He was most interested in learning why she suddenly appeared in Punta Arenas at almost the same time as his SOF team.

Hollis did not like being left in the dark, and he was in an intensely testy mood.

The man who hailed him was still standing on the bridge wing. Hollis looked into mesmeric green eyes — very opaline green indeed. They belonged to a lean, broad-shouldered man whose uncovered black hair was speckled with white flakes of ice. He stared at the two officers for all of five seconds, time enough to complete a survey. Then he removed his right hand slowly from a coat pocket and stuck it out.

"Colonel Hollis, Major Dillinger, my name is Dirk Pitt."

"Seems you know more about us than we do you, Mr. Pitt."

"A situation that will be quickly rectified," Pitt said cheerfully. "Please follow me to the Captain's cabin. The coffee's on, and we can talk where it's warm and private."

They gratefully stepped out of the cold and trailed Pitt down one deck to Stewart's quarters. Once inside, Pitt introduced Gunn, Giordino and Captain Stewart. The SOF officers shook hands all around and gratefully accepted the coffee.

"Please sit down," said Stewart, offering chairs.

Dillinger sank into a chair, but Hollis shook his head.

"Thank you, I'd rather stand." He cast a questioning look at the four men from NUMA. "If I can speak frankly, would you mind telling me what in hell is going on?"

"Obviously it concerns the *Lady Flamborough*," said Pitt.

"What's there to discuss? The terrorists have destroyed her."

"She's still very much afloat," Pitt assured him.

"I've received no word to that effect," said Hollis. "The last satellite photo shows no trace of her."

"Take my word for it."

"Show me your evidence."

"You don't screw around, do you?"

"My men and I flew here to save lives," Hollis said roughly. "No one, not even my superiors, has demonstrated to me that people on board that ship can still be saved."

"You have to understand, Colonel," said Pitt, his voice abruptly cutting like a whip, "we're not dealing with your usual gun-happy terrorists. Their leader is extremely resourceful. Until now he's outwitted the best security brains in the business. And he keeps right on doing it."

"Yet someone saw through the disguise," said Hollis, throwing a left-handed compliment.

"We were lucky. If the *Sounder* hadn't been surveying in that part of the sea, our discovery of the *General Bravo* might have taken a month. As it is, we've cut the hijackers' lead time down to one or two days."

Hollis's pessimism began to melt away. This man wasn't giving an inch. He wondered if the rescue operation might take place after all. "Where is the ship?" he asked bluntly.

"We don't know," answered Gunn.

"Not so much as an approximate position?"

"The best we can offer is an educated guess," said Giordino.

"Based on what?"

Gunn looked expectantly at Pitt, who smiled and carried the ball again.

"Intuition."

Hollis's hopes began to crumble. "Are you using tarot cards or a crystal ball?" he asked sardonically.

"Actually, I favor tea leaves," replied Pitt, tit for tat.

There was a brief silence, long and cold. Hollis rightly figured aggression wasn't going to get him anywhere. He finished his coffee and turned the cup round and round.

"All right, gentlemen. I regret coming on a little too strong. I'm not used to dealing with civilians."

There was no malice in Pitt's face, just a look of amusement. "If it will make you feel more comfortable, I carry the rank of Major in the Air Force."

Hollis frowned. "May I ask what you're doing on a NUMA vessel?"

"Call it a permanent assignment — a long story we don't have time to get into."

Dillinger caught it first. Hollis should have caught it the minute they were introduced, but his mind was saturated with questions.

"Are you by chance related to Senator George Pitt?" asked Dillinger.

"Father and son."

A small piece of the curtain lifted and the two officers saw a shaft of light beneath. Hollis pulled up a chair and settled in. "Okay, Mr. Pitt, please tell me what you've got."

Dillinger cut in. "The last report showed The *Lady Flamborough* heading for the Antarctic. You say she's still on the surface. New photos will easily pick her out amid the ice floes."

"If you're betting on the SR-ninety Casper," said Pitt, "save your money."

Dillinger gave Hollis a bleak look. They were outdistanced. This oddball group of ocean engineers had as much information in hand as they did.

"From a hundred thousand kilometers an SR-ninety can reveal three-dimensional images so sharp that you can distinguish the stitching on a soccer ball," stated Hollis.

"No question. But suppose the ball is camouflaged to look like a rock."

"I still don't know —"

"You'd see more clearly if we showed you," said Pitt. "The crew has set up a demonstration on deck."

The open deck on the stern had been covered over with a large, opaque blanket of white plastic, firmly secured to keep it taut and prevent it from billowing under the constant breeze. Captain Stewart stood by with two crew members who manned a fire hose.

"During our survey of the area around the *General Bravo* we recovered a roll of this plastic," Pitt lectured. "I believe it accidentally fell off the *Lady Flamborough* when the two vessels rendezvoused. It was sitting on the seabed among empty barrels of paint the hijackers used to remodel the cruise liner to resemble the Mexican container ship. Granted, the evidence is inconclusive. You'll have to take my word for that. But it all points to another makeup job. Nothing showed on the last satellite photo because all eyes were searching for a ship. The *Lady Flamborough* no longer looks like one. The hijack leader must be into art appreciation. He took a page from the controversial sculptor Christo, who's famous for his outdoor sculptures in plastic. He wraps the stuff around buildings, coastlines and islands. He hung a monstrous curtain in Rifle Gap, Colorado, and made a fence running for miles in Marin County, California. The chief hijacker went one better and wrapped the entire cruise liner. The liner is not a huge ship. The basic outline of her hull could have been altered by props and scaffolding. With the sheets all cut and numbered as to position, a hundred hostages and hijackers might have done the job in ten hours flat. They were working at it when the Landsat orbited overhead. The enhanced blowup was not clear enough to reveal details of the activity. When the Seasat followed half a day later there was nothing to identify, no features conforming to a ship, any ship. Am I going too fast?"

"No . . ." Hollis said slowly. "But none of it makes a hell of a lot of sense."

"He must be from Missouri," Giordino said wryly. "Shall we show him?"

Pitt gave a brief nod to Captain Stewart.

"Okay, boys," said Stewart to his crewmen. "Once over lightly."

One man turned the valve while the other aimed the nozzle. A fine spray was turned on the plastic sheeting. At first the wind carried half the mist over the side. The crewman adjusted the angle, and soon the plastic was coated with a watery film.

Before a full minute passed, the frigid atmosphere turned the water to ice.

Hollis observed the transformation pensively. Then he walked up to Pitt and held out his hand. "My respects, sir. You made a sound call."

Dillinger stared like a rube who'd been suckered at a traveling carnival. "An iceberg," he muttered angrily. "The sons of bitches made the ship into an iceberg."

49

Hala awoke cold and stiff. It was midmorning, yet there was still a level of darkness. The cargo container facade, combined with the ice-coated plastic shrouding the cruise liner, shut out most of the light. What little penetrated into the VIP suites was just sufficient to reveal the figures of Presidents Hasan and De Lorenzo on the bed next to her. Under one pitifully inadequate blanket, they huddled against one another for warmth, their frozen breaths hanging in vaporlike clouds above their heads before condensing and freezing on the walls.

The cold itself might have been tolerated, no matter how miserable, but the high humidity made the freezing temperatures unbearable. Their condition was further aggravated by not having had anything to eat since leaving Punta del Este. The hijackers made no effort to provide food for the passengers and crew. Ammar's inhuman callousness took its toll as the cold sapped their strength, and fear of the unknown drugged their minds.

For the first part of the voyage, the prisoners had survived on nothing but water out of the faucets in the bathroom showers and washbasins. But the pipes had frozen, and the torment of thirst was added to the ache of hunger.

The *Lady Flamborough* had been refitted to sail tropical seas and carried only a minimum supply of blankets. Everyone who came on board in Puerto Rico or Punta del Este had packed for a temperate climate and had left all winter clothing in closets at home. The prisoners bundled up as best they could, wearing several layers of lightweight shirts, pants and socks. They wrapped their heads in towels to retain body heat. The cold-weather gear they sorely missed most was gloves.

There was no warmth anywhere. Ammar had refused all pleas to circulate heat throughout the ship. He could not afford the luxury. Interior heat would have melted the ice film on the plastic sheeting and sabotaged the deception.

Hala was not the only prisoner awake. Most had found it impossible to drop off into a sound sleep. They lay as if in a hypnotic trance, aware of their surroundings but unable to make any kind of physical effort. Any thoughts of resistance had rapidly drained away under the onslaught. Instead of fighting the hijackers, Captain Collins and his crew were reduced to struggling to stay alive against the numbing cold.

Hala raised to her elbows as Senator Pitt came into the room.

He made a strange appearance, wearing a gray business suit over a blue pinstripe. He gave Hala a smile of encouragement, but it was a pathetic effort. The fatigue of the past five days had taken away his youthful look, and he looked closer to his true age.

"How you holding up?" he asked.

"I'd give my right arm for a cup of hot tea," she said gamely.

"For my part, I'd give more than that."

President De Lorenzo sat up and dropped his feet on the deck. "Did someone say hot tea?"

"Just fantasizing, Mr. President," replied the Senator.

"I never thought I'd find myself starving and freezing to death on a luxurious cruise ship."

"Nor I," said Hala.

President Hasan gave a slight moan as he changed position and lifted his head.

"Is your back bothering you?" asked President De Lorenzo, his face reflecting concern.

"I'm too cold to hurt," Hasan said with a tight smile.

"Can I help you up?"

"No, thank you. I think I'll just remain here in bed and conserve whatever strength I have left." Hasan looked at De Lorenzo and smiled thinly. "I wish we had met and become friends under more comfortable circumstances."

"I've heard the Americans say, 'Politics makes strange bedfellows.' We seem to be a literal example."

"When we get out of this, you must be my guest in Egypt."

De Lorenzo nodded. "A reciprocal agreement. You must also visit Mexico."

"An honor I gladly accept."

The two Presidents solemnly shook hands on it — no longer pampered heads of state but two men whose lives shared a fate they could not control and were determined to end with dignity.

"The engines have stopped," said Hala suddenly.

Senator Pitt nodded. "The anchors were just dropped. We're moored, and they've shut down the engines."

"We must be near land."

"No way of telling with the port windows hidden."

"Too bad we're blind," said Hasan.

"If one of you will guard the door, I'll make a try at forcing the window," said Pitt. "Once I make a break in the glass without alerting a guard, I'll carve a hole in the fiberboard. With luck we might be able to see where we are."

"I'll listen at the door," Hala volunteered.

"The cold is bad enough without letting more in," said De Lorenzo dispiritedly.

"The temperature is the same outside as in here," the Senator replied bluntly.

He was not about to waste time in debate. He went immediately to the large glass viewing window in the sitting room. The port measured two meters high by one wide. There was no promenade deck running along outside. The staterooms and suite entrances faced the center of the ship. The windowed outer walls rose flush from the hull.

The only open areas patrolled by the hijackers were the pool and lounge decks above and the observation decks fore and aft.

The Senator rapped the glass with his knuckles. The return sound came like a dull thump. The glass was thick. It had to be to withstand the crushing impact of huge waves and hurricane-force winds.

"Anyone wear a diamond ring?" he asked.

Hala slipped her hands out of the pockets of a light raincoat, held them up and wiggled her fingers, displaying two small rings mounted with opals and turquoise. "Muslim suitors are not in the habit of spoiling their women with lavish gifts."

"I could use a full carat."

President Hasan pulled a large ring from one of his pinky fingers. "Here is a three-carat."

The Senator eyeballed the stone in the dim

light. "This should do nicely. Thank you."

He worked quickly but carefully, making little noise, cutting an opening just large enough to slip a finger through. He stopped every so often to blow on his hands. When his fingers began to go numb, he held them under his armpits until they limbered up again.

He did not care to contemplate what the hijackers would do to him if they caught him. He could almost envision his bullet-riddled corpse floating in the current.

He cut a circular line around the small center hole, retracing the line until the gouge went deeper and deeper. The tricky part was to prevent a piece of the glass from falling down the side of the steel hull and tinkling as it fell.

He curled a finger into the hole and pulled. The circle of glass gave way. He slowly eased it backward and set it on the carpet. Not a bad job. Now he had an opening large enough to stick his head through.

The fiberboard making up the false cargo containers stood half an arm's length from the window and covered the entire length of the midship's superstructure. The Senator cautiously slipped his head past the opening, careful not to slice his ears on its razor-sharp edges. He peered from side to side, but saw only the narrow slot between the fake containers and the steel sides of the ship. Upward, he viewed the crack of light that was the sky, but it appeared dimmed as if socked in by fog. He should have seen a thin band of moving water below. Instead his eyes took in an immense sheet of plastic that was attached by bracing along the waterline. He stared at it in amazement, not having the faintest idea of its purpose.

The Senator felt secure. If he couldn't see the hijackers guarding the decks, they couldn't see him. He returned to the bedroom and rummaged through his suitcase.

"What do you need?" asked Hala.

He held up a Swiss Army knife. "I always carry one of these in my shaving kit." He grinned. "The corkscrew comes in handy for impromptu parties."

Senator Pitt took his time and warmed his hands before going back to work. He grasped the red handle, eased his arm through the opening in the glass and began to twist, using the small blade as a drill, and then the large blade to carve away the sides and increase the circumference.

The process went agonizingly slowly. He dared not run the blade more than a scant millimeter past the outer wall of the fiberboard. There was the nagging fear an alert guard might peer over the side and glimpse the tiny metallic movement. He carved very carefully, removing each layer of the fiberboard before attacking the next.

All feeling went out of his hand, but he did not warm it. His fist was frozen stiffly around the red handle. The small knife felt like an extension of his arm.

At last the Senator scraped away enough wood shavings for an eyehole large enough to observe a fairly large area of sea. He leaned his head through the glass and pressed his cheek against the cold surface of the board.

Something shut off his view. He poked his finger in the eyehole and felt it touch the plastic sheeting. He was more confounded than ever to learn it covered the hollow containers as well as the lower hull.

He cursed under his breath. He needn't have been so afraid of penetrating the wood. No one would have seen his knife blade under the plastic anyway. He threw off caution and quickly cut a slot in the opaque material. Then the Senator looked again.

He did not see the open sea, nor did he find himself viewing a shoreline.

What he saw was a towering cliff of ice that extended far beyond his limited line of sight. The glistening wall was so close he could have touched it with an extended umbrella.

As he stared he heard a deadened bass drumlike sound. It reminded the Senator of the rumble from a minor earthquake.

He stepped back abruptly, reeling at the implication of what he'd discovered.

Hala saw him stiffen. "What is it?" she

asked anxiously. "What did you see?"

He turned and looked at her blankly, his mouth working until words finally formed. "They've anchored us against a huge glacier," he said finally. "The ice wall can break away at any time and crush the ship like paper."

50

Twenty thousand meters above the Antarctic peninsula, the delta-wing reconnaissance plane slipped through the rarefied air at 3,200 kilometers per hour. She was designed to fly twice that altitude at twice the speed, but her pilot held her at 40 percent throttle to conserve fuel and give the cameras a chance to sharpen earth images under the slower speed.

Unlike her ancestor, the SR-71 "blackbird," whose natural titanium wings and fuselage wore the color of deep indigo, the "stealth" technology of the more advanced SR-90 created an incredibly tough, lightweight plastic skin that was tinted gray-white. Nicknamed "the Casper" after the cartoon ghost, she was almost as impossible to detect by eye as she was by radar.

Her five cameras could capture half the length of the United States in one hour with only one pass. Her photographic package filmed in black-and-white, color, infrared, three-dimensional, and a few imagery techniques that were highly classified and totally unknown to commercial photographers.

Lieutenant Colonel James Slade had little to do. It was a long, boring reconnaissance from his base in California's Mojave Desert. The only time he took manual control in flight was during refueling operations. The Casper's engines had a heavy thirst. She had to be refueled twice on each leg of the flight by aerial tankers.

Slade examined the instruments with a critical eye. The Casper was a new plane, and she had yet to reveal all her bugs. Thankful to find normal readings across the board, he sighed and pulled a miniature electronic game from a pocket of his flight suit. He began pressing the buttons below a small viewing window, trying to get a tiny diver past a giant octopus to reach a treasure chest.

After a few minutes he tired of the game and gazed ahead and down at the frozen isolation that was Antarctica. Far below, the curved, beckoning finger of the northern peninsula and its adjoining islands sparkled under a diamond-clear sky.

The ice and rock and sea created a beautiful vastness, awesome to the eye, intimidating to the soul. The sight may have looked appealing from twenty kilometers overhead, but Slade knew better. He'd once flown supplies to a scientific station at the South Pole and quickly learned the beauty and the hostility in the permanent domain of cold went hand in hand.

He well remembered the chilling temperatures. He didn't believe it possible to spit and see the saliva freeze before it hit the ground. And he never forgot the ferocious winds that scourge the coldest of all continents. The 160-kilometer gusts were unimaginable until he experienced them for the first time.

Slade could never fathom why some men were so attracted to that frozen hell. He had a facetious urge to call a travel agent after he returned to base and inquire about reservations at a good resort hotel close to the polar center.

Suddenly a female voice spoke over one of the three cockpit speakers.

"Attention, please. You are about to cross the outer limit of your flight path where seventy degrees longitude and seventy degrees latitude intersect. Disengage auto pilot and come around a hundred and eighty degrees beginning . . . now. The new heading for your return is programmed into the computer. Please enter the appropriate code. Have a good trip home."

Slade followed the instructions and made a lazy turn. As soon as the computer locked on the return heading he went back on auto pilot and shifted to a more comfortable position in his cramped seat.

Like so many other men who flew reconnaissance missions, he fantasized about the face and body that went with the disembodied voice. Rumor had it she weighed three hundred pounds, was sixty years old and a grandmother twelve times. No pilot with a sound imagination could believe such a myth-shattering thought. She had to look like Sigourney Weaver. Maybe it *was* Sigourney Weaver. He decided to explore the tantalizing possibility on his return home.

That delicate problem solved, Slade rechecked his instrument panel and then relaxed while the icebound land drifted away behind his tail. Over the sea again, he returned to his little electronic treasure game.

He saw little purpose in continuing to watch the world roll by, especially since Tierra del Fuego was covered by thick blankets of charcoal clouds. He'd studied enough geography to know it was a wretched land of constant wind, rain and snow.

Slade was almost thankful he couldn't see the monotonous landscape. He left it to Casper's infrared camera to penetrate the dark overcast and record the desolate, dead end of the continent.

Captain Collins stared into Ammar's mask and had to force himself not to avert his gaze. There was something evil, something inhuman in the eyes of the urbane leader of the hijackers. Collins could sense a chilling unconcern for mere human life about the man.

"I demand to know when you're going to release my ship," said Collins in a precise tone.

Ammar set a cup of tea on a saucer, patted his lips with a table napkin and looked at Collins detachedly.

"Can I offer you some tea?"

"Not unless you offer it to my passengers and crew as well," Collins replied calmly. He stood erectly in his summer white uniform, bitterly cold and shivering.

"The very answer I expected." Ammar turned the empty cup upside down and leaned back. "You'll be happy to know my men and I expect to leave sometime tomorrow evening. If you give me your word there will be no foolish attempt to retake the ship or escape to the nearby shore before we depart, no one will be harmed and you can resume command."

"I'd rather you heat the ship and feed everyone now. We're desperately short of warm clothing and blankets to ward off the cold. No one has eaten in days. The pipes have frozen, blocking all water. And I don't have to mention the sanitation problems."

"Suffering is good for the soul," Ammar said philosophically.

Collins glared at him. "What utter tripe."

555

Ammar shrugged wearily. "If you say so."

"Good God, man, there are people sick and dying on this ship."

"I doubt seriously whether any of your crew and passengers will die of exposure or from starvation before my departure," said Ammar curtly. "They'll simply have to survive some discomfort for the next thirty hours or so until you can restart the engines and heat the ship."

"That may be too late for any of us if the wall of the glacier breaks off."

"It looks solid enough."

"You don't realize the danger. A massive ice slab might fall any moment. The weight could smash the *Lady Flamborough* like a ten-story building collapsing on an automobile. You must move the ship."

"A risk I cannot avoid. The ice film on the plastic would melt, giving away our location, and satellite infrared cameras could detect our radiated heat."

Collins's face was lined with helpless rage. "You're either a fool or you're insane. What good has any of this proven? What profit will you get out of it? Are we being held for ransom or as hostages in return for freeing your fellow terrorists behind bars somewhere? If you're simply walking off and leaving us, I fail to see the purpose."

"You have an irritating degree of curiosity, Captain, but a dedication of purpose after

556

my own heart. You will learn the reasons behind our capture of your ship soon enough." Ammar rose and nodded at the guard who stood behind Collins. "Return the Captain to confinement."

Collins refused to move. "Why can't you provide hot tea, coffee, soup, anything that will alleviate the suffering?"

Ammar did not bother to turn as he walked from the dining salon. "Goodbye, Captain. We won't meet again."

Ammar went directly to the communications room. Ibn was standing, watching a teletype hum out the latest wire-service news. His electronics man was seated at the radio, listening to an incoming transmission while a voice recorder copied it on paper. The radio and teletype were powered by a portable generator.

Ibn turned at Ammar's approach, gave a brief nod in recognition and tore a long sheet of paper from the teletype.

"The international news media are still reporting the *Lady Flamborough* as lost," he reported. "Salvage ships are only now arriving off Uruguay to conduct an underwater search. My compliments, Suleiman; you fooled the world. We'll be safely back in Cairo before the West learns the truth."

"What news of Egypt?" asked Ammar.

"Nothing worth celebrating yet. Hasan's cabinet ministers still control the government. They stubbornly hold on to power. They've played it smart by not sending in security forces to smash the demonstrations. The only bloodshed was caused by our fundamentalist brothers who mistakenly blew up a busload of Algerian firemen attending a convention in Cairo. It was thought the bus was part of a government police convoy. The Cairo news network is claiming Akhmad Yazid's movement is a front for Iranian fanatics. Many supporters are wavering in their loyalty and there has been no mass demand for Hasan's cabinet to dissolve the government."

"That idiot Khaled Fawzy was behind the bus explosion," snarled Ammar. "The military, where do the armed forces stand?"

"Defense Minister Abu Hamid will not commit himself until he views the bodies of President Hasan and Hala Kamil to confirm their deaths."

"So Yazid has yet to make a triumphal takeover."

Ibn nodded and his expression turned grave. "There is another news item. Yazid has announced that the cruise ship crew and passengers still live, and he will personally negotiate with the terrorists and arrange for the release of everyone. He has gone so far as to offer his life in return for Senator George Pitt to impress the Americans."

A numbing, paralyzing rage swelled within

Ammar, sharpening his senses and opening his thoughts like envelopes inside his mind. After a few moments, he looked at Ibn.

"By Allah, the Judas goat has led us to slaughter," he said incredulously. "Yazid has sold out the mission."

Ibn nodded in agreement. "Yazid has used and betrayed you."

"That explains why he stalled off ordering me to kill Hasan, Kamil and the rest. He wanted them unharmed until Machado and his scum could remove you and me and our people."

"What do Yazid and Topiltzin gain by keeping the hostages alive?" asked Ibn.

"By playing the saviors of two presidents, the Secretary-General of the United Nations and an important United States politician, Yazid and Topiltzin will gain the admiration of international leaders. They automatically become stronger while their opponents lose ground. They are then free to assume the reigns of their governments in peaceful takeovers, widening their power base and increasing their benevolent images in the eyes of the world."

Ibn bent his head in resignation. "So we've been thrown to the vultures."

Ammar nodded. "Yazid meant for us to die from the beginning to guarantee our silence on this and other missions we've performed for him."

"What of Captain Machado and his Mexican crew? What happens to them after they've eliminated us?"

"Topiltzin would see to it they vanished after their return to Mexico."

"They would have to escape the ship and island first."

"Yes," Ammar replied thoughtfully. He paced the communications room angrily. "It seems I badly underestimated Yazid's cunning. I was smug in thinking Machado was impotent because he knew nothing of our arrangements for escaping to a safe airfield in Argentina. But thanks to Yazid, our Mexican comrade has implemented his own departure plans."

"Then why hasn't he murdered us by now?"

"Because Yazid and Topiltzin won't give him the order until they're ready to act out their sham negotiations for the hostage release." Suddenly Ammar turned and gripped the shoulder of the radio man, who quickly removed his headphones. "Have you received any unusual messages directed to the ship?"

The Egyptian communications expert looked curious. "Strange you should ask. Our Latin friends have been in and out of here every ten minutes, asking the same question. I thought they must be stupid. Any acknowledgment to a direct transmission would be intercepted by American-European intelligence listening facilities. They'd fix our position within seconds."

"So you've intercepted nothing suspicious."

The Arab communications man shook his head. "Even if I did, any message would certainly be in code."

"Shut down the equipment. Make the Mexicans think you're still listening for something. Whenever they ask about an incoming message, play dumb and keep saying you've heard nothing."

Ibn stared at Ammar expectantly. "My instructions, Suleiman?"

"Keep a sharp watch on Machado's crew. Get them off balance by acting friendly. Open the lounge bar and invite them to drink. Give the worst guard duty to our men, so the Latins can relax. This will lower their defenses."

"Shall we kill them before they kill us?"

"No," said Ammar, a flicker of sadistic pleasure in his eyes. "We'll leave that job to the glacier."

51

"Can't be less than a million icebergs down there," said Giordino bleakly. "Be easier picking a midget headwaiter out of a colony of penguins. This could take days."

Colonel Hollis was in the same mood. "There has to be one matching the *Lady Flamborough*'s contour and dimensions. Keep looking."

"Bear in mind," said Gunn, "Antarctic bergs tend to be flat. The superstructure under the plastic shroud will give the ship a multipinnacle shape."

Dillinger's eye was enlarged four times its size through a magnifying glass. "The definition is amazing," he muttered. "Be even better when we see what's on the other side of those clouds."

They were all grouped around a small table in the communications compartment of the *Sounder*, examining a huge color photo from the Casper. The aerial reconnaissance film had been processed and sent through the survey ship's laser receiver less than forty minutes after the aircraft landed.

The well-defined detail showed a sea of bergs broken away from the Larsen Ice Shelf on the eastern side of the peninsula, while hundreds more could be distinguished near glaciers off Graham Land to the west.

Pitt's concentration was aimed elsewhere. He sat off to one side, studying a large nautical chart draped across his lap. Once in a while he looked up, listening, but did not contribute to the conversation.

Hollis turned to Captain Stewart, who stood next to the receiver, wearing a headset with attached microphone. "When can we expect the Casper's infrared photo?"

Stewart raised a hand as a signal not to interrupt. He pressed the headset against his ears, listening to a voice at CIA headquarters in Washington. Then he nodded toward Hollis. "The photo lab at Langley says they'll begin transmitting in half a minute."

Hollis paced the small compartment like a cat listening for the sound of a can opener. He paused and stared curiously at Pitt, who was unconcernedly measuring distances with a pair of dividers.

The Colonel had learned a great deal about the man from NUMA in the past few hours, not from Pitt himself, but from the men on the ship. They talked of him as though he were some kind of walking legend.

"Coming through now," announced Stewart. He removed the headset and waited patiently for the newspaper-size photo to emerge from the receiver. As soon as it rolled free, he carried it over and placed it on the table. Then everyone began scrutinizing the shoreline around the upper end of the peninsula.

"The technicians at the CIA photo lab have computer-converted the specially sensitive film to a thermogram," explained Stewart. "The differences of infrared radiation are revealed in various colors. Black represents the coldest temperatures. Dark blue, light blue, green, yellow and red form an increasingly warmer scale to white, the hottest."

"What reading can we expect from the *Lady Flamborough?*" asked Dillinger.

"Somewhere in the upper end between yellow and red."

"Closer to a dark blue," Pitt broke in.

Everyone turned and glared at him as though he'd sneezed during a chess match.

"That being the case she won't stand out," Hollis protested. "We'd never find her."

"Heat radiation from the engines and generators will show as plain as a golf ball on a green," Gunn argued.

"Not if the engineering room was shut down."

"You can't mean a dead ship?" Dillinger asked in disbelief.

Pitt nodded. He stared at the others with a passing casual gaze that was more disturbing than if he had thrown a wet blanket over the enthusiasm of a breakthrough.

He smiled and said, "What we have here is a persistent urge to underrate the coach on the other team."

The five men looked at each other and then back at Pitt, waiting for some kind of explanation.

Pitt laid his nautical charts aside and rose from his chair. He walked to the table, picked up the infrared photo and folded it in half, revealing only the lower tip of Chile.

"Now then," Pitt continued, "haven't you noticed that every time the ship went through a change of appearance or altered course, it came immediately after one of our satellites passed overhead."

"Another example of precise planning," said Gunn. "The orbits of scientific data-gathering satellites are tracked by half the countries of the world. The information is as readily attainable as phases of the moon."

"Okay, so the hijack leader knew the orbiting schedules and guessed when the satellite cameras were aimed in his direction," said Hollis. "So what?"

"So he covered all avenues and shut down power to prevent detection by infrared photography. And, most important, to keep the warmth from melting the thin layer of ice coating the plastic shroud."

Four out of five found Pitt's theory quite plausible. The holdout was Gunn. He was the fastest intellect in the bunch. He saw the flaw before anyone else.

"You're forgetting the subzero temperatures around the peninsula," said Gunn. "No power, no heat. Everyone on the ship would freeze to death in a few hours. You might say the hijackers were committing suicide at the same time they murdered their prisoners."

"Rudi makes good sense," Giordino said. "They couldn't survive without some degree of warmth and protective clothing."

Pitt smiled like a lottery winner. "I agree with Rudi one hundred percent."

"You're driving in circles," said Hollis in aggravation. "Make sense."

"Nothing complicated: The *Lady Flamborough* didn't enter the Antarctic."

"Didn't enter the Antarctic," repeated Hollis mechanically. "Face the facts, man. The last satellite photo of the ship showed her halfway between Cape Horn and the tip of the peninsula, steaming hell-bent to the south."

"She had no place else to go," protested Dillinger.

Pitt tapped a finger on the ragged mass of islands scattered around the Straits of Magellan. "Want to bet?"

Hollis stood frowning, baffled for a mo-

566

ment. And then he caught on. His confusion vanished and total understanding beamed in his eyes. "She doubled back," he said flatly.

"Rudi had the key," Pitt acknowledged. "The hijackers weren't about to commit suicide, nor were they going to risk detection by infrared photos. They never had any intention of heading into the ice pack. Instead, they cut northwest and skirted the barren islands above Cape Horn."

Gunn looked relieved. "The temperatures are not nearly as severe around Tierra del Fuego. Everyone on board would be damned uncomfortable without warmth, but they'd survive."

"Then why the iceberg scam?" queried Giordino.

"To appear as if they calved from a glacier."

"Calved, like in cow?"

"Calving is the breaking away of an ice mass from an ice front or wall," Gunn clarified.

Giordino stared down at the infrared photo. "Glaciers this far north?"

"Several flow down the mountains and meet the sea within eight hundred kilometers from where we're docked here in Punta Arenas," replied Pitt.

"Where do you reckon she is?" Hollis asked.

Pitt took a chart showing the desolate fringe islands west of Tierra del Fuego. "Two possibilities within the *Lady Flamborough's* sailing range since she was last spotted by satellite." He paused to place an X beside two names on the chart. "Directly south of here, glaciers flow from Mounts Italia and Sarmiento."

Hollis said, "They're off the beaten track all right."

"But too close to the oil fields," said Pitt. "A low-flying oil-company survey plane might notice the phony ice cover. Me, if I was calling the plays for the hijackers, I'd head another hundred and sixty kilometers northwest. Which would put them near a glacier on Santa Inez Island."

Dillinger studied the small island's irregular shoreline on the chart for a moment. He glanced at the colored photograph, but the southern foot of Chile was blotted by clouds. He pushed it aside and peered through the magnifying glass at the upper half of the infrared image Pitt had folded to condense the search region.

After a few seconds he looked up in wonder and delight. "Unless Mother Nature makes icebergs with a pointed bow and a rounded stern, I think we've found our phantom ship."

Hollis took the glass from his subordinate and examined the tiny oblong shape. "It's the right contour all right. And as Pitt said, there's no sign of heat radiation. She's reading almost as cold as the glacier. Not quite pure black, but a very dark blue."

Gunn leaned in. "Yes, I see. The glacier flows into a fjord that empties in a bay crowded with small islands. One or two medium-size bergs, broken from the glacial wall. No more. The water is reasonably free of ice." He paused, a curious expression in the eyes behind the glasses. "I wonder why they moored the *Lady Flamborough* directly under the glacier's forward wall."

Pitt's eyes narrowed. "Let me have a look." He squeezed between Dillinger and Gunn, bent over and gazed through the powerful glass. After a time he straightened, his face clouded with a rising anger.

"What do you see?" asked Captain Stewart.

"They mean for every one to die."

Stewart looked at the others, puzzled. "How does he know?"

"When an ice slab fractures off the glacier and falls on the ship," Giordino said stonily, "she'll be shoved under the water and mashed into the bottom. No trace of her would ever be found."

Dillinger gave Pitt a hard look. "After all the lost opportunities, do you think they finally intend to murder the crew and passengers?"

"I do."

"Why not before now?"

"The myriad of deceptions was a stall for time. Whoever ordered the hijacking had reasons for keeping Presidents Hasan and De

569

Lorenzo alive. I can't tell you why —"

"I can," said Hollis. "Akhmad Yazid is the instigator. He planned to take control of Egypt soon after it was announced that President Hasan and U.N. Secretary-General Hala Kamil were abducted and presumed killed by unknown terrorists at sea. After he and his close supporters established a solid power base, he would claim his agents had found the ship, and then act the benevolent man of God and negotiate the hostages' release."

"Crafty bastard," murmured Giordino. "A Nobel Peace Prize candidate for sure if he saved President De Lorenzo and Senator Pitt as a bonus."

"Naturally, Yazid would see that Hasan and Kamil met with an unfortunate accident on their return to Egypt."

"And he'd still come out pure as the driven snow," Giordino grunted.

"A grand sting," admitted Pitt. "Yet, according to the latest news reports, the military has remained neutral, and Hasan's cabinet has refused to resign and fold the present government."

Hollis nodded. "Yes, throwing Yazid's carefully calculated schedule out the window."

"So he's plotted himself into a corner," said Pitt. "End of stalling tactics, end of masquerades; this time around he has to send the *Lady Flamborough* into oblivion, or face the very

570

real threat of intelligence sources ferreting out his role in the operation."

"A theory with no leaks," agreed Hollis.

"So while we stand here the hijack leader is playing Russian Roulette with the glacier," said Gunn in a low voice. "He and his terrorist team may have already abandoned the ship and escaped by boat or helicopter, leaving the crew and passengers confined below, helpless."

"Could be we've missed the boat," Dillinger speculated somberly.

Hollis didn't see it that way. He scribbled a number on a slip of paper and handed it to Stewart. "Captain, please signal my communications officer on this frequency. Tell him the Major and I are returning to the airfield and to assemble the men for an immediate briefing."

"We'd like to go along," said Pitt with quiet determination.

Hollis shook his head. "No way. You're civilians. You've had no assault training. Your request is out of line."

"My father is on that ship."

"I'm sorry," he said, but didn't sound it. "Write it off to tough luck."

Pitt looked at Hollis, and his eyes were very cold. "One call to Washington and I could queer your entire service career."

Hollis's mouth tightened. "You get your kicks making threats, Mr. Pitt?" He took a

571

step forward. "We're not playing touch football here. A lot of bodies are going to mess the decks of that ship in the next twelve hours. If my men and I do our jobs the way we've been trained, a thousand phone calls to the White House and Congress won't make a damn." He took another step toward Pitt. "I know more rotten tricks than you'd learn in a lifetime. I could tear you to shreds with my bare hands —"

No one in the room saw the movement, saw where it came from. One instant Pitt was standing casually with his arms at his sides, the next he was pressing the muzzle of a Colt forty-five-caliber automatic into Hollis's groin.

Dillinger crouched as if ready to spring. That was as far as he got. Giordino came from behind and pinned the Major's arms to his sides in a bear hug that clamped like a steel trap.

"I won't bore you with our résumés," Pitt said calmly. "Take my word. Rudi, Al and I have enough experience to hold our own in a shooting war. I promise we won't interfere. I presume you'll lead your Special Operations Forces against the *Lady Flamborough* in a combined air and sea assault. We'll stay out of your way and follow from the land side."

Hollis was far from frightened, but he was dazed. He couldn't begin to imagine how Pitt produced a large-caliber weapon with such lightning speed.

"Dirk is asking little of you, Colonel," said Gunn in a patient tone. "I suggest you demonstrate a small degree of mature logic and go along."

"I don't believe for a second you'd murder me," growled Hollis at Pitt.

"No, but I can guarantee you won't have a very productive sex life."

"Who are you people? Are you with the company?"

"The CIA?" said Giordino. "No, we didn't qualify. So we enlisted with NUMA instead."

Hollis shook his head. "I don't understand any of this."

"You don't have to," said Pitt. "Is it a deal?"

Hollis considered for half a second. Then he leaned forward until his nose was only a few millimeters from Pitt's and spoke as would a drill instructor to a raw recruit. "I'll see you weirdos are airlifted by an Osprey to within ten kilometers of the ship. No closer, or we'll lose the element of surprise. From there you can damn well hike in. If I'm lucky, you won't arrive until it's all over."

"Fair enough," Pitt agreed.

Hollis backed off then. He looked at Giordino and snapped, "I'd be grateful if you'd release my second in command." Then he re-faced Pitt. "We're shoving off, *now.* In fact, if you don't leave with Major Dillinger and me, you ain't going. Because, five minutes after boarding my command aircraft, our entire assault team will be airborne."

Pitt eased the automatic from Hollis's groin. "We'll be right behind you."

"I'll tag along with the Major," said Giordino, giving Dillinger a friendly pat on the back. "Great minds run in the same channels."

Dillinger gave him a sour look indeed. "Yours might run in a gutter but mine don't."

The room cleared out in fifteen seconds. Pitt hurried to his cabin and snatched up a tote bag. He made a quick trip to the bridge and conversed with Captain Stewart.

"How long for the *Sounder* to reach Santa Inez?"

Stewart stepped into the chart room and made a quick calculation. "Pushing throttles to the stops, our diesels should put us off the glacier in nine or ten hours."

"Do it," Pitt ordered. "We'll look for you around dawn."

Stewart shook Pitt's hand. "You take care, you hear?"

"I'll try not to get my feet wet."

One of the ship's scientists stepped over from the bridge counter. He was black, medium height, and wore a stern expression that looked as if it was chiseled there. His name was Clayton Findley, and he spoke in a deep, rich bass voice.

"Excuse me for eavesdropping, gentlemen,

but I could have sworn you mentioned Santa Inez Island."

Pitt nodded. "Yes, that's right."

"There's an old zinc mine near the glacier. Closed down when Chile halted government-subsidized production."

"You're familiar with the island?" Pitt asked in surprise.

Findley nodded. "I was chief geologist of an Arizona mining company who thought they might make the mine pay through efficient, cost-cutting operations. They sent me down along with a couple of engineers to make a survey. Spent three months in that hell hole. We found the ore grade about played out. Soon after, the mine was shuttered and the equipment abandoned."

"How are you with a rifle?"

"I've hunted some."

Pitt took him by the arm. "Clayton, my friend, you are a gift from the gods."

52

Clayton Findley did indeed prove to be a godsend.

While Hollis briefed his men inside an unused warehouse, Pitt, Gunn and Giordino helped Findley sculpt a diorama of Santa Inez Island from mud scooped beside the airport's runway on an old Ping-Pong table. He refreshed his memory of what he'd forgotten from Pitt's nautical chart.

He hardened the miniature landscape with a portable heater and highlighted the features with cans of spray paint scrounged by one of Hollis's men. Gray for the rocky terrain, white for the snow and ice of the glacier. He even molded a scale model of the *Lady Flamborough* and set it at the foot of the glacier. At last he stood back and admired his handiwork.

"That," he said confidently, "is Santa Inez."

Hollis interrupted his briefing and gathered his men around the table. Everyone stared at the diorama in thoughtful silence for a few moments.

The island was shaped like the center piece of a jigsaw puzzle produced by a drunken cutter. The ragged shoreline was a nightmare of spurs and hooks, gashed by barbed fjords and gnarled bays. It backed on the Straits of Magellan to the east and faced the Pacific Ocean to the west. It was dead ground, not fit for a graveyard, 65 kilometers wide by 95 kilometers in length and peaked by Mount Wharton 1,320 meters high.

Beaches and flat ground were virtually non-existent. The low-lying mountains rose like rockbound ships, their steep slopes falling in forlorn agony to meet the cold sea.

The ancient glacier sat like a saddle on the island. It was the result of cold and overcast summers that did not melt the ice. Barren escarpments of solid rock flanked the frigid mass, standing in sullen silence as the glacier gouged its irresistible passage toward the water where it calved section after section the way a butcher slices sausage.

Few areas of the world were more hostile to man. The entire island chain of the Magellans was uninhabited by permanent settlers. Through the centuries, men had come and gone leaving behind wrathful names like Break Neck Peninsula, Deceit Island, Calamity Bay, Desolation Isle and Port Famine. It was a hard place. The only vegetation that survived was stunted, twisted evergreens that merged with kind of a scrubby heath.

Findley swept a hand over the model. "Imagine a barren landscape with snow at the higher altitudes, and you pretty much get a picture of the real thing."

Hollis nodded. "Thank you, Mr. Findley. We're much obliged."

"Glad to help."

"All right, let's get down to the hard facts. Major Dillinger will lead the air-drop force, while I'll be in command of the dive team."

Hollis paused briefly to scan the faces of his men. They were lean, hard, purposeful-looking men dressed entirely in black. They were a tough breed of fighters who had survived torturous survival training to earn the distinction of serving with the elite Special Operations Force. A hell of a team, Hollis thought proudly to himself. The best in the world.

"We've trained long and hard for ship seizures at night," he continued. "But none where we've given away so many advantages to the enemy. We lack critical intelligence information, the weather conditions are miserable, and we're faced with a glacier that can shatter at any minute. Perplexing problems, tough problems that stand in the way of success. Before we launch our assault in a few hours, we want as many answers as possible. If you see a grave flaw in the operation, sing out. So let's begin."

"Island inhabitants?" Dillinger asked Findley straight away.

"None after we closed the mine."

"Weather conditions?"

"Rains almost constantly. It's one of the most heavily watered regions on the continent. You rarely see the sun. Temperatures this time of year run a few degrees below freezing. Winds are constant and can get violent at times. The windchill factor is a bitch, and it's almost certain to be raining."

Dillinger gave Hollis a grave look. "We don't stand a prayer of a pinpoint air drop at night."

Hollis appeared grim. "We'll have to go in with the mini-copters and scale down with ropes."

"You brought helicopters?" asked Gunn incredulously. "I didn't think they had the speed and range —"

"— To fly this far so fast," Hollis finished. "Their military designation has too many letters and digits to memorize. We call them Carrier Pigeons. Small, compact, they carry a pilot in an enclosed cockpit and two men on the outside. Comes equipped with an infrared dome and silenced tail rotors. They can be broken down or assembled in fifteen minutes. One of our C-140s can transport six of them."

"You have another problem," said Pitt.

"Go ahead."

"The *Lady Flamborough's* navigation radar can be tuned for aircraft. Your Carrier Pigeons may have low profiles, but they can be read on a screen in time for the hijackers to prepare a nasty reception party."

"So much for surprise from the air," said Dillinger morosely.

Hollis looked at Findley. "Any adverse conditions we should know about for an assault from the fjord?"

Findley smiled faintly. "You should have an easier time than the Major. You'll enjoy the advantage of frost smoke."

"Frost smoke?"

"Foglike clouds formed from the contact of cold air with warmer water near the glacial wall. It can rise anywhere from two to ten meters. Combined with the certain rain, your dive team should be cloaked from the time they begin their approach until they climb onto the decks."

"One of us gets a bit of luck after all," said Dillinger.

Hollis rubbed his chin thoughtfully. "We're not dealing with a textbook operation here. It could turn real messy if the air drop is a foulup. All surprise would be lost, and without it the twenty-man dive team isn't strong enough to engage forty armed hijackers without support."

"Since it's suicidal for your men to parachute onto the ship," said Pitt, "why not drop them farther up the glacier? From there they can make their way to the edge, and then rappel down ropes onto the main deck."

"We'd be looking at an easy descent," agreed Dillinger. "The ice wall is above the ship's superstructure and near enough for us to clear the gap."

Hollis nodded and said, "The thought crossed my mind. Any one see an obstacle with this tactic?"

"Your biggest danger, as I see it," said Gunn, "is the glacier itself. It can have an endless labyrinth of crevasses and treacherous snow crusts that give way under a man's weight. You'll have to take it slow and damned careful crossing it in the dark."

"Any other comment?" There was none. Hollis gave a side glance to Dillinger. "How much time will you require from air drop to attack readiness?"

"It would help if I knew wind velocity and direction."

"Nine days out of ten it blows from the southeast," answered Findley. "Average velocity is about ten kilometers an hour, but it can easily gust to a hundred."

Dillinger stared pensively for a few moments at the small mountains rising behind the glacier. He tried to visualize the scene at night, sense the severity of the wind. He ticked off the time inside his head. Then he looked up.

"Forty to forty-five minutes from air drop to ship assault."

"Pardon me for telling you your job, Major," said Pitt. "But you're cutting it too thin."

Findley nodded. "I agree. I've hiked the glacier on many occasions. The ice ridges make it slow going."

In a smooth, greased movement, Dillinger pulled a long, wicked-looking Bowie knife, angled between hilt and blade, from a sheath behind his back and used the spiked tip as a pointer. "The way I see it, we'll make our jump on the backside of the mountain to the right of the glacier. This should hide our C-140 transport from the ship's radar. Using the prevailing winds, which hopefully will run true to pattern, we'll glide our 'stealth parachutes' around the mountain for seven kilometers, landing within one kilometer of the glacier's forward wall. Time from jump until we regroup on the ice, I'd judge eighteen minutes. Time to walk to glacier's edge; another twenty minutes. Six more minutes to prepare rappel operation. Total time; forty-four minutes."

"I'd double it if I were you," said Giordino disapprovingly. "You'll have a hell of a time meeting a deadline if some of your men fall in a crevasse. The dive team won't be aware of the delay."

Hollis shot Al a look he usually reserved for war protesters. "This isn't World War One,

Mr. Giordino. We don't have to synchronize watches before we go over the top. Each man is custom-fitted with a miniaturized radio receiver in his ear and a microphone inside his ski mask. No matter whether Major Dillinger and his team are late or mine is early, so long as we are in constant communication, we can coordinate a joint assault —"

"One other thing," Pitt broke in. "I assume your weapons are silenced."

"They are," Hollis assured him. "Why?"

"One burst from an unsilenced machine gun could bring down the wall of the glacier."

"I can't speak for the hijackers."

"Then you better kill them quick," muttered Giordino.

"We don't train to take terrorists as prisoners," Hollis said with a cold, ominous grin. "Now then, if our visitors can restrain their criticisms, are there any questions?"

Dive-team leader Richard Benning raised his hand. "Sir?"

"Benning?"

"Will we be approaching the ship underwater or on the surface?"

Hollis simply used a ballpoint pen as a pointer. He tapped it on a small island in the fjord that was behind a point of land and out of sight from the ship. "Our team will be ferried by Pigeon Carrier to this island. Distance to the *Lady Flamborough* is about three kilometers. The water is too cold for a swim that far, so we'll stay dry and move in by rubber boats. If Mr. Findley is correct about the frost smoke, we should be able to approach without detection. If it's dissipated, we'll enter the water two hundred meters away and dive until we reach the hull."

"A lot of balls will be iced if we have to wait very long for Major Dillinger's team to get in place."

A small wave of laughter echoed from the eighty men gathered around the diorama.

Hollis sighed and gave a broad smile. "I don't intend to freeze mine. We'll give the Major an ample head start."

Gunn raised his hand.

"Yes, Mr. Gunn," Hollis said wearily. "What's on your mind now? Did I forget something?"

"Just curiosity, Colonel. How will you know if the hijackers somehow get wind of the assault and lay a trap?"

"One of our aircraft is filled with advanced electronic-surveillance equipment. It will fly a circular pattern seven miles above the *Lady Flamborough,* detecting any radio transmissions sent by the hijackers to their collaborators outside the region. They'd scream like madmen if they thought a Special Operations Force was closing the net around them. The communications men and translators can intercept all transmissions and alert us in plenty of time."

Pitt made a casual motion with one hand. "Yes, Mr. Pitt."

"I hope you haven't forgotten the NUMA party."

Hollis lifted an eyebrow. "No, I haven't forgotten." He turned to the geologist. "Mr. Findley, where did you say the old abandoned mine was located?"

"I neglected to place it," replied Findley matter-of-factly. "But since you're interested —" He paused and placed a match cover on the side of a small mount overlooking the glacier and the fjord. "She sits here, about two and a half kilometers from the forward edge of the glacier and the ship."

Hollis turned to Pitt. "That's where you'll be. You can serve as an observation post."

"Some observation post," grumbled Giordino. "In the dark and rain and sleet, we'd be lucky to see our own shoelaces."

"Cozy and safe and out of harm's way," Pitt said pontifically. "We may light a fire in the stove and have ourselves a picnic."

"You do that," Hollis said with some satisfaction. He looked around at the assembled men. "Well, gentlemen, I won't bore you with a gung ho pep talk. Let's just do our jobs and save some lives."

"And win just one for the Gipper," Giordino muttered.

"What did you say?"

"Al was saying what an honor it was to be part of an elite fighting force," said Pitt.

Hollis gave Giordino a stare that would cut glass. "Special Operations Forces do not give out honorary memberships. You civilians will stay back out of the way." Hollis turned to Dillinger. "If any of these NUMA people attempt to set foot on the ship before I give permission, shoot them. That's an order."

"A pleasure," Dillinger grinned sharkishly.

Giordino shrugged. "They certainly know how to vent wrath around here."

Pitt did not share Giordino's caustic mood. He understood perfectly Hollis's position. His men were professional, a team. He gazed around at them, big, quiet men, ranged in a rough circle around the model. None was over twenty-five.

As he stared into their faces he couldn't help wondering which ones were going to die in a few short hours.

53

"How much longer?" Machado asked Ammar as he sprawled on Captain Collins's settee.

With no ship's power, the Captain's cabin was dimly lit by four flashlights strategically hung from the ceiling. Ammar shrugged indifferently while he read from the Koran. "You spend more time in the communications room than I do. You tell me."

Machado made a spitting gesture at the deck. "I am sick of waiting around like a pregnant duck. I say shoot the lot of them and get the hell away from this barren purgatory."

Ammar looked at his peer in the business of murder. Machado was sloppy in his habits. His hair was oily and his fingernails wedged with dirt. One whiff at two paces was enough to recognize he seldom bathed. Ammar respected Machado as a dangerous threat, but beyond that there was only disgust.

Machado rolled off the settee to his feet

and restlessly roamed the cabin before settling in a chair. "We should have received instructions twenty-four hours ago," he said. "Topiltzin is not one to hesitate."

"Neither is Akhmad Yazid," said Ammar while keeping his eyes focused on the Koran. "He and Allah will provide."

"Provide what? Helicopters, a ship, a submarine, before we're discovered? You know the answer, my Egyptian friend, yet you sit like your Sphinx."

Ammar turned a page without looking up. "Tomorrow at this time you and your men will be safely back in Mexico."

"What guarantee can you give we won't all be sacrificed for the good of the cause?"

"Yazid and Topiltzin cannot risk our capture by international commando forces," Ammar said wearily, "for fear we might talk under torture. Their blossoming empires would be chipped to pieces if one of us revealed their involvement. Trust me, arrangements have been made for our escape. You must be patient."

"What arrangements?"

"You'll learn that part of the plan as soon as instructions arrive concerning the fate of our hostages."

The deep-dyed falsehood was beginning to fray at the edges. Machado might see the light at any time. As long as one of Ammar's men operated the ship's communications network, no signals were received while the radio was set on the wrong frequency. Yazid, and probably Topiltzin too, Ammar thought, must be sweating if they thought he had ignored the original plan and murdered everyone on board, instead of keeping them alive for propaganda purposes.

"Why not act on our own, lock them all below, sink the ship and be done with it?" Machado's voice came thick with exasperation.

"Killing the entire British crew, the American Senator and other non-Mexican or Egyptian nationals would not be wise. You may enjoy the excitement and constant intrigue of being the object of an international manhunt, Captain. Me, I'd prefer to live out my life in comfortable convenience."

"Stupid to leave witnesses."

The fool had no idea how right he was, Ammar thought. He sighed and laid down the Koran. "Your only concern is President De Lorenzo. Mine is President Hasan and Hala Kamil. Our relationship ends there."

Machado stood and crossed the cabin, jerking open the door. "We better hear something damned quick," he grumbled nastily. "I can't keep my men in check much longer. They have this growing urge to place me in charge of the mission."

Ammar smiled agreeably. "Noon . . . if we haven't heard from our leaders by noon, I will turn over command to you."

Machado's eyes widened for an instant in suspicion. "You'd agree to step down and place me in charge?"

"Why not? I've accomplished what I set out to do. Except for the disposition of President Hasan and Miss Kamil, my job is finished. I'll gladly hand the final headaches to you."

Machado suddenly grinned the devil's own grin. "I'm going to hold you to that promise, Egyptian. Then maybe I'll see the face behind the mask." Then he stepped outside.

The door latch had hardly clicked after Machado's departure when Ammar removed the miniature radio from under his coat and pressed the transmit switch.

"Ibn?"

"Yes, Suleiman Aziz?"

"Your location?"

"The stern."

"How many on shore?"

"Six have been ferried to the old mine pier. There are fifteen of us left on board, including you. The going is slow. We only have one three-man boat. The large eight-man inflatable was slashed beyond repair."

"Sabotage?"

"It could only be the handiwork of Machado's men."

"Have they caused any more problems?"

"Not yet. The cold keeps them off the outside decks. Most are sitting in the lounge drinking tequila from the bar. The rest are sleeping. You were wise to instruct our men to become friendly with them. Their discipline has loosened considerably."

"The charges?"

"All explosives have been placed in a fracture running parallel with the glacier's face. The detonation should bring down the entire frontal wall on the ship."

"How soon before our withdrawal can be completed?"

"The use of paddles makes for slow going under a heavy ebb tide. We can't use the boat's motor for fear of alerting Machado's men. I'd estimate another forty-five minutes to clear everyone off the ship."

"We must be safely away before daylight."

"Everyone will do their utmost, Suleiman Aziz."

"Can they run the ferry operation without you?"

"Yes."

"Bring one man and meet me at Hasan's cabin."

"We're going to execute them?"

"No," replied Ammar. "We're taking them with us."

Ammar switched off the radio and slipped the Koran into a pocket of his coat.

His betrayal by Akhmad Yazid would be revenged. It was galling to see his magnificent plan turn to shambles. Ammar had no intention of carrying through with the original operation, knowing Machado had been hired to kill him and his hijack team. He was angered more by the loss of his fee than by being stabbed in the back.

Therefore, he reasoned, he would keep Hasan and Kamil alive, and yes, De Lorenzo too, at least temporarily, as bargaining chips. He might recoup after all by turning the tables and throwing all guilt on Yazid and To-piltzin.

He needed time to think and create a new plan. But first things first.

He had to sneak his hostages off the ship before Machado and his motley crew caught on to his sleight of hand.

Hala's heart sank when the door opened and the hijacker's leader stepped into the cabin suite. She stared at him for a moment, seeing only the eyes behind the ridiculous mask and the machine gun casually held in one hand, and wondered with female curiosity what kind of man he might be under different circumstances.

He entered and spoke in a quiet but fear-some voice. "You will all come with *me*."

Hala trembled and lowered her gaze to the floor, angry at herself for showing fear.

Senator Pitt was not intimidated. He jumped to his feet and crossed the cabin in three strides, stopping only when the toes of his shoes nearly touched Ammar's.

"Where are you taking us and for what purpose?" the Senator demanded.

"I am not sitting in front of one of your camel-witted Senate investigation committees," said Ammar icily. "Do not cross-examine me."

"We have a right to know," the Senator insisted firmly.

"You have no rights!" snapped Ammar. He roughly pushed the Senator aside and moved into the room, his gaze taking in the pale, apprehensive faces.

"You're going for a little boat ride, followed by a short journey by train. My men will pass out blankets to ward off the damp chill."

They all looked at him as if he was crazy but none argued.

With a dreadful feeling of hopelessness, Hala slowly helped President Hasan to his feet. She was tired of living under the constant threat of death. She felt as though she no longer cared.

And yet, something within her, a spark, a will to defy, still smoldered.

The fearlessness of a soldier going into battle who knows he is going to die and has nothing to lose by fighting to the end slowly crept over her. She was determined to survive.

Captain Machado entered the communication room and found it empty. At first he thought Ammar's radio operator had taken a brief break for a call of nature, but he looked in the head and found it empty too.

Machado stared at the radio panel for a long moment, his eyes strained and red from lack of sleep, his face showing a puzzled expression. He stepped onto the bridge and approached one of his own crewmen who was peering into the radarscope.

"Where is the radio operator?" he asked.

The radar observer turned and shrugged. "I haven't seen him, Captain. Isn't he in the communications room?"

"No, the place is deserted."

"Would you like me to check with the Arab leader?"

Machado shook his head slowly, not quite able to get a grip on the Egyptian radio operator's disappearance. "Find Jorge Delgado and bring him here. He knows radios. Better us than the stupid Arabs to oversee the communications."

While they were talking, neither man noticed the strong blip that appeared on the radarscope, indicating a low-flying aircraft passing over the center of the island.

Even if they had been alert, there was no detecting the radar-invisible "stealth parachutes" of Dillinger's Special Forces team as they opened them and began gliding toward the glacier.

54

Pitt sat in the Spartan confines of the tilt-rotor Osprey. The bullet-shaped craft lifted off the ground like a helicopter but flew like a plane at speeds in excess of six hundred kilometers per hour. He was wide-awake; only a dead man could sleep in those aluminum seats with ultrathin pads for cushions, the weather turbulence, and the engine noise that roared through the barest of soundproofing. Only a dead man, that is, except Giordino. He was deflated like a life-size balloon figure — there was no other description for it — with just enough air to give it form. Every few minutes, as if his brain was set on an automatic timer, he changed position without cracking an eye or missing a breath.

"How does he do it?" asked Findley in frank amazement.

"It's in the genes," Pitt answered.

Gunn shook his head admiringly. "I've seen him sleep in the darndest contortions in the darndest places, and I still can't believe it when I see it."

The young copilot turned and peered around the back of his seat. "Doesn't exactly suffer from stress syndrome, does he?"

Pitt and the others laughed and then became quiet, all wishing they didn't have to leave the cozy warmth of the aircraft for the icy nightmare outside. Pitt relaxed as best he could. He felt some measure of satisfaction. Though he was not included in the assault — better to leave that to trained professionals in the art of hostage rescue — he was positioned close enough to tag along on the heels of Hollis and his SOF teams, and he had every intention of following Dillinger's men down the scaling ropes after the attack was launched.

Pitt sensed no foreboding premonition nor imagined any omen of death. He did not doubt for an instant his father was alive. He couldn't explain it, even to himself, but he felt the Senator's presence. The two had a tight bond over the years. They could almost read each other's minds.

"We'll be at your landing point in six minutes," announced the pilot with a cheerfulness that made Pitt cringe.

The pilot seemed blissfully unconcerned at flying over jagged, snowcapped peaks he couldn't see. All that was visible through the windshield was the flash of sleet striking the glass, and the darkness beyond.

"How do you know where we are?" asked Pitt.

The pilot, a laid-back Burt Reynolds type, shrugged lazily. "All in the wrists," he quipped.

Pitt leaned forward and peered over the pilot's shoulder. No hands were on the controls. The pilot was sitting with his arms folded, staring at a small screen that looked like a video game. Only the Osprey's nose showed at the bottom of the graphic display, while the flashing picture was filled with mountains and valleys that hurtled past under the simulated aircraft. In a split-screen panel in an upper corner, distances and altitudes blinked in red digital numbers.

"Untouched by human hands," said Pitt. "The computer is replacing everyone."

"Lucky for us they haven't developed a knack for sex." The pilot laughed. He reached out and made a slight adjustment with a tiny knob. "Infrared and radar scanners read the ground and the computer converts it to three-dimensional display. I plug in the auto pilot, and while the aircraft darts around the terrain like a Los Angeles Raiders running back, I deep-think about such wondrous subjects as the Congressional budget and our State Department's foreign policy."

"That's news to me," muttered the copilot wryly.

"Without our little electronic guide here,"

the pilot continued, undaunted, "we'd still be sitting on the ground at Punta Arenas waiting for daylight and clearing weather —" A chime sound issued from the display screen, and the pilot stiffened. "We're coming up on our programmed landing site. You better get your people ready to disembark."

"What were your instructions from Colonel Hollis for dropping us off?"

"Just to set you down behind the mountain summit above the mine to hide from the cruise ship's radar. You'll have to hoof it the rest of the way."

Pitt turned to Findley. "Any problem on your end?"

Findley smiled. "I know that mountain like my wife's bottom, every nook and crack. The summit is only three kilometers from the mine entrance. An easy hike down the slope. I could do it blindfolded."

"From what I see of this rotten weather," Pitt muttered darkly, "that's exactly what you'll have to do."

The howl of the wind replaced the whine from the Osprey's turbines as the NUMA crew quickly exited through the cargo hatch. There was no time wasted, no words spoken, only a silent farewell wave to the pilots. Within a minute, the four men, carrying only two tote bags, were bent into the sleet and trudging up the rocky slope toward the mountain's summit.

Findley silently took the lead. Visibility was almost as bad on the ground as it was in the air. The flashlight in Findley's hand was one degree above useless. The flaying sleet reflected the flashlight's beam, revealing the broken terrain no more than one or two meters ahead.

In no way did they remotely resemble an elite assault team. They carried no visible weapons. No two wore the same type of clothing to ward off the cold. Pitt had on gray ski togs; Giordino wore dark blue. Gunn was lost in an orange survival suit that looked two sizes too large. Findley was outfitted like a Canadian lumberjack complete with a woolly Basque stocking cap pulled low over his ears. The only items they had in common were yellow-lensed ski goggles.

The wind was blowing at about twenty kilometers per hour, Pitt estimated — bitter but bearable. The rocky, uneven surface was slippery from the wet, and they slid and stumbled, frequently losing their balance and falling heavily.

Every few minutes they had to wipe the buildup of sleet from their goggles. Soon, from the front, they looked like snowmen, while their backs were quite dry.

Findley raked the ground ahead with his flashlight, dodging large boulders and sparse, grotesque shrubs. He knew he had reached the summit when he stepped onto an outcrop of bare rock and was struck by the full force of the wind.

"Not much further," he said over the howl of the wind. "Downhill all the way."

"Too bad we can't rent a toboggan," said Giordino gloomily.

Pitt pulled back his glove and peered at the luminous hands of his old Doxa dive watch. The assault was set for O-five hundred. Twenty-eight minutes away. They were running late.

"Let's make time," he shouted. "I don't want to miss the party."

They made good time for the next fifteen minutes. The mountain's slope became more gradual, and Findley found a narrow, winding track that led to the mine. Farther downhill the stunted pines became thicker, the rock became smaller, looser, and their boots were able to get a firmer grip.

Thankfully, the driving wind and sleet began to ease up. Holes in the clouds appeared and stars became visible. They were able to see now without the hindrance of the goggles.

Findley grew more confident of his surroundings as a high ore tailing materialized in the blackness. He skirted the pile and swung onto a small, narrow-gauge railroad track and began following it into the dark.

He was about to turn and shout "We're

here," but was cut off. Pitt suddenly and unexpectedly reached out, grabbed the back of Findley's collar and jerked him to a halt so abruptly his feet flew out from under him, and he crashed on his buttocks. As he fell, Pitt snatched the flashlight and switched it off.

"What in hell — ?"

"Quiet!" Pitt rasped sharply.

"You hear something?" asked Gunn softly.

"No, I smell a familiar odor."

"Familiar odor?"

"Lamb. Somebody is barbecuing a leg of lamb."

They all leaned their heads back and sniffed the air.

"By God, you're right," murmured Giordino. "I *do* smell lamb on a grill."

Pitt helped Findley to his feet. "Appears that someone has jumped your claim."

"They must be dumber than a toad if they think there's any ore worth processing around here."

"I doubt they're excavating for zinc."

Giordino moved off to one side. "Before you doused the light, I saw a glint over here somewhere." He moved one foot around in a semicircle. It struck an object that clinked, and he picked it up. He turned so he was facing away from the mine and flicked on a tiny penlight. "A bottle of Château Margaux 1966. For hardrock miners, these guys have real style."

"Odd goings-on here," said Findley. "Who-ever moved in isn't getting their hands dirty."

"Lamb and vintage Bordeaux must have come from the *Lady Flamborough*," Gunn concluded.

"How far away are we from where the glacier meets the fjord?" Pitt asked Findley.

"The glacier itself is only about five hun-dred meters to the north. The wall facing the fjord is slightly less than two kilometers west."

"How was the ore transported?"

Findley gestured in the direction of the fjord. "By this narrow-gauge railroad. The tracks run from the mine entrance to the ore crusher, then down to the dock, where the ore was loaded on ships."

"You never said anything about a dock."

"Nobody asked." Findley shrugged. "A small loading pier. The pilings extend into a cove slightly off to one side of the glacier."

"Approximate distance from the ship?"

"A baseball outfielder with a good arm could lob a ball from the dock against the hull."

"I should have seen it," Pitt murmured bit-terly. "I missed it, everyone missed it."

"What are you talking about?" demanded Findley.

"The terrorists' support team," answered Pitt. "The hijackers on the ship need an advance base for their escape. They couldn't disembark at sea without detection and capture unless they had a submarine, which is impossible to find without legitimate government backing. The abandoned mine site makes a perfect hiding place for helicopters. And they can use the narrow-gauge railroad for commuting back and forth from the fjord."

"Hollis," said Gunn briefly. "We'd better inform him."

"Can't," said Giordino. "Our friendly neighborhood Colonel refused to provide us with a radio."

"So how do we warn Hollis?" Gunn put in.

"No way." Pitt shrugged. "But we might help by finding and disabling their helicopters while pinning down any terrorist force in the mine camp to keep them from catching Hollis and his assault teams in a vise."

"There could be fifty of them," protested Findley. "We're only four."

"Their security is lax," Gunn pointed out. "They don't expect anyone to drop in from the interior of a deserted island in the middle of a storm."

"Rudi's right," said Giordino. "If they were alert they'd have been onto us by now. I vote we evict the bastards."

"We have surprise on our side," Pitt continued. "As long as we stay careful and keep undercover in the dark, we can keep them off balance."

"If they come after us," asked Findley, "do we throw rocks?"

"My life is guided by the Boy Scout motto," replied Pitt.

He and Giordino knelt in unison and unzipped the tote bags. Giordino began passing around bulletproof vests while Pitt handed out the weapons.

He held up a semiautomatic shotgun for Findley. "You said you hunted some, Clayton. Here's an early Christmas present. A twelve-gauge Benelli Super Ninety."

Findley's eyes gleamed. "I like it." He ran his hands over the stock as lightly as though it were a woman's thigh. "Yes, I like it." Then he noticed that Gunn and Giordino carried Heckler-Koch machine guns modified with silencers. "You can't buy this stuff at a corner hardware store. Where did you get it?"

"Special Operations Forces issue," Giordino said nonchalantly. "Borrowed them when Hollis and Dillinger weren't looking."

Findley was further amazed when Pitt shoved a round drum in an ancient Thompson submachine gun. "You must like antiques."

"There's something to be said for old-fashioned craftsmanship," said Pitt. He looked at his watch again. Only six minutes remained before Hollis and Dillinger attacked the ship. "No shooting until I give the word. We don't want to screw up the Special Forces assault. They have precious little chance of surprise as it is."

"What about the glacier?" Findley asked. "Won't our gunfire send out shock waves that could fracture the forward wall of ice?"

"Not from this range," Gunn assured him. "Our concentrated fire will seem more like the distant bang of firecrackers."

"Remember," ordered Pitt, "we want to stall off a gun battle as long as we can. Our first priority is to find the helicopters."

"A pity we don't have any explosives," mumbled Giordino.

"Nothing ever comes easy."

Pitt gave Findley a few seconds to get his bearings. Then the geologist nodded and they moved out, skirting the backs of the old, weathered buildings, keeping to the shadows, stepping as quietly as possible, the crunch of their soles against the loose gravel muffled by the stiff breeze that reversed and now came sweeping down the mountainside.

The buildings around the mine were mostly built of wooden support beams covered by corrugated metal sheeting that showed signs of corrosion and rust. Some were small sheds, others rose two to four stories into the sky, their walls trailing off into the gloom. Except for the smell of the roasting lamb, it seemed like an old American West ghost town.

Abruptly Findley stopped behind a long shed and held up a hand, waiting for the other three to close around him. He peered around the corner once, twice, and then turned to Pitt.

"The recreation and dining-hall building is only a few paces to my right," he whispered. "I can make out cracks of light spilling out from under heavy curtains."

Giordino tested the air with his nose. "They must like their meat well done."

"Any sign of guards?" asked Pitt.

"The area looks deserted."

"Where could they hide the helicopters?"

"The main mine is a vertical shaft dropping to six levels. So that's out as a parking garage."

"Where, then?"

Findley gestured into the early-morning blackness. "The ore-crushing mill has the largest open space. There's also a sliding door used for storing heavy equipment. If the copter's rotor blades were folded they could easily squeeze three of them inside."

"The crushing mill it is," said Pitt softly.

There was no more time to waste; Hollis and Dillinger's joint attack would begin at any minute. They were halfway past the dining hall when the door suddenly opened and a shaft of light filtered through the rain, cutting them off below the knees and illuminating their feet. They froze, guns in firing position.

A figure was silhouetted by the interior light

606

for a few seconds. He stepped over the threshold briefly and scraped a few morsels from a dish onto the ground. Then he turned and closed the door. Moments later Pitt and the others flattened their backs against the crushing-mill's wall.

Pitt turned and put his mouth to Findley's ear.

"How can we sneak in?"

"Conveyor belts run through openings in the building that carried the bulk ore to the crusher and back to the train after it became slurry. The only problem is they're way over our heads."

"Lower access doors?"

"The big equipment-storage door," Findley answered, his murmur as soft as Pitt's, "and the main front entrance. If I remember correctly there's also a stairway that leads into a side office."

"No doubt locked," said Giordino morosely.

"A bright thought," Pitt conceded. "Okay, the front door it is. No one inside will be expect total strangers coming to call. We'll go in clean and quiet, like we belong. No surprises. Just three of their buddies strolling from the dining hall."

"I bet the door squeaks," Giordino muttered.

They walked unhurriedly around a corner of the crushing mill and entered unchallenged through a high, weathered door that swung on its hinges noiselessly.

"Curses," Giordino whispered through clenched teeth.

The interior of the building was enormous. It had to be. A giant mechanical machine sat in the center like a giant octopus with conveyor belts, water hoses and electrical wiring for tentacles. The ore crusher consisted of a massive horizontal cylinder containing various-sized steel balls that pulverized the ore.

Huge flotation tanks sat along one wall that had received the slurry after crushing. Overhead, maintenance catwalks reached by steel ladders crisscrossed above the massive equipment. A cord of lights hung from the catwalk railings, their power produced by a portable generator whose exhaust popped away in one corner.

Pitt had guessed wrong. He had figured at least two, perhaps even three, helicopters to evacuate the hijackers. There was only one — a large British Westland Commando, an older but reliable craft designed for troop transport and logistic support. It could carry thirty or more passengers if they were tightly crammed in. Two men in ordinary combat fatigues were standing on a high mechanic's stand peering through an access panel beside the engine. They were engrossed in their work and paid no notice to their predawn visitors.

Slowly, cautiously, Pitt advanced into the

great open crushing room, Findley on his right, Giordino covering the left, Gunn trailing. And still the helicopter's two crewmen did not turn from their work. Only then did he see an uncaring guard sitting on an overturned box behind a support beam with his back to the door.

Pitt gestured to Giordino and Findley to circle around the helicopter in the shadows and search for other hijackers. The guard, having felt the rush of cold air from the opening-and-closing door, half turned to see who had entered the building.

Pitt walked slowly toward the guard, who was dressed in black combat fatigues, with a ski mask over his head. Pitt was only two meters away when he smiled and lifted a hand in a vague greeting.

The guard gave him a quizzical look and said something in Arabic.

Pitt gave a friendly shrug and replied in gibberish that was lost under the sound of the generator's exhaust.

Then the guard focused his eyes on the old Thompson machine gun. The two seconds between puzzlement, and alarm, followed by physical reaction, cost him painfully. Before he could bring up his weapon and whip sideways, Pitt had chopped the butt of the Thompson against his skull under the black ski mask.

Pitt caught the guard as he slumped and

propped him back against the beam as though he were dozing. Next he ducked under the forward fuselage of the helicopter and approached the two mechanics working on the engine. Reaching the stand, he grasped the rungs of its ladder and gave it a great heave, tipping it backwards.

The mechanics flew through the air, so startled they didn't shout. Their only reaction was to throw up their hands in a futile attempt to claw the air before thumping onto the hard wooden plank floor. One struck his head and blacked out immediately. The other landed on his side, his right arm breaking with an audible snap. A painful gasp burst from his lips, only to be silenced by the sudden impact of the Thompson's butt against his temple.

"Nice work," said Findley, dispensing with silence.

"Every move a picture," Pitt muttered loftily.

"I hope that's the lot."

"Not quite. Al has four more behind the 'copter."

Findley cautiously stepped under the aircraft and was astounded to see Giordino sitting comfortably in a folding chair, staring fiercely at four scowling captives entirely encased up to their chins in sleeping bags.

"You always had a fetish for neat packages," said Pitt.

Giordino's eyes never left his prisoners. "And you were always too loud. What was all the noise?"

"The mechanics took a nasty fall off the maintenance stand."

"How many did we bag?"

"Seven, all told."

"Four must be part of the flight crew."

"A backup pilot and copilot plus two mechanics. They weren't taking any chances."

Findley motioned to one of the mechanics. "One of them is coming around."

Pitt slung his Thompson over a shoulder. "I think we'll fix it so they can't go anywhere for a while. You do the honors, Clayton. Bind and gag them. You should find some straps inside the copter. Al, keep a sharp eye on them. Rudi and I are going to look around outside."

"We'll ensure their complete immobilization," said Giordino, speaking like a bureaucrat.

"You better. They'll kill you if you don't."

Pitt motioned to Gunn and they stripped off the upper clothing from two of their prisoners. Pitt snatched the ski mask and pulled the black sweater from the unconscious guard. He wrinkled his nose from the smell of the unwashed sweater and slipped it over his own head.

Then they walked out the door, making no effort to appear inconspicuous. They strode

611

briskly, confidently, staying in the center of the road that ran between the buildings. At the dining hall they cut into the shadows and peered around the edge of a window through a crack in the curtains.

"There's got to be a dozen of them in there," Gunn whispered. "All armed to their molars. Looks like they're ready to vacate the premises."

"Damn Hollis," Pitt grunted softly. "If only he'd given us some means of communicating with him."

"Too late now."

"Late?"

"It's 05:12," answered Gunn. "If the assault had gone according to schedule, Hollis's support forces and medics would be flying over toward the ship by now."

Gunn was right. There was no sound of the Special Operations Forces' helicopters.

"Let's find the ore train," ordered Pitt. "We'd be smart to put it out of commission and cut all transportation between the mine and the ship."

Gunn nodded, and they moved silently along the wall of the dining hall, ducking under the windows and halting at a corner where they paused to cautiously scan the immediate neighborhood. Then they swung across an open space until they reached the railroad track, stepped across the rails and began sprinting between the ties.

A chill crept up Pitt's back as he tailed Gunn, and he clenched his fists around the stock and forward grip of the Thompson with a growing sense of despair. The wind and rain had stopped and the stars were quickly fading in the eastern sky.

Something had gone terribly wrong.

55

To Hollis, it seemed hours since they had launched the boats.

The compact Carrier Pigeon helicopters had flown low along the rugged coastline and deposited Hollis's team on a small island at the mouth of the fjord without a hitch. The launching was executed smoothly with effortless efficiency, but the swift, four-knot tidal current was far stronger than anyone had anticipated.

Then the silent electric motor on the lead five-man tow boat had mysteriously quit after the first ten minutes. Precious time was lost as the Special Forces men broke out the paddles and put their backs into a desperate race to close on the *Lady Flamborough* before first light.

Matters had been further complicated by the total breakdown in communications. To his dismay, Hollis was unable to raise Dillinger or any of the land team. He had no way of knowing whether Dillinger had boarded the ship or was lost on the glacier.

Hollis paddled and cursed the deceased motor, the current and Dillinger with every stroke. His carefully calculated timetable was down the drain. The attack was far behind schedule, and he couldn't risk calling it off.

His only salvation was the "fog smoke" Findley had described. It swirled around the small boats and the fiercely determined men, cloaking them like a protecting blanket.

The mist and the darkness made it impossible for Hollis to see more than a few meters ahead. He navigated and watched over his tiny fleet through an infrared scope. He kept them tightly grouped within a three-meter radius, quietly giving directions over his miniature radio whenever one began to stray.

He turned the scope on the *Lady Flamborough.* Her beautiful lines now looked like a grotesque ice carving floating in front of the cracked porcelain wall of an antique bathtub. Hollis judged her to still be a good kilometer away.

After exacting its toll, the tide suddenly began to slacken and their speed soon picked up almost a knot. The welcome relief came almost too late. Hollis could see his men were wearing down under the constant, arduous paddling. They were men hardened by rigid training, and all lifted weights on a regular basis. They dug the paddles into the water noiselessly and heaved against the merciless tide, but their muscles were beginning to stiffen and each stroke became an effort.

The protective mist was beginning to thin. In his mind was the fear that they would become sitting ducks in the water. Hollis looked upward, his confidence ebbing with the tide. Through the mist's open patches he could see a sky that was turning from black to an ever lighter blue.

His boats were in the middle of the fjord, and the nearest shore that offered any degree of cover was half a kilometer farther away than the *Lady Flamborough*.

"Put your backs into it, men," he urged. "We're in the home stretch. Go for it."

The weary fighters reached deep for their reserve strength and increased the length and speed of their strokes. It felt to Hollis as if the inflatable boats were spurting through the water. He put aside the infrared scope and paddled furiously.

They might make it, just might make it, he thought hopefully as they began to rapidly close on the ship.

But where was Dillinger? he wondered bitterly. What in hell had happened to the assault team on the glacier?

Dillinger was having no picnic himself. He was even more vague on the situation. Immediately after jumping from the C-140 transport, he and his men had been immediately hurled all over the sky by the heavy, erratic winds.

Tight-faced, Dillinger stared up and around to see how his team was managing. Each man carried a small blue light, but the driving sleet made it impossible for him to see them. He lost them almost the instant his chute opened.

He reached down and pressed the switch of a little black box strapped to his leg. Then he spoke into his tiny transmitter.

"This is Major Dillinger. I have turned on my marker beacon. We have a seven-kilometer glide, so try and stay close to me and home in on my position after you land."

"In this crap we'll be lucky to come down on the island," some malcontent muttered.

"Radio silence except for emergency," Dillinger ordered.

He looked down and saw nothing beyond his survival-and-weapons pack that dangled on a two-meter line beneath his harness. He took his bearings from the luminous dial of a combination compass and altimeter that extended in front of his forehead like the mirror worn by ear, nose and throat physicians.

Without reference points or a homing beacon dropped on the landing zone in advance — a luxury too great to risk alerting the hijackers — Dillinger had to literally fly by the seat of his pants and mentally judge glide angle and distance.

His primary concern was overshooting the

edge of the glacier and landing in the fjord. He hedged his bet and came down short — nearly a full kilometer too short.

The glacier materialized through the darkness, and Dillinger saw he was descending directly over a crevasse. A sudden side gust caught his rectangular canopy and it began to oscillate. He jockeyed the shrouds to compensate and twisted into a landing attitude just as his dangling pack struck the inner wall of the crevasse and bounced over the lip. A thin layer of snow cushioned his impact and he made a perfect landing on his feet, only two meters from the ice fracture.

He popped his release and the parachute collapsed before it could be caught by the wind. He didn't bother to roll it up and hide it in the ice for later retrieval. There was no time to waste. The taxpayers would have to eat the lost chute.

"This is Dillinger. I'm down. Home in on my position."

He pulled a plastic whistle from a pocket of his coat and blew through it once every ten seconds while facing in a different direction. For the first few minutes there was nobody to be seen.

Then, slowly, the first of his men appeared and jogged toward him. They had been widely scattered. Their progress across the uneven surface of the glacier took them far longer than Dillinger had anticipated.

618

Soon the others straggled in. One man had suffered a broken shoulder, another had cracked an ankle. His sergeant favored a wrist Dillinger suspected was broken, but the man carried on as though it was little more than a slight sprain, and Dillinger needed him too badly to write him off.

He turned to the two injured men. "You won't be able to keep up with the rest of us, but follow along in our tracks as best you can. Just make sure your lights are hooded." Then Dillinger nodded at his sergeant, Jack Foster. "Let's rope together and move out, Sergeant. I'll take the lead."

Foster gave a brief salute and began checking the team.

The going was treacherous across the broken ice surface, yet they moved along at an easy dogtrot. Dillinger had no fear of falling into an open lead; the line around his waist was anchored to enough beef and brawn to lift a track off the ground. Twice he called for a brief stop to catch his bearings, and then they were off again.

They crawled over jagged ice ridges and one open lead that all but defeated them. They wasted seven minutes before an ice grapnel bit in the opposite side and the lightest man on the team crossed hand over hand to secure the grip. Another ten minutes was gone before the last man made it over.

A sense of urgency mushroomed inside

619

Dillinger. His team was down two men and they were falling farther and farther behind the timetable. He sullenly regretted not taking Giordino's unsolicited advice and doubling his estimated time from air drop to attack.

He prayed the dive team wasn't waiting, freezing to death in the water beneath the *Lady Flamborough*'s hull. He tried repeatedly to signal Hollis and apprise the Colonel of his tardy situation, but there was no reply. The first faint traces of dawn were breaking behind him, revealing the surface of the glacier. There was a numbing desolation about it, a terrifying strangeness. He could also see the faint glimmering of the fjord — and suddenly he realized why there was a communications breakdown.

Hollis could see the ship clearly now without the infrared scope. And if a hijacker with a keen eye had looked in the right direction, he'd have spied the shadows of the inflatable boats outlined against the dark gray water. Hollis hardly dared breathe as the distance narrowed.

Hoping against hope, Hollis never let up on his plea for radio communications with Dillinger. "Shark to Falcon, please respond." He was about to try for the hundredth time when Dillinger's voice abruptly boomed through his earpiece.

"This is Falcon, go ahead."

"You're late!" Hollis hissed quietly. "Why didn't you respond to my calls?"

"Just now came within range. We were out of horizontal sight of you. Our signals couldn't penetrate the ice wall."

"Are you in position?"

"Negative," Dillinger said flatly. "We've stumbled on a delicate situation which will take a while to correct."

"What do you call delicate?"

"A string of explosives in an ice fracture behind the glacial front, armed and ready to be detonated by radio signal."

"How long to disarm?"

"Could take an hour just to find them all."

"You've got five minutes," Hollis said quickly. "We can't wait any longer or we'll be dead."

"We'll all be dead if the charges go off and the ice wall falls on the ship."

"We'll gamble on surprise to stop the terrorists from detonating. Make it fast. My boats can be discovered at any moment."

"I can just make out your shadows from the glacial rim."

"Your team goes in first," Hollis ordered. "Without total darkness to cover our ascent up the hull we badly need the distraction."

"I'll meet you on the sun deck for cocktails," Dillinger said.

"The tab will be on me," Hollis replied,

621

suddenly buoyant with expectation. "Good luck."

Ibn saw them.

He stood on the old ore-loading pier along with Ammar, their four hostages and twenty men of the Egyptian hijacking force. He peered through binoculars at the figures in all-black gear who were poised on the brink of the glacier. He watched as they slid down ropes, slashed their way through the plastic sheet and vanished inside.

He lowered the glasses slightly and focused on the men in the boats clustered below the hull. He observed them shoot grappling hooks from small launchers, and then climb the attached lines to the main-deck level.

"Who are they?" asked Ammar, standing next to him, also gazing through binoculars.

"I cannot say, Suleiman Aziz. They appear to be an elite force. I hear no battle sounds; their weapons must be heavily silenced. Their assault operation was most efficient."

"Too efficient for any rabble Yazid or Topiltzin could have scraped up on short notice."

"I believe they may be an American Special Operations Force."

Ammar nodded in the brightening light. "You may be right, but how in Allah's name did they find us so quickly?"

"We must leave before their support forces arrive."

"Have you signaled for the train?"

"It should be here shortly to transport us up to the mine."

"What is it?" asked President De Lorenzo. "What is happening?"

Ammar brushed off De Lorenzo. For the first time a flicker of foreboding came through in his voice. "It seems we left the ship at a most appropriate moment. Allah smiles. The intruders are not aware of our presence here."

"In another thirty minutes this island will be crawling with United States fighting men," said Senator Pitt, calmly turning the screw. "You might be well advised to surrender."

Ammar suddenly turned and stared savagely at the politician. "Not necessary, Senator. Don't look for your famed cavalry to charge to the rescue. If and when they arrive, there will be no one left to save."

"Why didn't you kill us on the ship?" Hala asked bravely.

Ammar's teeth showed under the mask in a hideous smile and he did not give her the courtesy of an answer. He nodded at Ibn. "Detonate the charges."

"As you wish, Suleiman Aziz," Ibn replied dutifully.

"What charges?" demanded the Senator. "What are you talking about?"

"Why, the explosives we placed behind the

glacial wall," Ammar said as if it was common knowledge. He gestured toward the *Lady Flamborough*. "Ibn, if you please."

Totally expressionless, Ibn took a small transmitter from a coat pocket and held it out in front of him so the forward end pointed at the glacier.

"In the name of God, man," pleaded Senator Pitt. "Don't do it."

Ibn hesitated, staring at Ammar.

"There are hundreds of people on that ship," said President Hasan, shock showing in every line of his face. "You have no reason to murder them."

"I do not have to justify my actions to anyone here."

"Yazid will be punished for your atrocity," Hala murmured in a tone edged with fury.

"Thank you for making it easier," Ammar said, smiling at Hala, whose face became a study in bewildered incomprehension. "Enough of these maudlin delays. Quickly, Ibn. Get on with it."

Before the stunned hostages could utter further protests, Ibn flicked the power switch of the transmitting unit to "on" and pressed the button that activated the detonators.

56

The explosion came like a curiously muffled clap of thunder. The forward mass of the glacier creaked and groaned ominously. Then nothing appeared to happen. The ice cliff remained firm and upright.

Detonations should have occurred at eight different locations inside the fracture, but Major Dillinger and his men had discovered and disarmed all but one charge before their search was cut off.

The distant thump came just as Pitt and Gunn were closing in on the two hijackers who were busily firing up the old mine locomotive. The hijackers paused, listening for a few moments, exchanging words in Arabic. Then they laughed between themselves and turned back to their work.

"Whatever caused the boom," whispered Gunn, "came as no surprise to those guys. They act as if they expected it."

"Sounded like a small explosion," Pitt replied softly.

"Definitely not the glacier breaking away. We'd have felt tremors in the ground."

Pitt stared at the small narrow-gauge locomotive, which was coupled to a coal tender and five ore cars. It was a type used around plantations, industrial plants and mining operations. Quaint, stout and sturdy, with a tall stovepipe smoke-stack and round porthole windows in the cab, it looked like the Little Engine That Could, standing there puffing wisps of steam around its running gear.

A railroad man would have classed the wheel arrangement as an 0-4-0, indicating no leading truck wheels followed by four drive wheels with no trailing truck beneath the cab.

"Let's give the engineer and his fireman a warm sendoff," Pitt murmured wryly. "It's the friendly thing to do."

Gunn looked at Pitt queerly and shook his head in bewilderment before crouching and running toward the end of the train. They split up and approached from opposite sides, taking cover under the ore cars. The cab was brightly illuminated by the open firebox, and Pitt gestured with an upturned palm, signaling Gunn to wait.

The Arab who acted as engineer was busy turning valves and watching the steam-pressure gauges. The other shoveled coal from the tender across the platform into the flames. He fed a load of the black lumps onto the fiercely burning firebox, paused to mop his sweating face, and then slammed the door to the firebox shut with his shovel, sending the cab into a state of semidarkness.

Pitt pointed at Gunn and then at the engineer. Gunn waved an acknowledgment, grasped the grab irons and leaped up the steps into the cab.

Pitt arrived first. He calmly approached the fireman head-on and said pleasantly, "Have a nice day."

Before the confused and astonished fireman could respond, Pitt had swiftly snatched the shovel out of the Arab's hands and beat him over the head with it.

The engineer was in the act of turning around when Gunn whipped him across the jaw with the heavy silencer joined to the Heckler & Koch's stubby muzzle. The Arab dropped like a bag of cement.

While Gunn guarded against intruders, Pitt propped both hijackers so they hung half out of the cab's side windows. Next he thoughtfully studied the maze of pipes, levers and valves.

"You'll never do it," Gunn said shaking his head.

"I know how to start and drive a Stanley Steamer," Pitt said indignantly.

"A what?"

"An antique automobile," Pitt answered. "Pull open the door to the firebox. I need some light to read the gauges."

Gunn did as he was asked and held out his hands to warm them from the flames leaping through the opening. "You better figure it out quick," he said impatiently. "We're lit up like a Las Vegas chorus line."

Pitt pulled down a long lever and the little engine slipped forward a scant centimeter. "Okay, that's the brake. I think I've figured what handle does what. Now, when we roll past the crushing mill, jump and hustle inside."

"What about the train?"

"The Cannonball Express," Pitt replied with a wide grin, "does not make stops."

Pitt released the ratchet on the forward-reverse lever and pushed it away from him. Next he squeezed the ratchet on the throttle bar and eased it open. The locomotive crept slowly ahead, accompanied by the clanging jerk of the coupled ore cars. He shoved the throttle to its stop. The drive wheels whirled full circle several times before they bit the rusty rails. The train lurched forward and got underway.

The labored puffing came in faster spurts as the little engine picked up speed and chugged by the front of the dining hall. The door opened and a hijacker leaned out and raised a hand as if to wave. He snapped it back down when he saw the two bodies leaning from the cab's side windows. He disappeared into the building as if jerked by an immense rubber band, wildly shouting a warning.

Pitt and Gunn both unleashed a blast of gunfire through the windows and door of the building. Then the engine was past and heading toward the crushing mill. Pitt glanced at the ground and judged the speed to be somewhere between fifteen and twenty kilometers.

Pitt pulled the overhead whistle lever and tied it down with a drawstring from inside his ski jacket. The spurt of steam through the brass whistle cut the air like a razor.

"Get ready to jump," he yelled at Gunn above the ear-splitting scream.

Gunn didn't reply. He stared at the rough gravel flashing past as though it were hurtling by at jet speed a thousand meters below.

"Now!" shouted Pitt.

They hit the ground on the run, skidding and sliding but somehow managing to keep their footing. There was no hesitation, no pause to catch their breath. They ran alongside the train and straight up the steps of the crushing-mill's stairs, and didn't stop until they both stumbled, then tripped over the threshold and crashed to the floor inside.

The first thing Pitt saw was Giordino standing above him, unconcernedly holding his machine gun in a muzzle-up position.

"I've seen you kicked out of some pretty

raunchy pubs," Giordino said in a dour voice, "but this is the first time I've ever seen you tossed off a train."

"No great loss," said Pitt, coming to his feet. "It didn't have a club car."

"The gunfire. Yours or theirs?"

"Ours."

"Company on the way?"

"Like mad hornets out of a vandalized nest," replied Pitt. "We don't have much time to prepare for a siege."

"They'd better be careful where they aim or their helicopter might get broken."

"An advantage we'll play to the hilt."

Findley had finished tying the guard and the two mechanics together in the center of the floor, and he stood up. "Where do you want them?"

"They're as safe as anywhere there on the floor," answered Pitt. He looked swiftly around at the cavernous interior of the building with the crushing mill squatting in the center. "Al, you and Findley grab whatever equipment or furniture you can lift and convert the ore crusher into a fort. Rudi and I will delay them as long as we can."

"A fort within a fort," said Findley.

"It would take twenty men to defend a building this big," Pitt explained. "The hijackers' only hope of capturing their helicopter intact is to blow the main door and rush us en masse. We'll pick off as many as we can from the windows and then retreat to the mill for a last-ditch defense."

"Now I can sympathize with Davy Crockett at the Alamo," moaned Giordino.

Findley and Giordino began fortifying the huge mill while Pitt and Gunn set up shop at windows on opposite corners of the building. The sun was beginning to cast its rays over the slopes on the other side of the mountain. Darkness was almost gone.

Pitt could feel the wave of anxiety that washed through his mind. They might prevent the Arabs who were rapidly surrounding the crushing mill from escaping, but if the hijackers on the ship eluded the Special Forces teams and made a run for the mine, he and his pitiful little force would be overwhelmed.

He looked darkly out the window at the little engine as it roared down the track on its final run, picking up momentum with every turn of its drive wheels. Sparks belched from the stack as a long plume of smoke trailed sideways, driven by a flanking wind. The ore cars rattled and swayed on the narrow rails. The sound of the whistle turned from a shrill shriek to the mournful wail of a lost soul in hell as the train hurtled into the distance.

57

The shock and disappointment showed clearly in Ammar's eyes when he realized the glacial front was not about to fall. He whirled to face Ibn.

"What went wrong?" he demanded, his voice ragged with growing anger. "There should have been a chain of explosions."

Ibn's face was like stone. "You know me well, Suleiman Aziz. I do not make mistakes. The explosives should have detonated. The commando team we saw drop from the glacier to the ship must have found and disarmed most of them."

Ammar stared briefly at the sky, threw up his hands and let them drop again. "Allah weaves strange patterns into our lives," he said philosophically. Then a slow smile spread across his lips. "The glacier may fall yet. Once our helicopter is airborne, we can make a pass and drop grenades into the ice fracture."

Ibn matched Ammar's smile. "Allah has not deserted us," he said reverently. "Do not forget, we are safe here on shore while the Mexicans have inherited the job of fighting the Americans."

"Yes, you're right, old friend, we're in Allah's debt for our well-timed deliverance." Ammar stared contemptuously at the ship. "We'll soon see if Captain Machado's Aztec gods can protect him."

"He was a maggot, that one —" Suddenly Ibn stopped and cocked an ear, then gazed up the mountain slope. "Gunfire, coming from the mine."

Ammar listened, but he heard something else — the distant cry of the locomotive's whistle. The sound was continuous and grew louder. Then he saw the plume of smoke and watched in sudden puzzlement as the train shot down the mountainside, careening wildly on the curving switchbacks before barreling across a long, straight stretch toward the pier.

"What are those fools doing?" Ammar gasped as he saw the train thundering wildly down the track, heard the whistle filling the predawn with its high-pitched scream.

The hijackers and their hostages were not prepared for the incredible spectacle now avalanching upon them like a monster on a rampage. They stood petrified in disbelieving fascination.

"Allah save us!" a man uttered in a hoarse voice.

"Save yourself!" Ibn snapped. He was the

first to recover, and he began shouting for everyone to clear the tracks. There was bedlam as everyone scattered away from the rails just as the ore cars, pulled by the out-of-control little engine, her drive rods whipping in blurred motion, shot onto the pier.

The wooden pilings and flooring shuddered at the sudden onslaught. The tail-end ore car bounced off the tracks but, held by its coupling, was dragged like a screaming, unruly child by his ear across the tarred planking. Clouds of sparks sprayed as the steel wheels clattered against the rails. Then the engine ran out of track and soared off the end of the pier.

The train seemed to arc through the air for an instant in slow motion before the engine finally dropped and dived into the fjord. Miraculously, the boiler failed to explode when its heated walls met the icy water. The engine vanished with a great hiss and a cloud of steam, followed by a loud grinding of tortured metal as the ore cars piled in on top of each other.

Ammar and Ibn dashed to the pier's end and stared helplessly at the bubbles and steam rising from the water.

"The bodies of our men were hanging from the cab," said Ammar. "Did you see them?"

"I did, Suleiman Aziz."

"The sound of gunfire you heard a minute ago!" Ammar said in a white rage. "Our men must be under attack at the mine. There is still a chance to escape if we hurry and help them before the helicopter is damaged."

Ammar paused only long enough to give orders for one of his men to bring up the rear with the prisoners. He set off up the narrow-gauge tracks at a half-run, the other members of his hijacking force trailing behind in single file.

Growing fear and uncertainty swelled inside Ammar's mind. If the helicopter was destroyed, there could be no escape, no place to hide on the barren island. The American Special Forces would hunt them down one by one, or leave them either to freeze or starve to death.

Ammar was determined to survive if for no other reason than to kill Yazid and find the devil who was responsible for hounding him to Santa Inez Island and devastating his intricate plans.

The sounds of the battle increased and reverberated down the mountain. He was panting heavily from the exertion of running uphill, but he gritted his teeth and increased his pace.

Captain Machado was standing in the wheelhouse when he heard, felt, really, the muted detonation on the glacier. He stiffened for a moment, listening, but the only sound was the light tick of a large eight-day clock above the bridge windows.

Then his face suddenly paled. The glacier, he thought, it must be ready to break off.

Machado hurried to the communications room and found one of his men staring dumbly at the teletype.

He looked up blankly at Machado's entrance. "I thought I heard an explosion."

Suspicion unfolded inside Machado's gut. "Have you seen the radioman or the Egyptian leader?"

"I've seen no one."

"No Arabs at all?"

"Not in the past hour." The radar operator paused. "I haven't seen any of them since I left the dining salon and came on duty. They should be guarding the prisoners and patrolling the outside decks, since those are the jobs they stupidly volunteered for."

Machado studied the empty chair at the radio thoughtfully. "Maybe they weren't so stupid."

He stepped to the counter in front of the helm and looked through the narrow view cuts in the plastic sheeting directly in front of the bridge windows. There was enough daylight now to clearly see the forward part of the ship.

His eyes found several wide tears in the plastic. Too late he saw the ropes running from the top of the glacier down through the openings. Too late he swung around to voice an alarm over the ship's communication system.

He came to a dead stop before he uttered a sound.

There was a man standing in the doorway.

A man who wore all-black dress; hands and what little face that showed through the ski mask were also blackened. Night-vision goggles hung around his neck. He wore a large bulletproof chest piece with several pockets and clips holding both fragmentation and stun grenades, three murderous-looking knives and a number of other killing devices.

Machado's eyes suddenly squinted. "Who are you?" he demanded, knowing full well he was staring at death.

As he spoke he made a lightning snatch of a nine-millimeter automatic pistol from a shoulder holster and snapped off a shot.

Machado was good. Wyatt Earp, Doc Holiday and Bat Masterson would have been proud of him. His shot struck the intruder square in the center of the chest.

With older bulletproof vests, the pure force behind the blow could snap a rib or stop a heart. The vests worn by the SOF men, however, were the latest state of the art. They could even stop a 308 NATO round and distribute the impact so it left only a bruise.

Dillinger shuddered slightly from the bullet, took one step back and pulled the trigger of his Heckler & Koch, all in the same motion.

Machado wore a vest too, but the older model. Dillinger's burst tore through and riddled his chest. His spine arched like a tightly strung bow and he staggered backward, falling against the Captain's chair before dropping to the deck.

The Mexican guard raised his arms and shouted, "Don't fire! I am unarmed —"

Dillinger's short burst into the throat cut off the Mexican's plea, knocking him into the ship's compass binnacle, where he hung suspended like a limp rag doll.

"Don't move or I'll shoot," Dillinger said belatedly.

Sergeant Foster stepped around the Major and looked down at the dead terrorist. "He's dead, sir."

"I warned him," Dillinger said casually as he slipped another clip into his weapon.

Foster kicked the body over on its stomach with his boot. A long bayonet knife slipped out of a sheath below the collar and rattled on the deck. "Intuition, Major?" asked Foster.

"I never trust a man who says he's unarmed —"

Suddenly Dillinger stopped and listened. Both men heard it at the same time and looked at each other, puzzled.

"What in hell is that?" asked Foster.

"They were a good thirty years before my

time, but I'd swear that's a whistle from an old steam locomotive."

"Sounds like it's coming down the mountain from the old mine."

"I thought it was abandoned."

"The NUMA people were to wait there until the ship was secure."

"Why would they stoke up an old locomotive?"

"I don't know." Dillinger paused and stared distantly, a sudden certainty growing within him. "Unless . . . they're trying to tell us something."

The detonation on the glacier caught Hollis and his team in the dining salon immediately after a wild shootout.

His dive team had sliced their way through the plastic and found a tight passage between the fake cargo containers. They had passed warily through a doorway into an empty bar and lounge outside the dining salon, fanned out, dodging behind pillars and furniture, four men covering the staircase and two elevators, and surprised Machado's Mexican terrorist team.

All but one terrorist was down. He still stood where he'd been hit, hate and vague astonishment reflected in his dying eyes. Then his body collapsed and he fell to the carpet, staining its rich, thick pile a deep crimson.

Hollis and his team advanced, warily stepping over and around the bodies. A blood-chilling creak of the ice wall sounded throughout the ship, rattling the few undamaged bottles and glasses behind an ornate bar.

The Special Operations men stared uneasily at one another and at their Colonel, but they stood firm and ready.

"Major Dillinger's team must have missed one," Hollis mused calmly.

"No hostages here, sir," said one of his men. "All appear to be terrorists."

Hollis studied several of the lifeless faces. None of them looked like they came from the Middle East. Must be the crew from the *General Bravo,* he thought.

He turned away and pulled a copy of the ship's deck layout from a pocket and studied it briefly, while he talked into his radio.

"Major, report your status."

"Met light resistance so far," replied Dillinger. "Have only accounted for four hijackers. The bridge is secure and we've released over a hundred crew members who were locked in the baggage hold. Sorry we didn't find all the charges."

"Good work. You did well to disarm enough to keep the glacier from calving. I'm heading for the master staterooms to free the passengers. Request the engine-room crew return to their station and restore power. We don't dare hang around under the ice cliff a minute longer than we have to. Watch yourselves. We took out another sixteen hijackers, all Latins. There must be another twenty Arabs still on the ship."

"They may be on shore, sir."

"Why do you say that?"

"We heard a whistle from a locomotive a couple of minutes ago. I ordered one of my men to climb the radar mast and check it out. He reported a train roaring down the mountain from the mine like a bowling ball. He also observed it run off a nearby pier that was crowded with two dozen terrorists."

"Forget it for now. Let's rescue the hostages first and see to the shore when we've secured the ship."

"Acknowledged."

Hollis led his men up the grand staircase and moved, quiet as a whisper, into the hallway separating the staterooms. Suddenly they froze in position as one of the elevators hummed and rose from the deck below. The door opened and a hijacker stepped out, unaware of the assault. He opened his mouth, the only movement he was able to make before one of Hollis's men tapped him heavily on the head with the silenced muzzle of his gun.

Incredibly, there were no guards outside the staterooms. The men began kicking in the doors, and upon entering, found the Egyptian and Mexican advisers and Presidential staff aides, but no sign of Hasan and De

Lorenzo.

Hollis broke open the last door at the hallway, burst inside and confronted five men in ship's uniforms. One of them stepped forward and gazed at Hollis in contempt.

"You might have used the door latch," he said, regarding Hollis with suspicion.

"You must be Captain Oliver Collins?"

"Yes, I'm Collins, as if you didn't know."

"Sorry about the door. I'm Colonel Morton Hollis, Special Operations Forces."

"By Jesus, an American!" gasped First Officer Finney.

Collins's face lit up as he rushed forward to pump Hollis's hand. "Forgive me, Colonel. I thought you might be one of them. Are we ever glad to see you."

"How many hijackers?" asked Hollis.

"After the Mexicans came on board from the *General Bravo,* I should judge about forty."

"We've only accounted for twenty."

Collins's face reflected the ordeal. He looked haggard but still stood tall. "You've freed the two presidents and Senator Pitt and Miss Kamil?"

"I'm afraid we haven't found them yet."

Collins rushed past him through the doorway. "They were held in the master suite just across the passageway."

Hollis stood aside in surprise. "No one in there," he said flatly. "We've already searched this deck."

The Captain ran into the empty suite, but saw only the rumpled bedclothes, the usual light mess left by passengers. His stiff-backed composure fell away and he looked positively stunned.

"My God, they've taken them."

Hollis spoke into his microphone. "Major Dillinger."

Dillinger took five seconds to respond. "I read you, Colonel. Go ahead."

"Any contact with the enemy?"

"None, I think we've pretty well rounded them up."

"At least twenty hijackers and the VIP passengers are missing. You see a sign of them?"

"Negative, not so much as a stray hair."

"Okay, finish securing the ship and have her crew move her out into the fjord."

"No can do," said Dillinger solemnly.

"Problems?"

"The murdering bastards really did a number on the engine room. They smashed up everything. It'll take a week to put the ship back in operation."

"We've got no power at all?"

"Sorry, Colonel. Here we are, and here we sit. These engines aren't taking us anywhere. They also wrecked the generators, including the auxiliaries."

"Then we'll have to take the crew and passengers off by lifeboat, using the manual winches."

"No go, Colonel. We're dealing with genuine sadists. They also trashed the lifeboats. Bashed the bottoms out."

Dillinger's dire report was punctuated by a deep growling noise that emanated from the glacier and traveled through the ship like a drum. There was no vibration this time, only the growl that turned into a heart-stopping rumble. It lasted nearly a minute before it finally faded and died.

Hollis and Collins were both brave men — no one would ever doubt it — but each read fear in the other's eyes.

"The glacier is ready to calve," said Collins grimly. "Our only hope is to cut away the anchor chains and pray the tide carries us out into the fjord."

"Believe me, you won't see ebb tide for another eight hours," said Hollis. "You're talking to a man who knows."

"You're just full of cheery news, aren't you, Colonel."

"Doesn't look encouraging, does it?"

"Doesn't look encouraging," Collins repeated. "Is that all you have to say? There are nearly two hundred people on board the *Lady Flamborough.* They must be evacuated immediately."

"I can't wave a wand and make the glacier go away," Hollis explained calmly. "I can take a few out in inflatable boats and call in our helicopters to airlift the rest. But we're talking a good hour."

Collins's voice came edged with impatience. "Then I suggest you get on with it while we're all still alive —" He halted as Hollis abruptly swung up a hand for silence.

Hollis's eyes narrowed in bewilderment as a strange voice suddenly burst over his earphone.

"Colonel Hollis, am I on your frequency? Over."

"Who the hell is this!" Hollis snapped.

"Captain Frank Stewart of the NUMA ship *Sounder* at your service. Can I give you a lift somewhere?"

"Stewart!" the Colonel burst out. "Where are you?"

"If you could see through all that crap hanging on your superstructure, you'd find me cruising up the fjord about half a kilometer off your port side."

Hollis exhaled a great sigh and nodded at Collins. "A ship is bearing down on us. Any instructions?"

Collins stared at him, numb with disbelief. Then he blurted, "Good God, yes, man! Tell him to take us under tow."

Working feverishly, Collins's crew slipped the bow and stern anchor chains and made ready with the mooring hawsers.

In a feat of superb seamanship, Stewart

645

swung the *Sounder*'s stern under the *Lady Flamborough*'s bow in one pass. Two heavy rope mooring lines were dropped by the crewmen of the cruise ship and immediately made fast to the survey ship's deck bitts. It was not the most perfect tow arrangement, but the ships were not going for distance across stormy seas, and the temporary expedient was accomplished in a matter of minutes.

Stewart gave the command for "slow ahead" until the slack was taken up from the tow lines. Then he slowly increased speed to "full ahead" while he looked over his shoulder, one eye on the glacier, one on the cruise liner. The *Sounder*'s two cycloidal propellers, one forward and one aft, thrashed the water as her great diesel engine strained under the load.

She was half the *Lady Flamborough*'s tonnage and never meant for tug duty, but she dug in and drove like a draft horse in a pulling contest, black exhaust pouring from her stack.

At first nothing seemed to happen, and then slowly, imperceptibly, a small bit of froth appeared around the *Sounder*'s bow. She was moving, hauling the reluctant cruise liner from under the shadow of the glacier.

Despite the danger, the passengers, crew and Special Forces fighters all tore away the plastic sheeting and stood on the decks, watching and willing the straggling *Sounder* forward. Ten meters, then twenty, a hundred, the gap between ship and ice widened with agonizing slowness.

Then at last the *Lady Flamborough* was clear.

Everyone on both ships gave a rousing cheer that echoed up and down the fjord. Later, Captain Collins would humorously call it the cheer that broke the camel's back.

A loud cracking sound trailed the celebrating voices and grew into a great booming rumble. To those watching, it seemed as if the air was electrified. Then the whole forward face of the ice cliff toppled forward and pounded into the fjord like a huge oil tanker being launched on its side. The water seethed and boiled and rose in a ten-foot wave that surged down the fjord and lifted the two ships like corks before heading out toward the open sea.

The monstrous, newly calved iceberg settled into the deeply carved channel of the fjord, its ice glinting like a field of orange diamonds under the new sun. Then the rumble rolled down from the mountainside and echoed in the ears of the stunned onlookers, who couldn't believe they were somehow alive.

58

At first there was complete confusion, with much shouting and wild shooting. The Egyptians had no idea of the size of the force that fired on them in the dining hall during the passage of the train. They snuffed the lights and shot at the early-morning shadows until they realized the shadows weren't shooting back.

The dirt roads between the wooden buildings took on an eerie silence. For several minutes the Egyptian hijackers made no effort to leave the dining hall.

Then, suddenly, a half-dozen men — two from the front and four at the rear of the building — broke from the doors, scrambling, crouching, and diving headlong behind predetermined shelter. Once in position, they laid down a circle of fire to cover the rest of the men, who then followed on their heels.

Their leader, a tall man wearing a black turban, directed the men's movements by blowing sharp bleeps on a whistle.

After a rocky start, the Egyptian terrorist team was everything Pitt was afraid of — highly trained, practiced and tough. When it came to house-to-house street fighting, they were the best in the world. They were even well led. The leader in the black turban was competent and methodical.

They searched building by building, working toward the crushing mill until they half-circled it like a crescent. No haphazard assault by Ammar's hand-picked killers. They moved with stealth and purpose.

Their leader called out in Arabic. When there was no reply, another terrorist shouted from a different location. They were hailing the guard and mechanics inside the crushing mill, Pitt guessed correctly.

They were too close now for Pitt to risk revealing himself at the window. He removed the terrorist's ski mask and clothing and threw it in a pile on the floor, then rummaged through a pocket of his ski jacket and retrieved a small mirror attached to a narrow stretch handle. He eased the mirror above the window sill and extended the handle, twisting it like a periscope.

He found the target he was looking for, 90 percent concealed, but enough showing for a killing shot.

Pitt turned the fire-select lever from FULL AUTO to SINGLE. Then he swiftly raised up, aimed and squeezed the trigger.

The deadly old Thompson spat. Black Turban took two or three steps, his face blank and uncomprehending; then he sagged, fell forward and pitched to the ground.

Pitt dropped down, lowered his gun and peered into the mirror again. The terrorists had disappeared. To a man, they had dodged behind buildings or crawled furiously under abandoned and rusting mining equipment. Pitt knew they weren't about to quit. They were still out there, dangerous as ever, waiting for instructions from their second-in-command.

Gunn took his cue and pumped a ten-round burst through a thin wooden door on a shed across the road. Very slowly the door swung open, pushed by a body that twisted and dropped.

Still there was no return fire. They were nobody's fools, thought Pitt. Now that the Arabs realized they were not up against a superior force but harried by a small group, they took their time to regroup and consider options.

They also realized now that their unknown assailants had captured their helicopter and were holed up in the crushing mill.

Pitt ducked, scurried over and crouched beside Gunn. "How's it look on your side?"

"Quiet. They're playing it nice and easy. They don't want to dent their helicopter."

"I think they're going to create a diversion

at the front door and then make a rush through the side office."

Gunn nodded. "Sounds logical. About time we found better cover away from these windows anyway. Where do you want me?"

Pitt looked up at the catwalks above. He pointed at a row of small skylights encircling a small winch tower. "Climb up and keep watch. Yell when they launch the attack and welcome them with a concentrated burst through the front door. Then get your ass back down here. They won't have any scruples about peppering the walls above the copter."

"On my way."

Pitt moved around to the side office, paused at the threshold and turned to Giordino and Findley.

"How's it coming?" he asked.

Giordino looked up from shoveling a pile of leftover ore for a barricade. "Fort Giordino will be finished on schedule."

Findley stopped work and stared at him. "F before G, Fort Findley."

Giordino looked at Findley morosely for a second before returning to his work. "Fort Findley if we lose, Giordino if we win."

Shaking his head in awe, Pitt wondered why he was blessed with such incredible friends. He wanted to say something to them, express his feelings of gratitude for risking their lives to stop a band of scum when they could have bolted for the boondocks and hid out until Hollis and his team arrived. But they knew: men like this needed no words of appreciation or encouragement. There they'd stay, and there they'd fight it out. Pitt hoped to God none would die uselessly.

"Argue about it later," he ordered, "and ready a reception committee if they get past me."

He turned and entered the damp and musty-smelling office. He checked his Thompson and set it aside. After quickly building a barrier with two overturned desks, a steel filing cabinet and a heavy iron potbellied stove, he lay down on the floor and waited.

He didn't wait long. One minute later he came to unmoving attention as he thought he heard the faint crunch of gravel outside. The sound stopped and then came again, soft but unmistakable. He raised the Thompson and propped the grips on the filing cabinet.

Too late, Gunn gave a yell of warning, when suddenly an object crashed through the transom window above the door and fell, rolling across the floor. A second came right behind. Pitt dropped low and tried to burrow into the steel cabinet, cursing his lack of forethought.

Both grenades went off with an ear-bursting blast. The office erupted in a great roar of shattered furniture and flying wood and yellowed paper. The outer wall was blown outward and most of the ceiling caved in.

Pitt was dazed by the concussion and the deafening clap of the twin blast. He'd never experienced an explosion in a close proximity before, and he was stunned right down to his toes.

The potbellied stove had taken the main force of the shrapnel, yet held its shape, the rounded sides perforated with jagged holes. The file cabinet was bent and twisted and the desks badly mutilated, but the only apparent injuries Pitt could find on himself were a thin but deep cut in his left thigh and a five-centimeter gash on his cheek.

The office had vanished and left in its place a pile of smoldering debris, and for one apprehensive moment Pitt had a vision of being trapped in a blazing fire. But only for a moment — the rain-soaked old wood of the building sizzled a bit in several places but refused to ignite.

With a conscious effort of will Pitt switched the Thompson to FULL AUTO, and aimed the barrel at the splintered remains of the front door. Blood was streaming down the side of his face and under his collar. His eyes never flickered as a barrage of automatic fire came pouring over his head from the guns of four men who charged through the shattered openings in the outer wall.

Pitt felt neither remorse nor fear as he fired

a long burst that blew away his attackers like trees before a tornado. They threw up their weapons, arms flailing in the manner of frenzied dancers on a stage, and spun crazily to the debris-piled floor.

Three more terrorist fighters followed the first wave and were as ruthlessly stopped by Pitt — all except one, who reacted with incredible swiftness and flung himself behind a smoking, shredded leather sofa.

Cannonlike blasts went off in Pitt's ear as Findley dropped to his knees behind him and pumped three loads from his shotgun into the lower base of the sofa. Leather, burlap padding and wood sprayed the air. A moment of quiet, and then one of the terrorist's arms flopped lifelessly beyond the sofa's carved feet.

Giordino appeared through the smoke and gunpowder fumes, grasping Pitt under the arms and dragging him back into the crushing-mill area and behind an old ore car.

"Must you always make a mess?" he said, grinning. Then his face softened with concern. "You hurt bad?"

Pitt wiped the blood away from his cheek and stared down at the crimson stain spreading through the fabric covering his leg. "Damn! A perfectly good pair of ski pants . . . ruined. Now that really pisses me off."

Findley knelt down, cut away the pants leg and began bandaging the wound. "You were lucky to survive the blast with only a couple of cuts."

"Dumb of me not to figure on grenades," Pitt said bitterly. "I should have guessed."

"No sense in blaming yourself." Giordino shrugged. "This isn't our line of work."

Pitt looked up. "We better get smart real fast if we want to be around when the SOF guys arrive."

"They won't try another assault from this direction," Findley said. "The blast knocked down the stairway outside. They'd be sitting ducks if they tried scrambling up ten feet of broken timber."

"Now might be a ripe opportunity to burn the helicopter and get the hell out of here," Findley said unhappily.

"The news gets worse, and it gets better," Gunn said, dropping from a ladder to the floor. "I saw another twenty of them charging up the railroad track like a prairie fire. They should be here in another seven or eight minutes."

Giordino looked at Gunn suspiciously. "How many?"

"I stopped counting at fifteen."

"The opportunity to flee the coop gets even riper," muttered Findley.

"Hollis and his men?" asked Pitt.

Gunn shook his head wearily. "No sign of them." He paused to draw a deep breath and turned to stare at Pitt. "The terrorist reinforcements, they were trailed by four hostages with two guards. I could just recognize them through my binoculars. One was your Dad. He and a woman were helping two other men along the tracks."

"Hala Kamil, bless her," Pitt said with vast relief. "Thank God, the old man is alive."

"The other two?" asked Giordino.

"Most likely Presidents Hasan and De Lorenzo."

"So much for early retirement," said Findley gloomily as he placed the final piece of tape over Pitt's bandage.

"The terrorists are only keeping the Senator and the others alive to ensure a safe escape," said Pitt.

"And won't hesitate to murder them one by one until we hand over their helicopter," predicted Gunn.

Pitt nodded. "Without a doubt, but if we surrendered, there's no guarantee they wouldn't murder them anyway. They've already tried to assassinate Hala twice and most certainly want Hasan dead too."

"They'll call a truce and negotiate."

Pitt looked at his watch. "They won't haggle for very long. They know their time is running out. But we might gain a few extra minutes."

"So what's the plan?" asked Giordino.

"We stall and fight for as long as it takes." Pitt looked at Gunn. "Were the hostages surrounded by the hijackers?"

"No, they were a good two hundred meters in the rear, trailing the main party up the railbed," Gunn replied. "They were herded by only two terrorists." He stared back into Pitt's green eyes, and then nodded in slow understanding. "You want me to take out the guards and protect the Senator and the rest until Hollis shows?"

"You're the smallest and the fastest, Rudi. If anybody can get clear of the building undetected and circle around behind those two guards while we distract them, you can."

Gunn threw out his hands and dropped them to his sides. "I'm grateful for the trust. I only hope I can pull it off."

"You can."

"That leaves only three of you to hold the fort."

"We'll have to make do." Pitt awkwardly rose to his feet and limped over to the pile of terrorists' clothing he'd tossed on the floor. He returned and held it out to Gunn. "Wear this. They'll think you're one of them."

Gunn stood there rooted, reluctant to desert his friends.

Giordino came to his rescue by laying a beefy hand on the smaller man's shoulder and steering him to a maintenance passage that dropped beneath the floor and ran around the giant crushing mill.

"You can get out through here," he said

smiling. "Wait until things heat up before you make your break."

Gunn found himself half under the floor in the passage before he could protest. He took one last look at Pitt, the incredibly durable, indestructible Dirk Pitt, who gave him a jaunty wave. Peered at Giordino, old steady and reliable, whose concern was masked by a lighthearted expression. And finally Findley, who flashed a sparkling smile and held up both thumbs. They we're all part of him and he was heartsick at leaving, not knowing if he would see any of them alive again.

"You guys be here when I get back," he said. "You hear?"

Then he ducked under the flooring and was gone.

59

Hollis paced beside the postage-stamp-sized landing pad that the *Lady Flamborough's* crew had hurriedly fabricated over the swimming pool. A Carrier Pigeon helicopter settled onto the pad as a small team of men waited to board.

Hollis stopped when he heard a fresh outburst of gunfire from the direction of the mine, his face reflecting concern.

"Load and get 'em airborne," he shouted impatiently to Dillinger. "Somebody's alive up there and fighting our battle."

"The mine must have been the hijackers' escape point," said Captain Collins, who paced at Hollis's side.

"And thanks to me, Dirk Pitt and his friends stumbled right into them," snapped Hollis.

"Any way you can get there in time to save them and the hostages?" asked Collins.

Hollis shook his head in grim despair. "Not one chance in hell."

■ ■ ■ ■

Rudi Gunn was thankful for the sudden downpour of heavy rain. It effectively shielded him as he crawled away from the crushing mill under a string of empty ore cars. Once clear of the buildings, he dropped down the mountain below the mine for a few hundred meters, and then circled back.

He found the narrow-gauge tracks and began walking silently on the crossties. He could see only a short distance around him, but within a few minutes of escaping the terrorists' assault on the crushing mill, he froze in position when his eyes distinguished several vague figures through the rain ahead. He counted four sitting and two standing.

Gunn faced a dilemma. He assumed the hostages were resting while the guards stood. But he couldn't shoot and check his assumption later. He would have to rely on his borrowed terrorist clothing to bluff his way close enough to tell friend from foe.

His only drawback, and a vital one, was he only knew two or three words of Arabic.

Gunn took a breath and walked forward. He said, *"Salaam,"* repeating the word two more times in a calm, controlled voice.

The two figures who were standing took on more detail as he approached, and he saw they held machine guns lowered and pointed his way.

One of them replied with words Gunn couldn't interpret. He mentally crossed his fingers and hoped they had asked the Arabic equivalent of "Who goes there?"

"Muhammad," he mumbled, relying on the prophet's name to carry him through, while lazily holding the Heckler & Koch across his chest with the muzzle aimed off to the side.

Gunn's heartbeat calmed considerably as the two terrorists lowered their guns in unison and turned their attention back to their guard duty. He moved casually until he was standing alongside them so his line of fire would not strike the hostages.

Then, while keeping his eyes aimed at the miserable people sitting on the ground between the track rails, and without even looking at the two guards, he squeezed the trigger.

Ammar and his men were on the verge of total exhaustion when they reached the outskirts of the mine. The persistent downpour had turned their clothes sodden and heavy. They struggled over a long mound of tailings and thankfully entered a shed that once housed mining-equipment parts.

Ammar dropped onto a wooden bench, his head drooped on his chest, his breath coming in labored gasps. He looked up as Ibn entered with another man.

"This is Mustapha Osman," said Ibn. "He says an armed group of commandos have killed their group leader and barricaded themselves in the crushing mill with our helicopter."

Ammar's lips drew back in anger. "How could you let this happen?"

Osman's black eyes registered panic. "We had . . . no warning," he stammered. "They must have come down from the mountain. They subdued the sentries, seized the train and shot up our living quarters. When we launched our counterattack they fired on us from the crushing-mill building."

"Casualties?" Ammar demanded coldly.

"There are seven of us left."

The nightmare was worse than Ammar thought. "How many in their assault party?"

"Twenty, maybe thirty."

"Seven of you have thirty of them under siege," snarled Ammar, his tone heavy with sarcasm. "Their number. This time the truth, or Ibn here will slit your throat."

Osman averted Ammar's eyes. He was frozen in fear. "There is no way of knowing for certain," he mumbled. "Perhaps four or more."

"Four men did all this?" said Ammar, aghast. He was seething but too disciplined to allow his anger to take control. "What of the helicopter? Is it damaged?"

Osman seemed to brighten a degree. "No, we were careful not to fire at the section of the building where it is parked. I'd stake my father's honor it has not been hit."

"Only Allah knows whether the commandos have sabotaged it," said Ibn.

"We'll all see Allah soon if we don't recapture it in flying condition," Ammar said quietly. "The only way we can overpower the defenders is to strike hard and penetrate from all sides and crush them by sheer weight of numbers."

"Perhaps we can use the hostages to bargain our way out," said Ibn hopefully.

Ammar nodded. "A possibility. Americans are weak when it comes to death threats. I'll parley with our unknown scourge while you position the men for the assault."

"Take care, Suleiman Aziz."

"Be ready to attack when I remove my mask."

Ibn gave a slight bow and immediately began giving orders to the men.

Ammar ripped a tattered curtain from one window. The fabric had once been white, but was now faded to a dingy yellow. It would have to do, he thought. He tied it to an old broom and stepped from the shed.

He moved along a row of miners' bunkhouses, keeping out of sight of the crushing mill until he was across the street. Then he extended the curtain around a corner and waved it up and down.

No gunfire tore through the ragged flag of truce, but nothing else happened either. Ammar tried shouting in English.

"We wish to talk!"

After several moments a voice yelled back. *"No hablo inglés."*

Ammar was taken back momentarily. Chilean security police? They were far more efficient than he thought. He could speak fluently in English and get by in French, but he knew little Spanish. Hesitation would get him nowhere. He had to see who stood in his way of a successful escape.

He held up the makeshift flag, raised his free hand and stepped out onto the road in front of the crushing mill.

The word for peace he knew was *paz.* So he shouted it several times. Finally a man opened the main door and slowly limped onto the road, stopped a few paces away and faced him.

The stranger was tall, with intensely green eyes that never flickered and yet ignored the dozen gunbarrels poking through windows and doorways in his direction. The eyes locked on Ammar only. The black hair was long and wavy, skin weathered a deep copper from long exposure to sun, slightly bushy eyebrows with firm lips fixed in a slight grin — all lent the masculine but not quite handsome face a deceptive look of humorous

detachment, with only a trace of cold hardness.

There was a cut in one cheek that oozed
blood and a wound on one thigh that was
heavily bandaged under the slashed fabric.

The shape might have been lean under the
bulky, out-of-place ski suit, but Ammar could
not make a clear assessment. One hand was
bare while the other was gloved and hung
loosely beneath one sleeve of the ski jacket.

Three seconds were all Ammar needed to
read this devil — three seconds to know he
was facing a dangerous man. He searched his
mind for the few meager words of Spanish
stored there. "Can we talk?" Yes, that would
do for openers.

"Podemos hablar?" he shouted.

The suggestion of a grin widened into a
casual smile. *"Porque no?"*

Ammar translated that as Why not? *"Hacer
capitular usted?"*

"Why don't we cut the crap?" Pitt said suddenly in English. "Your Spanish is worse than
mine. The answer to your question is No,
we're not going to surrender."

Ammar was too much a pro not to recover
immediately, yet he was confounded by the
fact that his adversary wore expensive skiing
clothes instead of battle gear. The first possibility that crossed his mind was CIA.

"May I ask your name?"

"Dirk Pitt."

"I am Suleiman Aziz Ammar —"

"I don't really give a damn who you are," Pitt said coldly.

"As you wish, Mr. Pitt," Ammar remarked calmly. Then one of his eyebrows lifted lightly. "You by chance related to Senator George Pitt?"

"I don't travel in political circles."

"But you know him. I can see a resemblance. The son perhaps?"

"Can we get on with this? I had to interrupt a perfectly good champagne brunch to come out here in the rain."

Ammar laughed. The man was incredible. "You have something of mine. I'd like it returned in first-rate condition."

"You're speaking, of course, of one unmarked helicopter."

"Of course."

"Finders keepers. You want it, pal, you come and get it."

Ammar clenched and unclenched his fists impatiently. This was not going as he had hoped. He continued in a silky voice.

"Some of my men will die, you will die, and your father will most certainly die if you do not turn it over to me."

Pitt didn't blink. "You forgot to throw in Hala Kamil and Presidents De Lorenzo and Hasan. And don't neglect to include yourself. No reason you shouldn't fertilize the grass too."

Ammar stared at Pitt, his anger slowly rising.

"I can't believe your stubborn stupidity. What will you gain by more bloodletting?"

"To put the skids under scumbags like you," said Pitt harshly. "You want a war, you declare it. But don't sneak around butchering women and children and taking innocent hostages who can't fight back. The terror stops here. I'm not bound by any law but my own. For every one of us you murder, we bury five of you."

"I didn't come out here in the wet to discuss our political differences!" said Ammar, fighting to control his wrath. "Tell me if the helicopter has been damaged."

"Doesn't have a scratch. And I might add that your pilots are still fit to fly. That make you happy?"

"You would be wise to surrender your weapons and turn over my craft and flight crew."

Pitt shrugged. "Screw you."

Ammar was shaken by his failure to intimidate Pitt. His voice turned abrupt and cold. "How many men do you have, four, perhaps five? We outnumber you eight to one."

Pitt nodded his head at the bodies scattered beside the crushing mill. "You're going to have to play catch-up ball. The way I see it, you're about nine stiffs down on the scoreboard." Then as an afterthought he said,

"Before I forget — I give you my word I won't sabotage your copter. It's yours in pristine shape providing you can take it. But harm any of the hostages, and I blow it from here to the nearest junkyard. That's the only deal I'll make."

"That is your final word?"

"For now, yes."

A thought crystallized in Ammar's mind, and he was swept by a sudden revelation. "It was *you!*" he rasped. "You led the American special forces here."

"Luck gets most of the credit," Pitt said modestly. "But after I found the wreck of the *General Bravo* and a misplaced roll of plastic, it all fell into place."

Ammar stood there for a moment in profound astonishment, then recovered and said, "You do your powers of deduction an injustice, Mr. Pitt. I readily concede the coyote has run the fox to ground."

"Fox?" said Pitt. "You flatter yourself. Don't you mean maggot?"

Ammar looked at Pitt through narrowed eyes. "I'm personally going to kill you, Pitt, and I'm going to take great pleasure in seeing your body shot to pieces. What say you to that?"

There was no fury in Pitt's eyes, no hatred etched in his face. He stared back at Ammar with a kind of bemused disgust one might display in exchanging looks with a cobra behind glass at a snake farm.

"Give my regards to Broadway," he said, turning his back on Ammar and walking casually back to the door of the crushing mill.

Furious, Ammar hurled down the flag of truce and strode swiftly in the opposite direction. As he moved he eased an American Ruger P-85 semiautomatic 9-millimeter from the inside pocket of his coat.

Suddenly he whirled, whipped off his mask and went into the classic crouched stance with the Ruger gripped in both hands. The instant the sights lined up dead center on Pitt's back, Ammar pulled the trigger six times in lightning succession.

He saw the bullets tear into the middle of Pitt's ski jacket in a ragged grouping of uneven holes, watched as the concentrated impact knocked his hated enemy stumbling forward into the wall of the crushing mill.

Ammar waited for Pitt to fall. His antagonist, he knew with firm certainty, was dead before striking the ground.

60

Gradually Ammar became aware that Pitt was not acting as he should.

Pitt did not fall dead. Instead, he turned, and Ammar saw the devil's own smile.

Stunned, Ammar knew he'd been outwitted. He realized now Pitt had expected a cowardly attack from the rear and protected his back with a bulletproof shield under the bulky ski jacket.

And with a numbing shock he saw the gloved hand hanging from the sleeve was fake. A magician's trick. The real hand had materialized, a hand clutching a big Colt 45 automatic that protruded from the partially unzipped ski jacket.

Ammar aimed the Ruger again but Pitt fired first.

Pitt's first shot took Ammar in the right shoulder and spun him sideways. The second smashed through his chin and lower jaw. The third shattered one wrist as he threw it up to his face. The fourth passed through his face from side to side.

Ammar rolled to the gravel and sprawled on his back, uncaring and oblivious to the gunfire that erupted over him, not knowing that Pitt had leaped uninjured through the door of the crashing mill before Ammar's men belatedly opened fire.

He was only vaguely aware of Ibn dragging him to safety behind a steel water tank as a short burst of fire from inside the crushing mill sprayed the ground around them. Slowly his hand groped up Ibn's arm until he clutched the solid-muscled shoulder. Then he pulled his friend downward.

"I cannot see you," he rasped.

Ibn removed a large surgical pad from a pack on his belt and gently pressed it over the torn flesh that once held Ammar's eyes. "Allah and I will see for you," said Ibn.

Ammar coughed and spit out the blood from the shattered chin that had seeped down his throat. "I want that Satan, Pitt, and the hostages hacked to pieces."

"Our attack has begun. Their lives are measured in seconds."

"If I die . . . kill Yazid."

"You will not die."

Ammar went through another coughing spasm before he could speak again. "No matter . . . the Americans will destroy the helicopter now. You must escape the island another way. Leave . . . leave me. That is my final

671

request of you."

Wordlessly, without acknowledging the plea, Ibn lifted Ammar in his arms and began walking away from the scene of the battle.

When Ibn spoke, his voice was hoarse but soft. "Be of strong spirit, Suleiman Aziz," he said. "We will return to Alexandria together."

Pitt barely had time to leap through the door, whip off the two bulletproof vests from under the back of his coat, replace one in the front and return the second to Giordino before a hail of concentrated fire drilled through the thin wooden walls.

"Now the jacket is ruined," Pitt grunted, pressing his body into the floor.

"You'd have been dead meat if he'd plugged you in the chest," said Giordino, wiggling into his vest. "How'd you know he was going to shoot when your back was turned?"

"He had bad breath and beady eyes."

Findley began scrambling from window to window, throwing grenades as fast as he could yank the activating pins. "They're here!" he yelled.

Giordino rolled across the plank floor and poured a continuous fire from behind a wheelbarrow full of ore. Pitt snatched up the Thompson just in time to stop two terrorists who had somehow managed to climb into the shattered side office.

Ammar's small army charged the building

from all sides with guns blazing. There was no stopping the tide of the savage onslaught. They swarmed in everywhere. The sharp crackle of the terrorists' small-caliber AK-74s and the deep stutter of Pitt's 45-caliber Thompson were punctuated by the boom of Findley's shotgun.

Giordino fell back to the crushing mill, laying down a covering fire for Pitt and Findley until all three had reached the temporary protection of their Mickey Mouse fort. The terrorists were momentarily stunned to find no enemy cringing or throwing up their hands in surrender. Once inside the building they'd expected to inundate their unprotected enemy with sheer numbers. Instead, they found themselves caught naked by a withering fusillade from the mill and were cut down like milling cattle.

Pitt, Giordino and Findley decimated the first wave. But the Arabs were fanatically brave, and they learned fast. An intensified gunfire and the blast from several grenades engulfed the cavernous room ahead of the next assault.

Bedlam! The dead heaped the floor, and the Arabs took cover behind the bodies of their dead comrades. It was a frightening scene — guns blasting, grenades exploding, the shouts and curses in two languages from two cultures as different as night and day. The building shook from the reverberations of gunfire and the concussions of the grenades. Shrapnel and bullets flayed the sides of the great mechanical mill like sparks from a bucket of molten steel. The air was filled with the pungent smell of gunpowder.

Fire broke out in a dozen places and was completely ignored. Giordino threw a grenade that blew off the tail rotor of the helicopter. Even with the last hope of escape gone now, the Arabs irrationally fought all the harder.

Pitt's ancient Thompson slammed deafeningly and then stopped. He ejected the fifty-round rotary drum and inserted another — his last. There was a cold, calculated determination he'd never felt before. He and Giordino and Findley had no intention of throwing in the towel. They had long passed the point of no return and found no fear of death behind it. They hung on grimly, fighting for their very existence, tenaciously giving better than they received.

Three times the Arab terrorists were driven back and three times they charged forward in the face of the murderous fire. Their badly diminished force regrouped again and launched a final suicide assault, closing the ring tighter and tighter.

The Arab Muslims could not understand their enemy's ferocity, how they could fight with such bloody-minded precision, why they were so outrageously defiant. The Americans fought desperately only to live, while they themselves sought a blessed death and martyrdom as salvation.

Pitt's eyes stung from the smoke, and tears streamed down his cheeks. The whole crushing mill was vibrating. Bullets ricocheted off the steel sides like angry hornets, four of them tearing through Pitt's sleeve and slightly grazing the skin.

Recklessly the Arabs threw themselves against the crushing mill and scurried over the makeshift barricade. The shooting match quickly turned into a man-to-man struggle as the two groups met in a savage, brawling mass of bodies.

Findley went down as two bullets struck him in his unprotected side, yet he remained on his knees, feebly swinging his empty shotgun like a baseball bat.

Giordino, wounded in five places, gamely heaved ore rocks with his right hand, his left arm dangling useless from a bullet through the shoulder.

Pitt's Thompson fired its last cartridge, and he hurled the big gun in the face of an Arab who suddenly reared up before him. He yanked the Colt automatic from his belt and fired at any face that lurched through the smoke. He felt a stinging sensation at the base of the neck and knew he'd been hit. The Colt quickly emptied, and Pitt fought on, chopping the heavy gun like a small club. He began to taste the beginnings of sour defeat.

Reality no longer existed. Pitt felt as if he were fighting a nightmare. A grenade went off, a crushing explosion that deafened him by its closeness. A body fell on top of him, and he was caught off balance and thrown backward.

His head struck against a steel pipe and an expanding ball of fire flashed inside his head. And then, like a wave breaking in the surf, the nightmare swept over and smothered him.

61

The Special Operations Forces landed and regrouped behind the ore tailings that shielded their approach from the mine buildings. They quickly spread out in a loose battle formation and waited for the command to move in. The snipers established their positions around the mine, lying flat and watching for movement through their scopes.

Hollis, with Dillinger at his side, crawled up to the summit of the tailings and cautiously peered over. The scene had the look of a graveyard.

The ghost mine was an eerie stage for a battle, but the cold rain and barren mountainside seemed an appropriate backdrop for a killing ground. The dull gray sky fell and gave the decaying buildings the look of a place that didn't belong to any world.

The firing had stopped. Two of the outer buildings were blazing fiercely, the smoke rolling into the low overcast. Hollis counted at least seven bodies littering the road on one side of the crushing mill.

"I hate to sound mundane," said Hollis, "but I don't like the look of it."

"No sign of life," agreed Dillinger, peering through a pair of small but powerful binoculars.

Hollis carefully studied the buildings for another five seconds and then spoke into his transmitter. "All right, let's mind our step and move in —"

"One moment, Colonel," a voice broke in.

"Hold the order," snapped Hollis.

"Sergeant Baker, sir, on the right flank. I have a group of five people approaching up the railroad track."

"They armed?"

"No, sir. They have their hands in the air."

"Very good. You and your men round them up. Watch for a trap. Major Dillinger and I are on our way."

Hollis and Dillinger snaked around the mine tailings until they found the railroad and began jogging along it toward the fjord. After about seventy meters, several human figures took form through the pouring rain.

Sergeant Baker came forward to report.

"We have the hostages and one terrorist, Colonel."

"You've rescued the hostages?" Hollis exclaimed loudly. "All four of them?"

"Yes, sir," replied Baker. "They're pretty

well worn out, but otherwise they're in good shape."

"Nice work, Sergeant," said Hollis, pumping Baker's hand in undisguised exuberance.

Both officers had memorized the faces of the two presidents and the United Nations Secretary-General during the flight from Virginia. They were already familiar with Senator Pitt's appearance from the news media. They hurried forward and were enveloped in a great surge of relief as they recognized all four of the missing VIPs.

Much of their relief turned to surprise when they saw the terrorist prisoner was none other than Rudi Gunn.

Senator Pitt stepped forward and shook Hollis's hand as Gunn made the introductions. "Are we ever glad to see you, Colonel," said the Senator, beaming.

"Sorry we're late," mumbled Hollis, still not sure what to make of it all.

Hala embraced him, as did Hasan and De Lorenzo. Then it was Dillinger's turn, and he went red as a tomato.

"Mind telling me what's going on?" Hollis asked Gunn.

Gunn took grim delight in rubbing it in. "It seems you dropped us off at a very critical point, Colonel. We found almost twenty terrorists at the mine, along with a hidden helicopter they planned to use in clearing off the island. You didn't see fit to include us in your communications, so Pitt tried to warn you by sending a runaway train down the mountain into the fjord."

Dillinger nodded in understanding. "The helicopter explains why the Arab hijackers deserted the ship and left the Mexicans to fend for themselves."

"And the train was their transportation to the mine," Gunn added.

Hollis asked, "Where are the others?"

"Last I saw of them before Pitt sent me to rescue his father and these people, they were under siege inside the crushing mill building."

"The four of you took on close to forty terrorists?" Dillinger asked incredulously.

"Pitt and the others kept the Arabs from escaping as well as creating a diversion so I could rescue the hostages."

"The odds were better than ten to one against them," stated Hollis.

"They were doing a pretty good job of it when I left," answered Gunn solemnly.

Hollis and Dillinger stared at each other. "We'd better see what we can find," said Hollis.

Senator Pitt came over. "Colonel, Rudi has told me my son is up at the mine. I'd like to tag along with you."

"Sorry, Senator. I can't permit it until the area is secure."

Gunn put his arm around the old man's

shoulder. "I'll see to it, Senator. Don't worry about Dirk. He'll outlive us all."

"Thank you, Rudi. I appreciate your kindness."

Hollis was not so confident. "They must have been wiped out," he muttered under his breath to Dillinger.

Dillinger nodded in agreement. "Hopeless to think they could survive against a heavy force of trained terrorists."

Hollis gave the signal and his men began moving like phantoms through the mine buildings. As they neared the crushing mill they began to find the litter of dead awesome. They counted thirteen bodies crumpled in rag-doll positions on the road and ground outside.

The crushing-mill building was riddled with hundreds of bullet holes and showed the splintered results of grenades. Not a single pane of glass was left intact anywhere. Every entry door had been blown into splinters.

Hollis and five men cautiously entered through holes blown in the walls while Dillinger and his team approached from the shattered opening that was once the front main entrance. Small fires burned and smoldered everywhere, but had not yet joined to build a major conflagration.

Two dozen bodies were heaped about the floor, several stacked against the front of the ore crusher. The helicopter stood amazingly clean and pristine with only its tail section in mangled condition.

Three men still lived among the carnage — three men who looked so smoke-blackened, so bloody, in such awful shape, that Hollis couldn't believe his eyes. One man was lying on the floor, his head resting in the lap of another, whose arm was held in a gore-stained sling. One stood swaying on his feet, blood streaming from wounds on one leg, the base of his neck where it met the shoulder, the top of his head and the side of his face.

Not until Hollis was only a few meters away did he recognize the battered men before him. He was absolutely stunned. He couldn't see how those three pitiful wrecks had kept the faith and won out over fearsome odds.

The Special Operations Forces grouped around in silent admiration. Rudi Gunn smiled from ear to ear. Hollis and Dillinger stood there wordlessly.

Then Pitt painfully straightened to his full height and said, "About time you showed up. We were running out of things to do."

■ ■ ■ ■

PART IV:
SAM'S ROMAN CIRCUS

■ ■ ■ ■

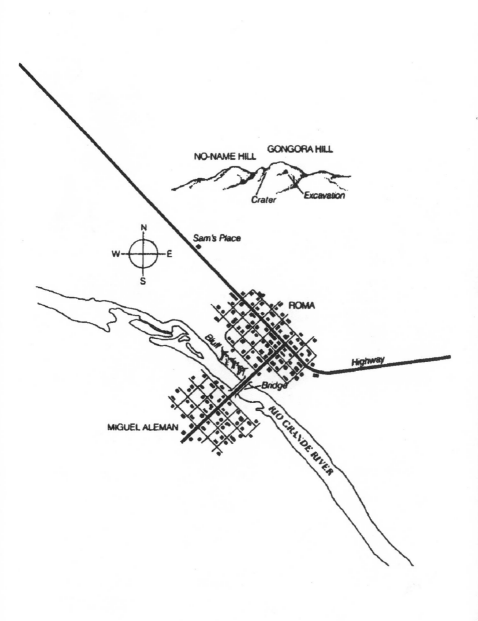

NO-NAME HILL   GONGORA HILL

Crater   Excavation

Sam's Place

N
W—E
S

ROMA

Bluff

Highway

Bridge

MIGUEL ALEMAN

RIO GRANDE RIVER

62

October 27, 1991
Washington, D.C.

Dale Nichols and Martin Brogan stood waiting on the White House steps as the President stepped from his helicopter and walked swiftly across the lawn.

"You have something for me?" the President asked expectantly as he shook hands.

Nichols could not contain his excitement. "We've just received a report from General Dodge. His Special Operations Forces have retaken the *Lady Flamborough* intact in Southern Chile. Senator Pitt, Hala Kamil and Presidents De Lorenzo and Hasan were rescued in good condition."

The President was weary from a series of nonstop conferences with the Canadian Prime Minister in Ottawa, but he brightened like a streetlight. "Thank God. That *is* good news. Were there any casualties?"

"Two SOP men were wounded, neither seriously, but three NUMA people were shot up pretty badly," reported Brogan.

"NUMA people were on the scene?"

"Dirk Pitt was responsible for tracking down the cruise ship. He and three others kept the hijackers from escaping along with their hostages."

"So he helped save his own father."

"He certainly deserves a major share of the credit."

The President rubbed his hands together happily. "It's almost noon, gentlemen. Why don't we celebrate with a bottle of wine over lunch, and you can give me a full report."

Secretary of State Douglas Oates, Alan Mercier, the President's National Security Adviser, and Julius Schiller also joined the group for lunch. After dessert, Mercier passed around copies of the transcribed report from General Dodge.

The President toyed with his fork as he read the transcript. Then he looked up, a mixture of surprise and triumph on his face.

"Topiltzin!"

"He's in it up to his ears," said Brogan. "Topiltzin provided the Mexican terrorist crew and the vessel for the switch with the cruise ship."

"So he *did* conspire with his brother on the *Lady Flamborough* hijacking," the President said confidentially.

Nichols nodded. "The facts add up that

way, but it won't be easy to prove."

"Any idea as to the identity of the master-mind behind the operation?"

"We have a make," replied Brogan briefly. "This is a condensed file on the man." He paused to hand the President another folder. "He did a remarkable job of disguising himself to look like the Captain of the ship during the capture, and then he changed to a mask. Later, Dirk Pitt met face to face with him during a truce before the fighting. The name he gave was Suleiman Aziz Ammar."

"Seems odd this Ammar got lax and dropped his name," mused Schiller. "Must be an alias."

Brogan shook his head. "The name is real enough. We have a comprehensive packet on him. So does Interpol. Ammar must have figured Pitt was as good as dead, and had nothing to lose by correctly identifying himself."

The President's eyes narrowed. "According to your file he's suspected of being directly or indirectly involved with over fifty murders of prominent government officials. Is this possible?"

"Suleiman Aziz Ammar is rated at the very top of his profession."

"A diehard terrorist."

"Assassin," Brogan corrected the President. "Ammar specializes only in political assassination. Cold-blooded as they come. Big on disguise and detailed planning. As the words of the song go, 'Nobody does it better.' Half his hits were so clean they were written off as accidents. He's a Muslim, but he's taken on jobs for the French and Germans and even the Israelis. Gets top dollar. He's amassed a considerable fortune for his successful operations in and around the Mediterranean."

"Was he captured?"

"No, sir," Brogan admitted. "He was not among the dead or wounded."

"The man escaped?" the President asked sharply.

"If he still lives, Ammar cannot get far," Brogan assured him. "Pitt thinks he pumped at least three bullets into him. An extensive manhunt has been activated. There is no escape from the island. He should be found in a few hours."

"He'll be a major intelligence coup if he can be persuaded to talk," said Nichols.

"General Dodge has already alerted his field commander, Colonel Morton Hollis, to take every precaution in capturing Ammar alive. But the Colonel thinks there is good reason to believe Ammar will kill himself when cornered."

Nichols shrugged resignedly. "Hollis is probably right."

"There were no other survivors among the hijackers?" the President asked Brogan.

"Eight we can interrogate. But they appear

to be only Ammar's hired mercenaries and not radical Yazid followers."

"We'll need their confessions to prove Ammar was working for Yazid and Topiltzin," said the President without optimism.

Schiller did not feel there was a setback. "Look on the bright side, Mr. President. The ship and hostages have been rescued without injury. President Hasan knows damn well Yazid wanted him dead and was behind the hijacking. He'll go after Yazid now with a vengeance."

The President looked at him, and then his eyes traveled from face to face. "Is that the way you gentlemen see it?"

"Julius has a good grasp of Hasan," said Mercier. "He can be real nasty if he's crossed."

Doug Oates nodded in agreement. "Barring unforeseen developments, I think Julius's projection is right on the money. Hasan may not go so far as to risk riots and ignite a revolution by arresting Yazid and trying him for treason. But he'll certainly take off the gloves and do everything short of murder to destroy Yazid's credibility."

"There will be a backlash against Yazid," Brogan predicted. "Egypt's Muslim fundamentalist moderates do not condone terrorist tactics. They'll turn their backs on Yazid while the country's parliament gives President Hasan overwhelming support. Also, in my best rose-colored view, the military will climb down out of its ivory tower and reaffirm its loyalty to Hasan."

The President took a final swallow of wine and set the glass on the table. "I must confess, I like what I hear."

"The crisis in Egypt is far from over," warned Secretary Oates. "Yazid may be pushed out of the limelight for a while, but in President Hasan's absence the Moslem Brotherhood of fundamentalist fanatics has formed an alliance with the Liberal and Socialist Labor parties. Together, they'll work to undermine Hasan's rule, to bring Egypt under Islamic law, cut ties with the United States and scuttle Israeli peace agreements."

The President tilted his head at Schiller. "Do you subscribe to Doug's doomsday canvas, Julius?"

Schiller nodded grimly. "I do."

"Martin?"

Brogan's solemn expression told it all. "The inevitable has only been stalled off. Hasan's government must eventually fall. The military's support will be here today and gone tomorrow. My best brains at Langley project a fairly bloodless coup eighteen to twenty-four months from now."

"I recommend we take a hands-off, wait-and-see attitude, Mr. President," said Oates. "And study our options in dealing with another Muslim government."

"You're suggesting an isolationist approach," said the President.

"Maybe it's time we took that stance," suggested Schiller. "Nothing of substance your predecessors attempted in the last twenty years worked."

"The Russians will lose too," added Nichols. "And our big consolation is in keeping Paul Capesterre, also known as Akhmad Yazid, from creating another Iranian disaster. He would have worked to destroy our Middle East interests at any cost."

"I do not entirely agree with your overall picture," said Brogan. "But in the time we have left we still have the opportunity to cultivate the next man to rule Egypt."

A questioning frown crossed the President's face. "Who do you have in mind?"

"Egypt's Defense Minister, Abu Hamid."

"You think he'll seize the government?"

"When the time is ripe, yes," Brogan explained patiently. "He has the power of the military in his pocket, and he's shrewdly sought strong support from the moderate Muslim fundamentalists. In my opinion, Abu Hamid is a shoo-in."

"We could do much worse," murmured Oates with a thin smile. "He hasn't been above accepting favors and tapping some of the billions of dollars we've poured into Egypt. Abu Hamid would not be the type to kick a gift horse in the mouth. Oh, sure, he'd make the required noises condemning Israel and cursing the U.S., for the sake of the religious fanatics, but underneath the rhetoric he'd keep a friendly line of communications open."

"The fact that he's on close terms with Hala Kamil won't hurt us either," Nichols said flatly.

The President was silent, staring into the glass of zinfandel as if it was a crystal ball. Then he raised the glass.

"To a continued friendly union with Egypt."

"Hear, hear," said Mercier and Brogan in unison.

"To Egypt," murmured Oates.

"And Mexico," added Schiller.

The President glanced at his watch and rose, followed by his advisers. "Sorry to cut this short, but I have a meeting with a group of Treasury people. Congratulate everyone involved in rescuing the hostages for me." He turned to Oates. "I want to meet with you and Senator Pitt the minute he returns."

"To discuss any words he had with President Hasan during their ordeal?"

"I'd be more interested in hearing what he learned from President De Lorenzo on the crisis south of our border. Egypt is of secondary importance compared to Mexico. We can safely assume Akhmad Yazid has been benched for the rest of the season, but Topiltzin is a far worse threat. Concentrate on him, gentlemen. God help us if we can't stabilize the upheaval in Mexico."

63

Slowly, reluctantly, Pitt rose from the black depths of a sound sleep to the brightly lit surface of consciousness only to find it was accompanied by stiff, aching pain. He tried to go back and reenter the comforting void, but his eyes blinked open, and it was too late. The first thing he focused on was a smiling red face.

"Well, well, he's back among the living," said First Officer Finney cheerfully. "I'll go and inform the Captain."

As Finney passed through the door, Pitt moved his eyes without moving his head and found a little baldheaded man sitting in a chair beside the bed. The ship's doctor, Pitt recalled, but the name escaped him.

"I'm sorry, Doctor, but I can't recollect your —"

"Henry Webster," he second-guessed Pitt, smiling warmly. "And if you're wondering where you are, you're in the finest suite on board the *Lady Flamborough,* which is cur-

696

rently under tow by the *Sounder* for Punta Arenas."

"How long have I been unconscious?"

"While you were making your report to Colonel Hollis, I was tending to your wounds. Soon afterward, I put you under heavy sedation. You've been out for about twelve hours."

"No wonder I'm starving."

"I'll see our chef personally sends down one of his specialties."

"How are Giordino and Findley?"

"Most admirable of you to inquire of your friends before yourself. Giordino is a very durable man. I took four bullets from him, none in critical areas. He should be ready to party by New Year's Eve. Findley's wounds were far more serious. Bullets entered his right side and lodged in a lung and kidney. I did what I could for him on the ship. He and Giordino were airlifted to Punta Arenas and flown to Washington soon after I put you out. Findley will be operated on by bullet-wound specialists at the Walter Reed Medical Center. If there are no complications, he should pull through in fine shape. By the way, your friend Rudi Gunn felt they needed him more than you did, so he accompanied them home."

Before Pitt could make a reply, a digital thermometer was slipped in and out of his mouth.

Dr. Webster studied the reading and nodded. "As for you, Mr. Pitt — you'll mend nicely. How are you feeling?"

"I don't think I'm up to entering a triathlon, but except for a throb in my head and a stinging sensation in my neck, I'll manage."

"You're a lucky man. None of the bullets struck a bone, internal organ or artery. I stitched up your leg and neck, or, more accurately, your trapezius muscle. Also your cheek. Plastic surgery should hide the scar, unless of course you think women find it adds to your sex appeal. The smack on your head caused a concussion. X-rays showed no sign of a hairline fracture. My prognosis is that you'll be swimming the English Channel and playing the violin within three months."

Pitt laughed. Almost immediately he tensed as the pain struck from every side. Webster's look became one of quick concern.

"I *am* sorry. My bedside manner tends to get a bit too jolly, I'm afraid."

Pitt relaxed and the agony soon subsided. He loved English phrasing and humor. They were a class act, he thought. He smiled gamely and stared at Webster with unconcealed respect. He knew the doctor had downplayed his skill and labors out of modesty.

"If that hurt," said Pitt, "I can't wait to get your bill."

It was Webster's turn to laugh. "Careful, I wouldn't want you to ruin my superb needlework."

Pitt gingerly eased himself to a sitting position and held out his hand. "I'm grateful for what you did for the three of us."

Webster rose and shook Pitt's outstretched hand. "An honor doctoring you, Mr. Pitt. I'll take my leave now. It seems you're the man of the hour. I think you have some distinguished visitors gathering outside."

"Goodbye, Doc, and thank you."

Webster gave a wink and a nod. Then he walked over to the door, opened it and motioned everyone inside.

Senator Pitt entered followed by Hala, Colonel Hollis and Captain Collins. The men shook hands, but Hala leaned down and lightly kissed Pitt.

"I hope you've found our ship's service satisfactory," said Captain Collins jovially.

"No man ever recuperated in a fancier hospital," Pitt replied. "I'm only sorry I can't bask in such luxury for another month."

"Unfortunately, your presence is required up north by tomorrow," said Hollis.

"Oh, no," Pitt moaned.

"Oh, yes," said the Senator, holding up his watch. "The *Sounder* will be towing us into dock at Punta Arenas in another ninety minutes. An Air Force transport is waiting to fly you and Ms. Kamil and me to Washington."

Pitt made a helpless gesture with both hands. "So much for my luxury cruise."

Next came the usual round of solicitous questions concerning his condition. After a few minutes Hollis turned the conversation to his current problem.

"Would you know Ammar if you saw him again?" he asked Pitt.

"I could pick him out of a lineup easily enough. Didn't you find him? I gave you a detailed description of his height, weight and looks before Doc Webster knocked me out."

Hollis handed him a small stack of photos. "Here are pictures taken and processed by the ship's photographer of the hijackers' bodies, including those taken prisoner. Do you see Suleiman Aziz Ammar among them?"

Pitt slowly sifted through the photographs, studying the close-up features of the dead. They had seemed faceless during the battle, he recalled. He wondered with morbid curiosity which ones were dead by his hands. Finally he looked up and shook his head.

"He's not in here among the living or the dead."

"You're sure?" asked Hollis. "The wounds and deathlike expressions can badly alter facial features."

"I stood closer to him than I am to you under conditions that aren't easily forgotten. Believe me, Colonel, when I say Ammar isn't among those pictured."

Hollis pulled a larger photo from an envelope and passed it to Pitt without comment.

After a few seconds, Pitt gave Hollis a questioning look. "What do you want me to say?"

"Is that Suleiman Aziz Ammar?"

Pitt handed the photograph back. "You know damn well it is, or you wouldn't magically produce a picture taken of him at a different time in a different place."

"I think what Colonel Hollis is holding back," said Dirk's father, "is that Ammar or his remains have yet to be found."

"Then his men must have hidden his body," Pitt said firmly. "I didn't miss. He took a shot in the shoulder and two in the face. I saw one of his men drag him to cover after he fell. No way he's walking around."

"It's possible his body was buried," admitted Hollis. "An extensive air and land search failed to detect any sign of him on the island."

"So the fox hasn't been run to ground," Pitt said softly to himself.

The Senator looked at him. "What was that?"

"Something Ammar said about a coyote and a fox when we met," Pitt replied pensively. Then he looked around at his audience. "I bet he's eluded the net. Anyone care to give me odds?"

Hollis gave Pitt a dark look instead. "You better hope he's deader than a barracuda in the desert, because if he isn't, the name of Dirk Pitt will head his next hit list."

Hala swept gracefully to the head of Pitt's bed, wearing a gold silk dressing gown with a modernized hieroglyphic design. She placed her hand lightly around his shoulder.

"Dirk is very weak," she said in an even voice. "He needs a good meal and rest until it comes time to debark the ship. I suggest we leave him alone for the next hour."

Hollis slipped the photos back in the envelope and rose. "I'll have to say my goodbyes. A helicopter is waiting to take me back to Santa Inez to continue the search for Ammar."

"Give my best to Major Dillinger."

"I shall." Hollis seemed uneasy for a moment; then he approached the bed and shook hands. "I apologize, Dirk, to you and your friends. I sadly underrated you all. Anytime you want to transfer from NUMA to Special Operations Forces, I'll be the first to sign a recommendation."

"I wouldn't fit in too well." Pitt grinned. "I have this allergy to taking orders."

"Yes, so you've demonstrated," Hollis said, smiling faintly.

The Senator came over and squeezed Pitt's hand. "See you on deck."

"I'll bid my farewell there also," said Captain Collins.

Hala said nothing. She herded the men from the room. Then she softly closed the door and turned the lock. She walked back until she stood beside the bed. The folds of the gown plunged and there was something in the casual way it draped her body that convinced Pitt she was naked beneath.

She proved it by loosening the sash and shrugging the gown from her shoulders. He heard the whisper of the silk as it slid down her soft flesh. She posed like a bronze statue, breasts thrust out, hands flattened against her thighs, one leg slightly in front of the other. She reached down and pulled back the bedcovers.

"I owe you something," she said huskily.

Pitt caught his reflection in the mirrors on the closet doors. He wore only white gauze. The top of his head and the side of his face were swathed in bandages, as was one side of his neck and the wounded leg. He hadn't shaved in a week and the whites of his eyes were streaked with red. In his mind he looked like a derelict any self-respecting bag lady would reject.

"I'm a sorry excuse for Don Juan," he muttered.

"You're handsome in my eyes," Hala whispered as she gently lay beside him and lightly trailed her fingers through the hairs of his chest. "We must hurry. We have less than an hour."

Pitt let out a long sigh. He would catch hell from Doc Webster if he overexerted and pulled out his stitches. Abject surrender. Why is it, he wondered, men plan more covert schemes than an intelligence agency to seduce women, only to have them turn on under crazy circumstances when you least expect it? He was more convinced than ever that James Bond really didn't have it all that great.

When Ammar awoke, he saw only blackness. His shoulder felt as though a piece of coal were burning inside his flesh. He tried to lift his hands to his face but one hand exploded with pain. Then he remembered bullets striking his wrist and shoulder. He raised his good hand to touch his eyes but the fingertips felt only a tightly bound cloth that wrapped around his head, covering his face from forehead to chin.

He knew his eyes were beyond saving. Not for him a life of blindness, he thought. He groped around for a weapon, anything to kill himself. All he touched was a damp, flat rock surface.

Ammar became desperate, unable to repress the fear of helplessness. He struggled to his feet, stumbled and fell.

Then two hands gripped his shoulders.

"Do not move or make a cry, Suleiman Aziz," came the whispered words of Ibn. "The Americans are searching for us."

Ammar clutched Ibn's hands for assurance. He tried to speak, but could no longer utter coherent words. Only animal-like guttural sounds came through the blood-caked wrapping supporting his shattered jaw.

"We are in a small chamber inside one of the mine tunnels." Ibn spoke softly into his ear. "They came very close, but I had time to build a wall that concealed our hiding place."

Ammar nodded and desperately tried to make himself understood.

It was as though Ibn could reach through the pitch-darkness and read Ammar's thoughts. "You wish to die, Suleiman Aziz? No, you will not die. We will go together but not one minute before Allah decides."

Ammar slumped in despair. He had never felt so disoriented, so completely out of control. The pain was unbearable, and the thought of living out his days in a maximum-security jail cell, blind and mutilated, devastated him. All instinct for self-preservation had deserted him. He could not stand being dependent on anyone for his hourly existence — not even Ibn.

"Rest, my brother," said Ibn gently. "You will need all your strength when it comes time for us to escape the island."

Ammar collapsed and rolled to his side. His shoulders came against the tunnel's uneven floor. It was wet, and the moisture seeped through his clothing, but he was suffering too much pain to notice the added discomfort.

He became more and more despondent.

His failure had become a horror. He saw Akhmad Yazid standing over him, smirking; then a curtain slowly formed and parted deep in the recesses of Ammar's mind. A faint glow appeared, a glow that bloomed and then burst in a blinding flash, and in that one chilling moment he glimpsed the future.

He would survive through revenge.

Mentally he spoke the word over and over until at last his self-discipline returned.

The first decision he came to grips with was who should die at his own hands, Yazid or Pitt? He could not act alone. He was no longer physically capable of assassinating both men himself. Already a plan was forming. He would have to trust Ibn to share in the revenge.

Ammar anguished over the decision, but in the end he had no choice.

Ibn would draw the coyote, while Ammar's final act would be to slay the viper.

64

Pitt refused to fly home on a stretcher. He sat in a comfortable executive chair, leg propped on the seat of a facing chair, and stared out the window at the snow-capped spires of the Andes. Far off to the right he could see the green plateaus that marked the beginning of the Brazilian highlands. Two hours later a distant gray haze advertised the crowded city of Caracas, and then he was gazing at the horizon line where the turquoise of the Caribbean met a cobalt-blue sky. From 12,000 meters the wind-creased water looked like a flat sheet of crepe paper.

The Air Force VIP transport jet was cramped — Pitt could not stand to his full height — but quite luxurious. He felt as though he were sitting inside a rich kid's high-priced toy.

His father was not in a talkative mood. The Senator spent most of the flight working out of a briefcase, making notes for his briefing to the President.

What little conversation took place was one-sided. When Pitt asked how he happened to be on the *Lady Flamborough* at Punta del Este, the Senator didn't bother to look up when he responded.

"A Presidential mission," he said tersely, closing off any further questions on the subject.

Hala also kept to herself and attended to business. She had the aircraft's in-flight telephone in constant use, firing off instructions to her aides at the United Nations building in New York. Her only acknowledgment of Pitt's presence was a brief smile when their eyes happened to meet.

How quickly they forget, Pitt thought idly.

He turned his mind to the search for the Alexandria Library treasures. He considered cutting in on Hala's phone monopoly for a progress report from Yaeger. But he drowned his curiosity with a dry martini, courtesy of the aircraft steward, instead, deciding to wait and learn whatever there was to learn at first hand from Lily and Yaeger.

What river had Venator sailed before burying the priceless objects? It could be any one of a thousand that course into the Atlantic between the Saint Lawrence in Canada to the Río de la Plata of Argentina. No, not quite. Yaeger theorized the *Serapis* had taken on water and made repairs off what was to become New Jersey. The unknown river had to be south, much farther south than the rivers that flow into Chesapeake Bay.

Could Venator have led his fleet into the Gulf of Mexico and up the Mississippi? Today's stream must be far different from what it was sixteen hundred years ago. Perhaps he had sailed into the Orinoco in Venezuela, which could be navigated for two hundred miles. Or maybe the Amazon?

He let his mind wander through the irony of it all. If Junius Venator's voyage to the Americas was absolutely proved by the discovery of the buried Library artifacts, history books needed to be revised and new chapters written.

Poor Leif Eriksson and Christopher Columbus would be relegated to also-ran footnotes.

Pitt was still daydreaming when he was interrupted by the steward telling him to fasten his seat belt.

It was dusk and the aircraft had dipped its nose and was dropping into the long glide toward Andrews Air Force Base. The twinkling sprawl of Washington slid past, and Pitt soon found himself hobbling down the steps on a cane hastily bent from an aluminum tube and presented by the grateful crew of the *Lady Flamborough.* He set foot on the concrete at almost exactly the same spot as on his arrival from Greenland.

Hala came down and bid him goodbye. She

was continuing on with the plane to New York.

"You've become a treasured memory, Dirk Pitt."

"We never did make our dinner date."

"The next time you're in Cairo, it's on me."

The Senator overheard and came over. "Cairo, Ms. Kamil. Not New York?"

Hala gave him a smile worthy of the beautiful Nefertiti. "I am resigning as Secretary-General and returning home. Democracy is dying in Egypt. I can do more to keep it alive by working in the midst of my people."

"What of Yazid?"

"President Hasan has vowed to place him under house arrest."

A frown crossed Senator Pitt's face. "Be careful. Yazid is still a dangerous man."

"If not Yazid, there is always another maniac waiting in the wings." Her soft dark eyes belied the fear that rode in her heart. She gave him a daughterly hug. "Tell your President Egypt will not become a nation of insane fanatics."

"I'll pass along your words."

She turned back to Pitt. She was on the brink of falling in love with him but fought her feelings with every bit of will she possessed. Her legs felt weak as she took both his hands and stared upward into his ageless face. For an instant, in her mind's eye, she saw herself entwined with his body, caressing his muscled skin, and then just as quickly she erased the thought. She had found brief fulfillment with him, long denied, but she knew she could never divide her love for one man with that for Egypt.

Her life belonged to those who had no life except misery and poverty.

She kissed him tenderly.

"Do not forget me."

Before Pitt could answer, Hala had turned and hurried up the steps into the aircraft. He stood looking at the empty entrance for a long moment.

The Senator read his thoughts and interrupted them. "They've sent an ambulance to take you to the hospital."

"Hospital?" Pitt said vacantly, still watching as the door closed. The jet engines whistled as the pilot increased the rpm and began to taxi toward the main strip.

Pitt tore the bandages from around his head and face and threw them into the jet's exhaust, where they were caught and sent swirling through the air like airborne snakes.

Only when the plane was airborne did he make his reply. "I'm not going to no damned hospital."

"Overdoing it a bit, don't you think?" the Senator said with paternal concern, full knowing it was a waste of breath to preach to his independent-minded son.

"How are you getting to the White House?"

asked Pitt. The Senator nodded toward a waiting helicopter about a hundred meters away. "The President arranged my transportation."

"Mind dropping me at NUMA?"

His father looked at him slyly. "You're speaking figuratively, of course."

Pitt grinned. "You never let me forget which side of the family my sadistic sense of humor came from."

The Senator slapped his arm around Pitt's waist. "Come on, you crazy nut, let me help you over to the helicopter."

The tension built like a twisting knot in his stomach as Pitt stood in the elevator, watching the numbers rise toward NUMA's computer complex. Lily was standing in the foyer as the doors parted and he limped out.

She wore a big smile that froze when she saw the tired, bedraggled look, the long scab on his cheek, the hump of the bandage beneath a knit fisherman's turtleneck sweater borrowed from his father, the dragging leg and cane. Then she bravely broke out the smile again.

"Welcome home, sailor."

She stepped forward and threw her arms around his neck. He winced and groaned under his breath. She jumped back.

"Oh, I'm sorry."

Pitt clutched her. "Don't be." Then he

mashed his lips against hers. His beard scraped against her skin and he smelled of gin — and delightfully masculine.

"There's something to be said for men who only come home once a week," she said finally.

"And for women who wait," he said, stepping back. He glanced around. "What have you and Hiram found out since I left?"

"I'll let Hiram tell you," she answered airily, taking him by the hand and leading him across the computer installation.

Yaeger charged out of his office. Without a word of greeting or sympathy for Pitt's wounds, he came straight to the heart of the breakthrough.

"We've found it!" he announced grandly.

"The river?" Pitt asked anxiously.

"Not only the river, but I think I can put you within two square miles of the artifacts' cavern."

"Where?"

"Texas. A little border town called Roma."

Yaeger had the smug, complacent look of a Tyrannosaurus rex that had just dined on a brontosaurus. "Named for seven hills, just like the capital of Italy. Pretty low, insignificant hills, I admit. But there are also reports of Roman artifacts supposedly having been dug up in the area. Scoffed at by accredited archaeologists, of course, but what do they know?"

"Then the river is —"

"The Rio Bravo, as it's called in Spanish."
Yaeger nodded. "Better known on this side as
the Rio Grande."

"The Rio Grande." Pitt repeated the words
slowly, savoring each syllable to the full, finding it difficult to accept the truth after dozens
of missed hunches, wild guesses and dead-
end speculations.

"It's really a great shame," Yaeger suddenly
said morosely.

Pitt glanced at him in faint surprise. "Why
do you say that?"

Yaeger shook his head heavily. "Because
there'll be no living with the Texans as soon
as they learn what they've been sitting on for
the last sixteen centuries."

65

At noon the next day, after landing at the
Corpus Christi Naval Air Station, Pitt and
Lily, along with Admiral Sandecker, were
driven by a Seaman First Class to NUMA's
ocean research center on the bay. Sandecker
directed the driver to stop beside a helicopter
squatting on a concrete pad beside a long
dock. There were no clouds, the sun was
alone in the sky. The temperature was mild
but the humidity high, and they quickly
began to sweat after exiting the car.

NUMA's chief geologist, Herb Garza, gave
a friendly wave and approached. He was
short, plump, brown-skinned, with a few
pockmarks on his cheeks and gleaming black
hair. Garza wore a California Angels baseball
cap and a fluorescent orange shirt that was
so blasting Pitt could still see it after he
momentarily closed his eyes.

"Dr. Garza," said Sandecker curtly. "Good
to see you again."

"I've looked forward to your arrival," Garza

said warmly. "We can take off as soon as you board." He turned and introduced the pilot, Joe Mifflin, who wore "Smilin' Jack" sunglasses and struck Pitt as being about as animated as a door knob.

Pitt and Garza had worked together on a project along the western desert stretch of coast in South Africa. "How long has it been, Herb?" said Pitt. "Three, four years?"

"Who counts?" Garza said with a broad smile as they shook hands. "Good to be on the same team with you again."

"May I introduce Dr. Lily Sharp."

Garza graciously bowed. "One of the ocean sciences?" he asked.

Lily shook her head. "Land archaeology."

Garza turned and stared at Sandecker with a curious expression. "This isn't a sea project, Admiral?"

"No, I'm sorry you weren't fully informed, Herb. But I'm afraid we'll have to keep the real purpose of our work a secret for a little longer."

Garza shrugged indifferently. "You're the boss."

"All I need is a direction," said Mifflin.

"South," Pitt told him. "South to the Rio Grande."

They dropped down the coast along the Intercoastal Waterway, passing over the hotels and condominiums of South Padre Island.

Then Mifflin ducked the green helicopter with the NUMA letters on the side under a layer of popcorn puffed clouds and swung west below Port Isabel where the waters of the Rio Grande spilled into the Gulf of Mexico.

The land below was a strange blend of marsh and desert, flat as a parking lot, with cactus growing amid tall grass. Soon the city of Brownsville appeared through the windshield. The river narrowed as it flowed under the bridge connecting Texas to Matamoros, Mexico.

"Can you tell me what we're supposed to survey?" asked Garza.

"You grew up in the Rio Grande Valley, didn't you," Sandecker queried without answering.

"Born and raised up river at Laredo. Took my undergraduate courses at Texas Southernmost College in Brownsville. We just passed over it."

"Then you're familiar with the geology around Roma?"

"I've conducted a number of field trips in the area, yes."

It was Pitt's turn. "Compared to now, how did the river flow a few centuries after Christ?"

"The stream wasn't much different then," answered Garza. "Oh, sure, the course has shifted during earlier flooding, but seldom more than a couple of miles. Quite often over the centuries it returned to its previous course. The major change is that the Rio Grande would have been considerably higher then. Until the war with Mexico the width ran from two hundred to four hundred meters. The main channel actually was much deeper."

"When was it first seen by a European?"

"Alonzo de Pineda sailed into the river's mouth in 1519."

"How did it stack up to the Mississippi back then?"

Garza thought a moment. "The Rio Grande was more akin to the Nile."

"Nile?"

"The headwaters begin in the Rocky Mountains of Colorado. During the spring flooding season, as the winter snows melted, the water swept down the lower reaches in huge surges. The ancient Indians, like the Egyptians, dug ditches so the high water ran to their crops. That's why the river you see now is a mere trickle of its former self. As the Spanish and Mexican settlers moved in, followed by the Texas Americans, new irrigation works were built. After the Civil War, railroads brought in more farmers and ranchers, who siphoned off more water. By 1894, shallow and dangerous shoals put an end to steamboating. If there had been no irrigation, the Rio Grande might have been the Mississippi River of Texas."

"Steamboats ran on the Rio Grande?" asked Lily.

"For a short time traffic was quite heavy as trade developed up and down and on both sides of the river. Fleets of paddle steamers made regular runs from Brownsville to Laredo for over thirty years. Now, since they built the Falcon Dam, about the only craft you see on the lower river are outboard boats and inner tubes."

"Could sailing vessels have navigated as far as Roma?" asked Pitt.

"With room to spare. The river was easily wide enough for tacking. All a ship with sails had to do was wait for easterly offshore breezes. One keelboat made it as far northwest as Santa Fe in 1850."

They fell quiet for a few minutes as Mifflin followed the meandering turns of the river. A few low, rolling hills appeared. On the Mexican side, little towns first settled nearly three hundred years ago sat in dusty seclusion. Some houses were built of stone and adobe and topped by red tile, while the outskirts were dotted with small primitive huts having thatched roofs.

The agricultural part of the valley, with its citrus groves and fields of vegetables and aloe vera, gave way to arid plains of mesquite trees and white thistle. Pitt expected a muddy brown river, but the Rio Grande pleasantly surprised him by running a deep green.

"We're coming up on Roma now," announced Garza. "The sister city across the river is called Miguel Alemán. Not much of a town. Except for some tourist curio stores it's mostly a border crossing on the road to Monterrey."

Mifflin pulled up and soared over the international bridge, and then dropped low on the river again. On the Mexican side men and women were washing cars, mending fishing nets and swimming. Along the bank a few pigs wallowed in the silt. On the American side a yellowish sandstone bluff rose from the riverbank up to the main section of downtown Roma. The buildings appeared to be quite old and some were rundown, but all seemed in sound condition. One or two were in stages of reconstruction.

"The buildings look very quaint," said Lily. "There must be a lot of history behind their walls."

"Roma was a busy port during the commercial and military boating era," Garza lectured. "Prosperous merchants hired architects to design some very interesting homes and business structures. And they've lasted quite well."

"Any one more famous than the others?" asked Lily.

"Famous?" Garza laughed. "My pick would

be a residence built in the middle 1800s that was used as 'Rosita's Cantina' when the movie *Viva Zapata* was filmed in Roma with Marlon Brando."

Sandecker gestured for Mifflin to circle the hills above the town. He turned to Garza. "Is Roma named after Rome because it's surrounded by seven hills?"

"Nobody really knows for sure," replied Garza. "You'd be hard-pressed to pick out seven distinctive hills. A couple have noticeable peaks, but mostly they just run into each other."

"What's the geology?" Pitt inquired as he stared downward.

"Cretaceous debris for the most part. This whole area was once under the sea. Fossil oyster shells are common. Some have been found that measure half a meter. There's a nearby gravel pit that illustrates the various geological periods. I can give you a quick lecture if you care to have Joe set us down."

"Not just yet," said Pitt. "Are there any natural caves in the region?"

"None visible on the surface. But that doesn't mean they aren't down there. No way of knowing how many caves, formed by the ancient seas, are hidden under the upper layer. Go deep enough in the right spot and you'll likely strike a good-size limestone deposit. Old Indian legends tell of spirits living underground."

"What sort of spirits?"

Garza shrugged. "Ghosts of the ancients who died in battle with evil gods."

Lily unconsciously clutched Pitt's arm. "Have any artifacts been discovered near Roma?"

"A few arrow and spear flints, stone knives and boat-stones."

"What are boat-stones?" asked Pitt.

"Hollow stones in the shape of boat hulls," answered Lily with mounting excitement. "Their exact origin or purpose is obscure. It's thought they were used as charms. They supposedly warded off evil, especially if an Indian feared a witch or power of a shaman. An effigy of the witch was tied to a boat-stone and thrown into a lake or river, destroying the evil forever."

Pitt put another question to Garza. "Any objects turn up that confound the historic time scale?"

"Some, but they were considered to be fake."

Lily put on her best casual expression. "What sort of objects?"

"Swords, crosses, bits and pieces of armor, spear shafts, mostly made of iron. I also recall the story of an old stone anchor that was dug out of the bluff beside the river."

"Probably Spanish in origin," ventured Sandecker guardedly.

Garza shook his head. "Not Spanish, but

722

Roman. State Museum officials were justifiably skeptical. They wrote them off as a nineteenth-century hoax."

Lily's hand bit deeper into Pitt's arm. "Any possibility of my having a look at them?" she asked in an anxious voice. "Or have they been lost and forgotten, packed away in the dust of a state university basement?"

Garza pointed out the window toward the road running north from Roma. "As a matter of fact, the artifacts are right down there. They've been kept and collected by the man who found most of them. A good old Texan boy named Sam Trinity, or Crazy Sam as he's known by the locals. He's poked around this area for fifty years, swearing a Roman army camped here. Makes a living by running a small gas station and store. Has a shack in the rear he grandly calls a museum of antiquity."

Pitt smiled slowly. "Can you set us down beside his place?" he asked Mifflin. "I think we ought to have a talk with Sam."

66

The sign stretched nine meters in length behind the highway turnoff. The giant horizontal board was supported by sun-bleached, weather-cracked mesquite posts that uniformly leaned backward at a drunken angle. Garish red letters on a faded silver background proclaimed

SAM'S ROMAN CIRCUS

The gas pumps out front were shiny and new and advertised methanol-blended fuel for forty-eight cents a liter. The store was built from adobe and designed like the Indian mesa dwellings of Arizona with the roof poles protruding through the walls. The interior was clean and the shelves were neatly stacked with curios, groceries and soft drinks. It was an echo of a thousand other small, isolated oases that stood beside the nation's highways.

Sam, though, didn't match the decor.

No baseball cap advertising Caterpillar

tractors. No scuffed cowboy boots or straw range hat or faded Levi's. Sam was attired in a bright green Polo shirt, yellow slacks and expensive custom lizard golf shoes complete with cleats. His evenly trimmed white hair lay flat beneath a sporty plaid cap.

Sam Trinity stood in the doorway of his store until the dust from the helicopter's rotor blades slowly rolled away under a light breeze. Then he stepped past the asphalt drive, holding a two iron Bob Hope-style and came to a halt about six meters from the opening door.

Garza dropped out first and walked up to him. "Hello there, dirt-kicker."

Trinity's dark calfskin face stretched into a big Texas smile. "Herb, you old taco. Good to see you."

He pulled up his sunglasses, revealing blue eyes that squinted under the bright Southern Texas sun. Then he dropped them again like a curtain. He was very tall, skinny as a fence pole, arms slender, shoulders narrow, but his voice had vigor and resonance.

Garza made the introductions, but it was obvious the names were hardly absorbed by Trinity. He simply waved and said, "Glad to meet yaal. Welcome to Sam's Roman Circus." Then he noticed Pitt's face, cane and limp. "Fall off your motorcycle?"

Pitt laughed. "The short end of a saloon brawl."

"I think I like you."

Sandecker stood jauntily with legs apart and nodded at the two iron. "Where do you play golf around here?"

"Just down the road in Rio Grande City," Trinity replied genially. "Several courses between here and Brownsville. I just got back from a quick round with some old army buddies."

"We'd like to poke around your museum," said Garza.

"Be an honor. Help yourself. Not every day someone drops in by whirlybird to look at my artifacts (he pronounced it 'arteefacts'). You folks like something to drink, sody pop, beer? I've got a pitcher of margaritas in the icebox."

"A margarita would taste wonderful," said Lily, dabbing her neck with a bandanna.

"Show our guests around to the museum, Herb. The door's unlocked. I'll join you in a minute."

A truck and trailer pulled in for gas, and Trinity paused to chat a moment with the driver before entering his living quarters adjoining the store.

"A friendly cuss," muttered Sandecker.

"Sam can be friendlier than a down-Texas ranch wife," said Garza. "But get on his bad side and he's tougher than a ninety-cent steak."

Garza led them into an adobe building

726

behind the store. The interior was no larger than a two-car garage, but was crowded with glass display cases and wax figures in Roman legionary dress. The artifact room was spotless; no dust layered the glass walls. The artifacts were rust-free and highly burnished.

Lily carried an attaché case. She carefully laid it on a display case, unsnapped the latches and pulled out a thick book with illustrations and photographs that resembled a catalogue. She began to compare the artifacts with those pictured in the book.

"Looking good," she said after a few minutes of study. "The swords and spearheads match Roman weapons of the fourth century."

"Don't get excited," said Garza seriously. "Sam fabricated what you see here and probably aged them with acid and the sun."

"He didn't fabricate them," Sandecker said flatly.

Garza regarded him with skeptical interest. "How can you say that, Admiral? There's no record of pre-Columbian contact in the gulf."

"There is now."

"That's news to me."

"The event occurred in the year A.D. 391," explained Pitt. "A fleet of ships sailed up the Rio Grande to where Roma now stands. Somewhere, in one of the hills behind town, Roman mercenaries, their slaves and Egyptian scholars buried a vast collection of artifacts

727

from the Alexandria Library in Egypt —"

"I knew it!" burst Sam Trinity from the open doorway. He was so excited he almost dropped the tray of glasses and pitcher he was carrying. "By golly, I knew it! The Romans really walked the soil of Texas."

"You've been right, Sam," said Sandecker, "and your doubters wrong."

"All these years no one believed me," Sam muttered dazedly. "Even after they read the stone, they accused me of chiseling the inscription myself."

"Stone, what stone?" Pitt asked sharply.

"The one standing over in the corner. I had it translated at Texas A and M, but all they told me was, 'Nice job, Sam. Your Latin ain't half bad.' They've kidded me for years for dreaming up a first-rate fish story."

"Is there a copy of the translated message?" asked Lily.

"There, on the wall. I had it typed and hung in a glassed frame. I cut off the part where they panned it."

Lily peered at the wording and read it aloud as the others crowded around her.

"This stone marks the way to where I ordered buried the works from the great Hall of the Muses.

"I escaped the slaughter of our fleet by the barbarians and made my way south, where I was accepted by a primitive pyramid

728

people as a sage and a prophet.

"I have taught them what I know of the stars and science, but they put little of my teachings to practical use. They prefer to worship pagan gods and follow ignorant priests' demands for human sacrifice.

"Seven years have passed since my arrival. My return here is filled with sorrow at the sight of the bones of my former comrades. I have seen to their burial. My ship is ready and I shall soon set sail for Rome.

"If Theodosius still lives I shall be executed but accept the risk gladly to see my family one last time.

"To those who read this, should I perish, the entrance to the storage chamber is buried under the hill. Stand north and look straight south to the river cliff."

Junius Venator

10 August 398

"So Venator survived the massacre only to die seven years later on the return voyage to Rome," said Pitt.

"Or perhaps he made it and was executed without talking," added Sandecker.

"No, Theodosius died in 395," said Lily in wonder. "To think the message was here all this time and ignored as a counterfeit."

Trinity's eyebrows lifted. "You know this

Venator guy?"

"We've been tracking him," admitted Pitt.

"Have you searched for the chamber?" Sandecker asked.

Trinity nodded. "Dug all over these hills, but found nuthin' but what you see here."

"How deep?"

"Used a backhoe about ten years ago. Made a pit six meters down, but only found that sandal over there in the case."

"Could you show us the site where you discovered the stone and other artifacts?" Pitt asked him.

The old Texan looked at Garza. "Think it's okay, Herb?"

"Take my word, Sam, you can trust these people. They're not artifact robbers."

Trinity nodded vigorously. "All right, let's take a ride. We can go in my Jeep."

Trinity steered the Jeep Wagoneer up a dirt road past several modern homes and stopped in front of a barbed-wire fence. He got out, unhooked a section of the wire and pulled it aside. Then he climbed back behind the wheel and continued on over a trail that was grown over and barely perceptible.

When the four-wheel-drive Jeep crested a long, sloping rise, he stopped and turned off the ignition. "Well, here it is, Gongora Hill. A long time ago somebody told me it was named after a seventeenth-century Spanish poet. Why they named this dirt heap for a poet beats grits out of me."

Pitt gestured at a low hill four hundred meters to the north. "What do they call that ridge over there?"

"Has no name I ever heard of," replied Trinity.

"Where did you discover the stone?" asked Lily.

"Hold on, just a little further."

Trinity restarted the engine and slowly edged the Jeep down the slope, dodging the mesquite and low underbrush. After a two-minute bumpy ride, he braked beside a shallow wash. He stepped from the car and walked to the edge and looked down.

"Right here I found a corner of it sticking out of the bank."

"This dry wash," observed Pitt, "winds between Gongora and the far hill."

Trinity nodded. "Yeah, but no way the stone traveled from there to the slope below Gongora unless it was dragged."

"This is hardly a flood plain," agreed Sandecker. "Erosion and heavy rains over a long time period might have carried it fifty meters from the summit of Gongora, but not half a kilometer from the next summit."

"And the other artifacts," asked Lily, "where did they lie?"

Trinity swept a hand on an arc toward the river. "They were scattered a little further down the slope and continued almost through the center of town."

"Did you conduct a survey with transits and mark each location?"

"Sorry, miss, not being an archaeologist, I didn't think to pinpoint the holes."

Lily's eyes flashed disappointment, but she made no reply.

"You must have used a metal detector," said Pitt.

"Made it myself," Trinity answered proudly. "Sensitive enough to read a penny at half a meter."

"Who owns the land?"

"Twelve hundred acres hereabouts have been in my family since Texas was a republic."

"That saves a lot of legal hassle," Sandecker said approvingly.

Pitt looked at his watch. The sun was beginning to fall beyond the string of hills. He tried to visualize the running fight between the Indians and the Roman-Egyptians toward the river and the fleet of ancient ships. He could almost hear the shouting, the screams of pain, the clash of weapons. He felt as if he had been present that fateful day so long ago. He returned to the present as Lily continued her questioning of Trinity.

"Strange that you didn't find any bones on the battlefield."

"Early Spanish sailors who were ship-wrecked on the Texas Gulf Coast and managed to make their way to Veracruz and Mexico City," Garza answered her, "told of Indians who practiced cannibalism."

Lily made an expression of utter distaste. "You can't know for certain the dead were eaten."

"Perhaps a small number," said Garza. "And what remains that weren't dragged off by tribal dogs or wild animals were later buried by this guy Venator. Any they missed turned to dust."

"Herb's right," said Pitt. "Any bones that remained on surface ground would disintegrate in time."

Lily became very still. She gazed almost mystically at the nearby crest of Gongora Hill. "I can't begin to believe we're actually standing within a few meters of the treasures."

An icy calm seemed to settle over them for a few moments. Then Pitt finally echoed the other's thoughts.

"A lot of good men died sixteen centuries ago to preserve the knowledge of their time," he said softly, eyes staring into the past. "I think it's time we dig it free."

67

The next morning Admiral Sandecker was passed through the compound gate by Secret Service guards. He drove along a winding lane to the President's hideaway cottage on the Lake of the Ozarks in Missouri. He stopped his commercial rental car in the drive and removed his briefcase from the trunk. There was a crisp chill in the air, and he found it invigorating after the steamy temperatures along the Rio Grande.

The President, dressed in a warm sheepskin jacket, came down the steps from the porch and greeted him. "Admiral, thank you for coming."

"I'd rather be here than in Washington."

"How was your trip?"

"Slept most of it."

"Sorry to bring you up here in a mad rush."

"I'm fully aware of the urgency."

The President put a hand on Sandecker's back and steered him up the steps toward the cottage door. "Come in and have some breakfast. Dale Nichols, Julius Schiller and Senator Pitt are already attacking the eggs and smoked ham."

"Assembled the brain trust, I see," Sandecker said with a cagey smile.

"We spent half the night discussing the political impact of your discovery."

"Little I can tell you in person that wasn't in the report I sent by courier."

"Except you neglected to include a diagram of your proposed excavation."

"I would have gotten around to it," Sandecker said, standing his ground.

The President was not put off by Sandecker's feistiness. "You can show everyone over breakfast."

They broke off the conversation for a few moments as the President led him through the log-constructed house. They walked through a cozy living room decorated more for modern living than a hunting lodge. A small fire crackled away in a large rock fireplace. They entered the dining room, where Schiller and Nichols, dressed as fishermen, rose as one to shake hands. Senator Pitt merely waved. He wore a sweatsuit.

The Senator and the Admiral were close friends because of their closeness to Dirk. Sandecker caught a hint of warning from the elder Pitt's somber expression.

There was one other man the President hadn't mentioned — Harold Wismer, an old crony and adviser of the President who enjoyed enormous influence and worked outside the White House bureaucracy. Sandecker wondered why he was present.

The President pulled out a chair. "Sit down, Admiral. How do you like your eggs?"

Sandecker shook his head. "A small bowl of fruit and a glass of skim milk will do me fine."

A white-coated steward took Sandecker's order and disappeared into the kitchen.

"So that's how you keep that wiry shape," said Schiller.

"That and enough exercise to keep me in a perpetual state of sweat."

"All of us wish to congratulate you and your people on a magnificent find," Wismer began without hesitation. He stared through rimless glasses with pink lenses. A snarled beard almost hid thin lips. He was bald as a basketball; brown eyes wide to give a slight popped look. "When do you expect to move dirt?"

"Tomorrow," Sandecker answered, suspecting the rug was about to be pulled out from under him. He pulled a blowup of a geological survey map showing the topography above Roma from his briefcase. Then he followed it with a cutaway drawing of the hill indicating the planned excavation shafts. He laid them out on a free section of the table. "We intend to dig two exploratory tunnels into the main hill eighty meters below the summit."

"The one labeled 'Gongora Hill'?"

"Yes, the tunnels will enter on opposing sides of the slope facing the river and then angle toward each other, but on different levels. One or both should strike the grotto Junius Venator inscribed on Sam Trinity's stone, or, with luck, one of the original entry shafts."

"You're absolutely sure a treasure trove of artifacts from the Alexandria Library is at this place," Wismer said, tightening the noose. "You have no doubts."

"None," asserted Sandecker in a salty tone. "The map from the Roman ship in Greenland led to the artifacts found in Roma by Trinity. The pieces slot together nicely."

"But could the — ?"

"No, the Roman objects have been authenticated." Sandecker cut Wismer off abruptly. "This is no hoax, no attempt at fraud, no wild stunt or game. We know it's there. The only question is how extensive is the hoard."

"We don't mean to suggest the Library's treasures do not exist," said Schiller quickly, a little too quickly. "But you must understand, Admiral, the international repercussions of such an enormous discovery might be difficult to predict, much less control."

Sandecker stared at Schiller unblinking. "I fail to see how bringing the knowledge of the ancient world to light will cause Armageddon. Also, aren't you a little late? The world already knows about the treasure. Hala Kamil announced our search in her address to the United Nations."

"There *are* considerations," said the President seriously, "you may not be aware of. President Hasan may claim the entire trove of relics belongs to Egypt. Greece will insist on the return of Alexander's gold casket. Who can say what claims Italy will put forth?"

"Maybe I took the wrong tack, gentlemen," said Sandecker. "It was my understanding we promised to share in the discovery with President Hasan as a means of propping up his government."

"True," admitted Schiller. "But that was before you nailed down the location beside the Rio Grande. Now you've brought Mexico into the picture. The fanatic Topiltzin can make a case on the fact that the burial site originally belonged to Mexico."

"That's to be expected," said Sandecker. "Except that possession is nine tenths of the law. Legally the artifacts belong to the man who owns the property they're buried on."

"Mr. Trinity will be offered a substantial sum of money for his land and the rights to the relics," said Nichols. "I might also add, his payment will be tax-free."

Sandecker regarded Nichols skeptically. "The hoard might be worth hundreds of millions. Is the government prepared to go that high?"

"Of course not."

"And if Trinity won't take your offer?"

"There are other methods of making a deal," Wismer said with cold determination.

"Since when is the government in the art business?"

"The art, sculpture and the remains of Alexander the Great are only of historic interest," said Wismer. "The knowledge in the scrolls, that's the area of vital interest."

"That depends on the eye of the beholder," Sandecker said philosophically.

"The information contained in the scientific records, particularly the geological data, could have enormous influence on our future dealings with the Middle East," Wismer continued doggedly. "And there is the religious angle to consider."

"What's to consider? The Greek translation of the original Hebrew text of the Old Testament was made at the Library. This translation is the basis for all books of the Bible."

"But not the New Testament," Wismer corrected Sandecker. "There may be historic facts that dispute the founding of Christianity locked away under that hill in Texas. Facts that would be better, left hidden."

Sandecker gave Wismer a cold stare, then turned his eyes to the President. "I smell a conspiracy, Mr. President. I'd be grateful for the reason behind my presence here."

"Nothing sinister, Admiral, I assure you. But we all agree, this has become a vast and intricate operation that must be conducted within stringent guidelines."

Sandecker was not slow; the trap had sprung. He'd known almost from the beginning what was going down. "So after NUMA —" he paused and stared at Senator Pitt — "and especially your son, Senator, have done all the dirty work, we're to be pushed aside."

"You must admit, Admiral," said Wismer in an official tone, "this is hardly a job for a governmental agency whose bureaucratic responsibilities lie underwater."

Sandecker shrugged off Wismer's words. "We've taken the project this far. I see no reason why we can't see it through to the end."

"I'm sorry, Admiral," said the President firmly, "but I'm taking the project out of your hands and turning it over to the Pentagon."

Sandecker was stunned. "The military!" he blurted. "Whose harebrained idea was that?"

An embarrassed look came into the President's eyes. Then they flicked to Wismer for an instant. "It makes no difference who conceived the new plan. The decision is mine."

"I don't think you understand, Jim," said the Senator quietly. "What you stumbled upon goes far beyond mere archaeology. The knowledge under that hill could very well reshape our Middle East foreign policy for decades to come."

"Reason enough why we have to approach this thing as if it was a highly secret intelligence operation," said Wismer. "We must keep the discovery classified until all documents are thoroughly examined and their data analyzed."

"That could take twenty or even a hundred years, depending on the number and condition of the scrolls after underground storage for sixteen hundred years," Sandecker protested.

"If that's what it takes. . . ." The President shrugged.

The steward brought the Admiral's fruit bowl and glass of milk, but Sandecker had lost his appetite.

"In other words, you need time to add up the value of the windfall," Sandecker said acidly. "Then negotiate political bargains for the ancient charts showing the locations of lost mineral and oil deposits around the Mediterranean. If Alexander hasn't turned to dust, his bones will be traded to the Greek government toward renewed leases for our naval bases. All this before the American people find out you've given away the store."

"We cannot afford to go public," Schiller explained patiently. "Not until we're prepared to move. You fail to realize the tremendous foreign policy advantages you've laid in the government's lap. We can't simply throw them away in the name of public curiosity about historic objects."

"I'm not naive, gentlemen," said Sandecker. "But I do confess to being a sentimental old patriot who believes the people deserve better from their government than they receive. The treasures from the Library of Alexandria do not belong to a few politicians to barter away. They belong to all America by right of possession."

Sandecker didn't wait for them to answer. He took a quick swallow of milk, then retrieved a newspaper out of his briefcase and casually tossed it on the center of the table.

"Because everyone is so wrapped up with the big picture, your aides missed a small item from Reuters wire service that was carried in most of the newspapers around the world. Here's a copy of a St. Louis paper I picked up at the car-rental agency. I circled the piece on page three."

Wismer picked up the folded paper, opened it and turned to the page indicated by Sandecker. He read the heading aloud, and then began the text.

"Romans land in Texas?
"According to top-level administration sources in Washington, the search for a vast underground depository of ancient rel-

ics from the famed Library of Alexandria, Egypt, has ended a few hundred meters north of the Rio Grande River in Roma, Texas. Artifacts found over the years by a Mr. Samuel Trinity have been acknowledged as authentic by archaeologists.

"The search began with the discovery of a Roman merchant ship, dated from the fourth century A.D., in the ice of Greenland —"

Wismer stopped, his face reddening with anger. "A leak! A goddamned leak!"

"But how . . . who?" wondered Nichols in shock.

"Top-level administration sources," Sandecker repeated. "That can only mean the White House." He looked at the President, then at Nichols. "Probably a disgruntled aide one of your supervisors either passed over for promotion or sacked."

Schiller looked glumly at the President. "A thousand people will be swarming over the place. I suggest you order out a military force to secure the area."

"Julius is right, Mr. President," said Nichols. "Treasure hunters will dig those hills to pieces if they're not stopped."

The President nodded. "All right, Dale. Open a line to General Metcalf of the Joint Chiefs."

Nichols quickly left the table and entered the study, which was manned by Secret

Service and White House communications technicians.

"I strongly advise we clamp a lid on the entire operation," said Wismer tensely. "We should also spread a story that the discovery is a hoax."

"Not a good idea, Mr. President," counseled Schiller wisely. "Your predecessors found out the hard way; it doesn't pay to lie to the American people. The news media would smell a coverup and chew you to bits."

"I'll side with Julius," said Sandecker. "Close off the area, but go through with the excavation, hiding nothing and keeping the public informed. Believe me, Mr. President, your administration will be far better off putting the Library artifacts out in the open as they're recovered."

The President turned and looked at Wismer. "Sorry, Harold. Perhaps it's all for the best."

"Let us hope so," said Wismer, solemnly staring at the newspaper story. "I don't want to think about what might happen if that lunatic Topiltzin decides to make an issue of it."

68

Sam Trinity stood and watched Pitt connect a pair of electrical leads from two metal boxes that sat on the open tailgate of his Jeep. One had a small viewing monitor and the other a wide slot with paper unreeling from it like a flattened tongue.

"A wild-looking rig," observed Trinity. "What do you call it?"

"The fancy name is electromagnetic reflection profiling system for subsurface exploration," Pitt replied as he jacked in the leads to a strange double-humped contraption with four wheels and a push bar. "In plain speech, it's a ground-probing radar unit, the Georadar One, manufactured by the Oyo Corporation."

"I didn't know radar could go through dirt and rock."

"It can provide a good profile down to ten meters, and deep as twenty under ideal conditions."

"How's it work?"

"As the portable probe moves across the terrain its transmitter sends an electromagnetic pulse into the ground. The reflecting signals are picked up by a receiver and then relayed to the color processor and graphic recorder here in the Jeep. That's pretty much the gist of it."

"Sure you don't want me to tow the transmitter buggy?"

"I have better control if I push it by hand."

"What are we looking for?"

"A cavity."

"You mean cavern."

Pitt grinned and shrugged. "Same thing."

Trinity gazed across the ridge of hills they were standing on toward the summit of Gongora Hill, four hundred meters away. "Why are we looking on the backside of the wrong hill?"

"I want to run some tests on the unit before we tackle the prime site," Pitt replied vaguely. "Also, there's the slight possibility Venator buried more artifacts someplace else." He paused and waved to Lily, who was peering through a surveyor's transit a short distance away. "We're ready," he shouted.

She waved back and approached, carrying a board with a sheet of graph paper tacked to it. "Here's your search grid," she said, pointing a pencil at the markings on the paper. "The boundary stakes are set in place. I'll walk behind the Jeep and monitor the instruments. Every twenty meters or so I'll plant a small flag marker so we can keep our lanes straight."

Pitt nodded at Trinity. "Ready, Sam?"

Trinity moved behind the steering wheel and started the Jeep's engine. "Say the word."

Pitt turned on the unit and made a few adjustments. Then he took the handle of the probe wagon in his hands and pointed ahead. "Go."

Trinity dropped the Jeep into drive and crawled forward while Pitt followed, pushing the transmitter-receiver unit five meters in the rear.

A light cloud overcast dulled the sun to a dim yellow ball. Thankfully, the day was mild and comfortable. Back and forth they traveled, dodging brush and trees. The morning wore into afternoon as the monotony associated with search and surveys stretched time out of all proportion.

They ignored lunch, stopping only at Lily's command as she studied the recordings and made notations.

"A good reading?" Pitt asked, taking a breather, sitting on the back of the tailgate.

"We're on the edge of something that looks interesting," answered Lily, engrossed in the recordings. "May be nothing, though. I'll know better after we cover the next two lanes."

Trinity graciously passed around bottles of

Mexican Bohemia beer from an ice chest in the Jeep. It was during these short breaks that Pitt noticed a growing number of cars parked at the bottom of Gongora Hill. People were fanning out over the slope with metal detectors.

Sam noticed too. "A lot of good my 'No Trespassing' signs did," he grumbled. "You'd think they was advertising free drinks."

"Where are they coming from?" asked Lily. "How did they find out about the project so soon?"

Trinity peered over the rims of his sunglasses. "Mostly local folks. Somebody must have blabbed. By this time tomorrow they'll be rolling in from every state in the Union."

The telephone in the Jeep buzzed, and Trinity answered. Then he passed the receiver out the window to Pitt.

"For you. Admiral Sandecker."

Pitt took the call. "Yes, Admiral."

"We were back-stabbed; we're no longer on the excavation," Sandecker informed him. "The President's advisers have talked him into turning the operation over to the Pentagon."

"It was to be expected, but I'd have preferred the Park Service. They're better equipped for an archaeological dig."

"The White House wants to break into the storage chamber and remove the scrolls for study as quickly as possible. They fear a nasty confrontation with countries that might demand to share in the discovery."

Pitt struck his fist against the roof of the Jeep. "Dammit! They can't go down there and throw everything into trucks as though it was secondhand merchandise. The scrolls could crumble to dust if not handled properly."

"The President has accepted responsibility for the gamble."

"The past has no priority over politics, is that it?"

"Not the only problem," said Sandecker tersely. "Some aide inside the White House leaked everything to a foreign wire service. Word is spreading like the plague."

"Crowds are already converging on the site."

"They're not wasting any time."

"How does the government get around the fact the property belongs to Sam?"

"Let's just say Sam is going to get an offer he can't refuse," Sandecker replied angrily. "The President and his cronies have a grand scheme to make a political bonanza out of the information contained in the Library scrolls."

"My father among them?" asked Pitt.

"I'm afraid so."

"Who exactly is taking over?"

"A company of Army engineers from Fort Hood. They and their equipment are being transported by truck. A security force should be dropping in on you any time by helicopter to seal off the perimeters."

Pitt thought a moment, then: "Could you use your clout to arrange for us to hang around?"

"Give me a cover story."

"Except for Hiram Yaeger, Lily and I know more about the search than anyone who will be excavating. Claim we're vital to the project as consultants. Use Lily's academic credentials as a backup. Say we're conducting an archaeological survey for surface artifacts. Say anything, Admiral, but con the White House into allowing us to remain on the site."

"I'll see what I can do," Sandecker said, warming to the idea, although he didn't have the vaguest idea of what Pitt was shooting for. "Harold Wismer should be the only barrier. If the Senator throws his support our way I think we can handle it."

"Let me know if my dad drags his feet. I'll get on him."

"I'll be in touch."

Pitt handed the receiver back to Trinity and turned to Lily. "We're off the case," he informed them. "The Army is taking over the excavation. They're going to haul the artifacts away as fast as they can throw them in the back of a truck."

Lily's eyes widened in shock. "The scrolls will be destroyed," she gasped. "After sixteen hundred years in an underground vault the parchment and papyrus manuscripts must be treated delicately. They could disintegrate from a sudden temperature change or the slightest touch."

"You heard me give the Admiral the same appraisal," Pitt said helplessly.

Trinity looked washed out. "Waal," he drawled, "shall we call it a day?"

Pitt looked at the stakes that marked the outer limit of the search grid. "Not yet," he said slowly, deliberately. "Let's finish the job. The show is never over till it's over."

69

The Mercedes stretch limousine stopped at the yacht club dock in the harbor of Alexandria. The chauffeur opened the door and Robert Capesterre climbed from the back seat. Wearing a tailored white linen suit with a powder-blue shirt and matching tie, he no longer looked like Topiltzin.

He was guided down a stone stairway to a waiting launch. He sat back in the soft cushions and enjoyed the ride across the harbor and through the entrance where one of the Seven Wonders of the Ancient World, the famed lighthouse known as the Pharos of Alexandria, once stood, a towering 135 meters high. Only a few stones built into an Arab fort were all that remained of its ruins.

The launch headed for a large yacht that was moored around the harbor and off the long wide beach. Capesterre had walked her decks on previous occasions. He knew her length to be forty-five meters. She was Dutch-built, with sleek, aircraft-style lines. She had transoceanic range and a cruising speed of thirty knots.

The pilot eased back on the throttle and slipped the launch into reverse as it approached the boarding steps. Capesterre was met on deck by a man dressed in an open silk shirt, shorts and sandals. They embraced.

"Welcome, brother," said Paul Capesterre. "It's been too long."

"You look healthy, Paul. I'd say you and Akhmad Yazid have gained about eight pounds."

"Twelve."

"Almost seems strange to see you out of uniform," said Robert.

Paul shrugged. "I get tired of Yazid's Arabic gear and that stupid turban." He stood back and smiled at his brother. "You're a fine one to talk. I don't see you in your Aztec god outfit."

"Topiltzin is temporarily on holiday." Robert paused and nodded at the deck. "You've borrowed Uncle Theodore's boat, I see."

"He hardly has use for it any more since the family left the drug business." Paul Capesterre turned and led his brother into the dining salon. "Come along, I've had lunch set. Now that I've learned you finally developed a taste for champagne, I've dusted off a bottle of Uncle Theodore's finest vintage."

Robert took an offered glass. "I thought

President Hasan placed you under house arrest."

"The only reason I bought the villa is because of a hidden escape tunnel that runs underground for a hundred meters and comes up in a mechanic's repair shop."

"Also owned by you."

"Of course."

Robert raised his glass. "Here's to Mother and Father's grand scheme."

Paul nodded. "Although at the moment, your end in Mexico looks more promising than mine in Egypt."

"You're not to blame for the *Lady Flamborough* fiasco. The family approved the plan. No one could foretell the cunning of the Americans."

"That idiot Suleiman Aziz Ammar," said Paul harshly, "he blundered the operation away."

"Any news of survivors?"

"Family agents report most were killed, including Ammar and your Captain Machado. Several were taken prisoner, but they know nothing of our involvement."

"Then we should consider ourselves lucky. With Machado and Ammar dead, no intelligence agency in the world can touch us. They were the only link."

"President Hasan didn't have any trouble putting two and two together or I wouldn't be under house arrest."

"Yes," agreed Robert, "but Hasan can't act against you without solid evidence. If he tried, your followers would rise up and prevent any trial. The family's advice is to keep a low profile while consolidating your power base. At least for another year, to see how the wind blows."

"For now the wind blows at the backs of Hasan, Hala Kamil and Abu Hamid," said Paul wrathfully.

"Be patient. Soon your Islamic fundamentalist movement will sweep you into the Egyptian parliament."

Paul looked at Robert with a cagey expression in his eyes. "The discovery of the Alexandria Library treasures might speed things a bit."

"You've read the latest news reports?" asked Robert.

"Yes, the Americans claim they've found the storage chamber in Texas."

"Possession of the ancient geological charts could be to your advantage. If they point the way to rich oil and mineral reserves, you can claim credit for turning Egypt's economy around."

"I've considered that possibility," said Paul. "If I read the White House correctly, the President will use the artifacts and scrolls as bargaining chips. While Hasan begs and haggles for a paltry share of Egypt's heritage, I can go before the people and raise the issue

as an outrage against our revered ancestors."
Paul hesitated, his mind leapfrogging. Then
he continued, his eyes narrowing. "With the
right semantics I think I can twist Muslim
law and the words of the Koran into a rally-
ing cry that will crack Hasan's government."

Robert laughed. "Try and keep a straight
face when you speak. The Christians may
have burned most of the scrolls in A.D. 391,
but it was the Muslims in 646 who destroyed
the Library forever."

A waiter began serving Scottish smoked
salmon and Iranian caviar. They ate for a few
minutes in silence.

Then Paul said, "I hope you realize the
burden of seizing the artifacts falls on your
shoulders."

Robert stared over the rim of his champagne glass. "You talking to me or Topiltzin?"

Paul laughed. "Topiltzin."

Robert set down the glass and slowly raised
his hands in the air as if beseeching a fly on
the ceiling. His eyes took on a hypnotic look
and he began to speak in a haunting tone.

"We will rise up by the tens of thousands,
by the hundreds of thousands. We will cross
the river as one and take what was buried on
our land, land that was stolen from us by the
Americans. Many will be sacrificed, but the
gods demand we take what rightfully belongs
to Mexico." Then he dropped his hands and
grinned. "Needs a little polishing, of course."

"I believe you've borrowed my script," said Paul, applauding.

"What's the difference so long as we're family?" Robert took a final forkful of salmon. "Delicious. I could eat smoked salmon by the boatload." He washed it down with the champagne. "If I can seize the treasures and hold on to them, then what?"

"I only want the maps. Whatever else can be smuggled out goes to the family to keep or sell on the black market to wealthy collectors. Agreed?"

Robert thought a moment, and then nodded. "Agreed."

The waiter brought a tray of glasses, a bottle of brandy and a box of cigars.

Paul slowly lit a panatella. He looked questioningly through the smoke at his brother. "How do you intend to grab the Library treasures?"

"I had planned to launch a massive, unarmed invasion of the American border states after I gained power. This strikes me as a good opportunity for a test run." Robert stared at his glass as he swirled his brandy. "Once I set the wheels of my organization in motion, the poor in the cities and the peasants of the country will be gathered up and transported north to Roma, Texas. I can assemble three, perhaps as many as four hundred thousand on our side of the Rio Grande in four days."

"What about American resistance?"

"Every soldier, border patrolman and sheriff in Texas will be helpless to stop the crush. I plan to put the women and children in the first wave across the bridge and river. Americans are a maudlin lot. They may have slaughtered villagers in Vietnam, but they won't massacre unarmed civilians on their own doorstep. I can also play on White House fears of a nasty international incident. The President won't dare issue orders to shoot. Static resistance will be inundated by a human tide that will sweep up through Roma and occupy the underground vault containing the Library treasures."

"And Topiltzin will lead them?"

"And I will lead them."

"How long do you think you can hold on to the vault?" asked Paul.

"Long enough for ancient-language translators to assess and remove any scrolls pertaining to long-lost mineral deposits."

"That could take weeks. You won't have the time. The Americans will build up their forces and push your people back into Mexico within a few days."

"Not if I threaten to burn the scrolls and destroy the art objects." Robert patted his lips with a napkin. "My jet should be refueled by now. I'd better return to Mexico and set the operation in motion."

Respect for his brother's inventive reasoning showed in Paul's eyes. "With their backs against the wall, the American government will have no option but to deal. I like that."

"Certainly the largest horde of people to invade the United States since the British in the Revolutionary War," said Robert. "I like that even better."

70

They began arriving in the thousands the first day, in the tens of thousands the next. From all over northern Mexico people inspired by the impassioned ravings of Topiltzin traveled by car, overloaded bus and truck, or walked to the dusty town of Miguel Alemán across the river from Roma. The asphalt roads from Monterrey, Tampico, and Mexico City were glutted with a continuous stream of vehicles.

President De Lorenzo tried to stop the human avalanche rolling toward the border. He called out the Mexican armed forces to block the roads. The military might as well have tried to stop a raging flood. Outside of Guadalupe, a squad of soldiers about to be swept away by a crush of bodies fired into the crowd, killing fifty-four, most of them women and children.

De Lorenzo had unwittingly played into Topiltzin's hands. It was exactly the reaction Robert Capesterre had hoped for. Riots broke out in Mexico City, and De Lorenzo realized he had to back off or face mushrooming unrest and the lighted match of a possible revolution. He sent a message to the White House with his sincere regrets for failing to stem the tide, and then he called off the soldiers, many of whom deserted and joined the crusade.

Unrestrained, the throng swarmed toward the Rio Grande.

The Capesterre family's hired professional planners and Robert's Topiltzin followers raised a five-square-kilometer tent city and set up kitchens and organized food lines. Sanitation facilities were trucked in and assembled. Nothing was overlooked. Many of the poor who flooded the area had never lived nor eaten so well. Only the clouds of dust and exhaust smoke from diesel engines swirled beyond human control.

Hand-painted banners appeared along the Mexico bank of the river proclaiming, "The U.S. stole our land," "We want our ancestors' land returned," "The antiquities belong to Mexico." They chanted the slogans in English, Spanish and Nahuatl. Topiltzin walked among the masses, agitating them into a frenzy rarely seen outside Iran.

Television news teams had a field day taping the colorful demonstration. Cameras, their cables meandering to two dozen mobile field units, stood tripod to tripod on top of

Roma's bluff, lenses panning the opposite shore.

Unwary correspondents who wandered through the crowds did not know that the peasant families they interviewed had been carefully planted and rehearsed. In most cases the simple, impoverished-looking people were trained actors who spoke fluent English, but answered questions in a stumbling, broken accent. Their tearful appeals to live permanently in California, Arizona, New Mexico and Texas drew a wave of sob-sister support across the nation when the segments ran on the evening news and the morning talk shows.

The only ones who stood grim and unimpressed were the dedicated men of the U.S. Border Patrol. Until now, the threat of a massive incursion had only been a nightmare. Now, they were about to witness the realization of their worst fears.

Border patrolmen rarely had call to draw their firearms. They treated illegal immigrants humanely and with respect before shipping them back home. They took a dim view of the Army troops covering the U.S. side of the river like nests of camouflaged ants. They saw only disaster and slaughter in a long line of automatic weapons and the twenty tanks whose deadly guns were trained on Mexico.

The soldiers were young and efficient as fighting units. But they were trained for combat with an enemy who fought back. They were uneasy about facing a wave of unarmed civilians.

The commanding officer, Brigadier General Curtis Chandler, had barricaded the bridge with tanks and armored cars, but Topiltzin had planned for that contingency. The riverbank was packed with every kind of small boat, wooden raft and truck inner tube gleaned within two hundred miles. Footbridges made of rope were stretched out and knotted to be carried across by the first wave and positioned.

General Chandler's intelligence officer estimated an initial rush of twenty thousand before the flotilla returned, loaded and ferried the next wave. He couldn't begin to guess the number of swimmers. One of his female agents had penetrated the dining trailer used by Topiltzin aides and reported the storm would be launched in the late evening after the Aztec messiah had whipped his devotees into near-frenzy. But she couldn't learn which evening.

Chandler had served three tours in Vietnam; he knew firsthand what it was like to kill fanatical young women and boys who struck without warning out of the jungle. He gave orders to fire over the heads of the mob when they began their move across the water.

If the warning barrage did not stop them — Chandler was a soldier who performed his duty without question. If ordered, he would use the forces under his command to repel the peaceful invasion regardless of the cost in blood.

Pitt stood on the second-story sun deck of Sam Trinity's store and peered through a telescope used by the Texan to gaze at the stars. The sun had dropped over the western range of hills and daylight was fading, but the staged spectacle on the other side of the Rio Grande was about to begin. Batteries of multicolored floodlights burst out, some sweeping patterns in the sky while others beamed on a tall tower that had been erected in the center of the town.

He focused on and magnified a tiny figure wearing a white ankle-length robe and colorful headdress who stood on a narrow platform atop the tower. Pitt judged from the upraised and brisk movement of the arms that the center of attraction was engaged in a fervent speech.

"I wonder who the character is in the jazzy costume stirring up the natives?"

Sandecker sat with Lily, examining the underground profile recordings from the survey. He looked up at Pitt's question. "Probably that phony Topiltzin," he grunted.

"He can sway a crowd with the best of the Evangelists."

"Any sign they'll attempt the crossing

764

tonight?" asked Lily.

Pitt leaned back from the telescope and shook his head. "They're hard at work on their fleet, but I doubt if it will come for another forty-eight hours. Topiltzin won't launch his big push until he's certain he commands the lead news story of the day."

"Topiltzin is an alias," Sandecker informed him. "His real name is Robert Capesterre."

"He's got himself a thriving racket."

Sandecker held up one thumb and forefinger an inch apart. "Capesterre is that far away from taking over Mexico."

"If that convention on the other side of the river is any indication, he's after the entire American Southwest too."

Lily stood up and stretched. "This sitting around is driving me crazy. We do all the work, and the army engineers get all the glory. Preventing us from watching over the excavation and keeping us off Sam's property — I think it's rude of them."

Pitt and Sandecker both smiled at Lily's feminine choice of words. "I could put it a little stronger than *rude*," said the Admiral.

Lily chewed nervously on the tip of a pen. "Why no word from the Senator? We should have heard something by now."

"I can't say," replied Sandecker. "All he told me after I explained Dirk's setup, was that he'd somehow work a deal."

"Wish we knew how it was going," Lily

murmured.

Trinity appeared on the stairs below wearing an apron. "Anybody care for a bowl of my famous Trinity chili?"

Lily gave him an uneasy look. "How hot is it?"

"Little lady, I can make it as mild on your stomach as a marshmallow or as fiery as battery acid. Any way you like it."

"I'll go with the marshmallow," Lily decided without hesitation.

Before Pitt and Sandecker could put in their order, Trinity turned and stared through the dusk at a stream of headlights approaching up the road. "Must be another army convoy," he announced. "Been no cars or trucks come this way since that General closed off the roads and rerouted all the traffic to the north."

Soon they counted five trucks led by a hummer, the vehicle that replaced the durable jeep. The truck bringing up the rear pulled a trailer with a canvas-covered piece of equipment. The convoy did not turn off the road toward the engineers' encampment on Gongora Hill or continue into Roma as expected. The trucks followed the hummer into the driveway of Sam's Roman Circus and stopped between the gas pumps and the store. The passengers climbed from the hummer and looked around.

Pitt immediately recognized three familiar

faces. Two of the men were in uniform while the third wore a sweater and denims. Pitt climbed carefully over the railing and lowered himself until he was only a few feet off the ground. Then he let go and landed directly in front of them, uttering a low groan at the sudden pain from his wounded leg. They were as startled by his sudden appearance as he was by theirs.

"Where'd you drop from?" asked Al Giordino with a broad smile. He looked pale under the floodlights and his arm was in a sling, but he looked testy as ever.

"I was about to ask you the same thing."

Colonel Hollis stepped forward. "I didn't think we'd meet up again so quickly."

"Nor I," added Major Dillinger.

Pitt felt a vast wave of relief rush over him as he grasped their outstretched hands. "To say I'm glad to see you has to be the year's understatement. How is it you're here?"

"Your father used his powers of persuasion on the Joint Chiefs of Staff," explained Hollis. "I'd hardly finished my report on the *Lady Flamborough* mission when orders came down to assemble the teams and rush here by vehicle transportation, using back-country roads. All very hush and classified. I was told the field commander would not be apprised of our mission until I reported to him."

"General Chandler," said Pitt.

"Yes, steel-trap Chandler. I served under

him in NATO eight years ago. Still thinks armor alone can win wars. So he's got the dirty job of playing Horatio defending the bridge."

"What are your orders?" asked Pitt.

"To assist you and Dr. Sharp on whatever project you've got going. Admiral Sandecker is to act as a direct line to the Senator and the Pentagon. That's about all I know."

"No mention of the White House?"

"None that's down on paper." He turned as Lily and the Admiral, who had taken the long way down the inside stairs, rushed out the front door. As Lily embraced Giordino, and Dillinger introduced himself to Sandecker, Hollis pulled Pitt aside.

"What the devil is going on around here?" he muttered. "A circus?"

Pitt grinned. "You don't know how close you are."

"Where do my special forces fit in?"

"When the free-for-all starts," said Pitt, turning deadly serious, "your job is to blow the store."

71

The backhoe the Special Operations Forces had transported from Virginia was huge. Wide treads moved its massive bulk up the slope to a site marked by one of Lily's small marker flags. After ten minutes of instruction and a little practice, Pitt memorized the lever functions and began operating the steel behemoth on his own. He raised the two-and-a-half-meter-wide bucket and then brought it down like a giant claw, striking the hard ground with a loud clang.

In less than an hour a trench six meters deep and twenty meters in length had been carved on the rear slope of the hill. That was as far as the excavation progressed when a Chevrolet four-wheel-drive Blazer staff car came barreling through the underbrush with a truckload of armed soldiers trailing in its dust.

The wheels had not yet stopped turning when a captain with a ramrod-straight back and the eyes of a man driven by an inspired dedication to army discipline and standard operating procedure jumped to the ground.

"This is a restricted area," he snapped smartly. "I warned you people personally two days ago not to reenter. You must remove your equipment and leave immediately."

Pitt indifferently climbed down from his seat and stared into the bottom of the trench as though the officer didn't exist.

The Captain's face went red and he barked to his sergeant, "Sergeant O'Hara, prepare the men to escort these civilians from the area."

Pitt slowly turned and smiled pleasantly. "Sorry, but we're staying put."

The Captain smiled back, but his smile was scorching. "You have three minutes to leave and take that backhoe with you."

"Do you care to see papers authorizing us to be here?"

"Unless they were signed by General Chandler, you're chewing air."

"They come from a higher command than your general."

"You have three minutes," the Captain said flatly. "Then I will have you forcibly removed."

Lily, Giordino and the Admiral, who were sitting out of the sun in Trinity's borrowed Jeep Wagoneer, walked over to take in the show. Lily was wearing only a halter and tight shorts. She saucily paraded up and down in front of the line of soldiers.

Women who have never worked the streets as hookers cannot walk with a seductive swing and sway that appears like a natural phenomenon. They tend to exaggerate to the point of slapstick. Lily was no exception, but the men could not have cared less. They ate up the performance.

Pitt began to tense with anger. He hated pompous sapheads. "You have only twelve men, Captain. Twelve engineers with less than a hundred hours of combat training. I have forty men backing me, any two of whom could kill your entire force in less than thirty seconds with their bare hands. I'm not asking, I'm telling you to back off."

The Captain made a casual three-hundred-degree turn, but all he saw besides Pitt were Lily strutting in front of the troops, Admiral Sandecker, who was unconcernedly puffing a large cigar, and a man he hadn't seen before wearing an arm sling. They were both leaning against the Jeep as if they were half-asleep.

He glanced quickly at Pitt, but Pitt's eyes gave no hint of emotion. He made a forward motion with his hand. "Sergeant, move these people the hell out of here."

Before his men had taken two steps, Colonel Hollis seemed to appear as if by magic. The simulated colors of his camouflaged battle dress and grease-hued hands and face were incredibly faithful to the surrounding

771

foliage. Standing less than five meters away, he blended into the underbrush nearly to the point of invisibility.

"Do we have a problem?" Hollis asked the Captain about as charitably as a sidewinder eyeing a gopher.

The Captain's mouth dropped open and his men froze in position. He took a few steps closer and gawked at Hollis more carefully, seeing no obvious sign of rank.

"Who are you?" he blurted. "What is your outfit?"

"Colonel Morton Hollis, Special Operations Forces."

"Captain Louis Cranston, sir, 486th Engineering Battalion."

Salutes were exchanged. Hollis nodded toward the line of engineers, their automatic weapons at the ready. "I think you can give the order for your men to stand at rest."

Cranston was uncertain what to make of an unfamiliar colonel who appeared out of nowhere. "May I ask, Colonel, what a Special Forces officer is doing here?"

"Seeing that these people are allowed to conduct an archaeological survey without interference."

"I must remind you, sir, civilians are not permitted in a restricted military zone."

"Suppose I told you they have the authority to be here."

"Sorry, Colonel. I am under direct orders

from General Chandler. He was very explicit. No one, and that includes yourself, sir, who is not a member of the battalion is to be allowed to enter —"

"Am I to understand you intend to throw me out as well?"

"If you can't present signed orders from General Chandler for your presence," Cranston said nervously, "I will obey my instructions."

"Your hardnose position won't win you any medals, Captain. I think you'd better reconsider."

Cranston knew damned well he was being toyed with and he didn't like it. "Please, no trouble, Colonel."

"You load up your men and return to your base, and don't even think of looking back."

Pitt was enjoying the encounter, but he reluctantly turned away and climbed down into the trench. He began probing the dirt on the bottom. Giordino and Sandecker idly strolled over to the edge and watched him.

Cranston hesitated. He was outranked, but his orders were clear. He decided his stance was firm. General Chandler would back him if there was an investigation.

But before he could order his men to clear the area, Hollis took a whistle from a pocket and blew two shrill blasts.

Like ghosts rising from the graves of a horror movie, forty forms that looked more like bushes and undergrowth than men suddenly materialized and formed a loose circle around Captain Cranston and his men.

Hollis's eyes turned venomous. "Bang, you're dead."

"You called, boss?" said a bush that sounded like Dillinger.

Cranston's cockiness collapsed. "I . . . must report this . . . to General Chandler," he stammered.

"You do that," said Hollis coldly. "You can also inform him that my orders come from General Clayton Metcalf of the Joint Chiefs. This can be verified through communications to the Pentagon. These people and my team are not here to interfere with your excavation on Gongora Hill or get in the way of the General's operations along the river. Our job is to find and preserve Roman surface artifacts before they're lost or stolen. Do you read, Captain?"

"I understand, sir," replied Cranston, gazing around uneasily at the purposeful-looking men, whose facial expressions appeared frightful under the camouflage makeup.

"Found another one!" Pitt shouted, unseen below ground.

Sandecker excitedly waved everyone to the trench. "He's got something."

The confrontation was momentarily forgotten as the Engineers and SOF men clustered around the rim of the trench. Pitt was on his hands and knees, brushing away loose dirt from a long metallic object.

In a few minutes he pulled it free and very carefully passed it up to Lily.

The flippancy was gone now as she examined the ancient relic. "Fourth-century sword with definite Roman characteristics," she announced. "Neatly intact with little corrosion."

"May I?" asked Hollis.

She held it out to him and he gently clasped his hand around the hilt and lifted the blade above his head. "Just think," he murmured reverently, "the last man to hold this was a Roman legionary." Then he graciously passed it to Cranston. "How'd you like to fight a battle with this instead of an automatic firearm?"

"I'd prefer a bullet any day," Cranston said thoughtfully, "to being hacked to shreds."

As soon as the Engineers left on the short drive back to their encampment, Pitt turned to Hollis.

"My compliments on your camouflage. I only detected three out of your whole team."

"It was eerie," said Lily, "knowing you were all around us but not visible."

Hollis looked genuinely embarrassed. "We're more used to concealment in jungle or forest. This was a good field exercise for semi-arid terrain."

"An excellent job," added Sandecker,

pumping Hollis's hand.

"Let's hope General Chandler buys the good Captain's report," said Giordino.

"If he bothers to hear it," Pitt replied. "The General's most urgent business is to stop half a million aliens from flooding across the border and grabbing the Library's art and knowledge. He doesn't have time to fool with us."

"What about the Roman sword?" asked Hollis, holding it up.

"That goes back in Sam's museum collection."

Hollis looked at Pitt. "You didn't find it in the trench?"

"No."

"You get a turn on digging holes?"

Pitt acted as though he hadn't heard Hollis. He walked a short distance to the summit of the hill and looked down the slope into Mexico. The tent city had swelled to twice what it was the previous day. Tomorrow night, he thought. Topiltzin would unleash the storm tomorrow night. He turned to his left and stared up at the slightly higher Gongora Hill.

The Army Engineers were digging exactly where Lily had placed her stakes four days ago. They made two separate excavations. One was at the common tunnel, complete with overhead supports. The other was an open mine, a gouged crater in the side of the hill. Work was going slowly since General Chandler had pulled away most of the Engineers to help in the border defense.

Pitt turned and came back down the incline. He walked up to Hollis. "Who's your best demolition expert?"

"Major Dillinger is one of the best explosive ordinance men in the army."

"I need about two hundred kilograms of C-six nitroglycerin gel."

Hollis looked at him in genuine surprise. "Two hundred kilograms of C-six? Ten kilos can take out a battleship. Do you know what you're asking? The nitrogel mix is shock-hazardous."

"Also a battery of spotlights," Pitt pressed on. "We can borrow them from a rock-concert group. Spotlights, strobe lights, and eardrum-blasting audio equipment." Then he turned to Lily. "I'll leave it to you to find a carpenter who can knock together a box."

"Why in God's name do you want all that stuff?" Lily asked, eyes wide with curiosity.

"You don't want to know," Giordino moaned.

"I'll explain later," Pitt hedged.

"Sounds crazy to me," said Lily, uncomprehending.

The lady was only half right, Pitt thought. His plan was twice as crazy as anything she could conceive. But he kept everyone in the dark. He didn't think now was the right time to tell them he planned to take his act on the stage.

72

The green Volvo with the taxi markings stopped at the drive of Yazid's villa near Alexandria. The Egyptian army guards, who were posted by the personal order of President Hasan, stiffened into alertness at the gate as the taxi sat there without anyone's getting out.

Ammar sat in the back seat, his eyes and jaw heavily bandaged. He wore a blue silk robe and a small red turban. His only medical treatment since escaping Santa Inez had come during a two-hour visit to a back-street Buenos Aires surgeon before chartering a private jet to fly him across the ocean to the small airport outside the city.

He no longer felt pain in his empty eye sockets. The drugs took care of that, but it was still agony to speak through his shattered jaw. And although he felt a strange sense of tranquillity, his mind functioned as ruthlessly and efficiently as ever.

"We are here," said Ibn from the driver's seat.

Ammar visualized Yazid's villa in his mind — every detail as if he could actually see. "I know," he said simply.

"You do not have to do this thing, Suleiman Aziz."

"I have no more hopes or fears." Ammar spoke slowly, fighting the pain of each syllable. "It is the will of Allah."

Ibn swung from behind the wheel, opened the rear door and helped Ammar to climb out. He led Ammar up the driveway and turned him so he faced the heavily guarded gate.

"The gate is five meters in front of you," Ibn spoke haltingly in a voice heavy with emotion. He gently embraced Ammar. "Goodbye, Suleiman Aziz. I will miss you."

"Do what you promised, my faithful friend, and we will meet in Allah's garden."

Ibn quickly turned and retraced his steps to the car. Ammar stood without moving until he heard the sound of the engine fade in the distance. Then he approached the gate.

"Stop right there, blind man," ordered a guard.

"I have come to visit my nephew, Akhmad Yazid," said Ammar.

The guard nodded to another, who disappeared into a small office and came out with a folder containing twenty or so names.

"Uncle, you say. What's your name?"

Ammar enjoyed making his last play as an impostor. He had collected on an old debt from a colonel in Abu Hamid's Defense Ministry and received the list of names of those permitted entry into Yazid's villa. He selected one who couldn't be immediately contacted.

"Mustapha Mahfouz."

"Your name is here all right. Let's see your identification."

The guard studied Ammar's counterfeit ID, fruitlessly trying to compare the photo with the heavily bandaged features.

"What happened to your face?"

"The car bomb that exploded in the bazaar at El Mansura. I was struck by flying debris."

"Too bad," the guard said without sincerity. "You can blame your nephew. It was his followers who set it off." He gestured to a subordinate. "If he clears the metal detector, guide him up to the house."

Ammar held out his arms as if he expected to be frisked.

"No need for a body search, Mahfouz. If you're carrying a weapon, the machine will spot it."

The metal detector revealed nothing and did not sound.

The front door: Ammar gloated as the Egyptian army security guard led him up the steps to the front door. No having to sneak in

781

a side passage this time. He sorely wished he could see the look on Yazid's face when they met.

He was guided into what he perceived to be a large entry hall by the echo of the guard's boots on the tile floor. He was helped to a stone bench, and he sat down.

"Wait here."

Ammar heard the guard mumble to someone before returning to the gate. He sat in silence for several minutes. Then he heard approaching footsteps followed by a contemptuous voice.

"You are Mustapha Mahfouz?"

Ammar recognized the voice instantly. "Yes," he answered casually. "Do I know you?"

"We have not met. I am Khaled Fawzy, leader of Akhmad's revolutionary council."

"I've heard good things about you." The arrogant jackass, thought Ammar. He doesn't know me under the bandages or by the slow rasp of my speech. "It is indeed an honor to meet you."

"Come along," said Fawzy, taking Ammar by the arm. "I'll take you to Akhmad. He thought you were still on a mission for him in Damascus. I don't think he's aware of your injuries."

"The result of an assassination attempt three days ago," Ammar lied artfully. "I left the hospital only this morning and flew straight here to brief Akhmad first hand."

"Akhmad will be pleased to hear of your loyalty. He will also be saddened to learn of your injuries. Unfortunately your visit is poorly timed."

"I cannot meet with him?"

"He is at prayer," Fawzy said curtly.

Despite his suffering, Ammar could have laughed. He slowly became aware of another presence in the room. "It is vital he receive me."

"You may speak freely to me, Mustapha Mahfouz." The name was spoken with heavy sarcasm. "I will relay your message."

"Tell Akhmad it concerns his ally."

"Who?" Fawzy demanded. "What ally?"

"Topiltzin."

The name seemed to hang in the room for an interminable time. The stillness became intense. And then it was broken by a new voice.

"You should have stayed and died on the island, Suleiman," said Akhmad Yazid in a menacing tone.

Ammar's calm did not desert him. He had set his genius and last bit of strength for this moment. He was not about to wait for death. He was going to step forward and embrace it. Not for him a life of perpetual darkness and disfigurement — revenge was his deliverance.

"I could not die without standing in your

forgiving presence one last time."

"Save your babble and remove those stupid bandages. You're losing your touch. Your crude imitation of Mahfouz was fourth-rate for a man of your skills."

Ammar did not reply. He slowly unwrapped the bandages until the ends came free, and he dropped them on the floor.

Yazid audibly sucked in his breath when he saw the hideous disfigurement of Ammar's face. Sadistic blood ran in Fawzy's veins: he stared with the perverted thrill of one who enjoyed the sight of human wreckage.

"My payment for my service," Ammar slowly rasped.

"How is it you're alive?" Yazid asked, his voice shaken.

"My faithful friend Ibn hid me from the American Special Forces for two days until he fashioned a raft out of driftwood. After drifting with the current and paddling for ten hours, by the grace of Allah we were picked up by a Chilean fishing boat that set us ashore near a small airport at Puerto Williams. We stole an airplane and flew to Buenos Aires, where I chartered a jet to bring us to Egypt."

"Death does not come easy to you," muttered Yazid.

"You realize you signed your death warrant by coming here," Fawzy purred with anticipation.

"I expected little else."

"Suleiman Aziz Ammar," said Yazid with a trace of sadness. "The greatest assassin of his time, feared and respected by the CIA and the KGB, the creator of the most successful assassinations ever carried out. And to think you should end as a filthy, pathetic beggar in the streets."

"What are you saying, Akhmad?" asked Fawzy in surprise.

"The man is already dead." Yazid's disgust was slowly turning to satisfaction. "Our financial experts will arrange for his wealth and investments to be taken over in my name. Then he will be turned out in the streets with twenty-four-hour guards to make certain he remains in the slums. He will spend the rest of his days begging to exist. That is far worse than a quick death."

"You will have me killed when I tell you what I came to say," said Ammar conversationally.

"I'm listening," said Yazid impatiently.

"I dictated a complete thirty-page report of the entire *Lady Flamborough* affair. All names, conversations, times and dates were carefully itemized, everything, including my observations on the Mexican part of the operation and my opinion on the connection between you and Topiltzin. Copies are being read at this moment by the intelligence services of six countries and members of their news media. However you deal with me, Akhmad, knowing you're finished —"

He broke off abruptly, gasped as his entire head burst into excruciating agony. Fawzy, his face livid and teeth gnashed in rage, struck Ammar with his fist. The impact did not carry the solid weight of a planned punch. Fawzy's unthinking, explosive action came from complete loss of self-control. The blow glanced off one side of Ammar's injured jaw.

A man in good physical condition would have shrugged it off, but Ammar teetered on the brink of unconsciousness. Delicate scar tissue around his eyes and jaw split apart.

He staggered backward, blindly warding off Fawzy's wild punches with his hands and arms, fighting to clear his mind of the pain, face white, blood streaming.

"Stop!" Yazid shouted at Fawzy. "Can't you see the man is asking to die. He may be lying, hoping we'll kill him here and now."

Ammar regained a measure of mental control, positioning the sound of Yazid's voice, the sharp breaths of the maddened Fawzy.

He reached out with his left hand and moved slightly forward until he was certain he touched Yazid's right arm. Then he clutched it and made a lightning motion with his free hand behind his neck.

The carbon composite knife was pressed

tightly into the slight indentation just to the right of Ammar's upper spine by white surgical tape. Known as utility device by undercover operatives, it was designed to pass safety through metal detectors.

Ammar tore the thin, triangular-shaped, eighteen-centimeter blade from his back, whipped back his elbow like a piston, then rammed the knife into Yazid's chest just under the rib cage.

The vicious thrust lifted the revolutionary Muslim impersonator off his feet. Paul Capesterre's eyes bulged in shock and terror. His only sound was a hoarse gurgle.

"Farewell, vermin," Ammar croaked through his bleeding mouth.

And then the knife was jerked free and Ammar made a sweeping arc toward the spot where he sensed Fawzy was standing. The knife wasn't designed for a slashing attack, but his hand came in contact with Fawzi's face, and he felt the blade slice the cheek.

Ammar knew Fawzy was right-handed and always carried a gun, an old nine-millimeter Luger in a holster slung under the left armpit. He fell against Fawzy, blindly attempting to clutch the arrogant fanatic, while shoving the knife upward again.

Without sight, his timing was late.

Fawzy had swiftly drawn the Luger. He pushed the barrel into Ammar's stomach and triggered two rounds before the knife drove into his heart. He dropped the gun and clutched at his chest. He swayed a few steps to his side, staring down with a strange quizzical look at the knife protruding on an upward angle below his sternum. Finally his eyes rolled upward and he dropped to the floor only a meter from where Capesterre had fallen.

Ammar very slowly sank to the ceramic tile floor and settled on his back. There was no more pain, none at all. He saw visions without his eyes. He could feel his life ebbing away as if it were floating down a stream.

His fate had been decided by a man he'd only met briefly. The image came back of the tall man with the green eyes and the set grin. A wave of hate surged and just as quickly passed. Dirk Pitt — the name was etched in the darkening reaches of his mind.

He felt a euphoric contentment close over him. His last thought was that Ibn would take care of Pitt. Then the slate would be wiped clean. . . .

73

The President sat in a leather armchair and stared at four television monitors. Three were tuned to the major networks, while the fourth was a direct feed from an Army communications track at Roma. He looked tired, but his eyes glistened with intensity. They roved steadily from one monitor to the next; his face was set in concentration.

"I can't believe so many people can exist in so small an area," he said wonderingly.

"Their food has about run out," said Schiller, reading from an up-to-the-minute CIA report. "Drinking water is scarce, and the sanitation facilities are backed up."

"It's tonight or never," sighed Nichols wearily.

The President asked, "What kind of numbers are we looking at?"

"A computer head-count from an aerial photograph shows nearly four hundred and thirty-five thousand," replied Schiller.

"And they're going to pour through a corridor less than a kilometer wide," Nichols said grimly.

"Damn that murdering bastard!" the President said savagely. "Doesn't he realize or care that thousands will be killed or drowned in the crush alone?"

"A majority of them women and children," added Nichols.

"The Capesterres aren't known for charity and goodwill," muttered Schiller acidly.

"Still not too late to remove him." This from CIA director Martin Brogan. "Killing Topiltzin would be comparable to assassinating Hitler in 1930."

"Providing your hired gun got close enough," commented Nichols. "Afterward, he'd be butchered by the crowd."

"I was thinking of a high-powered rifle from four hundred meters."

Schiller shook his head. "Not a practical solution. A clear shot could only come from an elevation on our side of the river. The Mexicans would know immediately who was responsible. Then things could turn real ugly. Instead of a peaceful crowd, General Chandler's troops would be facing a maddened mob. They'd storm Roma with any weapons they could find, guns, knives, rocks and bottles. Then we'd have a real war on our hands."

"I concur," said Nichols. "General Chandler would have no choice but to open up with everything he had to save his men and any American Citizens in the area."

The President struck the arm of the chair with his clenched fist in frustration. "Is there nothing we can do to prevent mass slaughter?"

"Any way we look at it," said Nichols, "we're on the short end of the stick."

"Maybe we should say the hell with it and turn over the Alexandria Library's treasure to President De Lorenzo. Anything to keep it out of Topiltzin's filthy hands."

"A meaningless gesture," said Brogan. "Topiltzin's only using the artifacts as an excuse for a confrontation. Our intelligence sources report he plans the same immigrant invasions from Baja into Southern California and across the border at Nogales into Arizona."

"If only we can stop this madness," muttered the President.

One of four phones buzzed, and Nichols picked it up. "General Chandler, Mr. President. He's coming through on a scrambled frequency."

The President let out a long breath. "Staring into the face of the man I may have to order to kill ten thousand people is the least I can do."

The monitor faded for a moment and then came back with the head and shoulders of a man who was in his late forties. His face was gaunt and his heavily silvered hair was bare of helmet or cap. The stress of command showed in the lines around the blue eyes.

"Good morning, General," the President greeted him. "I regret I can see you and you can't see me, but there is no camera at this end."

"I understand, Mr. President."

"What is the situation?"

"A heavy rain is just starting to fall, which should prove a godsend for those poor people. They can replenish their water supplies, dust will be dampened, and the stench from their latrines is already beginning to diminish."

"Have there been any provocations?"

"The usual taunts and banners, but no violence."

"From what you can observe, have any of the crowd become discouraged and started drifting back to their homes?"

"No, sir," replied Chandler. "If anything, they're more enthused. They think their Aztec messiah brought the rain, and he's pounded his chest to convince them of it. Groups of Catholic priests have been circulating among the people, preaching and begging them to return to the church and their homes. But Topiltzin's goons quickly escort the good fathers out of town."

"Martin Brogan thinks they'll make their move tonight."

"My intelligence agrees with Mr. Brogan's

timetable." The General hesitated before asking the fateful question. "Any change in orders, Mr. President? I'm still to stop them at any cost?"

"Until I tell you different, General."

"I must state, sir, you've placed me in a very awkward situation. I cannot guarantee my men will cut down women and especially children if so ordered."

"I'm in sympathy with your position. But if the line is not held in Roma, millions of poor Mexicans will see it as an open invitation to pour into the United States unhindered."

"I can't argue the point, Mr. President. But if we let loose a wall of modern firepower into half a million people jammed shoulder to shoulder, history will convict us of committing a crime against humanity."

Chandler's words triggered the horror of Nazi vileness and the Nuremberg trials in the President's mind, but he stiffened his resolve. "Repugnant as the thought is, General," he said solemnly, "the consequences of inaction are unthinkable. My National Security experts predict that a wave of self-preservation hysteria will sweep the country, resulting in the formation of vigilante armies to beat back the flood of illegal immigrants. No Mexican-Americans will be safe. The death toll on both sides could climb to astronomical proportions. Conservative legislators will rise up and demand Congress vote a formal declaration of war against Mexico. I don't even want to think about what happens after that possibility."

Everyone in the room could clearly see the confusion of conflicting thoughts and emotions that were swirling through the General's mind. When he spoke it was in a quiet, controlled voice.

"I respectfully request we stay in close communication until the incursion."

"Understood, General," agreed the President. "My National Security advisers and I will gather in the Situation Room shortly."

"Thank you, Mr. President."

The image of General Chandler was cut to a closeup of a small barge being pulled into the water on rollers by nearly a hundred men straining on ropes.

"Well," said Schiller, shaking his head as if marveling at it all, "we've done all we can to contain the bomb but failed to keep the explosion from becoming irreversible. Now all we can do is sit by and be consumed."

74

They came an hour after dark.

Men, women and children, some barely able to walk, all held lighted candles. The low clouds that lingered after the rainstorm glowed orange from the sprawling ocean of flickering flame.

They came in one gigantic swell toward the shoreline, voices slowly rising in an ancient chant. The sound grew from a hum to a loud drone that rolled across the river and caused windows to vibrate in Roma.

Country refugees and city poor, who had abandoned their mud hovels, corrugated tin shacks and cardboard carton shelters in destitute villages or noxious slums, came as one. They were galvanized by Topiltzin's promise of a new dawning of the once-mighty Aztec empire on former lands in the United States. They were desperate people on the bottom rung of wrenching poverty, driven to grasp at any hope for a better life.

They moved at a snail's pace, one short step

at a time to the waiting fleet of boats. They came down the roads that were muddy and puddled from the rain. Small children whined in fear as their mothers carried or led them onto unstable rafts that dipped and bobbed during the boarding.

Hundreds were forced into the river by the crush behind. Frightened cries came from a multitude of young victims as they were pushed into water over their heads. Many went under or drifted away with the current before they could be rescued, a near-impossible job, since most of the men were grouped farther to the rear.

Slowly, in disorganized confusion, the hundreds of boats and rafts began to pull away for the opposite shore.

The American Army's floodlights, joined by those of the television crews, brightly illuminated the seething turmoil swelling across the river. The soldiers stared in uneasy fascination at the tragedy and the human wall advancing toward them.

General Chandler stood on the roof of Roma's police station in the center of the bluff. His face was gray under the lights, and there was a look of despair in his eyes. The scene was far more appalling than his worst fears.

He spoke into a small microphone clipped to his collar. "Can you see, Mr. President? Can you see the madness?"

The President stared fixedly at the huge monitor in the Situation Room. "Yes, General, the transmission is coming in clearly."

He sat at the end of a long table, flanked by his closest advisers, cabinet members and two of the four Joint Chiefs of Staff. They all gazed at the incredible spectacle that was displayed in stereophonic sound and vivid color.

The fastest boats had touched shore, and their passengers quickly scrambled out. Only when the first wave was fully across and the fleet on its way back for the next passengers did the mob assemble and press forward. The few men who had crossed over were walking up and down the shore with bullhorns, encouraging and urging the women forward.

Clutching their candles and their children while chanting in the Aztec language, the women began streaming up the lesser inclines skirting the bluff like an army of ants splitting around a rock in expectation of joining again on the other side.

The terror-haunted looks of the children and the determined faces of their mothers as they stared into the muzzles of the massed guns were clearly shown by the cameras. Topiltzin had claimed his divine powers would protect them, and they fervently believed him.

"Good lord!" exclaimed Doug Oates. "The entire first wave is made up of women and little kids."

No one commented on Oates's alarming observation. The men in the Situation Room watched with growing dread as another crowd of women began to lead their children across the bridge and toward the tanks and armored cars solidly blocking their way.

"General," said the President. "Can you fire a volley over their heads?"

"Yes, sir," replied Chandler. "I've ordered my troops to load blank rounds. The risk of hitting innocent people beyond the town is too great to use live ammo."

"A sound decision," said General Metcalf of the Joint Chiefs. "Curtis knows what he's doing."

General Chandler turned to one of his aides. "Give the command to fire a blank salvo."

The aide, a major, barked into a radio receiver. "Blank salvo, fire!"

The thunderous roar spat a wall of flame into the night. The concussion came like a gust of wind, blowing out many of the candles held by the throng. The ear-splitting clap from the tank cannon and the crackle of small-arms fire reverberated throughout the valley.

Ten seconds. Ten seconds it took between the commands to "fire" and "cease fire," and for the rumble to echo back from the low hills behind Roma.

A paralyzing silence, pierced by the pungent smell of cordite, fell over the stunned multitude.

Then the screams of the women shattered the quiet, quickly joined by the shrieks of the terrified children. Most dropped in horror to the ground while the rest remained standing, frozen in shock. A great outcry followed from the other side as the men, held back from crossing with their wives and children, feared the fallen were dead or wounded.

Pandemonium erupted, and for the next few minutes it looked as though the immigrant invasion had been stopped dead in its tracks.

Then spotlights from the Mexican shore blazed to life and were beamed to a figure standing atop a small platform supported on the shoulders of several men in white tunics.

Topiltzin stood with arms outstretched in a parody of Christ, shouting through speakers, ordering the women who were hugging the ground to rise up and press forward. Slowly the shock diminished and everyone began to realize there were no bloody, mangled bodies. Many laughed hysterically to find they were neither injured nor dead. A rolling cheer went up that turned deafening as the throng mistakenly thought Topiltzin's powers had miraculously swept aside the destruction and shielded them from harm.

"He turned it against us," said Julius Schiller ruefully.

The President shook his head sadly. "Just as it's happened so many times in our nation's history, our humane efforts backfire."

"Chandler's in for it," said Nichols.

General Metcalf nodded very slowly. "Yes, it all falls on his shoulders now."

The time for the fateful decision had arrived. There was no dodging the agonizing issue any longer. The President, sitting safely deep in the basement of the White House, remained strangely silent. He had deftly passed the time bomb to the military, laying the groundwork for General Chandler to become the sacrificial scapegoat.

He was between the proverbial rock and a hard place. He could not allow an army of foreigners to simply storm across the borders unhindered, but neither could he risk the downfall of his entire administration by directly ordering Chandler to slaughter children.

No President ever felt so impotent.

The chanting women and children were only a few short meters away from the troops entrenched a short distance back of the shoreline. Those at the head of the snakelike column of candles crossing the international bridge were already close enough to look up at the gun muzzles of the tanks.

General Curtis Chandler had a long and illustrious military career to look back upon, but nothing to look forward to except a guilt-stricken conscience. His wife had died the year before from a long illness, and they had no children. A one-star Brigadier General, he had no more rank to attain in the short time before his retirement. Now he stood on the bluff watching hundreds of thousands of illegal immigrants flood into his native land and wondered why his life had cruelly culminated at this place and time.

The expression on his aide's face bordered on frantic. "Sir, the order to fire."

Chandler stared at the little children nervously clutching their mothers' hands, their candles revealing their wide, dark eyes.

"General, your orders?" the aide implored.

Chandler mumbled something, but the aide couldn't hear it over the chanting. "I'm sorry, General, did you say 'Fire'?"

Chandler turned and his eyes glistened. "Let them pass."

"Sir?"

"Those are my orders, Major. I'm damned if I'll go to my grave a baby killer. And for God's sake don't even say the words 'Don't fire,' in case some dumb platoon commander misunderstands."

The Major nodded and hurriedly spoke into his microphone. "To all commanders,

General Chandler's orders; make no hostile move and allow the immigrants to pass through our lines, repeat, stand down and let them through."

With immeasurable relief, the American soldiers lowered their weapons and stood stiff and uneasy for a few minutes. Then they relaxed and began flirting with the women and, kneeling down, playing with the children and gently cajoling them to wipe away their tears.

"Forgive me, Mr. President," said Chandler, speaking into a camera. "I regret I must end my military career by refusing a direct order from my Commander-in-Chief, but I felt that under the circumstances . . ."

"Not to worry," replied the President. "You did a magnificent job." He turned to General Metcalf. "I don't care where he stands on the seniority list; please see that Curtis receives another star."

"I'll be more than happy to take care of it, sir."

"Good call, Mr. President," said Schiller, realizing the President's silence had all been a bluff. "You certainly knew your man."

There was a faint smile in the President's eyes. "I served with Curtis Chandler when we were Lieutenants of Artillery in Korea. He would have fired on a vicious, out-of-control, armed mob, but women and babies, never."

General Metcalf also saw through the facade. "You still took a terrible chance."

The President nodded in agreement. "Now I have to answer to the American people for the unopposed invasion of their land by masses of illegal aliens."

"Yes, but your show of restraint will be a strong bargaining chip for future negotiations with President De Lorenzo and other Central American leaders," Oates consoled him.

"In the meantime," added Mercier, "our military and law enforcement agencies will be quietly rounding up Topiltzin's followers and herding them back across the border before the threat of vigilante warfare breaks out."

"I want the operation to be conducted as humanely as possible," the President said firmly.

"Haven't we forgotten something, Mr. President?" asked Metcalf.

"General?"

"The Alexandria Library. Nothing stands in the way now of Topiltzin's looting the artifacts."

The President turned to Senator Pitt, who had been sitting quietly at the end of the table. "Well, George, the Army has struck out, and you're the last man at bat. You care to enlighten everyone on your stopgap plan?"

The Senator looked down at the table. He didn't want the others to see the uneasy apprehension in his eyes. "A desperation long shot, a deception created by my son, Dirk. I don't know how else to describe it. But if everything goes right, Robert Capesterre, a.k.a. Topiltzin, won't lay his hands on the knowledge of the ancients. However, if all goes wrong, as some critics already suggest, the Capesterres will rule Mexico and the treasure will be lost forever."

75

Thankfully, the outpouring of religious zeal and Topiltzin's maniacal grab for power did not end in bloodshed. There was no death by misunderstanding. The only real tragedy was that of the young victims who had drowned during the first crossing.

Unbound, the massive crowd flowed past the army units and through the streets of Roma toward Gongora Hill. The chanting had faded and they shouted slogans in the Aztec tongue that all American and most Mexican observers could not comprehend.

Topiltzin led the triumphal pilgrimage up the slope of the hill. The Aztec god imposter had carefully planned for his role of deliverer. Seizing the Egyptian treasures world give him the necessary influence and financing to push aside the long-reigning Institutional Revolutionary Party of President De Lorenzo without the inconvenience of a free election. All of Mexico was within four hundred meters of falling into Capesterre family hands.

News of his brother's death in Egypt had not yet reached him. His close supporters and advisers had deserted the communications truck during the excitement and missed the urgent message. They walked behind Topiltzin's hand-carried platform, driven by curiosity to see the artifacts.

Topiltzin stood erect in a white robe with a jaguar-skin cape draped on his shoulders, clutching a raised pole that flew a banner of the eagle and the snake. A forest of portable spotlights were aimed at his platform, bathing him in a multicolored corona. The glare distracted him, and he gestured for some of the lights to sweep the slope ahead.

Except for several pieces of heavy equipment, the excavation seemed deserted. None of the Army Engineers was evident near the crater or the tunnel. Topiltzin didn't like the look of it. He spread his hands as a signal for the advancing mob to halt. The order was repeated through loudspeakers until the forward wall of people slowly came to a stop, every face turned toward Topiltzin, reverently awaiting his next command.

Suddenly, a bansheelike wail rose from the summit of the hill and increased in volume until its shrill pitch forced the crowd to cover their ears with their hands.

Then, an array of strobe lights sparkled and flashed across the sea of faces. A light display with the magical dazzle of the northern lights danced in the night sky. The people stood rooted, gazing entranced at the extraordinary sight.

The light show grew to an indescribable intensity while the shriek whipped the air around the countryside with the eerie timbre of a sound track from a science-fiction movie.

Together the flashing lights and the eerie sounds built to a breathtaking crescendo, and then the strobe lights went out and the silence struck with stunning abruptness.

For a full minute the sound rang in everyone's ears, and the lights skyrocketed in their eyes. Then an unseen light source very slowly highlighted a lone figure of a man standing on the peak of the hill. The effect was startling. The light rays shimmered and glistened off metallic objects surrounding his body.

When the man was fully revealed, he was seen to be wearing the fighting gear of an ancient Roman legionary.

He wore a burgundy tunic under a polished iron cuirass. The helmet on his head and the greaves protecting his shins were shined to a high gloss. A gladius — a double-edged sword — hung at his side, clasped to a leather sling that went over the opposite shoulder. One arm held an oval shield while the opposite hand gripped an upright pilum thrusting spear.

Topiltzin stared with curious fascination. A game, a joke, a theatrical hoax? What were the Americans scheming now? His immense horde of believers stood in hushed silence and stared at the Roman as if he were a phantom. Then they slowly turned back to Topiltzin, waiting expectantly for their messiah to make the first move.

A bluff born of desperation, he decided finally. The Americans were playing their last card in an effort to block his superstitious, dirt-poor followers from approaching the treasures.

"Could be a trick to kidnap and hold you as a hostage," said one of his nearby advisers.

There was contemptuous speculation in Topiltzin's eyes. "A trick, yes. But a kidnap, no. The Americans know this mob would go on a rampage if I was threatened. The ploy is transparent. Except for the envoy whose skin I sent back to Washington, I've denied all appeals for talks with their State Department officials. This theatrical production is simply a clumsy attempt at a final face-to-face negotiation. I'd be interested to learn what offer they've thrown on the table."

Without uttering another word and without listening to further warnings from his advisers, he ordered the platform lowered to the ground, and he stepped off. The spotlights stayed on him as he advanced up the hill alone and arrogant. His feet did not show beneath the hem of his robe and he appeared to glide rather than walk.

He moved at a measured pace, fingering a holstered Colt Python .357 revolver on a belt under his robe. He also kept one hand on an orange smoke bomb in case he required a visual effect to screen a quick escape.

He approached until he could clearly see that the figure in the Roman legionary costume was a department store mannequin. It wore an insipid smile, and the painted eyes stared blankly into nothingness. The plaster hands and face were faded and chipped.

An unmistakable curiosity spread on Topiltzin's face as he studied the dummy, but there was also a look of wariness. He was sweating freely, and the white robe had wrinkled and gone limp.

Then a tall man in range boots, denims and a white turtleneck sweater stepped into the spotlights from behind a thicket of mesquite. He peered through opaline green eyes that were as cold as an Arctic ice floe. He stopped when he stood beside the mannequin.

Topiltzin felt he had the advantage. He wasted no time. He spoke first in English. "What did you hope to gain with the dummy and the light show?"

"Your attention."

"My compliments. You were successful. Now if you'll kindly relate your government's message."

The stranger stared at him for a long moment. "Anybody ever tell you your outfit looks like a bed sheet the day after a college fraternity toga party?"

Topiltzin's expression hardened. "Did your President hope to insult me by sending a clown?"

"I believe this is where I'm supposed to say, 'It takes one to know one.' "

"You have one minute to state your case —" he paused and made a sweeping gesture with his hand — "before I order my people to resume their march."

Pitt turned to the rear of the hill and looked questioningly toward the many kilometers of dark, open country. "March where?"

Topiltzin ignored the remark. "You can begin with your name, your title and function in the American bureaucracy."

"My name is Dirk Pitt. My title is *Mister* Pitt. My function is United States taxpayer, and you can go straight to hell."

Topiltzin's eyes blazed darkly. "Men have died horribly for showing disrespect to one who speaks directly to the gods."

Pitt smiled with the bored unconcern of the devil being threatened by a television evangelist. "If we have to talk, let's cut out the hype and hot air. You've misled the poor of Mexico with stage gimmicks while promising them new lifestyles over the rainbow you can't possibly deliver. You're a fraud; from top to bottom you're a fraud. So don't talk down to me. I'm not one of your garbage pickers. I'm not impressed with criminal scum like Robert Capesterre."

Capesterre opened his mouth, then snapped it shut. He took a step backward, surprise showing in his eyes, unable to fully believe what he'd heard.

Seconds passed while he stared at Pitt. At last he spoke in a hoarse whisper. "How much do you know?"

"Enough," Pitt replied casually. "The Capesterre family and their slimy business are the talk of Washington. Champagne corks popped all over the White House when word came in about your greasehead brother, the one who thinks he's a Muslim prophet. Poetic justice, him getting killed by the terrorist he hired to hijack the *Lady Flamborough* and murder the passengers."

"My brother —" Capesterre could not spit out the word "dead." "I don't believe you."

"You didn't know?" Pitt asked, mildly surprised.

"I talked to him less than twenty-four hours ago," Topiltzin said adamantly. "Paul . . . Akhmad Yazid is alive and well."

"A walking corpse is not one of his better imitations."

"What do you or your government hope to gain by these lies?"

Pitt stared at Capesterre coldly. "I'm glad you brought that up. The idea here is to save the Alexandria Library treasures, and we can't very well do that if you unleash your groupies inside the depository chamber. They'll steal whatever artifacts they think they can sell to buy or trade for food, and destroy what they don't value, especially the precious books and scrolls."

"They will not enter," Capesterre said firmly.

"You think you can stop them?"

"My followers do what I command."

"The books and artworks have to be catalogued and surveyed by qualified archaeologists and historians," Pitt said. "If you want any concessions from Washington, you must guarantee the Library will be treated as a scientific project."

Capesterre's eyes searched Pitt's for a moment. He slowly came back on balance and straightened to his full height. He was ten centimeters shorter than Pitt. He stood there wavering like a cobra about to strike. Then he spoke in a voice deep, toneless and menacing. "I do not have to make guarantees, Mr. Pitt. There will be no bargaining for concessions here. Your military failed to turn back my people at the river. The momentum is mine. The Egyptian treasures are mine. The entire Southwestern states —" his eyes blazed at Pitt with the look of a maniac — "will also be mine. My brother Paul will rule Egypt. Our younger brother will someday head the government of Brazil. That is why I am here.

812

That is why you are here as the lone defender of a world superpower in one final, pathetic attempt to negotiate. But your government has nothing left to negotiate. And if any attempt is made to stop our removal of the treasure to Mexico, I shall order it all burned and destroyed."

"I have to give you credit, Capesterre," Pitt muttered in disgust. "You think big. A pity you're allowed to run loose. You could make up a fifth Napoleon for a poker game in an asylum."

Irritation flickered at the edge of Capesterre's eyes. "Good-bye, Mr. Pitt. My patience is exhausted. I will genuinely enjoy sacrificing you to the gods and sending your flayed skin to the White House."

"Forgive me for not having any decorative tattoos."

Capesterre found Pitt's free-and-easy indifference unnerving. No one had ever talked down to him before. He turned and raised a hand toward the hushed mass of people.

"Don't you think you should inventory your new wealth before you turn it over to them?" Pitt asked. "Think of the world abuse that will be heaped on you for allowing your drones to trash Alexander the Great's golden casket."

Capesterre's hand slowly dropped. There was a flush at his temples. "What are you saying? Alexander's casket exists?"

"And so do his remains." Pitt motioned toward the excavated tunnel. "Would you like a guided tour before you throw open the storage chamber to your adoring public?"

Capesterre nodded. With his back to the crowd he slipped the Colt revolver from the belt beneath his robe and held it out of sight under a loose, draped sleeve. His other hand gripped the smoke bomb. "The slightest move by you or anyone hidden inside the tunnel to harm me, and I will blow your spine in two."

"Why would I possibly want to harm you?" Pitt asked with mock innocence.

"Where are the engineers who were working the excavation?"

"Every man who could carry a gun was sent to the defense line at the river."

The lie seemed to satisfy Capesterre. "Raise your shirt and drop your pants below your boots."

"In front of all these people?" Pitt asked, smiling.

"I want to see if you're armed or wired for sound."

Pitt pulled his turtleneck above his shoulders and lowered the denims to his ankles. There was no sign of a hidden transmitter or gun on his body or inside his boots. "Satisfied?"

Topiltzin nodded. He waved the gun toward the shaft entrance. "You lead, I'll follow."

"Mind if I carry the dummy inside? The weapons he's holding are real artifacts."

"You can leave them just inside the entrance." Then Capesterre turned and waved a signal to his advisers that all was safe.

Pitt rearranged his clothing, removed the weapons from the mannequin and entered the shaft.

The roof was slightly less than two meters high, and Pitt had to duck under the support beams as he walked. He deposited the spear and sword, but kept the shield, placing it over his head as if to ward off falling rock.

Knowing the shield was as useless as a sheet of cardboard against rounds from a .357-magnum handgun, Topiltzin made no protest.

The shaft sloped sharply down for twelve meters and then leveled off. The passage was lit by a string of lights that hung from the beams. The Army Engineers had cut the walls and floor almost perfectly flat so the going was easy. The only discomfort was the stuffy air and the dust that rose in swirls from their footsteps.

"Are you receiving sound and picture, Mr. President?" asked General Chandler.

"Yes, General," answered the President. "Their conversation is coming in quite clear, but they walked out of camera range when they entered the tunnel."

"We'll pick them up again in the casket

chamber, where we have another concealed camera."

"How is Pitt wired?" asked Martin Brogan.

"The microphone and transmitter are inserted in the front seam of the old shield."

"Is he armed?"

"We don't believe so."

All those in the Situation Room became silent as their eyes moved to a second monitor that was displaying the excavated chamber under Gongora Hill. The camera was focused on a gold coffin raised in the center of the chamber.

But not all eyes were on the second monitor. One pair had not left the first.

"Who was that?" Nichols blurted.

Brogan's eyes narrowed. "Who do you mean?"

Nichols pointed at the monitor whose camera was still aimed at the underground entrance of the hill. "A shadow passed in front of the camera and moved into the tunnel."

"I didn't see anything," said General Metcalf.

"I missed it too," the President agreed. He leaned toward the microphone sitting on the table in front of him. "General Chandler?"

"Mr. President," the General replied swiftly.

"Dale Nichols swears he saw someone enter the tunnel after Pitt and Topiltzin."

"One of my aides thought he caught someone too."

"So I'm not seeing things," Nichols sighed. "Do you have any idea who it might be?"

"Whoever it was," Chandler said, alarm showing on his face, "he wasn't one of ours."

76

"I see that you limp," said Capesterre.

"A little memento of your brother's mad scheme to murder President Hasan and Hala Kamil."

Capesterre gave Pitt a questioning look but he did not pursue the subject. His mind was taken up with keeping an eye on Pitt's every move while staying alert for the least sign of intrigue.

A little farther on the tunnel broadened into a circular gallery. Pitt slowed and came to a stop in front of a coffin supported on four legs that were carved in what looked like erect Chinese dragons. The entire work gleamed gold under the overhead lights. A stack of Roman legionary weapons leaned against one wall.

"Alexander the Great," Pitt announced. "The art and scrolls are stored in an adjoining chamber."

Capesterre moved closer in awe. He hesitantly reached out and touched the top of the casket. Then suddenly, he jerked his hand back and spun to face Pitt, his face a mask of rage.

"A trick!" he shouted, his voice echoing through the tunnels. "This is no two-thousand-year-old coffin. The paint isn't dry."

"The Greeks were very advanced —"

"Shut up!" Capesterre's right sleeve fell away, exposing the revolver. "No more smart talk, Mister Pitt. Where is the treasure?"

"Give me a break," Pitt begged. "We haven't hit the main depository chamber yet." He began to edge away from the coffin, feigning fear. He backed up until his shoulders touched the wall holding the ancient swords and spears. His eyes darted to the casket as if expecting its resident to sit up.

Capesterre caught the furtive glance and his lips glazed into a knowing smile. He pointed the revolver at the coffin. He pulled the trigger and four holes appeared on one side but exited in great shredded gouges on the opposite. The reports were deafening inside the rock chamber. They sounded as if the gun was fired under a giant bell.

Capesterre took hold of the lid over the coffin's upper half. "Your backup, Mr. Pitt?" he snarled. "How simple-minded of you."

"There was no place else to hide him," Pitt replied regretfully. The green eyes showed no fear and his voice was tightly controlled.

Capesterre threw open the lid and stared

inside. His face went deathly pale and he shuddered in horror before letting the lid drop with a loud thump. A low moan escaped his lips, growing into a long, drawn-out "no" sound.

Pitt turned slightly so the shield covered the movement of his right hand. He edged away from the chamber wall until he stood facing Capesterre's left side. Then he glanced uneasily at the hands of his watch. He was almost past his deadline.

Capesterre stepped fearfully toward the coffin again and lifted the lid; this time he let it fall open and backward. He forced himself to stare inside.

"Paul . . . it really is Paul," he stammered in shock.

"From what I was told," said Pitt, "President Hasan wasn't about to allow Akhmad Yazid's followers to entomb him in a shrine as a martyr. So the cadaver was airmailed here where you two can lie together."

Grief slowly replaced shock as Capesterre stared at his brother. Then his face twisted in bitterness and he asked in a vicious undertone, "What was your part in all this?"

"I headed the team that found the key to the Library treasure site. That was a dedicated effort. Then your brother's hired terrorists tried to kill me and my friends but only succeeded in ravaging my classic car. That was a big mistake. Next, you and your brother took my father as a hostage on the *Lady Flamborough.* You know the ship I'm talking about. Now that was really a blunder. I decided not to get mad, but get even. You're going to die, Capesterre. In another minute you're going to lie as cold and stiff as your brother. A damned small payment for the men whose hearts you cut out and all those children who drowned because of your insane power grab."

Capesterre's body tautened and the grief cleared from his eyes. "But not before I kill *you!*" he said savagely as he spun around and crouched.

Pitt had prepared for the attack. The sword he'd snatched from the stack by the wall was already raised above his head. He brought it down in a slashing sideways arc.

Capesterre frantically lifted the Colt. The muzzle was only centimeters from lining up on Pitt's head. The gleaming blade sliced through the air, glinting under the hanging lights. The gun, with Capesterre's hand clutching the grip, finger tightening on the trigger, seemed to detach from his arm and sail toward the ceiling. They rotated through the air, end over end, before dropping to the limestone floor, still locked together.

Capesterre's mouth sagged open and a thin scream echoed through the excavation. Then he sank to his knees, staring dumbly at the severed limb, unable to believe it was no longer a part of him, oblivious to the spreading stream of blood.

He knelt there, swaying side to side, the pain tightly held in check by shock. He slowly looked up at Pitt with dazed eyes. "Why this?" he whispered. "Why not a bullet?"

"A small payment for a man by the name of Guy Rivas."

"You knew Rivas?"

Pitt shook his head. "Friends of his told me how you mutilated him. How his family stood at the gravesite not knowing they were burying only his skin."

"Friends?" Capesterre asked blankly.

"My father and a man who lives in the White House," Pitt said coldly. He glanced at his watch again. He stared down at Robert Capesterre, but there was no pity on his face. "Sorry I can't stay and help with the mess, but I have to run." Then he turned and headed for the exit tunnel.

He took only two steps before he came to an abrupt halt. A short, swarthy man, wearing a pair of old and worn army combat fatigues, stood in the center of the chamber entrance holding a four-shot pistolized shotgun that was pointed at Pitt's stomach.

"No need to hurry, Mr. Pitt," he said with a heavy accent, his voice matter-of-fact. "No one is going anywhere."

77

Though they had been aware of a third party entering the tunnel, the sudden appearance of the menacing stranger still took everyone by surprise in the Situation Room. Calamity began to loom as they helplessly watched the scene being played out deep under Gongora Hill.

"General Chandler," said the President sharply, "what in hell is going on? Who is the intruder?"

"We're viewing him from our monitoring unit too, Mr. President, but the best guess is he's one of Topiltzin's men. He must have penetrated from the north, where our security line is spread thin."

"He's wearing a uniform," said Brogan. "Can he be one of your men?"

"Not unless our quartermaster is issuing Israeli Army battle fatigues."

"Get some men down there to help Pitt," ordered General Metcalf.

"Sir, if I sent a squad of men anywhere near

823

the excavation, the mob would think we were out to either harm or capture Topiltzin. They'd go berserk."

"He's right," said Schiller. "The crowd is getting edgy."

"The intruder stole inside the tunnel under their noses," Metcalf persisted. "Why can't a couple of your men do the same?"

"It was possible ten minutes ago, but not now," replied Chandler. "Topiltzin's crew have set up more floods. The whole slope is swimming in bright light. A rat couldn't run in there without being seen."

"The excavations face south toward the people," explained Senator Pitt. "There are no exits behind the hill."

"We're lucky as it is," Chandler continued. "The gunfire echoing from the tunnel sounded like distant thunder and no one was sure where it came from."

The President looked at Senator Pitt darkly. "George, if the crowd begins to surge forward, we'll have to end the operation before your son can escape."

The Senator passed a hand in front of his eyes and nodded solemnly. Then he looked up at the monitor.

"Dirk will make it," he said with quiet confidence.

Nichols suddenly came to his feet and pointed at the monitor. "The mob!" he rasped despairingly. "They're moving!"

While others debated his chances of survival 2,500 kilometers away, Pitt's main concern was the black mouth of the shotgun pistol. He didn't doubt for a second it was held in the hand of a man who had killed many times. The face behind the gun wore a bored expression. Ho-hum, another one, Pitt thought. If he didn't have his insides splashed against a wall in a few seconds, he would be crushed by tons of earth. He wasn't keen on either choice.

"You mind telling me who you are?" Pitt asked.

"I am Ibn Telmuk, close friend and servant to Suleiman Aziz Ammar."

Yes, thought Pitt, yes. The sight of the terrorist on the road in front of the crushing mill came back to him. "You guys go to any length for revenge, don't you?"

"It was his last wish that I kill you."

Pitt very slowly dropped his right arm so the sword hung down pointing at the chamber floor. He made the show of a brave man accepting defeat and relaxed his body, shoulders sagging, knees slightly bent. "Were you on Santa Inez?"

"Yes, Suleiman Aziz and I escaped back to Egypt together."

Pitt's dark eyebrows came together. He

hadn't thought it possible Ammar had lived after the shootout. God, time was running out. Ibn should have shot him without a word, but Pitt knew the Arab was only toying with him. The blast of fifty pellets would come in the middle of a sentence.

There was no reward in stalling. Pitt stared at Ibn, measuring the distance between them, figuring what direction he would leap. With casual ease, he edged the shield across his body.

Capesterre wrapped part of his robe around the bleeding stump, moaning from the increasing pain. Then he held up the blood soaked cloth in front of Ibn. "Get him!" he cried. "Look what he did to me. Shoot him down!"

"Who are you?" asked Ibn icily, without taking his eyes from Pitt.

"I am Topiltzin."

"His real name is Robert Capesterre," said Pitt. "He's a colossal fraud."

Capesterre scrambled over to Ibn until he was sitting at the Arab's feet. "Don't listen to him," pleaded Capesterre. "He is a common criminal."

For the first time Ibn grinned. "Hardly that. I've studied a file on Mr. Pitt. He's not common at anything."

Looking better, Pitt thought. Ibn was momentarily distracted by Topiltzin. He slipped sideways a few centimeters at a time, trying to place himself so that Capesterre lay between him and Ibn.

"Where is Ammar?" Pitt asked abruptly.

"Dead," replied Ibn. The grin was quickly replaced with lip-tightening anger. "He died after killing that pig Akhmad Yazid."

The bombshell stunned Capesterre. His gaze automatically turned to his brother's body in the coffin.

"So it was the man my brother hired to hijack the ship," Capesterre uttered in a hoarse croak.

Pitt fought the urge to say "I told you so," and moved another centimeter.

Ibn's eyes registered incomprehension. "Akhmad Yazid was your brother?"

"Two peas in a pod," said Pitt. "Would you recognize Yazid if you saw him?"

"Of course. His appearance is as familiar as the Ayatollah Khomeini or Yasir Arafat."

Pitt's mind raced with new modifications to his desperation plan, taking advantage of the few crumbs thrown his way. Everything hinged on how well he could read Ibn's mind and predict the killer's reaction to seeing Yazid.

"Then take a good look in the coffin."

"Do not even think of making a move, Mr. Pitt," said Ibn. His eyes hung warily on Pitt as he shuffled toward the coffin. When his right hip touched the pallbearer's handle he stopped and took a quick glance inside, and then back at his quarry.

Pitt had not moved a centimeter.

It all depended on the unexpected. Pitt planned on the classic double take. He took the gamble that Ibn's first cursory glimpse inside the coffin would cause a delayed reaction followed by a second longer look. And Ibn did exactly that.

In the Special Operations Forces command truck, parked half a kilometer west of the excavation, Hollis, Admiral Sandecker, Lily and Giordino gazed at a TV monitor, their attention solidly locked into the drama being acted out under Gongora Hill.

Lily stood motionless, her skin eggshell-white, while Sandecker and Giordino fidgeted in frustration like a pair of zoo tigers with a platter of fresh meat just beyond reach of their cage.

Hollis was pacing the small enclosure, nervously clutching a small ultrahigh-frequency detonation transmitter in one hand while the other held a phone receiver.

He was shouting at an aide of General Chandler's. "Like hell I'll detonate! Not until the crowd passes the danger perimeter."

"They've moved too close now," the aide, a colonel, countered.

"Another thirty seconds!" snapped Hollis. "Not before."

"General Chandler wants that hill blown

now!" demanded the Colonel, his voice rising. "That's an order that comes from the President."

"You're only a voice over a phone, Colonel," Hollis stalled. "I want the order direct from the President."

"You're asking for a court-martial, Colonel."

"It won't be the first time."

Sandecker shook his head fearfully. "Dirk will never make it, not now."

"Can't you do something?" pleaded Lily. "Talk to him. He can hear you over the speaker connected to the TV camera."

"We don't dare distract him," answered Hollis. "Break his concentration and that Arab will kill him."

"That's it!" Giordino muttered, infuriated. He tore out the command truck door, jumped to the ground and dashed over to Sam Trinity's Jeep. Before Hollis's men could stop him the car was bouncing through the brush toward Gongora Hill.

In one quick leap, Pitt uncoiled like a rattler and drove the shield against Ibn. The sword blurred and slashed again.

His muscled arm swung with all the strength of his shoulder behind it. He felt and heard the blade edge clang against metal before it struck something soft. An explosion went off, seemingly in his face. He flinched as the main force of the blast struck the middle of his shield and ricocheted against the rock ceiling. The armored plastic sheeting that had been riveted to the laminated wood by Major Dillinger that afternoon was dented but not penetrated. Pitt's sword hand finished the arc, and he launched a murderous back-hand swing.

Ibn was fast, but his shock at seeing Yazid cost him a precious second. He caught Pitt's attack out of the corner of one eye and squeezed off a badly aimed snap shot before the sword blade glanced off the breech of the shotgun and sliced through his hand, severing his thumb and fingers just behind the knuckles.

Ibn uttered a ghastly groan. The pistolized shotgun clattered to the hard limestone floor almost on top of the Colt Python still gripped in Capesterre's severed hand. But Ibn recovered enough to duck away from Pitt's slashing swing. Then, in one violent twisting motion, he lunged at Pitt.

Pitt was ready for the assault, but, as he dodged to one side his right leg folded under him. In a flashing instant he realized that one or two of the shotgun's pellets had missed the shield and struck him in the same leg that had been wounded on Santa Inez Island.

Before he could react and dance away, Ibn dropped on him like a panther. The black eyes gleamed satanically under the string of lights, the teeth ghoulishly bared. Pitt lost his grip on the sword hilt as Ibn knocked it away. His other arm was trapped under the inside straps of the shield. Then slowly, deliberately, Ibn's good hand closed around Pitt's throat.

"Kill him!" Robert Capesterre shrieked repeatedly like a mad man. "*Kill* him!"

Pitt heaved in a corkscrew motion and brought his fist up from the floor, striking Ibn in the Adam's apple. With the cartilage of the larynx crushed, most men would have gagged to death — the rest should have at least gone unconscious. Ibn did neither. He simply clutched his throat, made a terrible gurgling voice and reeled backward.

They both struggled drunkenly to their feet, Pitt hopping on one leg, Ibn gasping for air, his mangled right hand hanging useless. They stood there, facing each other like wounded pit bulls catching their breath for the next round, warily eyeing each other to see who would make the first move.

It came from an unexpected quarter. Capesterre suddenly came to his senses and threw himself on the Colt, frantically struggling one-handed to pry the frozen fingers from the grip. The dead hand fell away.

Then, like a game of musical chairs, Capesterre's grab triggered a like response from Ibn and Pitt. They quickly looked around for the weapons nearest them.

Pitt lost. The shotgun was in Ibn's corner.

So was the Roman sword. Any port in a storm, Pitt thought. He kicked out wildly with the foot of his wounded leg, connecting with Capesterre's rib cage, but suffering a grinding pain from the effort. He also hurled the shield like a Frisbee at Ibn, striking the Arab on the stomach and knocking the wind out of him.

A loud wailing cry gushed from Capesterre's lips. He dropped the Colt and Pitt caught it in midair. It was a near-perfect catch — His hand slipped around the bloodied grip and his finger through the trigger guard. Ibn, doubled over by the blow from the shield, was still awkwardly lifting the pistolized shotgun with his left hand when Pitt fired.

Pitt tightened his grip for the next recoil. The Arab stumbled backward against the chamber wall, and then his body fell forward onto the floor and his head struck with a repugnant thud.

Pitt stood panting through clenched teeth. Only then did he hear a frantic voice shout through the speaker on the TV camera.

"Get out of there!" Hollis was yelling. "For Jesus' sake, run for it!"

Pitt was temporarily disoriented. He was so busy fighting Ibn he forgot which passage led to the easier tunnel entrance and which to the more difficult open crater exit. He took a last fleeting glimpse of Robert Capesterre.

The face was ashen from the loss of blood but not, Pitt saw, with fear. Hate filled the eyes of Topiltzin.

"Enjoy your trip to hell," Pitt said.

Capesterre's reply was the smoke bomb. He had somehow pulled the primer pin. Smoke instantly burst and filled the interior of the chamber with a densely packed orange cloud.

"What happened?" the President asked, staring at the strange orange mist that blocked out the camera view of the chamber.

"Capesterre must have been carrying some kind of a smoke-warning device," Chandler answered.

"Why haven't the explosives gone off?"

"One moment, Mr. President." Chandler looked off-camera and conversed angrily with an aide. Then he turned back. "Colonel Hollis of the Special Operations Forces insists on a direct order from you, sir."

"Is he in charge of the detonation?" demanded Metcalf.

"Yes, General."

"Can you patch him into our communications network?"

"One moment."

Four seconds was all it took before Hollis's face was peering from one of the monitors in the Situation Room.

"I realize you can't see me, Colonel," said

833

the President. "But you recognize my voice."

"I do, sir," Hollis answered through tight lips.

"As your Commander-in-Chief, I'm ordering you to blow that hill, and blow it now."

"The mob is swarming up the hill," Nichols said in near-panic.

They all tensed and swung their eyes to the monitor sweeping the hill. The huge throng was slowly moving up the slope toward the summit, chanting Topiltzin's name.

"If you wait any longer you'll kill a lot of people," said Metcalf urgently. "For pity's sake, man, detonate."

Hollis's thumb was poised above the switch. He spoke into his transmitter. "Detonation!"

But he didn't press the switch. He used the enlisted man's gambit: Never refuse an order and be tried for insubordination, but answer to the affirmative and never carry it out. Inefficiency was one of the most difficult of charges to prove at a court-martial.

He was determined to squeeze every second he could for Pitt.

Holding his breath as though he were diving under water, eyes tightly closed against the stinging smoke, Pitt willed his legs to move, to run, to crawl, to do anything which would rush him clear of that horror chamber. He made it into a passage, not knowing if it led

834

to the tunnel shaft or the crater. He kept his eyes shut, feeling his way along the wall, half-hopping, half-hobbling on his bad leg.

He felt a burning rage to live. He simply couldn't believe he'd die now, not after having survived the last few minutes. Finally he opened his eyes. They burned as if stung by bees, but he could see. He had passed the worst of the smoke. It was only an orange vapor now.

The shaft through the limestone began to rise. He felt a slight increase in temperature and a light breeze. Then he stumbled outside into the night. The stars were there, almost blotted out by the bright lights shining up the hill.

But Pitt was not clear. There was a snag. He had the unsettling realization that he had exited through the crater tunnel. The slanting sides rose up another five meters. So close, yet so tormentingly far.

He began clawing his way up the incline, his wounded leg, totally useless now, dragging along behind. He could only dig in and push with one foot.

Hollis had gone silent. The Colonel had no words left to say. Pitt knew the explosion he'd so carefully planned was going to take him with it. Fatigue swept over him in great floating waves, yet he stubbornly crawled upward.

Then a dark form appeared over the rim of the crater and a massive hand reached down, grabbed the shoulder of Pitt's sweater and heaved him onto level ground.

With seemingly incredible ease Giordino threw Pitt into the open tailgate of the Jeep, leaped into the driver's seat and jammed the accelerator pedal flat onto the floorboard.

They had barely covered fifty meters when Hollis pressed the demolition switch. The ultrahigh frequency signal set off the two hundred kilograms of C-6 nitroglycerin gel deep inside the hill with a monstrous roar.

For one brief moment it was as if a volcanic eruption was about to hurtle from the bowels of the earth. The hill shook with a terrifying rumble. The great mass of Topiltzin followers were thrown to the ground, their mouths agape in horror, the concussion sucking the air from their lungs into a vacuum.

Then the whole summit of Gongora Hill rose almost ten meters into the air, hung there in the night as if clutched by a giant hand, and crumbled and fell inward, leaving a huge plume of billowing dust as a ghostly tombstone.

78

November 5, 1991
Roma, Texas

Five days later, a few minutes past midnight, the President's helicopter set down at a small airfield a few miles outside Roma. Accompanying him were Senator Pitt and Julius Schiller. As soon as the rotor blades swung and drooped to a stop, Admiral Sandecker walked up to the door and greeted them.

"Good to see you, Admiral," the President said graciously. "Congratulations on a splendid job, though I must say I didn't think NUMA could pull it off."

"Thank you, Mr. President," replied Sandecker with his usual cocky air. "We're all grateful you had enough confidence in our mad plan to give us the go-ahead."

"A neat scam, a very neat scam indeed." The President turned and looked at Senator Pitt. "But you have the Senator to thank for my backing. He can be very persuasive."

After a few words between Sandecker and

Schiller, they all climbed a short ladder through a concealed door into the bed of a huge tandem, ten-wheeler dump truck.

Two of the President's Secret Service agents, wearing work clothes, climbed into the cab with the driver. Four more piled into an old battered Dodge van parked in the rear.

The exterior of the truck had a worn, dusty and faded-paint look. But the interior of the four-and-a-half by two-and-a-half-meter bed was converted into a room containing a small kitchen bar and six roomy chairs. The top had been raised by side boards and covered with two centimeters of gravel to complete the disguise.

The door in the dump bed was closed, and they settled into the comfortable chairs mounted to the floor and snapped their seat belts.

"Sorry about the unusual transportation," said Sandecker. "But we can't afford to give the show away with choppers flying in and out of the site."

"This is my first ride inside a gravel truck," the President joked. "The suspension doesn't compare to the White House Lincoln limousine."

"We've converted six of these as undercover transports," explained Sandecker.

"A good choice," laughed the Senator, rapping the metal wall with his knuckles. "They already come bulletproofed."

The smile on the President's face died and he turned serious. "The secret has been kept?" he asked.

Sandecker nodded. "I've seen nothing to indicate otherwise from our end."

"There won't be any leaks from the White House this time around," Schiller guaranteed, picking up on the General's veiled insinuation. "The lid is nailed tight."

The President was silent for a moment. "We were damned lucky to get away with it," he said finally. "Topiltzin's mob of followers might have gone on an orgy of revenge after they realized he was dead."

"After the shock wore off," said Sandecker. "They wandered around the hill, staring into the explosion's crater as if it was a supernatural phenomenon. Bloody rioting was kept to a minimum because of the presence of women and children, that and the fact that Topiltzin's close supporters and advisers quietly ducked out and beat a fast retreat for Mexico. Leaderless, tired and hungry, the crowd slowly began filtering back across the border to their cities and villages."

"According to Immigration," said Schiller, "a few thousand took off north, but a third of them have already been rounded up."

The President sighed. "At least the worst is over. If Congress passes our aid plan to Latin America, it should go a long way in helping our neighbors to the south climb back on their financial feet."

"And the Capisterre family?" asked San-decker. "How will they be dealt with?"

"The Justice Department is going after any assets they have in this country." The President's face was expressionless, but his eyes had a steel-like glint. "This is just between us, gentlemen, but Colonel Hollis of our Special Operations Forces is planning an assault exercise on an island in the Caribbean that shall remain nameless. If any of the Capesterre family happen to be in the vicinity at the time . . . well, that's too damn bad for them."

Senator Pitt gave a sarcastic smile. "With Yazid and Topiltzin gone, our foreign relations will seem pretty tame for a while."

Schiller shook his head negatively. "We've only plugged two holes in the dike. The worst is down the road."

"Don't cry doom, Julius," said the President, now in a jovial mood. "Egypt is stable for the moment. And with President Hasan stepping aside for health reasons and turning over his office to Defense Minister Abu Hamid, the Muslim fundamentalists will be under enormous pressure to reduce their demands for an Islamic government."

"The fact that Hala Kamil has consented to marry Hamid won't hurt the situation either," Senator Pitt summed up.

The conversation was interrupted as the

truck came to a stop. The concealed door was opened from the outside and the ladder set in place.

"After you, Mr. President," invited Sandecker.

They stepped to the ground and looked around. The area was surrounded by an ordinary chain-link fence and dimly lit by widely spaced pole lights. A large sign beside the entrance gate read, SAM TRINITY SAND AND GRAVEL COMPANY. Except for a pair of gravel loaders, a large excavator bucket and several dump trucks and gravel trailers, the entire yard was deserted.

The underground security guard units and electronic detection equipment were virtually invisible to anyone walking around the equipment yard.

"Can I meet Mr. Trinity?" asked the President.

Sandecker shook his head. "Afraid not. A good man, Sam. A good patriot. After voluntarily signing over the rights to the artifacts to the government, he took off on a playing tour of the world's top one hundred golf courses."

"We compensated him, I hope."

"Ten million tax-free dollars," replied Sandecker. "And we damned near had to hogtie him to take it." Then Sandecker turned and pointed out a deep excavation a few hundred meters away. "The remains of Gongora Hill.

Now a gravel pit. We've actually made a profit on our sand-and-crushed-rock operation."

The President's face clouded as he stared into the huge open pit that was once the summit of the hill. "Did you happen to dig up Topiltzin and Yazid?"

Sandecker nodded. "Two days ago. We sent their remains through the rock crusher. I believe they're both part of a roadbed."

The President seemed satisfied. "Just what the bastards deserve."

"Where is the tunnel?" asked Schiller, looking around.

"In there." Sandecker gestured toward a well-used mobile home trailer that was converted to an office. A sign by one window advertised the "Dispatcher."

The four Secret Service agents in the van had already exited and begun patrolling the area while the two in the cab of the truck jumped to the ground and entered the office to check it out as a matter of routine.

After the President's party passed through two doors into a small, barren office at the rear of the mobile home, Sandecker invited them to step to the center of the room and hold onto a railing that protruded from the floor. He waved at a TV camera in one corner of the ceiling. Then the floor began to lower through the trailer and into the ground below.

"Pretty slick," said Schiller admiringly.

"Yes indeed," murmured the President. "I

can see why the project hasn't been penetrated."

The lift dropped through the limestone and
came to a jerking halt thirty meters under the
ground surface. They stepped off into a wide-
tunneled passageway lit with fluorescent-tube
lights. For as far as they could see the tunnel
was lined with sculptures.

A woman waited to greet them.

"Mr. President," said Sandecker, "may I
introduce Dr. Lily Sharp, director of the
cataloging program?"

"Dr. Sharp, we're all deeply in your debt."

Lily blushed. "I'm afraid I was only a small
cog in the wheel," she replied modestly.

After she was introduced to Schiller, Lily
began the guided tour of the treasures from
the Alexandria Library.

"We've studied and catalogued 427 different sculptures," she explained, "representing
the finest work of the early bronze age beginning in 3,000 B.C. and ending in the tran-
scendental style of the Byzantine era of the
early fourth century. Except for a few stains
from water seepage through the limestone,
which can be removed by chemicals, the
marble and bronze figures are in a remarkable state of preservation."

The President walked speechless through
the long passage, stopping every so often to
gaze in frank admiration at the magnificent
classic sculpture, some of it five thousand

years old. He was overwhelmed at the sheer numbers of it. Every age, every dynasty and empire was represented with the best its artists turned out.

"I'm actually seeing and touching the Alexandria museum collection," he said in reverence. "After the explosion I couldn't believe it wasn't all destroyed."

"The earth tremors stirred up some dust and caused a few bits and pieces of the limestone to fall from the roof," said Lily. "But the artifacts came through just fine. You're seeing the sculptures just as Junius Venator last saw them in A.D. 391."

After nearly two hours of studying the incredible display, Lily stopped at the last artifact before entering the main gallery. "The golden casket of Alexander the Great," she announced in a hushed tone.

The President felt as if he was about to meet God. He hesitantly approached the golden resting place of one of the greatest leaders the world had ever known and peered through the crystal windows.

The Macedonians had laid their king out in his ceremonial armor. His cuirass and helmet were pure gold. The Persian silk that once made up his tunic was mostly gone, rotted away after nearly twenty-four centuries. All that was left of the great subject of romantic legend were his bones.

"Cleopatra, Julius Caesar, Mark Antony, all

stood and gazed at his remains," lectured Lily.

Each took his turn, hardly able to conceive what lay beneath their eyes. Then Lily led them into the great storage gallery.

Nearly thirty people were hard at work. Several were examining the contents of the wooden crates stacked in the gallery's center. Paintings, stained and soiled, but restorable, along with delicate objects carved from ivory and marble or cast from gold, silver or bronze were catalogued and repacked in new cases for transport to a secure building complex in Maryland for restoration and preservation.

Most of the archaeologists, translators and preservation experts were gently handling the bronze cylindrical tubes that held the thousands of ancient books, translating the copper tags and recording descriptions of the contents. The containers and their delicate scrolls were also carefully packed for shipment to Maryland for study and research.

"Here it is." Lily gestured around the chamber proudly. "So far we've found the complete books of Homer, much of the lost teachings by the great Greek philosophers, early Hebrew writings, manuscripts and historical data showing new insight on Christianity. Maps illustrating previously unknown tombs of ancient kings, the locations of the lost trading centers, including Tarshish and Sheba, and geological charts of mines and oil deposits long forgotten. Enormous gaps in ancient chronological events will be filled. The history of the Phoenicians, Mycenaeans, Etruscans, and civilizations that were only rumored to exist, they're all here and accounted for in vivid detail. If restorable, the paintings will give us a true picture of what the immortals of the ancient world looked like."

For a moment the President had nothing to say. He was numbed. He couldn't begin to digest the immensity of the astonishing accumulation. As art, it was priceless. As knowledge, its value was incalculable.

Finally, he asked in a hushed voice, "How long before you'll be finished here?"

"We'll move the scrolls first, then the artwork," replied Lily. "The sculptures will go last. Working around the clock, we hope to have the passage and gallery emptied and the entire collection safely in Maryland by New Year's."

"Almost sixty days," said Sandecker.

"And the preservation and translation of the scrolls?"

Lily shrugged. "The preservation is the slow part. Depending on budget restrictions, we're looking at anywhere between twenty and fifty years to make all translations and gain a full understanding of what we have."

"Don't worry about funding," said the President excitedly. "The project will have the highest priority. I'll see to that."

"We can't fool the international community much longer into believing these magnificent treasures were destroyed," warned Schiller. "We've got to make an announcement, and soon."

"Too true," said Senator Pitt. "The uproar from our own people and those of foreign governments has not slackened since the explosion."

"Tell me about it," the President muttered dryly. "My popularity poll has dropped fifteen points; Congress is chewing my tail, and every foreign leader in the world wants to nail my hide on an outhouse door."

"If you gentlemen will forgive me," said Lily hesitantly, "but if you can hold off for another ten days, I think the project members and I can produce some extraordinary film and video tape of the major pieces of the inventory."

Senator Pitt looked at the President. "I think Dr. Sharp has just handed us a bombshell. A dramatic disclosure by the White House, backed by a documentary, sounds like a hell of an idea."

The President raised Lily's hand and patted it. "Thank you, Dr. Sharp. You've just made my life a bit easier."

"Have you given any more thought as to how you intend to disperse the artifacts?" asked Sandecker, not bothering to mask the irritation in his tone.

The President smiled broadly. "If I can sweet-talk Congress into appropriating the funds, and I'm pretty sure I can, a replica of the Alexandria Library will be constructed on the Washington mall, housing every piece Junius Venator brought to the Americas from Egypt, plus artifacts from the ancient Americas. And if other countries wish to view their heritage, we'll be glad to loan it on exhibit. But it remains the property of the American people."

"Oh, thank you, Mr. President!" Lily gasped, throwing her arms around him in unabashed enthusiasm.

Admiral Sandecker shook his hand. "Thank you, sir. I think you've just made everyone's day."

Schiller leaned over and spoke softly into Lily's ear. "Just make sure you translate the geological data first. We may keep the artworks but the knowledge should be shared with the world."

Lily merely nodded.

After the fever of excitement and the questions eased a bit, Lily led the Presidential group over to a corner of the gallery where Pitt and Giordino were sitting around a folding table with a Latin/Greek translator who was examining a cylinder's tag with a magnifying glass.

The President recognized them and swiftly walked over. "Good to see you alive and healthy, Dirk," he said with a warm smile. "On behalf of a grateful nation I wish to thank you for this astonishing gift."

Pitt came to his feet, leaning heavily on a cane. "I'm only happy it turned out so well. If not for my friend Al here and Colonel Hollis, I'd still be under Gongora Hill."

"Will you please clear up the mystery?" asked Schiller. "How did you know the Library treasures were beneath this lower hill instead of the higher Gongora?"

"I don't mind admitting," said the President, "you had the hell scared out of us. All we could think of was 'What if you blew the wrong hill.' "

"I apologize for being vague," answered Pitt. "Unfortunately, there was no time for a lengthy explanation to ease everyone's fears." He paused and gave his father a wide smile. "I'm only glad you all trusted me. But there was never a real doubt. Junius Venator's description of the location that was inscribed on the stone found by Sam Trinity, said to 'stand north and look straight south to the river cliff.' When I stood north of Gongora Hill and stared on a line due south, I found that the Roma bluff stood almost half a kilometer to the west on my right. So I moved farther west and slightly north to the first hill that fit Venator's directions."

"What's it called?" asked the Senator.

"This hill?" Pitt held up his hands in a

blank gesture. "So far as I can tell, it has no name."

"It does now," said the President laughing. "As soon as Dr. Sharp gives me the go-ahead to announce the greatest treasure discovery in the history of man, we'll say it came from No Name Hill."

A dawn mist was lifting from the river and the glow of a new sun rising over the Rio Grande valley when the Presidential party returned to Washington, their minds thoroughly awed by what they had seen.

Pitt and Lily sat on the summit of No Name Hill and smelled the dampness of morning and watched the lights of Roma blink out. It looked like a painting by Grant Wood.

Lily smiled into his eyes. They did not look hard and fierce now, only soft and pensive. The sun shone on his face, but he did not see it, only felt the warmth. She knew his mind was roving in the past.

She had come to learn he was a man no woman could ever completely possess. His love was an unknown challenge somewhere over the horizon, a mystery that beckoned with a siren lure only he could hear. He was a man a woman desired for an impassioned affair but never married. She knew their relationship was fleeting; she fully intended to take advantage of every moment that was left to her until she awoke one day and found him gone in search of the enigma waiting beyond the next hill.

Lily sat against him, head on his shoulder. "What did the tag read?"

"Tag?"

"The one on the scroll you and Al seemed so interested in."

"A tantalizing clue to more artifacts," he said quietly, still staring into the distance.

"Where?"

"Under the sea. The scroll was labeled 'Recorded Shipwrecks with Valuable Cargoes.' "

She looked up at him. "A map to underwater treasure."

"There is always treasure somewhere," he said almost distantly.

"And you're going to find it?"

He turned and smiled. "Never hurts to look. Unfortunately, Uncle Sam rarely gives me the time. I've yet to search the Brazilian jungles for the golden city of El Dorado."

She gave him an intuitive stare and then lay back, gazing at the fading stars. "I wonder where they're buried."

He slowly shook off the vision of sunken treasure and looked down. "Who?"

"The ancient adventurers who helped Venator save the Library collection."

He shook his head. "Junius Venator is a hard man to outguess. He could have buried his Byzantine comrades most anywhere between here and the river —"

She placed her hand gently on his head and drew him down to her level. Their lips met and pressed tightly for several moments. A hawk spiraled above them in the orange sky, but seeing nothing appetizing, it winged south into Mexico. Lily's eyes opened and she pulled back, smiling coyly.

"Do you think they'd mind?"

Pitt looked at her curiously. "Mind what?"

"If we made love over their grave. They might very well be lying beneath us."

He rolled them both over until she was on her back and he was above, looking down into her eyes. Then his lips curled into a sly grin.

"I don't think they'd care. I know I certainly wouldn't."

ABOUT THE AUTHOR

Clive Cussler's life nearly parallels that of his hero, Dirk Pitt®. Whether searching for lost aircraft or leading expeditions to find famous shipwrecks, he has garnered an amazing record of success. With his NUMA crew of volunteers, Cussler has discovered more than sixty lost ships of historic significance, including the long-lost Confederate submarine *Hunley*. Like Pitt, Cussler collects classic automobiles. His collection features eighty examples of custom coachwork and is one of the finest to be found anywhere. Cussler divides his time between the deserts of Arizona and the mountains of Colorado.

The employees of Thorndike Press hope you have enjoyed this Large Print book. All our Thorndike and Wheeler Large Print titles are designed for easy reading, and all our books are made to last. Other Thorndike Press Large Print books are available at your library, through selected bookstores, or directly from us.

For information about titles, please call:

(800) 223-1244

or visit our Web site at:

http://gale.cengage.com/thorndike

To share your comments, please write:

Publisher
Thorndike Press
295 Kennedy Memorial Drive
Waterville, ME 04901

HLB